the
thing
with
feathers

the thing with feathers

Anne Sweazy-Kulju

Dedication

This novel is for my daughter, Laura—thanks, Cornflake, for always being my champion; and for my husband and best friend, Steve. Without you, this book simply would not be.

Acknowledgements

I wish to say thank you to my husband, Steve, who, as it turns out, is the best amateur editor ever.

Thank you Vivian Woods, for listening and for your encouragement.

A special thanks to Amanda at Tate Publishing for believing in this story.

And of course, my heartfelt gratitude to James Bare, my very talented editor, for leading me through this rough country.

I wish to thank Glenn Beck, whose December 2010 "Challenge" is responsible for my knocking the dust off this manuscript and giving it a chance to be.

> Blessed is the man who perseveres under trial, because when he has stood the test, he will receive the crown of life that God has promised to those who love Him.
>
> James 1:12 (NIV)

Prologue

On that May afternoon in 1945, Cloverdale was headed for hell in a hand basket. Nature had gone haywire. Day was night, and Rebecca Tjaden knew she might be losing her dearest friend that day.

"Only time I ever saw her happy was when she was with you. Sean, do you know what happened to her to make her leave?" Rebecca's soft question broke through the hush in the room.

He was able to turn his head and look Rebecca's way only with greatest difficulty. "A blind *un*-luck of birth," he rasped. Then, a hoarse, bitter chuckle followed, full of the promise that Rebecca would finally hear the whole story.

He lay there quietly, staring at the ceiling, seeming to wrestle with some turmoil inside. He'd always been like that, the strong, silent type. Sean Marshall could be counted on to keep a confidence, and because people recognized that integrity in him, he was the keeper of many dark secrets.

Did he just say something? Rebecca looked up again from the book she was reading, thinking that maybe it was just a cough; but he had his arm outstretched, and he was pointing to the armoire in the corner.

She rose from her chair and walked over to the closet and opened the door. She looked his way and saw that he was shaking his head no. She opened the other side. His finger was shaking downward, to a sliding drawer in the bottom of the compaction armoire. She pulled out the drawer marked "Sundries." There was his old box camera, still his favorite after all those years, and an old wooden box about five inches across and deep and maybe eighteen or so inches long. It was locked with a sturdy brass hasp.

Rebecca looked at him questioningly. "Is this what you want?"

"The key," he said, hacking, "is on my key ring…little… brass…"

Rebecca rummaged through the top drawer of his dresser, where Sean kept his wallet, keys, and loose change. She found the small brass key and unlocked the box. Then she brought it over to the bed and sat back down in her chair with the box on her lap.

"Open it."

She did. The first thing she saw was the money. She raised her eyebrows at him. He shook his head no again. That wasn't what he wanted. Then she found an envelope folded in half. It was pale pink, badly faded, and worn from handling. She took the letter out, and her eyes went immediately to the bottom of the single sheet of paper with the beautiful penmanship. It read, "All my heart, Cindy." Rebecca was both curious and a trace jealous. She read the letter and looked up at the man in the bed.

"Sean…?"

His arm wavered again, pointing to the box. There was more. Rebecca looked again at the contents. There was a photograph, quite old from the looks of it, probably worth a fortune if it was one of Sean's earlier photos. She took it gingerly by the edges and brought it up close to her face so she could see it clearly.

"Oh!" She put the photograph back in the box as though it could bite her. She looked at Sean somberly, tears brimming in her eyes. "I never…oh, Lord, Sean." Her voice cracked.

"Beck-wheat, once I knew, what could I do? But I should have burned that photo years ago. And I would have, but it was the only proof I had. That doesn't matter any more. I don't want Victor to see it. Please take care of that for me." He stopped to catch his breath and stem off a coughing fit. "I want him to have the letter, though. He has so little to remember his mother by. Please see that Blair's portrait goes to him, too. And the watch— he should have the watch. It was Blair's most prized possession."

"I'll see to it, Sean."

The photograph explained everything. She took hold of his hand to calm him and squeezed it. She loved that man. She always had. But fate had other plans for the two of them. Together, they had tried to save a young girl's life. Rebecca was only now learning of the role she had played all those years ago. She remembered it like it was yesterday. So did Sean, and he began telling her the things she hadn't known. His voice came bursting out between coughs like the spat of machine gun fire. It would be a long and difficult story for him to tell, but it was time he told it to someone. It was only right that the someone be Rebecca.

As it turned out, it was the ugliest photograph he had ever taken over his long and successful career. It was the one picture Sean Marshall promised he would never show to anyone, at least not intentionally. He hadn't meant to snap the photo, hadn't given the action any thought at all. It just occurred to him, and his hands had done the rest. He could not even bring himself to look at the picture once he had seen to its development. He had buried it among other photos in a handmade wooden box secured with a brass lock.

"And that"—Sean exhaled and wiped his hands against the denim of his trousers as though the photo had dirtied them—"is the end of that."

And it was, for at *least* a decade or so.

Chapter 1

The mule labored beneath the large man's bulk as it trudged across the Idaho desert. The moon's glow was thin and spare and his dark, retreating shape was growing less distinguishable to the woman walking many yards behind him. She did not appear to care. She had been walking for a very long time, quite swollen and struggling mightily with her intensifying labor pains. She stumbled again, but that time, she did not push on.

"Get up!" the mule rider hollered over his shoulder at the woman. He did not stop.

The young mother-to-be glared holes in the backside of the shadowy wayfarer. Her hatred of the man was nearly a tangible thing. Slowly, she reached down to the desert floor and grabbed up a scrap of wood, a bleached and splintered discard from wagon wheel spoke, left over from the heydays of the Oregon Trail. Still boring daggers at the distant rider, she jammed the wood in her mouth and bit down hard. Then she hiked up her dusty skirt, none too dainty, and laid herself down in the dirt.

A scream split the night. Other screams followed, of course, all of which seemed capable of tearing the very fabric of time with their tortured piercing. Two men were within a hundred miles of hearing those awful wails. One man, a good Samaritan by the name of Milton Blair, held the hand of the stricken woman and cried for her agony, not knowing what else to do for her. The other man, far less good, supposed the Oregon Trail had claimed yet another pitiful traveler. He held no anguish, though it was his wife who was dying.

While the young stranger ministered to Bowman's wife, Bowman greedily surveyed the other man's belongings through the filthy windows of his jalopy.

"Are you a Bible salesman then?" Bowman asked, noting the stacks on the backseat.

"I retired as my congregation's minister last year. Now I travel and spread the good word. You may help yourself to one of those smaller Bibles, sir."

"How does one become a minister, if I may? How much study is there, and is there a seminary near?"

Bowman would need a profession when he reached the end of his travels, and he did not hanker for manual labor. In fact, he romanticized that he would achieve a position of greatness and respect in his future. Julius grew up angry at his circumstances in life; he'd been robbed. His father had failed to pass on the respect his name should have garnered because he'd been a mean drunk who was poor with money. But it was Julius to whom life was unfair.

This good Samaritan looked to have more than his fair share of blind luck, Julius noted. He wore nice clothing and owned a three year-old Model-T. And the man was already retired and traveling the country. The more Julius thought of it, the angrier he grew.

"In fact, I have no formal seminary training myself, sir. Mine was a Baptist congregation."

"I don't understand." Bowman scratched at the lice in his hair.

"Well, sir, the congregation simply voted to ordain me as their pastor, and it was done. Many Baptist congregations do it, as I understand it."

The stranger turned his attention from the suffering woman and observed the hungry manner in which Bowman was eyeing his property. Milton Blair was growing uncomfortable in the man's presence.

"Can I ask you to pour some more water from that canteen onto this handkerchief for me?" Milton asked.

Bowman was presently lost in thought. He absently took the cloth and dampened it more with the canteen of water, which the man kept on the front seat of his auto. Bowman was thinking that if the stranger were to become stricken by, say, putrid throat, while on travels through the Idaho desert, Bowman would inherit the man's abandoned property. That is desert law. If a passerby should come upon two fresh mounds in the great arid plains of Eastern Idaho, and if those mounds were to have the legend of diphtheria marked upon them, Bowman guessed that no man's curiosity was enough to want to investigate the tragedy further. Bowman's warped mind quickly conceived of a plan, a plan wherein one man's course, in a fluke chance of being in the wrong place at the wrong time, would soon be marked by tragedy and death. The other's was soon to offer excitement, providence, perhaps even a little pleasure.

Julius Bowman approached the grieving stranger from his back side and was upon him, his razor knife doing fatal damage before the traveler knew what happened. Julius let the body drop into the dirt. He stooped over his wife. She'd been a beauty. She was perfectly silent and still, with glazed eyes and a mouth poised in eternal agony. His eyes traveled lower. The mound was still present. She had not succeeded in pushing it out.

"Will ya grant me the child, Lord?" he shouted at the heavens.

The child, an heir, was all that mattered. Julius Bowman, formerly of Tennessee, enjoyed telling folks of his significance in royal history.

The bowman for the king had been Julius's ancestor. But the family inherited far more than the pathetic scrap of historical pride. In the days of kingship, it was common to marry within the family to assure a pure heir and a concentration of wealth and title. Truth be known, although a bowman was important to the royals for both hunting and security, the title was only a half step up from peasant or even a robber. Still, the Bowman family had always been hell-bent on preserving it. Later, it was learned that incestuous practices sometimes bred insanity, sometimes bleeders. The Bowmans' had no bleeders.

Julius Bowman had, himself, been born of incest to Bernard Bowman and to the title, which was barely on the skirt of actual nobility, in 1870 Europe. Leah Bowman had given birth to several daughters, even though Julius' father had beat her unmercifully each time for the offense. After the first girl, Marie, was born, his father took to putting an immediate end to the life of subsequent infant girls. He could hardly afford to feed them all. When Marie was of child-bearing age, Julius's father did in poor Leah, and made the girl his wife. Julius was the result of said union. By the time Julius was old enough to contribute to the future gene pool, his father was too old. It became Julius's responsibility. His father had assured Julius that he would be doing God's work.

"In order to know virtue, we must first acquaint ourselves with vice," he would often quote the Marquis De Sade, sometimes quoting the Bible in the same rant, perverting God's Word in the process.

When Julius balked, his father beat him severely, nearly starved him, and verbally abused and threatened him, all of which finally gained Julius's submission, if not his hatred. The union produced a female, and Julius and Marie were beaten for the transgression. That time, Julius was so angry that *he* broke the infant's neck. But times were changing in Europe. You could no longer murder your wife or infants and get away with it. Julius's deed became known to a priest, and he was forced to flee.

He fled to America in the year 1888 and settled in Tennessee, where he found that, while slavery was illegal, there were still ways; any bad white man could claim that a nigger had been stolen from him and swear the blackie into jail. Then, in place of keeping the nigger in jail (where the sheriff would otherwise have to provide meals), the man could buy up the black's services until such time as he or she was sentenced for. By the time the sentence was served, the white man could bring up some other false charges and buy up the services again. Bowman had bought his wife, Jenny, from a farm bordering a neighborhood of niggers. With her being a Quadroon and all, or a quarter black, it seemed like nobody wanted her, not even the niggers. He'd been able to buy her cheap.

"'And Joshua said to 'em, "Pass o'er before the ark of the Lord your God in the midst of Jordan and take you every man of you a stone upon his shoulder accordin' ta the number of the tribes of the children of Is-ra-el. Make it a sign for ya, that when your children ask their fathers, 'What mean you by these stones?' And ye shall answer, 'The stones shall be for a memorial for the children of Is-ra-el forever.'" Julius was fevered in the moment, for he believed the Lord had seen fit to give him another son.

From the moment he had bought his first woman, a fifteen-year-old half-breed, he'd been obsessed with having a son. But when she'd finally produced a boy child, she promptly poisoned it. She had hated Julius Bowman to such a degree that when he'd left to celebrate his good fortune at a local pub, she'd killed his son to spite him. And then he did the worst thing imaginable to the half-breed. He sold her down the river to a New Orleans landowner, one reputed to be a master of the whip.

"Ah," he said over the dead mother. "This stone I take shall be for a memorial unto this here peasant pioneer, who gave his life that I might possess his heritage. I shall name the boy Blair."

In the ensuing silence, he rent open the torso of the woman and pulled the child free. Somewhere in the steely desert night, an animal shrieked. Then it was Julius who shrieked.

"What raillery is this? This is a girl child!"

He was so scorched that he nearly broke the child's neck, but that time, something stopped him, something equally twisted as killing the child. It came to him that that child was intended to become his next wife. It was she who was to bear him a son, a pure legacy.

Julius Bowman arrived in Cloverdale on the Oregon Coast, not too far south of Tillamook Bay. It was a Saturday, late in the year 1911. He possessed a dead man's silver, Bible, and some home-made soap he hadn't bothered to use for himself or his ward. He still had the mule he'd started out on and, of course, the infant girl. Julius had tied the mule to Milton Blair's hard-used touring car, and since the mule was unencumbered, it easily managed to trot alongside at a comfortable pace of about 15 miles per hour. The car had finally given out in western Idaho.

The townsfolk were uncommonly goodhearted and trusting. They were duly sensitive to the man's misfortune of losing his young wife in childbirth, though some whispered that she had no business riding on the back of a mule so late in her pregnancy. Still, they were endeared by the circumstance of the good man—a Baptist minister, he told them—inclined to raise the baby girl on his own. It was decided immediately that Preacher Bowman should be hired to preach their sermons on Sundays. The town took up a collection to build a small home for the preacher, col-lecting a good deal from patrons of the local saloons when it became evident that the women collectors would not leave until every man had reached into his pocket.

On the day following Julius's arrival, the men put aside their tilling and the womenfolk prepared food aplenty, and Cloverdale saw a good, old-fashioned house-raising for Preacher Bowman. It was treated like a celebrated town picnic.

Chapter 2

By 1928, the main street in Cloverdale had grown boardwalks so the ladies wouldn't dirty their dust ruffles. Cloverdale had also been visited by a carnival not too far back, and they had their own stagecoach drop not too far north of the town, which dispatched visitors to the coast via modified car-truck. Sean passed by the Bowman barn, raised by a town effort a few weeks earlier, but with a roof not yet complete. He observed that it was already home to dozens of swallows. They whipped and flitted from open rafters to hay remnants in the fields and then back again. Industriously, they labored to form their nests and protect their young before the rains of April arrived. Rain was a far-off thought to Sean since the March afternoon boasted fine weather, warm sun and clouds like the candy Sean tried at the carnival a summer ago. It was a perfect day to hone his photography skills.

He spent every penny he earned selling salmon in the valley for five cents on a pound to buy the equipment. It had cost Sean near three dollars for the camera and three more for the developing and finishing outfit, but Sears, Roebuck and Co. professed the Conley box camera to be better than those sold by other dealers for as much as five dollars. The Conley was used by the best professional photographers. The lens had universal focus, and the shutter was purported to be instantaneous. He might be an ordinary dairy farmer for the time being, but he hoped one day to be an extraordinary photographer, something he'd told his parents many a time and to their great dismay. Sean's father worried what living a man would make taking pictures.

Sean passed by Preacher Bowman's cottage. It reminded Sean of one of those little cottages buried deep in the woods of a Grimm Brothers' tale, only there was nothing sweet or candy about the shutters and trim. In sixteen years, the preacher had not seen fit to add a single adornment or even an additional bedroom to the modest place the townsfolk had house-raised for him. Sean had only been four or so, so he didn't recall much about the day the cabin was built. He remembered only that the men had been busily felling the trees while the ladies worked on a clay fireplace and a stick-and-daub chimney, and they had let Sean play in the clay until he was pretty much statue art. The first windows had been made from flour sacks, and there were even some benches and a table for eating that were made from split logs. The Bowman cottage had been erected with community spirit and much of the banter and laughter of a church social. Sean could bet his suspenders that those walls hadn't heard a piece of laughter since that day.

He picked up his pace lickety-clip, and in no time at all, he could smell the river. He was anxious to catch a great blue heron or an otter at play. He thought that he might even try to double-expose an object to see what would be produced on the film. Sean daydreamed as he hiked among the low-growing blackberry bramble that was beginning to green. He nearly toppled when his foot became entangled, and as he worked his boot free, he became aware of the melodic voice of a girl somewhere near. That was probably Blair Bowman's voice, Sean supposed. She was an awful pretty girl but painfully shy. Now that Sean thought of it, he'd never heard laughter from Blair or even seen her smile. His curiosity piqued, Sean adjusted his pant leg back into his boot and hurried toward the merry voice by the river.

He was getting close and hearing things clearer. It was not Blair's voice alone but rather two voices. And it no longer sounded to Sean that Blair was laughing. Sean ducked from tree to tree until he caught a glimpse of movement in a small clearing on the river's bank. He strained to hear what Blair was saying. It seemed to Sean that he had heard her sobbing, not laughing. He moved a bit closer, using the dense brush and alder to conceal himself. And his blood froze. It was Preacher Bowman who was with his daughter. Man of God or not, Preacher Bowman scared the wits out of Sean. He thought better of his spying, lest he should be caught, and was readying to steal away when Blair's voice stalled him.

"Papa, please. Papa, don't."

"Quiet yourself, demon child."

Sean turned back toward the clearing even though he could sense dread. All the townsfolk bore heavy hearts for Blair Bowman. All sixteen years of her age had been raised under the stern hand of the preacher. Folks said that Blair's mother had died giving birth to her after traveling the Oregon Trail on the back of a mule for the entire ninth month of her pregnancy. Some folks thought the preacher wicked for entailing on his poor wife such misery and danger to life. Sean, too, thought the preacher must have been devoid of feeling for his wife as to expose the frail woman to such recklessness that insured her death. Though twenty-two years old and, by all standards, a man, Sean's parents would probably still switch him good if he were to voice such an opinion about Preacher Bowman. His parents were largely responsible for persuading the congregation to ordain Mr. Bowman as their Baptist minister. Sean was close enough now to hear Blair's words amid the sobbing.

"Papa…I have ripened. Miss Joseph warned all the girls about the blooding, Papa. I…could become pregnant."

The preacher's voice boomed from the clearing. "'Be fruitful and multiply, and replenish the earth.'"

Blair wailed at his response. "No! Papa, please. People would say of me—"

"That you are a demon child sent to test me, as you have been! A girl child, not a man child. But still, I am duty-bound to produce a son. The test? A test that I should succumb to lust and forget that this is God's will. That you should look like my wife and sound like her, nay, be the very image of her, is more the trial!"

The girl cried uncontrollably. Sean felt sick. His senses all of a sudden seemed sharp and too real, focused on misery. He became aware of the mighty carpenter ants milling on the tree he rested against, could now hear little but the angry buzz of yellow jackets nearby and the racket made by many birds, which, just minutes earlier, had sounded like lovely music. And the heat of the March day was suddenly stifling. There was no longer anything beautiful about that, Sean realized. He heard the sound of a slap and the rustling of a petticoat.

His face burned with humiliation for Blair. *What can I do? Should I rush to the clearing by the river and expose the preacher as a molester of children? Would Bowman kill me for my spying? Would he harm Blair?* Sean heard Blair cry out in pain. *I could run and get help, but who would I tell of it? No one would come. No one would believe this.* He cast his eyes downward in shame. They came to rest upon the camera.

Chapter 3

March, 1928

Cloverdale, Oregon

The shadow woke Sean. A bird had swooped in through his bedroom's open window. Sean jumped off the sagging mattress and grappled the pillowcase off his pillow. He finally persuaded the frightened Stellar's Jay to fly back outside by shooing it toward the opening using the pillowcase. That done, Sean rubbed the sleep from his eyes and drew his pants and suspenders over his summer skivvies. He reached under the bed for his boots, and his hand brushed against the wooden box. Sean sighed. The photograph weighed heavy on his mind. He knew that it was proof of the preacher's wickedness, but he wasn't sure he wanted to tell anyone. It was not because he was afraid of Preacher Bowman. If only it were as simple as that. No, Sean was afraid of what would happen to Blair if the town was to find out what her own father was doing with her. Somehow, Preacher Bowman would make it all look her fault.

That day was Sunday, and the Marshall family never missed Preacher Bowman's sermon. Sean's family spent a good deal of money to help build the tiny Baptist church so that the family beliefs were as well represented in Cloverdale, Oregon, as they had been in Tennessee. Even though Preacher Bowman was not an ordained minister until their small congregation had proclaimed him so, he knew the book and preached with fire and brimstone, and he, too, was from Tennessee. Thinking about all that, Sean was beginning to feel even more miserable. He just wasn't ready to show anyone the picture. Maybe he would try to talk to Blair. One thing was for sure: Sean was of no mind to attend services that day and face Preacher Bowman. He removed his pants and crawled back under the covers, hiking his knees to his chest. When his mother missed him at the breakfast table and came looking for him, he would feign stomach cramps. Then, when the family and farm hands left for church without him, Sean would have space to think about what he should do.

"Oh no you don't, young man! Get out of that bed before I switch you for your laziness. There is nothing the matter with you at all."

Mavis Marshall wasn't sympathetic to sudden illnesses that seemed to strike her boys on Sunday mornings but vanish by Sunday evenings.

Sean groaned melodramatically. He was unaccustomed to lying to his parents. "Ma, my gullet's aching awful bad."

Mavis slammed firm fists against her bony frame and gave her youngest son a firm glare. "You get yourself dressed an' down to the kitchen this instant or your gullet isn't the only part that will be aching you, Sean. You know I've been down there in my Sunday's-best since the sun rose, rolling out biscuits and frying pork to go with today's porridge. Now you hightail it down there and get some 'fore we leave for church."

Sean dejectedly pulled himself from the mattress and began pulling on his pants again.

"Lord, Mama. I'm a man now. A man oughta decide for himself if his gullet's in any condition to travel."

Sean knew his mother was not a nagger, a calamity-howler or a complainer, and she didn't tolerate any complaining or feeling sorry for oneself from her boys either. Sean knew that his feigned illness had not fooled her one little bit. She'd had him licked from the beginning.

Mavis simply turned and left. Sean could hear her heavy boots crossing the soft fir floorboards. He reached for his own boots, and there again was the box.

"Aw, hell," Sean murmured miserably.

With yearning, he remembered that when he was a small boy, before Preacher Bowman came to town, his father, Wyatt Marshall, would conduct the family worship on Sundays. They would get dressed in Sunday finery and assemble in the small parlor downstairs, and Wyatt would read from the Good Book. Wyatt would read the parables and leave time enough for the boys to work the lessons out. Sean had only been five years of age, and he couldn't remember particulars, but he'd gleaned a theme from his father's preachings; and it was friendship, truth, honesty, loyalty, and a reverence for God and one's parents. Sean missed those sermons and lessons. He hankered for a return of his family's unpainted version of faith, a simple interpretation that asked only for the good Christian to keep the faith of his father and live honestly before man and God. For living according to the Good Book, it was considered that God would see to it all would be well in the end. Those were the lessons he learned as a small boy from the man he most respected in the world. After what he'd witnessed of the preacher, Sean dreaded going to Bowman's church and listening to his speeches of hellfire; he felt it a blasphemy.

The church was newly whitewashed and practically shone in the bright sunshine. As the Marshalls' buckboard pulled up the road, Sean could see Preacher Bowman standing at the foot of the steps, greeting his flock. The day was hot, but Sean felt a sudden chill. The preacher was smiling and shaking hands. At his side was his silent daughter, Blair. Before the previous day, Sean hadn't paid much attention to her. But that day, he noticed that she was even prettier than he remembered, with doe-like brown eyes that were sad and brooding. She bowed her shoulders forward and stood with her arms wrapped protectively about her waist. She stared at the dirt beneath her boots all of the time. It occurred to Sean that Blair did not want to be noticed. She acted like someone who wished to be invisible. Sean could not take his eyes from her.

Blair appeared nervous and Sean wondered if she could feel him watching her. He'd be nervous if he were her—he'd always worry if anyone knew. The poor girl must be drubbed by a fear of her secret getting out. Blair lifted her eyes and Sean could tell she was clearly startled to see him standing before her, smiling. She seemed to jump right out of her skin and blanch at the sight of him. It made his heart ache for her all the more. He wanted to throw his arms around this fragile dark beauty, but instinctively, he knew better than to touch her.

"Hiya, Blair," was all Sean could think to say to her.

She backed away from Sean a half step and looked back at the ground. Everyone else had gone inside, and the church doors were closing. Sean witnessed an almost-manic darting of the girl's eyes like some poor wounded bird.

"That's a pretty dress you're wearing, Blair," Sean offered.

In truth Sean thought Blair's manner of dressing was odd. For one thing, the girl wore too many clothes for such a warm day—a blouse under her dress and a sweater over the top—and she'd put a cleaning scarf over her lovely dark curls and chose to wear her work boots with her Sunday dress. She looked up briefly at his compliment, and Sean could tell she distrusted it, and him. She looked away again.

"Really, Blair. You look so pretty today. I was wondering if you'd let me take your picture later."

At that, Blair jerked her head up and shouted in a strange, hoarse whisper, "No!" And with that, she ran behind the church.

Sean followed around the building but could see that she intended to run all the way back to her home.

Sean wished he could kick his own behind. *What a stupid thing to say! Maybe she don't aim to look pretty, you idiot. Heck, that'd probably be the last thing she'd want to do. Stupid!*

Inside the small church, Preacher Bowman was telling his rapt audience of the genius of Paul: "For I do not do the good I want, but the evil I do not want is what I do…Wretched man that I am! Who will deliver me from this body of death?'"

Preacher Bowman searched his audience for one with the answer, but they all were quiet.

"His name is Savior!" The preacher boomed. "He sets the prisoner free. He forgives sin and gives the guilty conscience peace. He does more, far more! By the indwelling presence of his Holy Spirit, he gives us the power to achieve a permanent victory over the most sordid, stubborn of the sins that haunt and harass us. In Christ, we find the secret of moral victory! We know how we ought to live. We know how we want to live. It is the power we lack to fight Satan's temptations. This church is your vale of soul-making. We are all here to do the will of God, to be trained for our eternal destiny as his sons and daughters by the disciplines of life. Amen!" the preacher thundered.

"Amen," answered the small congregation.

Sean watched the preacher's face grow red and huffy as he shouted his sermon at the parishioners. Sweat trickled down the sides of the preacher's fattened face. White spittle had taken refuge in the corners of his mouth. His mouth contorted with ecstasy while delivering his conviction of God's forgiveness for even the most sordid sins. Sean could not stomach any more of it. His gullet truly was peckish now. He hurried quietly out the doors into the harsh sunlight and gulped in the fresh spring air. He had to find a way to help Blair Bowman.

Chapter 4

There was a small lean-to at the backside of the tiny cottage, the roof of which sloped so drastically low that occasionally, the goats would use the wood pile to climb atop it. Blair liked to climb to the roof as well. It was a hideout where she gained some sense of privacy and could submit to her pain-free fantasy world. She ran from the church to the top of the lean-to, and as she picked at the fir needles, she hugged herself with protectiveness and began the almost-ritualistic habit of talking to herself. The self she spoke to was much stronger and far more sensible than the Blair on the outside, she thought. The Blair inside, she knew instinctively, was the only reason she survived. She decided to give herself an inner name which she would protect from the world.

He wasn't looking at you the same way Father does, her inner-self told her. *It was different…it was like…he cared about you.*

She picked up a handful of needles and threw them off the roof, watching them cascade down to the ground. *No. I should know better than that. Father's always said the day would come when tempting him would no longer be enough for me, when I would begin seducing other men. And that's what I must have done. Why would Sean Marshall care about me?* she returned.

But you didn't do anything. You didn't even look at him. He approached you and said you looked pretty, argued the inner self.

It was my fault. I should not look pretty. I should not tempt. I must be a demon, as Father says. She hugged herself tighter and began to sob.

I know you didn't mean to, the inner-self reassured her. *Good gravy, Blair. You dress stranger than a two-headed cow!*

Blair could not suppress a small smile to herself.

Why must it be a sin to be pretty anyway? Why can't a boy be interested in you without it being evil? Why don't you get to have a life that is normal? the inner-self asked desperately.

Blair fumbled for the worn folded paper she kept next to her heart. Pulling the paper free, she unfolded it carefully and her slender fingers smoothed it out against her skirt-draped knees. She found it soothing to recite the words from the now-faded penmanship of a favorite teacher—how Miss Joseph knew Blair would treasure the poem by Emily Dickinson, she could not fathom. Her mouth moved soundlessly as her eyes followed the lines:

"Hope" is the thing with feathers
That perches in the soul
And sings the tune without the words
And never stops–at all
And sweetest–in the Gale–is heard
And sore must be the storm
That could abash the little Bird
That kept so many warm
I've heard it in the chillest land
And on the strangest Sea
Yet–never–in Extremity,
It asked a crumb–of me.

Her shoulders slumped farther. Her suffering was silent.

After a long while, Blair heard the sounds of her father's wagon pulling up to the house. He would be furious with her for not having started Sunday dinner. Surely it must be nearing two o'clock. She scrambled from the roof and into the summer kitchen, grabbing flour and leavening from the shelf and pulling potatoes, carrots, and onions from the drawer. She tried to look as though she'd been busy with dinner preparations for some time by scattering flour here and there and pumping cool water over the chicken and placing it in the enamel roasting pan. Her trembling hands were well onto the peeling of a third potato when her father walked in.

"I did not see you inside the church, child. Where did you go?" Her father wanted to know where she was and who she was with all of that time.

Blair concentrated hard on peeling the potato without taking too much of the potato away.

I went to hell for a short holiday, the inner self whispered to Blair.

But what Blair said aloud was, "Sean Marshall started talking to me just outside the door, Father, and—"

"Ah!" the preacher yelled as though he'd been wounded. "It begins now! You surely are the temptress, Blair. More so than your mother ever was."

"No, Father! I wasn't tempting anyone. I was…I was minding myself. I didn't want him to talk to me. I don't know why he chose to. I ran all the way home," she added desperately in her defense.

"And you believe, to be certain, that you did not tempt the young man any more than you have tempted your own father? You know that you are the Genesis seductress, Blair. 'Come, let us make our father drink wine, and we will lie with him that we may preserve the seed of our father.'"

The preacher's breathing was becoming heavy and his speech husky, with the sing-song quality that made the back of Blair's neck grow cold. She knew that if she turned, she would see the glassy, faraway look in her father's eyes. Tears began to well up in her own eyes, and a fluttery fear rose in her stomach. She could not see the potato she was peeling at all clearly, and she cut herself with the paring knife. Quickly, she grabbed a sink cloth and wrapped it around her thumb.

Without turning, she said softly, "I don't wish to tempt anyone, Father. I never wanted—"

"Ha! Never wanted? Do you not remember how you wanted, even when you were but five years old? You would come to me with stories of the devil and demons and ask to come in to my bed. I would hold you like a father, and you would squirm and rub against me like the temptress you are."

"I was just a frightened child, Father. You frightened me with stories of the damned and then sent me to sleep in this dark room alone," Blair protested more to the sink than to her father. She could hear him breathing heavier still, and her legs were growing weak.

"When I began to understand the will of God, Blair, how He replaced your mother, who was too weak to bear children, with a stronger and younger wife for me, you did not protest!" She could hear him fumble with his belt. "I know what you want, demon child. Lust's passion will be served. It demands. It militates. It tyrannizes!" He quoted De Sade.

The first whip of the belt caught her high across the thighs and sent her to the floor on all fours. Tears were streaming down Blair's face, but she could not cry aloud. The best she could voice in the way of protest was a weak, "No," as her father pushed her flat to the floor and pulled viciously at her skirt and petticoat.

He stripped her from the waist down and proceeded to strike at her smooth, soft skin with the leather belt. Each strike revealed an ugly welt. The preacher recited a prayer while he viciously stroked his daughter's backside. She tried to scramble away, and her father tossed the belt aside and dropped to his knees behind her. Blair fell into a different world where she felt no pain or humiliation. It was like being removed from her ravaged body. Eventually, his voice penetrated her dreamlike state. "Your sobbing will not gain you any pity, Blair."

She was not aware that she had been crying.

"You will not make me feel guilt for implementing God's will. You might as well stop crying and clean yourself up. You are late with Sunday supper."

And then she was alone, curled on the cold kitchen floor with nausea in her stomach. How she wished she would die.

Chapter 5

Rescue Blair. But how? Sean grunted in desperation. His head pounded with the thoughts he'd contemplated during his hours hiking Marshall Mountain behind the homestead, shooting randomly with the treasured Conley but only half conscious of the photography mission on which he'd set out. There must be a way he could rescue Blair. He would not, could not, seek vengeance. Even though that was what he wanted more than anything, his religious doctrine prohibited it. The irony that the doctrine he chose to abide by was taught to him by the very object of his abhorrence did not escape him.

If God would allow it, Sean prayed, *I would like to see Pastor Bowman horse-whipped. At the very least, the charlatan man should be tarred, feathered, and run out of town.* But such call to action would harm Blair too. Folks in town are plain and simplistic. He did not doubt his neighbors would find the Preacher culpable and view Blair as a pitiable victim. But she would also be the girl who has intimate relations with her own father.

Only Sean had actually seen how it was, and only he knew that Blair had no choice. Much to his chagrin, he had actually documented the sin. But in this case, a picture would not say a thousand words. The townsfolk would not regard Blair as *entirely* blameless. In any case, Sean suspected that the humiliation of others knowing about her deplorable life within those four shabby walls would be far more devastating to Blair than the assigning of any blame.

Someone had to get Blair away from that house for good. Someone needed to rescue her from the evil that was her father, his pastor, without making public the need for it. So far, Sean could only think of one way to do that. It was this notion, more than the sun on his hatless head that gave him head pains. More accurately, it was knowing that he would have to break his relationship with Rebecca—Rebecca who was more than his sweetheart. Rebecca was also his best friend. He would have to break off his promised engagement with her and could not even be permitted to explain why. Sean wasn't certain he could do it. But if he were to commit himself to the salvation of an innocent, suffering human being, and if he were to do so with pureness in his ambition and not for pursuit of praise or glory or station in heaven, then he could not tell Rebecca. Because Rebecca, in all her fair-minded unselfishness, would give her blessing even as her heart broke, thereby breaking Sean's heart in the bargain.

It would be far easier to forget about the photograph he had locked away, and all of the ugliness that the photo betrayed—pretend that out-of-sight means out-of-mind. But what would happen to Blair? He'd tried but could not shake her tragic beauty from his mind. Whenever he closed his eyes visions came to him, unsought and unwelcome, of the Preacher in contorted ecstasy striking Blair's delicate body with cruel abandon, forcing his bulk upon her. Of course it affected his sleep, but worse is the fact that Sean had been awake for hours and the nightmare was still playing in his head. *Would he ever be able to rid his mind of it?* Sean had come to a sad realization that so long as Blair was trapped in her unseemly circumstances within that squalid cabin, his conscience would not permit him to forget it.

The hike made him sweat. It was another warm day, this one stock-still and muggy. From the top of the mountain, Sean could see the bay to the south, the Pacific directly in front and under him, and the entire valley to the east. Bald Eagles nested in the high trees up there, and as he looked up, he witnessed an immature Bald Eagle soaring above. It could not have been a more beautiful panorama, but it was mostly lost on Sean. He could think of nothing but Rebecca and the emotional pain he knew he would soon be inflicting upon her. Still, it was what he intended to do. Sean made his mind up. He would ask Blair Bowman to marry him.

Sean arrived back at the house to see Preacher Bowman's buck-board in front of the carriage house. Fortunately for Sean, his mother had insisted on a second, more secret entrance to the home, one that her boys and the hired hands could use to get up the stairs to their quarters without treading through Mavis's fine parlor with muddy boots. Sean had never seen his mother actually hostess a ladies' tea in the parlor that the men were all warned to stay clear of. But at times like that, Sean thought it just fine his mother had insisted on having her way. He came in through an English pantry in the back and then through a side door of the pantry, which opened into a closet in the library, which had a secret passageway that lead under the stairs and into a linen closet, which opened into the stairwell. When Sean arrived at his room, happy to have avoided greeting the guest downstairs, he yelled a whispered, "Yeah!" and kicked his heels once.

"Sean!" Mavis hollered from the foot of the stairs. "Come down here, young man."

"Dang." Sean muttered his favorite new word. "Sean, when you're safe and happy, why don't you learn to keep your mouth shut!" he admonished himself as he trudged dejectedly down the stairs. "Preacher Bowman," he accented with a slight nod in his way of greeting the loathsome man.

"Preacher Bowman stopped by to learn why you were not in church yesterday, Sean." Mavis eyed her youngest son over the tops of her bifocals.

"I told you that my gullet was aching me. I wasn't too sure my breakfast would stay down. I just hung around outside is all, wait-ing for ya." He could not bring himself to look at the preacher so close to him.

"Fiddlesticks, Sean. Preacher Bowman has already told us the reason why you did not attend his service. You and that pretty girl o' his were courtin'. Did you forget about Rebecca, Sean?"

Wyatt Marshall stuffed his pipe and toked. "I don't see harm in talking to a pretty girl, Mavis. It's not like the boy proposed marriage or anything. 'Probably time he gets to thinking about his future. Can't walk around takin' pictures for a living." Wyatt glanced at Sean. "And, yes, he needs to think about taking a wife. But I don't remember Sean proposing to Rebecca just yet anyhow." He noticed Sean looked mighty uncomfortable with the conversation.

"Wyatt, he did promise Rebecca—"

"And promises get broken, Mavis. Isn't that why we have courtships before engagements? I believe we should leave the boy to try things for himself."

"I just said hi to Blair and told her she looked pretty is all. And I'm not a boy, Pa. I'm twenty-two years old. I do a man's work on this farm, and I helped to build this house. Dang. When are you gonna start thinking of me as a man?"

"Just as soon as you start acting like one, Sean. I don't care if you miss a Sunday service here and again."

Preacher Bowman's and Mavis Marshall's eyes blazed at Wyatt for that.

"But, boy…I mean, son, you have to start thinking how you're gonna ever take a wife with nothing but picture-taking for a trade."

"Someday, that's how I intend to make my living."

Well, son, that's fine. I hope it works out for you. But that someday is a might well in the offing, I 'spect, and you need to start givin' thought to your more immediate future. I reckon Rebecca's beginning to make some plans of her own. She ain't getting younger waiting for you, Sean."

Sean looked angrily from his father to the preacher to his mother. Mavis Marshall changed the subject. "I understand that you found a banana box with the Hudson name stamped on it, Preacher Bowman. That so?"

"It is. Went to the valley for some canning supplies. Must be ready when the berries are, you know. Saw that box leaning against a fruit stand on the main road. Asked the man if he'd part with it for five cents, and he said he would."

"You know, Preacher, my family is related to them folks who started the Hudson Bay Company. I sure would like to get my hands on a box like that."

Mavis could hint no stronger than that without being rude. Still, Preacher Bowman made no offer.

"You folks ain't the only ones with distinguished lineage, Mavis. Why, did I ever tell you where the name Bowman comes from?"

"Yes," came the response from all three, but it mattered not at all.

"My ancestor was the bow man for the king, the next thing to royalty, really."

Sean and his father exchanged a quick glance.

"You know," Sean ventured, "Ma's line of Hudsons comes directly from Henry Hudson, the explorer, and Pa's great-great uncle was Chief Justice John Marshall." He knew the preacher would be jealous of that.

Bowman pretended he did not hear that as he tweaked his ear in false aggravation. "Well, I reckon I've stayed long enough. Boy, I want to see you in my church next Sunday." He winked at Sean. As he turned to take his leave, he told Wyatt, "I believe that boy might have a work/play inversion problem."

Sean was certain the preacher had called him boy just to irritate him. *I can make myself an irritation too, Preacher. I'll come 'round Blair so often that you won't have an opportunity to touch her,* Sean promised as his eyes tried to burn holes in the preacher's withdrawing backside. Under his breath and just loud enough for his father's ears, Sean muttered, "I believe you have a dental/rectal inversion problem."

Wyatt stifled a laugh, turned quickly and left the room.

Chapter 6

When Preacher Bowman arrived at his own home, he could see the girl sitting atop the lean-to again, pickin' off pine needles and such. He jumped to the ground with a huff of disgust for the strangeness in his daughter. Wasn't none of his doing, he'd convinced himself. The child had always been strange. She'd wanted to sleep with her father at a young age; was frightened as can be of God, though her father was a preacher; dressed herself funny and talked to no one save herself—an odd girl, but not of his doing. He was certain of that. The preacher told himself again that he was a man of God who had taken into account and carefully observed certain external factors that God gave him the intelligence to understand. That it was easy to dominate and define some factors more than others in order to bend his religion to fit his needs, did not often occur to him.

Every man has such needs, Bowman defensively promised himself. He glanced up at the heavens and recited one of his own father's favorite De Sade quotes to no one in particular: "'Sex is as important as eating or drinking and we ought to allow the one appetite to be satisfied with as little restraint or false modesty as the other.'"

He did not go outside his home for his manly releases. He did not seek out women of ill repute or become a party to adultery. He didn't need to since God had seen fit to deliver him a particularly suitable wife, specific in the way that her soul had been damned upon first breath, giving him his mission to save her soul and eventually the trial to save his own. And he would deliver. Sometimes, it was necessary to beat the devil out of her, but he accepted the mission without reservation. He had convinced himself that he was doing God's work.

In truth, he did sometimes become afraid and shrink from his own actions. But Preacher Bowman never pondered those doubts too much or for too long since to do so would raise other questions. If taken a step further, those questions might not live up to the constitutions of public opinion, respectability, and reputation, which was what truly mattered to the family name. Oh, it would surely be a danger if he were to become conscious of himself. The uncertainty he harbored deep inside would not kill his body but would certainly kill his soul. Tucked safely in the back of his demented mind, Bowman knew that he was a helpless victim of something evil that obsessed and possessed him. He was unable to help himself in any way against the demonic power of his morbid idea. It proliferated in him like a carcinoma. On the night of Blair's birth, the idea of using her for a wife just manifested, as of a quite natural idea. And in terms of his own family's ancestry, it was not new. So from that moment on, the idea remained unshakable. He questioned it momentarily sometimes, as he did now, but then his need would tell him more loudly that his secret fears of the unknown perils of the soul were...mythical.

"Blair!"

She bolted from the roof of the lean-to, skipping down the wood pile with the gracefulness of a doe, and rushed to the wagon. "I finished the wash, Father." She looked away from him as she spoke. "I just took a moment to rest."

He grunted. "When you're through watering the horses, you may get ready the canning shed. I have fresh jars and pectin in the back here. Be quick, child. It is getting late." Under his breath, he griped, "Child must have the weak mentality of her quadroon mother."

"Yes, Father." Blair grabbed the reins and pulled the horses around the back. "Like you're not a sandwich short of a box lunch," she murmured to herself.

Chapter 7

"Hiya, Blair." Again, the poor girl nearly jumped from her skin.

"Oh…uh…I'm awful sorry if I scared you, Blair. I just came by to…uh…well, to see if you could help me with something."

"Papa would be angry if he saw me talkin' when I should be tendin' to the horses," she said to her shabby boots.

"If I could help ya finish your chores, then will you help me with something?"

What does he want? she screamed to herself.

Then her voice inside grew firm. *You just stay quiet, Blair, an' let me handle this,* the voice said. The eyes glanced up through long, dark lashes quite seductively. "Don't know how's I can help you, Sean. Anywise, I have to unload the cannin' goods to the shed…"

"I'll do that for ya, Blair. Pretty girl shouldn't have to lift those heavy cases. Show me where they go."

It was the most Blair Bowman had ever said to anyone that she could recall. Her heart pounded for it, but the voice inside was very insistent.

Just quiet yourself and let me do all the talking, it said.

And Blair was far too meek to refuse the order. So she had become that other girl again, she marveled, the one who was sometimes her only friend but at other times looked upon her and her father when they did unmentionable things in the bedroom and called her names like *pathetic* and laughed cruelly at her whenever he beat her.

Having given the horses a quick brushing and a watering and stacking all the crates in the shed, she turned to Sean Marshall and batted her eyelashes.

"It…ah…I'm…uh…let's go down by the river and…uh…I want to take some pictures, and I need someone to kind of stand-in so I can adjust for the light. I mean, you don't have to model for me if it makes you uncomfortable. We can take some pictures of the critters we spot."

She rocked a little and smiled lightly. "Okay."

Chapter 8

Ruth Snyder and her lover, Judd Gray, were to be electrocuted at Sing-Sing. Mavis Marshall bypassed that article and the one about Babe Ruth's sixtieth home run for the Yankees, stopping at the piece about Amelia Earhart's flight across the Atlantic. She eyed her husband over the tops of the newspapers. Growing impatient, she willed her eyes to penetrate his paper that he might note she was disturbed by something. But Wyatt Marshall was a purposeful man, and he read his newspaper from headline to finish, stopping only for a sip of marvelous Brazilian coffee. Finally, Mavis's patience ran out.

"Wyatt, put down that paper!"

He neatly folded his paper so as not to lose his place and raised his eyebrows at his wife across the plank table. "What is it, Mother?" He had begun addressing her by the familiar name since the day of their first son's birth.

"What do you suppose has gotten into Sean? He's not called on Rebecca one time this week. And he seems to be spending an awful lot of his time with the Bowman girl. That boy worries me, Wyatt."

"Well now, Mother, I reckon Sean's right about one thing, and that is we need to recognize he is not a boy any longer. I'd taken my wife by the age he is now, had my profession picked out too," he added with just a sprinkle of disdain. "He may be a might slow in choosing, but it's his business, Mother. I think we ought'a not speculate too much about his courtships. Maybe he changed his mind about Rebecca. Ain't none of our business."

"It is our business, Wyatt. I distinctly felt the Preacher Bowman was a might displeased with the attention our son has been bestowing on his daughter."

"Well, we don't want to be offending anyone so close to royalty as the Preacher Bowman," Wyatt tried with humor, only to be met with a glare that could light a hurricane lamp. "Oh, Mother, stop your worrying. That poor Blair Bowman could use some attention from a nice b—man, like our son. Something's terrible odd about that girl. Preacher's not up to the task of raisin' that downhearted child without a mama. She needs more of a family than she's got with him."

Mavis started to object.

He rushed on. "I might as well be struck down for saying it, but I think there's something not quite square up there," he said, tapping his forehead, "with the good preacher himself."

Wyatt Marshall was actually minimizing what he truly thought of Preacher Bowman, but he would never say such a thing within earshot of his wife, knowing how she revered the church. Wyatt suspected that his wife didn't so much like the preacher as she liked the idea of being close to a man who was close to God, close enough to gain herself, and the rest of them, a private ladder to heaven. He smiled to himself. He never faulted his wife for all her pretensions. She was a good-hearted woman, and he loved her.

"They're an odd couple," were his final words on the subject.

He shook his head and went back to his paper. Wyatt Marshall could not possibly know how close to the truth his statement was.

Chapter 9

They played mah-jongg in the parlor. It was cooler that day, like ordinary March weather on Oregon's coast. Rebecca was being cool too and giving him the silent treatment.

"That's a good book." He gestured toward the well-handled copy of *Elmer Gantry* that was lying on the floor at Rebecca's feet. "I sure like Sinclair Lewis."

"Seems I've had a little extra time on my hands this week and not much to do with it but for reading." Rebecca looked up at Sean pointedly.

She wanted to stay mad at him, but one look at his handsome face smiling at her and her irritation just melted away. He was not large, but neither was he small. His muscles were firm and chiseled from farm work. Along with his high cheekbones and good, strong chin, his form could have been hewn by a talented sculptor out of a mighty spruce. His smile always reached up into his clear green eyes, as it did then. Whenever he'd shrug and lift his brows and wag his head from side to side with that lopish smile of his, as if to say, "please put up with me even if I am an idiot," Rebecca's heart would flip. She knew she would forgive him again, so what was the point of staying mad? Sean couldn't help himself from getting carried away with that camera of his. And it was just a camera, after all. It wasn't as though she was competing for him against another woman. She smiled back.

"Yeah, I have been kind of busy this week."

"Taking pictures, I 'spect?"

"Lots of pictures, yeah…Blair Bowman's been helping me. You know, modeling sort of, to help me with the natural light and such."

"Blair?" Rebecca looked him right in the eyes, and then she had to look away quickly. She saw something there. He was lost to her. *Blair Bowman?* Rebecca wished she could hate the girl, but it wasn't possible. Blair was to be pitied. Many townsfolk speculated on the quality of that poor girl's life. But if Blair captured Sean's heart, she would soon be the luckiest girl in Nestucca Valley. *And did she capture Sean's heart? Well, that was what I thought I saw in my sweetheart's eyes, wasn't it?*

"Rebecca…Rebecca, I don't expect you to understand, and I know you should hate me for this…I wish I could tell you why I'm doin' it, but—"

"I don't hate you, Sean." Rebecca's eyes betrayed her by spilling over with tears. She willed herself to stop as she stared at the game board pieces, but they grew all blurry, and then she could feel hot tears on her cheeks.

"I'm sorry, Rebecca. You know…I love you." Then it was Sean's turn to look away, his eyes watering.

"Then why?" Her voice cracked with pain.

"I can't say. If I told why, then it wouldn't be a selfless act. I mean…I've already said too much, Rebecca. I'm sorry, I…I just can't tell you why." He reached for her hand across the game table and gave it a light squeeze. "But…I'm going to ask Blair to marry me."

One audible sob was all. Sean could not hear how he had broken Rebecca's heart, but he could see. Her tears dripped onto the wooden board. He looked back at her through tears of his own and could see her slight shoulders shaking beneath her long, yellow hair. He got up from his chair and pulled her up to him and held her close as she cried. Sean stroked her hair and whispered to her that it would be all right, that they were doing the right thing. He promised her that someday they would both be rewarded for ending their love. She looked up once, questioningly, and then embraced him hard. Sean was such a good man. He surely had his reasons, and Rebecca didn't for an instant believe that it was because he had suddenly fallen in love with Blair Bowman. Though Blair was undeniably beautiful, Rebecca knew that Sean loved her.

Then why? she kept asking herself. Rebecca began listening with her own heart. *Sean's reason must be honorable. He'd said "selfless act." Did he mean sacrificial? Didn't he just tell me he loved me? Didn't he say it was the right thing to end our romance?*

She unwrapped her arms from his shoulders and took a step back. Slowly, she lifted her head and smiled at him through her tears. "I won't ever ask you why again, Sean. I trust that your reasons must be good ones. Will you still be my best friend?" Her voice broke with the torture.

"I pray it with all my heart, Rebecca." He held her to him again, fiercely, unready to let her go.

Chapter 10

The clanging of the dinner bell reached all corners of the two-hundred-acre homestead. The Marshall men and all the farm hands immediately dropped what they were doing and headed for the large, warm kitchen that was sure to provide a bounty of hearty dishes for Mavis Marshall's hungry men. Sean was the last one in the door. He took his seat across from his mother, beside his brother, Will, neither commenting on the wonderful smells coming from the roasted chickens nor lifting his head to acknowledge the presence of the others.

Mavis Marshall exchanged a look with her husband, who sternly shook his head no so that his wife would not pester Sean. Mavis snapped her napkin open and exaggeratedly placed it in her lap, trying to get her young son's attention. Finally, Wyatt Marshall cleared his throat. Everyone bowed their heads and folded their hands in front of them. Their growling stomachs were eager for someone to say grace so they could dig into the bounty of delicious-smelling foods before them.

"Sean, will you say grace for us?"

Sean thanked the Lord a might quickly, and while that was just fine with the other men at the table, Mavis was clearly displeased. Everyone began reaching for and passing around bowls of early garden peas, mashed potatoes and turnips with gravy, platters of roasted bird and buttermilk biscuits, fresh beets, and some of Mavis' treasured golden russet apples that she cooked with brown sugar and cinnamon. Two enameled pots holding strong, black coffee were placed at either end of the long-planked table. Once everyone had served himself or herself and the table noise quieted down, it became obvious to all that Sean was upset about something.

One of the farm hands who bunked in Sean's room, Johnny Arthur, threw a biscuit at Sean's head. "Hey, wake up. Been spending too much time with the ladies, Sean? Pretty Rebecca tire you out today?"

Sean picked the biscuit up off the floor and put it on his plate. Nothing went to waste in Mavis Marshall's kitchen. "Just not feeling well," he answered by way of explanation.

"Well, son, what do you suppose is wrong with you? Still some of that stomach trouble?" Wyatt reached over and placed his hand atop his son's.

Sean withdrew his hand from the table. "Naw. I'm okay, Pa. I just been doin' a lot of thinking, an' I'm kind of tired is all. Been thinking about what you an' Ma said about learning myself a real profession. Engineering interests me. I'd like to go to the college in the valley and learn to be an engineer of the surveying sort." He looked up into the surprised faces of his parents.

"That's wonderful, Sean," his mother answered guardedly. To her husband, she asked, "Can we afford it, Wyatt?"

"I suppose if we have another good year, we could manage it. How 'bout it, gentlemen? Can we have a good enough year so that Sean here can go to college?"

"Ya mean so we don't have to spend another dinner looking at his hang-dogged face? I'll work double hard, Pa." His brother, Will, ribbed him.

"Sure thing, Mr. Marshall," said another hand.

Sean irritably shrugged his brother off.

"I'm sorry, Sean. I was just kidding around. Means that much to ya, we'll all work extra hard so you can go." Will patted him lightly on the back.

He knew that his brother had no interest in the farm. Some men were not meant to be dairy farmers. A job like that you had to love, and it just wasn't for Sean, not that Sean didn't work hard. On the contrary, Sean got up earlier than anyone and was always last in from the fields. And he worked hard while he was at it.

That way, he didn't have to feel guilty about spending time with his photography hobby. No one else really understood Sean's passion for the camera or believed he'd ever make a living with it. But it was Sean's life, and if he wanted to work like an ox so he could enjoy a hobby, there wasn't anyone who faulted him for it.

"Sorry, Will." Sean looked over at his older brother. "Just got a lot on my mind is all. I know you all are just having some fun with me."

"Not much!" Johnny Arthur chimed in, which made everyone laugh.

"That's okay, little brother." Will laughed. "Here. Have another biscuit."

He dunked that one in gravy and grabbed his brother by the neck to shove it in his face. The two brothers wrestled right out of their chairs and brawled harmlessly on the floor.

Mavis watched her own biscuit in earnest as she buttered it, deliberately ignoring the scuffle between her sons. Wyatt passed the potatoes around again, glad that things were back to normal.

Chapter 11

April 1928

Cloverdale, Oregon

She slipped quietly from between rough blankets and tip-toed into the water closet. As soon as the door was closed and latched, she lifted her nightie and looked anxiously between her legs. She was immediately assaulted by the familiar musty smell of her father. She grabbed a cloth and dampened it in the basin, rubbing coarse soap softened with lavender oil into the washcloth before using it to make her body clean again.

Will it ever be clean again? she wondered.

All the soap and lavender oil in the county wouldn't make you clean, Blair. He's made you filthy. He's a pig, and so are you for letting him do those filthy things to you!

But I don't let him! Blair pleaded with her sanity. *He…rapes… me!*

She withdrew her hand from under her cotton night dress. Much to her dismay, the white cloth was still white. *How many days have I repeated this routine?* She was unsure, but enough days that Blair knew she should have had blood by now, enough days that panic sprouted. Yesterday at the schoolhouse, Priscilla Mason had told her that "grandma was visiting," when Blair had asked why she grabbed her stomach so. That was Priscilla's way of saying she was having her menses. Blair remembered that she was usually over her time before Priscilla's began. Miss Joseph had told the girls that cessation of menses indicated pregnancy. She'd promised them that the day menstruation ceased would surely be the happiest day of their married lives, for it meant the bringing of a new life into the world.

I'll bet Miss Joseph doesn't know it's going to happen to you, Blair! I bet Miss Joseph wouldn't think it so happy a day if she knew it was because you'd bedded your father!

Blair threw her hands to her ears as if that could stop the voice from within. It was a terrible and obtrusive voice, and it grew louder with the passing of each new day. Blair leaned over the wash basin and vomited.

The coffee pot lid rattled in the pot as Blair tried in vain to stop her shaking. She poured her father's cup and splashed just a few drops of the boiling brew over his poised hand. Blair screamed when her father jumped up. She ran to the sink for a towel.

"Damnation, child! What has gotten in to you?"

Blair started to say something, but no words would come out. She stood at the sink, facing him, her eyes wide and her mouth frozen, and then she just began to cry. As her father looked on in confusion, her crying grew louder and bordered on hysteria. The preacher walked over and very casually slapped her hard across the cheek. Blair's legs grew weak at what she suspected would follow next, and she fell to the floor in a bawling heap. Preacher Bowman just stood over her, wondering what it was all about.

"I think…Father…I'm pregnant."

He reached down and turned her face up to his. He stared at her for many seconds. "By Gosh, Blair! I believe you might be!"

It was Blair's turn to be confused. She thought she would surely receive a beating for allowing such a thing to happen. But her father did not appear angry at all. He looked as though he were actually happy. He was smiling at her. He picked her up gently in his arms and rested her in his most comfortable chair. Then he fetched some milk and apples for her and urged her to eat.

"You must stay healthy, Blair. You have a child to consider now."

He is actually doting on me, Blair marveled.

"A son! I know it will be a boy!" He started slicing the apple into pieces for her. He could not seem to stand still.

"But, Father…" Blair was appalled. "I can't have…what will people think of us? I can't stay here. I thought perhaps you would send me to Aunt Mary in Indiana or take me to one of those city doctors. I've…I've heard they can…rid a woman—"

"Never!" The preacher turned red as a rooster's comb. "This was God's plan all along, Blair. Can you not see that? You are such a foolish girl. Drink your milk!" And with that, the preacher stormed out the back door, letting it slam behind him.

Blair always hung the wash down by the river. A few feet back from the water's edge, there were two fairly straight Alder trees, ten feet apart, from which she had strung line to hold the wash. As she bent over the wringer, she placed her left hand over her middle and rested it there, feeling only the slightest swelling to her firm abdomen. But it wasn't her belly that told Blair she was pregnant. Rather, it was something else her hand felt. No. That wasn't right. It was something her heart felt through her hand. There was no doubt in her mind at all.

When Sean came out of the trees into the clearing, that was how he found Blair. She had one hand over her stomach, the other on the handle of the wringer, and her eyes focused on some distant horizon. She did not hear him softly call her name as he approached, so as not to startle her that time; and when he came up beside her and carefully put his hand on her shoulder, she whipped her head around, startling them both.

"Boy, I'm sorry, Blair. You were really concentrating on something, I guess. I gave a holler this time. I swear I was not trying to sneak up on you. Is everything all right?" He truly looked concerned for her.

"I'm fine," she said shortly and went back to turning the handle as though he were not there.

"Can I help you with that? I mean, I know a thing about doing wash. I help my ma all the time. I don't think anything so strenuous should be called women's work, do you?"

"Huh?" She was far off again.

"Blair, let me do that for ya. Are you sure you're okay?" Sean carefully pushed her aside and started in.

She did not answer right away. She walked a few feet closer to the water and sat down on a large stump.

Talk to him, you idiot, the inner voice told her. *In case you have not thought this through yet, he is freedom. Blair, he is our way out.*

"Huh?" she asked aloud.

"Did you say something, Blair?"

She turned around to look at him, really seeing him for the first time. He was awful handsome and was always so nice to her. She wondered why. She knew she wasn't very pretty, and she knew that people in town thought her odd. The Marshall family had money, stature, and good looks.

Why is Sean here?

Ugh! Just quiet and let me talk to him, girl. You would ruin everything if I let you.

Chapter 12

"You're awful nice to me, Sean. I wish I could do something nice for you too. Maybe I could give you a tour of the church graveyard. It's kind of interesting reading all those old headstones. Did you know we have Civil War veterans buried there?" Blair's inner-self asked him.

"I did. My grandpa on my ma's side was with Sherman's army in the March to the Sea. He wasn't with us long after the trip here by wagon. He's buried there. But a tour sounds fine," Sean said. "Say, maybe we could do it this evening, just before the sun goes down. See, I was hoping to try something different with my camera. I've been reading some about different photography methods. I was thinking of trying to leave the shutter open once it got a little dark and writing something in the air with a lantern just to see if it catches it on the film. Would you like to take me on that tour and then help me with the experiment? I'll put your name in lights!" He grinned.

He watched as Blair transformed before his very eyes. She tucked her chin coquettishly and looked up at him through her lashes. Boy, but Sean thought she looked even prettier when she did that. "Yes, I would, Sean."

He finished the last blouse in the basket and hung it up with wooden pins. He slapped his hands against his trousers and turned to face her. She was writing "Sean" in the dirt with a twig, he noticed. He smiled to himself. *She likes me. That must be the reason she's come out of her shell,* Sean thought, though it worried him a bit how that girl could run so hot and then so cold. It was like talking to two different people. "May I come by for you then around five o'clock?"

Blair had removed her boots and stockings. Then she hiked her dress up well past her petticoat and stepped into the cool water. She turned and gave him another fetching look over her shoulder. "I'll just wait for ya by the fence, Sean."

"Okay!" He removed his folded pork pie from his back pocket and placed it back on his head.

"Well, see ya then, Blair!"

She waggled playful fingers at him.

He turned and hurried back the way he had come but perhaps with just a bit more spring to his step.

Chapter 13

Preacher Bowman visited his church in order to thank the good Lord for the son He would soon bestow upon him. But after a few minutes of basking in the knowledge that his son would be forthcoming, the demons who frequently tortured him started in. The demons asked what the congregation would think about the preacher's unwed daughter having a baby. The demons said that the congregation would run him out of town when it was learned that he had fathered his child's child.

"They don't understand this bidding I do for Him," the preacher yelled at hiding devils. Sweat began pouring from his scalp and forehead.

Ordinary folks would fail to grasp the holy design. They had not the intelligence or the insightfulness to recognize that he was just a disciple devoted to God's destiny for him. Bowman prayed for answers, and in due time one came to him, but it surely came not from God. Bowman began making plans of his own.

They called him the music man. Bowman's trip to Dolph to find him took several hours because the town of Dolph kept getting moved around, until these days it was several miles farther up the Little Nestucca River. Dolph had a nice hotel and a stagecoach drop but not much else. And by the 1920s, there were no stagecoaches running from Portland or Salem. The roads that connected the Oregon Coast with the state capitol and other citified destinations were primarily the rough logging and fire access roads of dirt that traversed the Big Nestucca and Little Nestucca Rivers many times. Most visitors who drove their shiny new Chevy AA's and Ford Model-T's as far as Dolph, were only too happy to park their treasured vehicles in the Dolph garage and taxi out to the coast.

Old Man Bell, who ran the Dolph station, had purchased a couple of used creamery trucks from local farms to use as shuttles to the coast, mostly for visitors heading to the Tjaden Bath Houses and Wellness Spa. The undercarriages of the creamery trucks sat higher, which made them better at navigating potholes, fallen rocks, trees, and other road hazards without snapping an axle or punching a hole in their oil pans. Bell had customized the cargo beds to accommodate seat benches along the sides. Canopies were installed to protect passengers from rain, and curtained sides unfurled to act as barriers to all the dust those hard rubber tires kicked up.

Buckboards and horsing were still the primary means of travel for most folks who lived in the area. The Marshall family owned a Tin Lizzy, one of the last off the assembly line. They'd also had its back seat removed and a cargo bed placed in its stead.

The Marshall's. Bowman grunted at the thought of them. *And that boy of theirs!* He scowled. He knew he would have to do something about Sean Marshall buzzing around his Blair at some point. But at that moment he had much more pressing business to attend to.

Bowman had heard things about the man who taught note singing, recently arrived in Dolph. Mostly, the things Bowman had heard were not at all flattering. The man was reportedly a beggar, a womanizer, and an oddjobber—and none too trustworthy. He was making his way from village to village, teaching folks to sing by note, hosting "shape note singing meetings" in local churches. The preacher did not favor them and had told his congregation that he would not have such meetings in his church. Even though the songs were mostly hymns, psalms and anthems, Bowman indicted the classes as being particularly popular with the young folks, because they used the get-togethers to mingle with members of the opposite sex.

All the windows were opened in the church to allow for the heat, which the many bodies in the room were generating. It seemed to Preacher Bowman that the whole town had turned out for the get-together. Bowman took in the music man's notes of the scale, designated strangely by circles and squares and triangles that were drawn on the blackboard for all to see. Each visitor was provided a tune book.

He didn't look much like a song leader. He looked like a poor dirt farmer, and he smelled like he'd been barrel-rolled in an outhouse. But the man proved himself a fine musician in short order.

"You, over here…and you…sing some notes for me…okay. Let's put you here…"

He divided the voices into four harmonic parts—tenor, bass, treble, and alto—and then set his tuning fork for a comfortable range and commanded the group to vocalize in fa-la-la syllables. Bowman found the whole exercise ludicrous and was beside himself when the musician led him over to the bass group and directed him to sing along.

After a spell, the four parts of the choir took up different parts of a song, each singing different sets of words, and by some manner short of sorcery, they all came together at song's end in perfect harmony. The music was so pleasing that Angus Tjaden, on Bowman's left, kept grinning and nudging the preacher nonstop during the singing, making the preacher more uncomfortable still.

*Look at that idiot, tapping his feet and acting like a jack*ass, Bowman thought. *What else can you expect from a man who runs bath houses for a living?* He also professed himself to be a "doctor of spiritual and mental health" and was laying claim to an ability to heal all forms of illness, from diabetes to cancer. *Bah!* Bowman moved himself a bit farther from the man's elbow.

They sang every psalm they knew. Then, for the finale, the musician passed out tune sheets for a popular new song, "You're the Cream in My Coffee." Bowman feared the roof might blow right off, and the windows too, for the singing was loud and pure and shaking with pride. The collection of voices was truly unique. Every one of them could carry the notes, most of them surprisingly well.

"Well, that's it, er, that's all there is," the music man announced when the song was done. He began collecting his tune books and sheet music amid a cacophony of protests. A new chorus broke out among the parishioners, who were sad to have the session end.

"Oh, must that be the last one?" someone whined.

"One more?" several more voices pleaded.

"Can we do this again soon, Preacher?" asked Angus Tjaden.

Preacher Bowman bristled a, "We'll see," and led the music man back to his cottage for lunch.

Chapter 14

The song leader played his role as logger and felled the small tree near the house, the one marked with white-wash, and cut it into manageable pieces. He'd taken a wedge from the side of the shack, propped up where he'd left it, and he split the log pieces for firewood. He'd stacked more than half a cord before he was done. The man worked hard, and he worked fast. For his effort, he was promised a good meal and better pay than he'd ever had before. Of course Bowman couldn't guess what the logger's usual pay was, but then the music man wasn't too bright, either. He'd taken the preacher at his word. He was a man of God, after all.

Although he hadn't bothered to wash up first, the music man plunked himself down on the bench before the dining table. He smelled foul, and he clearly needed a shave. Blair thought him uncouth, especially given the amount of time she'd spent preparing the meal. She had selected a fine pork roast of about four pounds and trimmed it carefully. She spit the roast and had built up a good fire under it. All afternoon, she'd kept vigil over the fire, sprinkling it with both apple and hazelnut wood chips for flavor while she basted the roasting meat with the juice of a pomegranate.

She had also chopped potatoes and onions and put them in a heavy iron pot that she had heavily greased with the pork fat trimmed from the roast. Those potatoes roasted until they were an enticing golden brown, and their aroma could be smelled all the way to their neighbor's home hundreds of yards or so north. Spring vegetables wouldn't come for another two months, but Blair retrieved a large jar of carrots from her canning shed. These she had allowed to caramelize in a pan full of butter and brown sugar, and just a dash of pumpkin pie spices that she blended herself. She also baked a pumpkin pie to round out the meal, and had set it in the pie safe to cool. It was indeed a meal fit for a king. Blair thought the musician/logger eyed the dessert a might impolitely.

The music man had grown hopeful for his pay, although he found the whole matter strange. Earlier, he'd been certain the preacher was unimpressed with his music lesson.

The music man ate so much food that he'd found it necessary to splay himself out on the bench with his belt and his top trouser button undone. He sat there and belched away his discomfort while Blair cleaned up the dishware.

"My compliments, ma'am," the musician told her as he tipped the hat he had failed to take off before diving into his meal.

Blair mumbled a hurried, "thank you," and exited out the back door to her canning shed, where she hoped to disappear from the sight of the vulgar man.

"Seems she don't much care for song leaders neither." The musician reached for another piece of the pie.

"On the contrary." Preacher Bowman gave the man a knowing look.

"Serious? Naw. Pull my other leg, it has bells on!" he'd told him.

"I never knew a young girl who didn't attempt to lure a man she's interested in away from the prying eyes of her father." The preacher pushed his platter away from himself and smiled. "You'll probably be wanting your payment now. I believe I promised you better pay than you've ever had before. Well, my man, it waits for you in the canning shed out back." Bowman nodded his head toward the kitchen window. He encouraged the music man to get up and take a look.

The musician followed Bowman's gaze out the window that hung over the kitchen sink. He spotted the side of the small shed and his eyes caught barely a glimpse of Blair's floral skirt moving within. He tossed a confused look to the preacher, who gave the man a surreptitious wink and then resumed his seat at the table.

A lecherous look registered in the music man's deep-set eyes about the same instant the preacher's intentions reached his cramped mind. The musician reached for the back door handle and opened it, looking back at the preacher once more to be sure that *that* was what the preacher intended. He was rewarded with a silent nod.

Preacher Bowman reached for another slice of pie.

Chapter 15

Wyatt Marshall was pleased to hear Rebecca's beautiful soprano. He had to stand close to her to distinguish her voice among the boisterous others. In note singing, the tenor lead the choir instead of the alto. She sang with a wistfulness that matched the sadness of her smile. Whenever Wyatt tried eye contact with the young girl who had, up until a week ago, been a near constant feature in his home, she looked away.

When the singing was done and the overheated neighbors grouped out in front of the church, discussing mainly their music but also other provincial topics, Rebecca had sought Wyatt Marshall out among them.

"Mr. Marshall, how…how is everyone at your home today?"

He reached for Rebecca's hand. "All's well, dear. Though somethin' tells me you're most interested in how Sean's doing." He saw a flash of pain cross her face, and his heart melted. "Oh my dear, what's happened between you two? A lover's quarrel?"

"I honestly don't know, Mr. Marshall. He broke off…" She bit her lip and fought back tears.

Wyatt Marshall made himself look away while the girl struggled to maintain her composure. "Let's walk, my dear."

He led her away from the others by the arm. When they were some distance away, he turned to face her. "I don't know what goes through my young son's head these days, Rebecca. But I fear it is not about you, nor is it anything within your power or mine to change. All I know is that Sean's been struggling mightily with something lately. I'll promise you, dear, that I will make an effort to speak to him. Might be he just needs some time and space. I know he's been doing some planning about his future. Forks in the road of that nature can send any man into a tailspin." He patted her hand lightly.

Rebecca squeezed his hand in return, but she looked at the ground as they strolled along, revealing none of her thoughts. Wyatt Marshall was right about one thing. Sean had been planning some very big changes for his life. What Wyatt Marshall did not know, and Rebecca did, was that those plans no longer included her.

She looked back at all the folks milling around in front of the church and Wyatt saw the girl cringe slightly. He understood. Sean and Blair Bowman were obviously absent. His heart went out to the lovely girl at his side.

"I think"—Rebecca gently took her hand back—"I should be gettin' on. I have chores. Thank you, Mr. Marshall. Would you…would you tell Sean for me that I…please just tell him I said hello."

Wyatt nodded and began stuffing his pipe bowl as he watched Rebecca walk away. "Sure hope that boy knows what he's doin'," he said to no one in particular.

Chapter 16

When Blair turned around, the music man was standing there, leering at her in a most disturbing way. He took a step toward her, his hands reaching out for her breasts.

"What are you doing here? You stop right there, do you hear?"

Blair skirted around the work table she'd had her back up against, and she backed a couple steps out of the open shed, intending to make a run for it, when she tripped over a buckling tree root in the dirt. Splayed out now, with the man converging on her with that horrid look in his eyes, Blair screamed. Still, he kept coming. She kicked at him as she crab-walked backward in the dirt. He jumped on top of her, pinning her clawing hands out to her sides.

"So, that's what this is all about." His breath was foul. "You like it rough, huh? That daddy of yours is sure an understanding preacher. He don't judge you none. He just goes out an' gets ya what ya need. Let's see what we got here."

Blair squirmed beneath him with all her might but succeeded only in arousing the man more.

"Get off…stop…my God…" She fought him. "He'll kill you if he finds us!"

"Kill me?" He stopped long enough to laugh in her face. "Shoot, darlin'. Your ol' pappy gave you to me." He pulled his pants down and wrestled her skirt up.

Blair did not believe what she heard. Surely her father, if out of nothing more than sheer jealousy, would defend her against that violation. She turned her head toward the house and saw the silhouette of her father's head and shoulders looking out the window at them. She screamed for him. Then she saw him walk away.

"There!"

The music man was grunting, with one hand still pinning her arms over her head and the other hand ravaging her body. Blair yelped. The music man was hurting her, but when she cried out, it only seemed to spur the man on.

Somebody, please help me!

She fell into the safety of her haze. Through the fog, she could hear the man uttering obscenities. She could see the violent attack of his body on hers. She could feel him blowing rancid spittle in her face as he rhythmically shouted, "There! There! There!" The physical pain he inflicted by his selfish cravings could not compare with the much uglier crime he committed on poor Blair, of wounding her spirit and mind in ways that would surely never heal.

Get up, her inner-voice, with an identity of its own, told Blair. *It's over. Go clean yourself up, for heaven's sake.*

Blair rose slowly, shakily, observing the bruising that was already beginning to form all over her body. She walked gingerly down to the river. At the river's edge, she knelt and splashed water onto her front. She looked down at her breasts and touched one of them softly. It held bite marks and bruises and scratches.

Father saw what he did to me...and just watched. He just watched! A pinched wail escaped her. *Did my father, who was so joyful of my pregnancy mere days ago, arrange for me to be raped just so that he could place the blame on someone else? Or...oh, my God...did he want me to lose my baby?*

Blair crossed her hands over her womb in a symbol of protection. *Will my baby be all right?*

She began crying, quietly at first but graduating into uncontrollable sobs.

That was how Sean Marshall found her.

"Blair?" He could only see her from the back, kneeling at the edge of the river and crying. He approached slowly, knelt next to her, and lifted her face up to his. "Oh, Blair. Oh, my Lord." Sean took in the torn dress, the dirt on her face and breasts—no, not merely dirt, but bruising and a lot of it. He blinked furiously as his eyes took in the gouges and teeth marks. He looked angry enough to spit nails.

"I'll kill him," he whispered through clenched teeth as he removed his white handkerchief from his pocket. He dipped it into the cold, clear water of the Nestucca and began dabbing gently at the most offensive dirt and spit that covered her.

Even as Sean washed her, the voice in her head kept repeating, *I'll never be clean…I'll never come clean.*

After a while of Sean's ministerings, she began to snap out of the faraway place she'd been. She was surprised that darkness was already falling. She looked into Sean's face, really seeing him for the first time since he'd found her there.

"Will you?" she asked.

"Will I what, Blair?"

"Will you kill him for me? Please, Sean. Please kill him."

"God forgive me, Blair, but I want to. How could your own father do something like this?"

"He didn't." She looked down, too ashamed to meet his questioning look.

"But…I saw, once before…the two of you here by the river. I know what he's done to you, Blair."

That startled her. "What you must think of me. I have so much shame—"

"No, Blair. This isn't your fault. Your father, he's a monster."

"He says I seduce him. I came to his bed when I was little. I was frightened. He…he says I am a demon child."

"You were an innocent child. He's the parent who should be lookin' out for your well-being. Instead…no, it's him who is responsible for all of this. You are a victim, Blair. Look at you! No woman would ask for this." Sean dabbed at the tears flowing freely down her cheeks.

"He didn't do this. The music man did. But Father…let him."

Sean looked horrified. "Your father allowed that man to rape you?"

"I was his payment for teaching the note singing lesson and for chopping wood."

Somehow that was even worse. It was too much.

"It was not enough to brutalize his own daughter? Now he has lent you out to be brutalized?" Sean pulled her in and held her close. He would have to kill the preacher and that transient scum for what they'd done to Blair or else go insane. "How could he do such a thing?" Sean asked of the sky.

"Because I'm pregnant, Sean. My father made me pregnant, and now he has someone else to blame it on. Or maybe he wants me to lose the baby. Do you think I will lose the baby, Sean?" She began crying softly. "What am I going to do?"

Sean had been struggling over the course of several days with his idea for saving Blair. He had asked God for a sign telling him he would be doing the right thing. Now he guessed the news of Blair's pregnancy was that sign. If Sean had had doubts before, the sight of Blair before him cleaved them away.

"Blair, will you marry me?"

She took her palms from her wet eyes, but she would not lift her eyes to meet his. *Why would this good and handsome man waste his life on marrying me?* Blair thought. She couldn't allow him to do that. "I can't," she said.

"Blair? Please? I think we could be happy. I'd get you out of here anyway. You'd be away from him. And I could give your child my name. I can protect you, Blair. Say you will and come with me now. I promise I would never hurt you."

"Don't waste your life on me, Sean. I'm not worthy of one so decent as you. I can't let you do it."

He stroked her beautiful dark curls and wiped her tears. "I want to marry you, Blair. I know that in time we'd even grow to love each other. We can be happy. C'mon, Blair. Tell me you will."

She felt miserable and overjoyed, scared and hopeful. She was in Sean's arms, and those warm, comforting arms enveloped her completely. Her face was pressed to his shirt, and she could feel and hear his strong heart beating. His gentle fingers stroked her hair, and his eyes held nothing but compassion. There was no judgment there.

After all God had allowed her father to do to her, is this, in some way, compensation?

She never believed she deserved happiness. But Sean had told her that none of it was her doing. Her father, the preacher, was the wicked one. She was a victim.

Say yes! The inner-self urged.

Blair took a gulp of air and wiped her eyes. "All right, Sean. I will."

Chapter 17

Sean led Blair back to the Marshall house. He would never allow her to sleep in the cottage again. She was his responsibility now, and he aimed to live up to his promise to her that he would not allow her to be hurt again. Mavis Marshall took one look at the disheveled girl being ushered through the door by her youngest son and sheltered her like a mother hen did her chicks. To her credit, Mavis asked no questions. She merely took the girl from her youngest son's arm and led her to the bathing room. She filled the oversized claw-foot tub with warm, soapy water, adding a touch of rose water and glycerin to soothe the poor girl's skin. She helped the girl undress in silence, almost. Mavis could not call back the gasp that escaped her when the child removed her blouse.

Blair bit her lower lip at the exclamation, humiliated beyond words.

Mavis put a soft arm around the girl's shoulders, stroked her hair and whispered, "I'm going to burn these clothes, child. I want you to slip into the water and soak yourself awhile. I'll come back to check on you with a cup of hot tea."

Blair nodded somewhat mechanically and stepped into the inviting bathwater.

Mavis closed the door quietly behind her, the girl's ragged clothing piled in her arm. She handed them to Will, who stood talking quietly with Wyatt, Sean, and the two farm hands who received room and board, Johnny Arthur and Henry Kellerich. Will stared at the torn and blood-stained blouse that lay atop the pile. Sean could see that his brother was seething, and it may have been the first time he had ever seen Will so angry. Will had a reputation with the ladies, Sean knew. But he was not a womanizer. On the contrary, Will cherished the fair sex, and seemed to put every woman he knew up on a pedestal. When Will saw him usher in the tender young girl, with her delicate body battered and bruised and her lovely face stained with tears and more, Sean thought Will looked fit to do murder.

"Burn them," Mavis ordered. She pulled her husband aside and told him, "Wyatt, that sweet girl is covered with bruising and bleedin' and teeth marks, for heaven's sake. She's been… dear heaven…so horribly violated." Tears escaped her eyes and Wyatt drew her head to his shoulder. Mavis drew strength from her husband's touch. She squared her shoulders and announced, "The brute who's work this is must be dealt with in the strongest terms, and swiftly." She turned toward her sons and charged, "Who's responsible?"

"She says it was the music man, Ma. Came over to chop wood for the preacher and…" He shrugged. Sean would not lie to save a man like the preacher, but neither would he reveal the ugly secret he'd promised Blair would never be known to anyone but him.

Henry slapped Johnny on the back. "Let's get 'im."

They left to fetch the horses.

"Someone needs to tell the preacher what's happened, Wyatt."

"I will go over and visit with him about the matter," Wyatt promised.

Sean reached for his mother's arm and touched it softly, saying, "Ma, please, don't leave her alone. I, I want her to stay here from now on. She's scared of the cottage, an'…well, anyhow, I intend to make her my wife soon as possible."

Wyatt's pipe fell out of his mouth. "Son…are ya sure?"

"Pa, there's some things you don't know, an' I can't tell ya neither. But I have made up my mind on this. She's not goin' back to the preacher's house. I want her to stay here, with us."

Stunned, Mavis left the room to fetch some tea for Blair so the men could talk.

Wyatt Marshall and his youngest son were left standing face-to-face. "Sean, is this what has been laying so heavy on your mind these recent days?"

"Pa, I can't talk about it. I made promises."

Wyatt bent and retrieved his pipe from the soft fir floorboards. The tobacco had been strewn wide and wild. He plucked at snuff remnants he could find and stuffed them back into the pipe; his shaking hands visibly betrayed strained nerves.

Sean could see the effect his announcement had on his father—Wyatt Marshall was clearly rattled. Sean bent and swept up what remaining tobacco could be seen into his hand, and poured it into his father's palm. "I'm sorry, Pa."

Wyatt looked into his son's eyes. "And, Rebecca?"

"It's going to be alright, Pa."

Wyatt grabbed his son's hand between his and squeezed. He nodded, but said nothing. There was nothing to say. And yet, he harbored a gnawing worry that a great storm was building on the horizon. He worried for Sean.

Later that evening an angry mob, lead and incited by the preacher himself, pushed and prodded the music man toward the octopus tree. The eight branches of that particular spruce bent horizontal before reaching for the sky, giving the appearance of an octopus gone belly up. Henry Kellerich tied the noose and heaved it over a strong arm of the tree. He had no weak stomach for the task he set about doing. A German at heart, Kellerich was an advocate of swift, sure justice. He'd seen the girl come into the house with Sean, seen the beauty's haunted eyes and tear-stained face, her delicate body ravaged by the sick rotter standing too near to him for his liking. Johnny grabbed the man, whose hands had been tied tightly behind him, and shoved him toward the noose. The man stumbled and fell to his knees. He began crying, which only proved to disgust Kellerich all the more.

"Get up, you pagan," he jerked the man to his feet and threw the noose around his neck. "It's time to answer to your maker."

He and Johnny pushed the man up into the saddle of Johnny's horse, Paint, as the township urged the punishment to befall. The music man was wailing. He pleaded for a chance to explain himself but could not be heard above the jeers and insults from the crowd. His eyes searched out Bowman in the midst of the onlookers and he yelled, "The devil tricked me. He made me do it!" Just then, Johnny Arthur slapped his horse's hind quarters and the rope stretched taught as the horse unseated its rider.

"Then to the devil with you!" the preacher hollered piously above his parishioners' cheers as the life blinked out of the music man.

Chapter 18

April, 1928

Cloverdale, Oregon

"I know you don't care none for the man, Sean. I haven't asked you about your business, but, son, goin' to the Justice in the valley when her pa is a preacher? It don't set right, Sean. People are gonna ask questions."

"Well, let them ask their questions. Blair's never been anywhere outside of Cloverdale, so we're getting married in the valley and spendin' our honeymoon there."

He pulled the canopy over the Tin Lizzy and snapped it in place. The car was loaded with their things already. Now, with the canopy in place, they would keep dry even if the thunderstorm that was threatening decided to show itself. He just needed to fetch his bride-to-be and they would be ready to leave.

"Son, I guess there's no point in stalling about this. It's time for me to give you some instructions." Wyatt raised his eyebrows meaningfully.

"Oh, Pa." Sean groaned. "You don't got to. Heck, I been on a farm my whole life. I've watched the bulls with the cows before."

"Well, son, I hope you know there's quite a difference between dairy cows and ladies."

"Shh." Sean chuckled with a little embarrassment. "You know what I mean, Pa. I think I understand what goes where. Thanks anyway."

"Not so fast, boy, I mean, son. It ain't just a matter of what goes where. And if that's what you think, then you do need my advice. So now sit down. You got a minute you can spare your old pa."

They rested in the shade of the car, and Wyatt pondered only for a few seconds about what he should say.

"Women need to be caressed, and they need to be talked to. They need compliments and hugs just as much as they need the sex."

"Pa—"

Sean tried to interrupt, but his father held his hand out while he took a toke on his pipe.

"You better believe they need it, son. Don't make the mistake of thinking women have only a passing interest in the bedroom, that they are only fulfilling a wifely duty. They like it too. It just isn't ladylike to admit it is all. You've got to be gentle with Blair, and you got to always remember to talk nice. Say good things, and say them often. Women don't take a pledge of love as doctrine, Sean. There's something in the way the female mind works that makes it so they need to be reminded of it often. If you stop telling her you love her, she'll start thinking you've changed your mind. Then this giant fence gets built up with all those unsaid words of love, 'til that fence is just too darned high and there's no fight left for climbing. Do you understand me, Sean?"

"Yes, sir. Pa, is that so? I mean about women liking it as much as we do?"

Wyatt leaned into his son's ear and whispered like a confederate, "Just between you and me, I believe they like it more." He winked. "Now, are you absolutely certain you know what goes where?"

Sean shook his head and laughed with his father. "Thanks, Pa." He stood, dusted off the seat of his trousers, and turned to go.

"Sean." Wyatt turned Sean to face him by placing a concerned hand on his shoulder. "There's something else that needs saying and…somethin's not cricket. I know that much, but I don't know what it is. I suspect it has a good deal to do with the preacher and why you don't care none for the man. I trust your judgment, my boy, but I don't want you to get hurt. Have you thought this all the way through?"

"I have, Pa."

"Well, she's an awfully sweet girl, son. Pretty as a peach too. But frail, I fear. She's gonna need lookin' after more than most." He gave an amused chuckle. "Your ma is sure in all her glory havin' Blair around. She's the daughter…well, I don't s'pose you'd remember that you had a baby sister for a short while."

"Really? What happened?"

"Her name was Leslie. She just didn't make it. It is a hard thing for your ma to talk about. She made me swear to never mention it. You were only two years old when she died. Leslie left us in her sleep without so much as a cry or a whimper. Your ma so wanted a little girl, and our little Leslie was such a joy. Women like havin' baby girls to dress up like the dolls of their childhoods."

Sean smiled. "I'm really glad Ma's taken such a shine to Blair. But you're wrong about her, Pa. She's stronger than you'll ever know."

Wyatt Marshall nodded sadly. Something else needed to be said there, but how would he put it to words? So much about this pending matrimony was veiled and arcane, and it was clear both Blair and Sean wanted to keep it that way. "Sean, just remember that life is full of trials, and not one of us will win every trial every time."

His son gave him a questioning look, but Wyatt continued on.

"Oh, I expect I'm not saying this exactly right, but I need you to understand something. Sean, there's just no use pledging war with life's trials. I'm not saying a good man walks away from 'em, but a man needs to accept that sometimes the best you can hope for in this life are little victories here and there. There are going to be times in your life when you'll want more justice, when you'll feel you deserve much more. But vengeance is the Lord's wheelhouse, Sean, not ours. Remember, little victories. Anything more must be left up to God. In that, you must have faith, son. If there are any big battles to be wagered against—and I'm referring to genuine evil—those fights must be left to God. Believe in Him, Sean. Believe that He will set all things wrong with the world right again."

"I sure hope so, Pa, for Blair's sake." He kicked lightly at the grass beneath his feet with the toe of his boot. Finally, Sean asked his Pa what he really needed to know. "Have you ever, uh," he looked up. "I was just wonderin' if, if you…aw," Sean shook his head in frustration; he simply wasn't the sort who was comfortable speaking of such things. "Remember when you used to hold Sunday sermons in the parlor for us and our friends, and you always finished up the worship by saying how grateful we were for our blessings, and how the good Lord should use you as his instrument to do with as He saw fit, 'cause you gave your whole heart and soul, or life? I think you said something along those lines, anyway."

"Yes, son. I remember." Wyatt answered cautiously.

"Okay, good. Well, we—Will and I—always had our heads bowed and our eyes closed, but in my mind, I was sayin' those things right along with you, through all of those years. And I still include that last part in my prayers, because, well, I believe it."

"My sons are righteous men." Wyatt declared, with equal doses of pride and concern. He waited for his son to come out with what was really needling him.

"Pa, did you ever wonder what it would be like if He did it? I mean, if God really decided to tap you on the shoulder and ask you to do something that's gonna be, you know, hard to do? Did you ever wonder, if He did decide to tap you, how He would do it? Like, I always wondered if He would speak aloud to me, burning bush and all, or speak with a voice inside my own head. Or maybe He would come in a dream, or just kind of, I don't know, send me a message, sort of heart-to-heart, see?"

Wyatt Marshall sat back down on the stoop, heavily. This burden of his son's was a tremendous load. Wyatt would do almost anything to take that burden for Sean, whatever it was. But he realized no amount of prayer was going to change the facts: this was Sean's burden to bear. Wyatt was willing, sure enough, but he had not been called to the Lord's service. Sean had. With fresh pain clearly written on his face, Wyatt answered his son.

"I have wondered, Sean. I guess I always believed I would just know."

The men stared silently at one another as seconds ticked by. Finally, Wyatt asked his son the question left hanging in the air. "So, which one is it, Sean? How did our Lord tap you?"

"The last one. And, you do know, Pa. You just know." He smiled at his Pa. Sean thought his father looked beaten, wrung out. He appeared to have aged some over a matter of days. "Shoot, Pa, you look sad. Don't be. I think Blair an' me have a good life ahead. We're happy," he promised.

His father said nothing right away. But finally he stood, brushed off his seat again and faced his son. "Then I'm happy for you, Sean. You should be warned that the business of setting things right in the world might not happen soon enough to suit you. That's exactly why you've got to have faith that eventually, our Lord will dispense his justice and even things up. Justice might be slow, but it will come, son. Until then, keep watch o'er your backside." He took his hand from his son's shoulder and hugged him fiercely instead, slapping his back with both hands to emphasize his love for him.

"I…thanks, Pa. I love you."

"I love you too, son. Now, go an' get that lovely bride a yours an' get out of here."

Chapter 19

They were Mr. and Mrs. Sean Marshall. It made Sean feel like he was someone else, an altogether strange sensation. He wondered what his bride was thinking. He was surprised and pleased that Blair had not been too nervous about their being together. If anything, Sean was nervous enough for the both of them. He wasn't concerned he'd fail in any way, but he was worried about hurting Blair. To his relief, there'd been nothing to worry about. Blair had taken him by the hand, sensing his doubt, and had led them both through a wondrously tender union. He placed his hand over her belly and felt the warmth through the lacy white dressing gown Mavis had given her as a wedding gift. After long minutes of blissful silence, Sean spoke first.

"Blair, are you…okay?"

She smiled, and her hand joined his over the top of her belly. "I feel fine, Sean. I was just thinking about the baby."

"Say, Blair, do you already have a girl's name picked out? Because if you don't and if it is a girl, do you think we could name her Leslie?"

It would not be a girl, Blair knew. Her father always got what he set out for, and he'd said it would be a boy. "I wouldn't mind it at all. Leslie…it's a pretty name for a girl, Sean. But what if it's a boy?"

"Think it will be?" His thrill at the thought was evident.

"Could be just as easy."

"Hmm. Just before we left Cloverdale, Pa gave me, you know, a fatherly talk. And he gave me some advice for the both of us. He said we'd come across some battles in our life together and we shouldn't expect to win them all. Battles against evil, you know—"

"I reckon I do," Blair interrupted with contempt for the thoughts Sean's words brought to mind.

Sean turned onto his side and stroked his wife's cheek and gently tucked some stray curls away from her temple. "Anyhow, Blair, he said that we should leave it to God to fight the big trials since that's what our belief is all about, knowing He'll save or avenge us from the larger evils, so long as we keep faith. But Pa also said that we can hope to win the little battles for ourselves, little victories, he'd said. So I was thinking that if it is a boy, maybe we should name him Victory." He looked at her relaxed face, her deep brown eyes. "Whaddya say, Blair? No one but us knows we even won this little victory over evil, no one but us and the preacher. I think it's a masterful name for a son of ours."

"Victor…our little Victory." She squeezed his hand. She'd been surprised at her level of grief and worry over whether the music man might have harmed her baby. She was growing to love the small mound that was forming in her belly. It was time to give that love a name, wasn't it? "Yes. I like it, Sean. In fact, I love it."

Chapter 20

Talk around town said that Blair was made pregnant by the man who raped her. Rebecca wasn't so sure. She was the only person who knew that Sean had decided to step in and marry Blair before the act of rape had occurred. Sean could not have predicted such a horrible fate would befall Blair. But he'd known something.

Is it his child? A tight, frayed little voice in her head wondered. *No! You must not think such thoughts,* Rebecca admonished herself. She knew in her heart of hearts that Sean would not have done such a thing. His was an act of mercy, of charity. Without him actually saying so, Rebecca suspected that Sean's intentions concerning Blair were for her salvation. She'd promised Sean that she would never ask him why, and she wouldn't. But it was a black secret that concerned Blair's pregnancy, and Rebecca only prayed that Sean would not be harmed by it.

Chapter 21

"Guess tomorrow we ought'a be getting that barn roof finished, eh, Preacher? Rain's gone for a while, and things dried up. Best get to it while the gettin's good, make hay while the sun shines, as they say." Angus Tjaden elbowed the preacher's ribs.

"Yes, I s'pose now's a good a time as any," Bowman replied, tucking his scowl away. "Is the work party willing?"

"Wyatt Marshall says he can make himself available. Will and Sean told me they could be there to help, and me and my three boys will show. Couple o' the others here today said they'd try to get free for a while."

"Well then, I guess I better get to makin' a barrel of iced-up tea. I'll supply some fried cush as well to keep the men going," Bowman said. Cush was a southern tidbit made of well-salted cornmeal and bacon left sit to congeal, then cut into bars and fried in bacon grease. Bowman saw that Angus flinched some, then caught himself at it just a tick later. The man's cherub cheeks pinked up on the spot. Bowman knew folks hallowed Angus Tjaden as a neighbor and friend, and one of the main reasons was that big round face of his, plain as potatoes, which registered every emotion that swept across his five-gallon noggin. The man was incapable of deceit. *I guess talk of such paltry fixin's amid the fine-smoked salmon and oysters and other delectable dishes present at one'a his barbecues is too vulgar to mention.* Bowman burned.

"Well, that's good of ya to offer it, Preacher. You bein' on your own these days an' all, why not let the womenfolk handle the food? My Signey offered to send some cold fried chicken and slaw."

"Nonsense!" Bowman said. "The unwritten rules of a barn-raising dictate the holder to bring the food and drink. I can manage it." Bowman then softened a tad. Blair was gone and he couldn't cook much other than eggs and oatmeal for himself, both of which he would be pleased to never eat again. He shot a withering glance in his daughter's direction. He would not have minded some fried chicken and slaw. "Uh, but if Mrs. Tjaden is so inclined…" he added, noting the relief clearly written on Angus's face.

"Speaking of Mrs. Tjaden, is there to be another Mrs. Tjaden added to your clan soon, Angus?" Bowman noticed, and he was certain Sean Marshall had too, that Elrod, the eldest of the Tjaden boys kept buzzing around Rebecca.

A broad smile broke out across Angus's face as he followed Bowman's stare. "Oh, I would not be surprised a bit, not one little bit. Rebecca is a treasure, I tell you. And you, preacher—" Angus stopped himself from asking about Blair's pregnancy. Emotions were oddly strained between the preacher and his daughter. Angus cleared his throat and resumed, "All's well with you?"

Preacher Bowman grunted his reply, but studied Angus Tjaden's goodly and substantial face in a most unsettling way.

Chapter 22

May 14, 1928

Cloverdale, Oregon

The afternoon was a beauty; the sky was blue as a jay, a smattering of clouds waltzed with the delicate currents, and the kind-hearted sun kept its rays steady but moderate. Blair jumped up to fetch Wyatt a scoop of tea when she saw him approach.

"Fine day, Father." She smiled, one forearm resting upon her slightly bulging waist as she proffered the ladle.

"Certainly is, daughter. You rest yourself now. We can help ourselves."

Smiling, she sat back down on the pile of shake and squinted up at the men at work. It was a high pitch, that roof, and on top of a two-story barn. Wyatt rested with one hand laid on the back of his daughter-in-law's neck. His son had been correct. She was a might tougher than one would guess. Something dark in her past had made her so. Wyatt reflected on it now and then, certain that it had something to do with her father, the preacher, but not understanding why the two never talked to each other. He knew that Blair still struggled with some auspicious issue, a private matter, but he often saw the young woman's face change in a flicker at the mere mention of her father. Sometimes the girl's sudden changes unnerved him. They could come about so quickly and completely. But his son was happy, and she seemed to be happy in his company. There wasn't much more that Wyatt could have hoped for.

Preacher Bowman could only watch as his daughter, his wife, swelling with his son, conversed with her father-in-law. If there was one man in the whole valley who could ruin Bowman, it was Wyatt Marshall. No one had more money or inspired more respect than he. Whatever Wyatt said would be believed. Preacher Bowman had reason to fear the man.

Bowman watched as Marshall made his way back to the rooftop. The rafters had been covered with cross boards, and the shake was three quarters to the peak. The preacher had been resting for a spell. It would have looked inappropriate if he rested any longer. He climbed up after Wyatt.

"Can ya hand me another stack?"

Wyatt reached with the hand he was using to steady himself and slipped. His feet grappled for the cross boards even before his hands came down to catch him, but to no avail. Wyatt Marshall slipped off the roof. In a desperate grab, he caught a cross board and was holding on to his life with the strength of the last three fingers of his right hand. The hand was turned painfully while the rest of him dangled vertically over the peak of the barn.

Preacher Bowman had been shadowing Wyatt. He was the only man near when the accident happened. He scurried to the edge of the roof to help the man, grabbing for the outstretched left hand. That secured, the preacher grabbed hold of Wyatt's right wrist and clenched tightly.

"What has she told you about me?" he asked Wyatt through clenched teeth.

"What? Preacher, help me. I…I can't hang on."

"What did the little demon tell you about me? Answer me or so help me I'll let you drop."

Wyatt felt his grip loosening and he struggled to hang on. "Demon? Preacher, I don't—there's nothing—ah! Please help me!"

The preacher searched Wyatt Marshall's eyes and saw confusion suddenly change to understanding.

And Wyatt did understand. He had suspected all along that there was some dark secret that only those in the preacher's house knew of, and probably his son. His imagination would not have allowed him to guess just what that darkness was, until then. But in the flash of an instant, with his life literally hanging in the balance, everything became startlingly clear for Wyatt.

"'For I do not do the good I want, but the evil I do not want is what I do…'" The preacher let go of Wyatt's wrist.

Blair screamed.

The body of Wyatt Marshall hit the ground with a *whump*. His legs were twisted in a most gruesome way. It all seemed to happen in slow motion. The men came running from all directions, and everyone was shouting. Blair's mouth was still open, but she screamed silently. Her head rose up mechanically to look at the perch from which her kindly father-in-law had fallen. Her eyes met a look in her father's. It was a satisfied look. He'd killed Wyatt Marshall, and he looked satisfied, no, justified. She knew that look so very well. The day turned suddenly cold. Blair fainted.

Chapter 23

The body of Wyatt Marshall was laid in the back of a wagon and led to the homestead where Mavis waited. One of the Tjaden boys ran the entire distance to tell her there had been an accident and then cranked up Wyatt's Model-T in order to fetch a doctor. The nearest one was at least an hour's ride away, in Tillamook.

The lumber wagon pulled up in front of the house. Will and Sean had to restrain their mother by her shoulders from going to see her husband, whose fatal head injury became immediately apparent to those in attendance, the instant he was lifted by his oldest boy. The race to Tillamook would be a futile one. Wyatt Marshall had died instantly. Tiny, bony Mavis Marshall put up a hell of a fight against her two strong sons, but it soon became clear that she had derived most, if not all of her strength, from her husband. When she was told he was already gone, that strength ebbed from her like an outgoing tide, only for Mavis, the tide would never completely roll in again.

October, 1928

Cloverdale, Oregon

Wyatt's death occurred months earlier, but Mavis seemed to still suffer some sense of shock or other mental defect. She wandered around the house with all the jerkiness of a Chaplin movie and always with the wonder of someone who can't be made to accept. In her own mind, she didn't believe it. Every part of her world seemed suspended in a state of unreality. She went through the motions of being a functioning person, but she was numb and without motive. She kept waiting to wake up from a bad dream, but it surely was the longest nightmare she'd ever had. To Sean's dismay, his mother could not remember Wyatt's funeral. She did not remember the service or, later, the wake. She could not remember hearing the words over Wyatt's grave as the first shovelful of dirt was thrown atop the mahogany box, words that Sean could not forget.

"The good always die young," Angus Tjaden had said in the emotional eulogy he gave for his best friend, "because God wants the good ones for Himself."

To Sean, the words had not granted the peace of mind intended by their kind neighbor. Instead, they sounded hauntingly prophetic.

Blair had to remind Mavis to eat, and recently had begun sitting in a chair beside Mavis' bed to ensure that the emaciated woman *would* eat. Blair had scarce time for watching over Mavis, but she made time for the woman who had shown so much kindness to her. It simply meant that Blair's days would be a bit longer, a little more froward. She would rise earlier and, when necessary, would continue her chores on into the night hours. It was October. Winter was coming. There was much work to be done on the farm and one less man to see to it. Everyone took on a greater work load. Sean took his orders from his older brother, Will, who rightfully became the family's patriarch by default.

In Mavis's confused and sometimes trancelike state, she could not notice the changes in Blair. Her daughter-in-law would sit by her bedside and watch her eat, and oftentimes, Blair would read to her. Mavis was grateful to have Blair's companionship, even though she never really listened to the words Blair was reading. Mavis also failed to notice that the girl held no book in her hands. It seemed to Mavis that the larger Blair's pregnancy grew, the more often the girl would read for her.

Mavis went to sleep early on that day, perhaps coming down with a touch of flu. Blair accepted it as a chance to soak in a warm tub. She loved that tub. She dried herself and applied scented powder before slipping on the roomy nightdress. She was braiding her long, dark hair when her husband entered the bedroom. Sean was tuckered and bone-weary, but the sight of his lovely wife's reflection in the gilded mirror, nimbly tying her thick and glossy hair with pretty ribbons, brought a smile to his lips. Catching his gaze, she finished and walked over to him.

Sean kissed her head and sat down on the bed to remove his boots. Blair pushed his hands away and began untying the laces and pulling the boots free for him. That done, she rose up and playfully pushed him back onto the bed and unbuttoned his shirt. When her fingers reached his dungarees, he stopped her.

"Don't, Blair. It'll make me…"

"So?" Her eyes arched up seductively.

"I…we can't. Can we? I mean, I don't want to hurt the baby."

"I'll make it so we don't harm the little man. Just lay back and leave it to me."

She pulled his jeans off and spread his shirt open. She could not resist running her hands over his glistening torso, still tan from the outdoor work performed shirtless in the heat of September. She ran playful fingers through his soft swirls of chest hair before gathering up her nightdress.

She lay still on her back, twisting her braid with her fingers and staring out the window at the darkening late afternoon. Sean was awake too, she could tell, but he was lost in his own thoughts. Blair was trying to talk to herself, and she was angry. The inner-voice, the one Blair had learned to depend upon more and more for bolster, if not protection, was only supposed to be there for the hard parts. She was supposed to give Blair the strength she lacked to handle the hard things.

Well, he was hard, wasn't he? The voice giggled inside of Blair's mind.

Blair was actually jealous of herself. It was always the other Blair who made love to Sean. In the beginning, Blair might have needed her only because she'd been nervous. She didn't need her anymore. But no matter how hard she tried to rid of her other self during intimate moments with Sean, she always appeared and took over.

"Blair," he interrupted her argument with herself, "why don't you want me to use your name when we make love?" He turned on his side to see her in the half light of their bedroom.

"Wh—what?" Blair repeated, truly surprised.

"That's what you said. You know. When we were…"

"I said that?"

"You don't remember?" A troubled expression darkened her husband's face. "I must have called out your name. You bent down and whispered in my ear. You said, 'I don't want you to call me by *her* name when we make love.' What did you mean by that? Why wouldn't you want me to call you 'Blair'?"

Blair felt lost, frightened. If she could not control that other voice, would she eventually lose herself completely? "Well…I…" She shrugged. "Sometimes I like to pretend I'm someone else. Someone who is not…so…weak. When I was young there was a… doll. She wasn't mine—I never owned a doll. But a girl brought hers to our class one day and I remember thinking how beautiful she was. But she also looked smart and important. She was dressed up like a girl who might work and live in a big city. Anyway, I know it's silly, but I used to imagine that if I were that doll, I would be much stronger. So sometimes, whenever I felt— like I needed—help…"

"You mean, as long as you pretended you were that doll, or that doll was you, you felt stronger and more beautiful?"

"I guess so."

"But, Blair,"—he raised himself on his elbow and caressed her cheek—"you're so beautiful. And you're the strongest woman I have ever known."

"That's just the doll."

"No. That doll only exists inside of you. It can't survive without you. You're the strong one, Blair. And smart. Lord! Look what your mind did for you to help you survive. You endured all that pain and suffering and humiliation your father caused you. You're carrying his child inside you while you harbor the darkest of secrets. I don't know of another woman who could withstand all that. But you did. So, if pretending to have the strength of something else has helped you to do it, I guess I can understand that. You found strength somewhere inside yourself when most people would give up and die. I think you're an amazing woman, Blair, and…I love you. I'm bursting with love for you." He paused. "You don't need to be someone else when you're with me, do you?"

Blair started to say something but stopped. She didn't want to answer his question. She didn't want to hurt his feelings. Sean took the silence as his answer, and it wounded him deeply.

"I never meant to hurt you, Blair." His voice was full of sadness.

She slid closer to her husband and tucked herself beneath his chin. He cradled her and kissed her head.

"Sean?" Her voice sounded so small. "You never hurt me, Sean. You saved me. And I love you." She raised her head to look into his eyes. "I love you, and I love our life together, and I am completely in love with this baby growing inside me. I'm trying to make that other voice go away, but she won't. I used to have to call for her help when I needed her. Now I have trouble making her go away. But I'm trying, Sean. Really, I am."

"Okay. It's okay, Blair." He held his wife close, worried about who she was right then, fretting over who would give birth to the child growing large within her. But mostly, he worried for Blair's sanity.

Chapter 24

December 24, 1928

Cloverdale, Oregon

Victory entered into the world with the usual mixture of blood and pain and joy. The Christmas Eve baby arrived with thick, dark, curling hair and enormous dark brown eyes that made him the spitting image of his mother. Ever since the night Blair confessed an alternate personality to help her cope, Sean could never be entirely sure if it was Blair who was before him or not. It was cause for some concern, and Sean knew that his young wife should probably be seeing a doctor for her condition. But there were no Carl Jung's homesteading in the wild Oregon Territory. Sean had figured that he would treat his poor wife himself. He would treat her with even more love and more kindness and attention than ever.

For Blair's Christmas gift, Sean had taken a photograph of her to an enormously talented painter in Blaine, who produced from the picture a splendid portrait. All who saw the portrait hanging over Mavis's prized piano were taken back by the depth of the portrait's eyes and the slight upturning at the corners of the beautiful, full lips, like that of the famed Mona Lisa. One house guest commented on the portrait's mischievous smile, teasing Blair that she must know a secret that no one else knew. One of those secrets was that Blair did not remember posing for the photograph in the first place. And that was a secret that only Sean knew.

The only darkening of their blessed Christmas Day came from a visit by the Preacher Bowman, who demanded to see his grandson. Blair refused to be in the same room with her father and begged Sean to make him leave. But Sean knew that to do so would cause the townsfolk to wonder, and that led to talk. It was agreed that the preacher would be permitted to see his grandson while in Sean's presence. It was apparent to everyone that there was no love lost between the preacher, his daughter, and his son-in-law, but no one knew why. Sean and Blair had never brought their indictment to the rest of the Marshall family's attention, but they believed that the preacher had purposely killed Wyatt. Such accusation, however, could not be made without revealing a motive for the act. Again, the preacher went unpunished for the evil he had done.

Little victories, Sean reminded himself wistfully as he watched the preacher cuddle and coo his son. It occurred to Sean that his father had been right about something else too: justice would not come along fast enough to suit Sean.

May, 1929

Cloverdale, Oregon

It was a time for healing. Spring breathed new life into Mavis Marshall, who had for many months allowed both body and mind to wan in the confines of her bed. She had barely survived a malady of the chest since her small, malnourished body took in little with which to fight infection. But Blair had diligently nursed her mother back to some semblance of health. Although Mavis appeared to have aged twenty years in only half as many months, she did seem to possess a new zeal for life, due, in part, to Victor. A new baby in the house had given Mavis something to struggle for.

Victor was a precious little boy who delighted basking in the love he received from his parents, Gramma, and Uncle Will. Old enough to sit on his own, his inquisitive eyes were always moving and his exploring hands always reaching.

"Look how smart he is!" his uncle Will would exclaim at just about anything Victor would do.

"Just like his daddy. It just rubs off on him, I do believe." Blair would always follow, especially if she was within earshot of Preacher Bowman.

That day, Blair had dressed the tot in a white-and-navy sailor-like jumper with an adorable sailor hat. She had bought herself a lightweight shift of pale organza that flared just slightly at the calf-high hem. Fashion had become a new passion of Blair's. Skirts were coming up. It was the latest style, she assured her husband. She tied her long hair into a dozen narrow braids and then swept them all up at the nape of her neck with a wide lavender ribbon. Her only adornment was a long string of opera pearls, understated, but elegant. She wanted her husband to be proud of her, but she did not wish to upstage the bride. As she began descending the stairs, her husband, handsome in his own getup replete with suspenders, whistled appreciatively.

"You don't think it's too much, do you?" she asked with a hint of self-doubt.

Sean lifted the hem a tad and made a production of ogling her shapely calves. "Too much? I was jus' gonna ask you where's the rest of it?" He laughed. "Naw. I'm kidding ya darling. You look swell." He kissed her on the cheek. "There's my big boy!" Sean reached for the baby. He couldn't wait to show the baby off to Rebecca. She hadn't seen Victor in months, and Sean could not get over how fast babies grew.

Will and Henry stomped their dress shoes on the entry rug as they came in the front door.

"C'mon, people. It's time we got to the church. Ma ready?" Will looked at Blair.

"I'll just go check on her."

Fair, like his brother, Will Marshall was separated from drop-dead good looks the likes of which Sean possessed, by a pair of eyes just a tad too closely-set. But the mirth in his countenance and a wonderful sense of humor made him seem even more so. He was considered right handsome by the ladies, and women loved his distinguishing handlebar mustache.

Will took the opportunity to approach his little brother. "This don't bother ya none, does it, Sean? I mean, Rebecca used to be your girl."

"You kidding? I'm as happy as can be for Rebecca and Elrod."

His brother lifted his eyes questioningly.

"Really, Will. I'm happy for them. Hey, I'm a happily married man. Rebecca and I decided a long time ago that we'd just remain friends, and we are."

He punched his brother playfully, and Will grabbed for the back of Sean's neck. He dodged, spun around, and...stopped short when he saw the glare in Mavis Marshall's eyes.

"Sorry, Ma. We were jus' horsin' around." He quickly smoothed his hair back into place and shot an apologetic smile in his wife's direction.

She replied with a wry smile.

"Someone say it was time to go?" Mavis made for the door.

Sean hefted up the wedding gift from the Marshall family and made for the Model-T. Mavis Marshall thought the choice of gift frivolous for a young couple just starting out, but she had already said her piece about the matter. Anyway, Sean had been adamant. Handing over money was too impersonal, and picking out boudoir and bath items was too private. More than anything, he wished Rebecca merriment in her married life with Elrod, so he chose a first-rate phonograph and a selection of some of the most popular new songs: "My Heart Stood Still," "Makin' Whoopee," "Stardust," and "Tiptoe Through the Tulips." Knowing how Rebecca would love the player put Sean in high spirits on this sunny May Day. The only small cloud on the horizon was the awareness that it would be the first time Sean or Blair had stepped foot inside the tiny Baptist church in Cloverdale in over a year. They still worshipped in the privacy of their own home, and Sean sent the family's tithing to the Baptist church in Tillamook, but they had no use for Preacher Bowman's tabernacle and fully intended that day to be their last and final visit.

Chapter 25

May, 1929

Cloverdale, Oregon

Tiny finger sandwiches, bowls of nuts, and wedding cake did nothing to quell the aching racket Bowman's stomach was making. The Tjaden family had invited hoards of people to their reception and it appeared everyone came. The refreshments, times being what they were, scarcely made it around. None of the other guests seemed to mind—they were too busy dancing to that blasted phonograph to notice. *Where had his daughter learned to dance like that? It was a spectacle! And the hem of her dress—that was a spectacle.* As far as Bowman could tell, his daughter never threw so much as a glance in his direction the whole day long. People noticed, he was certain. Already there were fewer parishioners who attended his services, and there were far fewer tithings left for him in the church coffer. He didn't know what was chasing his flock away, but he could ill afford to lose any more. Bowman looked down at his garb and wondered if part of his troubles were due to his air of decline. *No matter how I try, I never get my garments as clean or as pressed as she did.* Bowman had made a request of the church in Tillamook to ask among the ladies if anyone was available to take in the laundry of a bachelor preacher. No takers as yet. He growled and lumbered back across the little cottage, which had not seen a good scrubbing in some time. *It wasn't supposed to be this way. He'd descended from the fringe of nobility. His family had lineage!*

His gut gurgled loudly, putting a sharp point on his sour mood. He was hungry. Sweeping deep-set eyes over the cupboard shelves he observed his stores were nearly empty. He had coffee and he could mix up some water biscuits…He paced some more. The Preacher had looked forward to that Tjaden shindig as an opportunity to eat something other than his usual fare of boiled wheat. He was hungry for a real meal. He'd not had one since his daughter left. He'd also not had a woman since Blair left. Bowman stopped his pacing. A large carpenter ant distracted him and he watched it trek in and out of the spaces between floor boards. *He could visit the reservation in Grand Ronde. The roadhouse there served a salmon filet barbecued on a cedar plank—it made his jowls juice thinking about it—and sometimes there were women, too.* He looked again in the envelope handed to him by Angus Tjaden, his fee for performing the ceremony earlier that day. He was doubly gladdened by that irksome man's generous heart. In spite of the poor financial state of the whole country, and some financial troubles of their own, or so he'd heard, the Tjaden's had slipped a nice gratuity in with his fee. Bowman grew bored watching the insect and violently ground his boot into the floor, smearing the ant across two boards. He tucked the envelope into his pocket and grabbed his coat and hat.

The bootlegger often joked that if it weren't for bad luck, he'd have none at all. One thing was certain; if good luck was to ever shine on Otis Welby, it would be when he least expected it. Well, shine it did that Saturday night in early May, 1929. And he certainly had not been expecting it.

By the time Otis got to the roadhouse it was after dark. He'd been running behind all day, and he looked every bit a tired man when he pulled his cart into the joint, loaded up with jugs of sour mash and homemade ale. It was his last delivery, he'd told Young Bear, so he enjoyed himself a cold ale while he waited for his sales ticket and cash. Young Bear almost dropped the mug he'd been drying, and Otis dropped his jaw, when a loud *bang-*

thump! from an upstairs room was followed by howls of laughter in a deep baritone, and also a female's giggle. Young Bear stared at the ceiling for a few seconds, maybe to see if it was going to crash in, but then shrugged his shoulders and resumed his polishing. Somebody was just a little over-zealous with the ol' slap-an'-tickle.

A few minutes later Otis was finished with his beer and Young Bear had finished counting out the money owed him. Welby took his turn to leave just as the noisy upstairs couple came down the steps, still laughing and carrying on. The Indian woman came into view first, who Otis recognized as a whore who frequented the establishment. She was followed by his town's preacher. And the man of the cloth was clearly intoxicated. Amusements stopped cold and mouths froze in brittle grins when Bowman came face to face with Otis Welby. It was Welby's turn to smile.

Chapter 26

October, 1929

Cloverdale, Oregon

Trouble had been just around the next bend, less than six months following the wedding of Rebecca and Elrod Tjaden, only they called it by other names: the Wall Street Crash, Black Wednesday, the Great Depression. For the Marshalls, it meant saying good-bye to Henry and Johnny, since they could no longer afford the cost of hourly wages on top of feeding the two extra hands. Much of the homestead's grazing acreage sat useless while Mavis and Blair worked hard at tripling the size of the vegetable garden. Sometimes a basket full of money wasn't enough to buy two loaves of bread, so Will and Sean put together a small gristmill for the family to grind their own grains and set about planting the untended portion of their grazing land with wheat and oats.

The Tjadens were hardest hit by the financial distress of the country. Their bath houses depended upon a constant supply of affluent customers who could afford excursions to Oregon's coast for the purpose of being pampered in the Tjaden's wellness camp. The majority of Angus's customers, if they weren't jumping to their deaths from high-rise windows, were flat broke. The tourist industry was moot. What paltry supply of customers remained were discouraged by the inconvenience of having the stage drop at Hebo removed. The closest drop was in the town of Dolph, which had been moved yet again, ever farther up the Little Nestucca River.

On top of that, Angus was being sued. Three different suits were filed against him for fraud. The truth of the matter was, Tjaden's wellness camp did heal people. Many folks came to Angus with complaints of muscle pain, fatigue, head pains, and joint troubles, and Angus cured them. He would feed his patients three highly nutritional square meals each day. He put the folks through a regular daily exercise program. He soaked them in steaming tubs of sulfur water, and he saw to it that each and every guest turned in early, guaranteeing a minimum of eight hours of sleep, and rose early to fill their lungs with fresh sea air. The problem was, Angus's cures worked too well. His patients showered him with praise, and somewhere along the line, some-one started referring to him as Doctor Tjaden. Will Rogers once said that a man's greatest downfall would come from believing his own advertising, or something along those lines. It was sure true enough Angus Tjaden's failing.

On a late afternoon in February of 1930, Sean was turning over soil with back-breaking speed and daydreaming about the new talked-about phenomenon, technocracy. It was a term used by those who believed that fast-developing technology would soon dominate the world. Sean believed it. He had just heard of a man who invented a photoflash bulb so that photography could take place no matter what the lighting conditions. Radios and teleprinters were already in danger of becoming old hat. Europe was experimenting with telepictures. Sean had a keen interest in radios and their workings. He decided that he would like to study in that area of engineering instead of surveying when he got together enough money to enroll at the Linfield college, if he ever got the money together. Times were tough, and money was too tight to mention. He sighed, leaned on his shovel for a moment's rest, and wiped the sweat from his brow.

When Sean looked up, he could see smoke on Tjaden Hill, a lot of smoke. Then he squinted and thought he could make out some licks of fire beyond the rise, the side of the hill where all the wellness camp cottages and bath houses lay. Sean pitched his shovel and ran for the house, ringing the dinner bell on the front porch in hopes that his brother, Will, who was out milking, would hear the racket and come running.

There was no danger of the fire moving toward the Marshall property. The wind was blowing the other way, and besides, the land was too wet from all the winter storms. Sean and Will rode to the Tjaden's house first. They found Signey "Sig" Tjaden on the front porch, surrounded by the younger children, wringing her hands nervously. As the Marshall boys approached, she lifted her hand and pointed west toward the flames that were clearly visible and hollered one word, taut with worry, before the men could dismount their horses.

"Angus!" she had screamed.

The boys took off in the direction of the fire, searching for the good-humored neighbor they had known and loved since they were both knee-high to a fly.

Chapter 27

February, 1932

Cloverdale, Oregon

Had it really been almost two years since they'd buried Angus? Where did the time go? Sean was thinking he was happy to have all that nastiness with the lawsuits and the fire investigation surrounding Angus Tjaden's death dealt with and discharged. The family kept their homestead and that was Sean's interest in the matter. He'd been beside himself when it looked he might lose Elrod and Rebecca. But here it was, 1932, a promising new year, and the fine February day was perfect for a road trip. Sean glanced sideways at his young son sitting up in the seat beside him. The boy's hair was thick and curly, and his lashes as long and dark as a beautiful maiden's. But Victor was all boy. Much as Blair tried to coddle the little boy and keep him close to her, Victor couldn't be stilled for long. There was always a garter snake or tiny green tree frog that vied for his attention, and nature almost always won over his mother's lap. It would be hard for the lad to sit still the entire ride to McMinnville. Sean kept having to bribe him with reminders of why they were going.

"Is mine gonna be red too, Daddy?" The boy looked up at his father, squinting because the sun was in his eyes.

"Yessiree, Victor. Red and bright as an apple."

They'd seen a picture of the tricycle in Mr. Wendt's drugstore in town. It had to be ordered by catalog from Sears and Roebuck, and only the store in McMinnville received the catalog orders. Victor had been waiting since his birthday on Christmas Eve until then, when the weather was finally accommodating, for them to go and pick up his present.

"Four years old, Victor." Sean shook his head. "I just can't believe you're getting that big."

The little boy smiled up at him. He was a happy child. They were all happy, considering. Life hadn't been too fair to the boy's mother, Lord knew. And it seemed like one tragedy after another had assaulted the Marshall household. But 1932, they hoped, was a bright new year, and Sean and Blair had decided, in spite of economic difficulties all over the world, that they would splurge that once on the coveted tricycle; thus, the trip to the valley. They would be staying overnight at a hotel, which would have been the closest thing to a vacation for he and Blair since their honeymoon. But Sean's mother wasn't in good enough health for the trip, having caught another winter cold that settled in her prone and vulnerable lungs, and Blair said that she should stay and watch over Mavis.

Sean frowned at the sight of a hand-painted sign on the side of a barn up ahead. It read, "Fascism Lives. Death to Stalin." It seemed like a lot of folks were upset about the unrest in central Europe. The papers reported on the terror Stalin used to rule the Soviet Union and on the atrocities committed by Mussolini in Italy, and Sean doubted that it would end there. The world was entering an age of dictators. Unrest usually meant an opportunity for men seeking power, and countries could begin falling like timbers. Rumor had it some young upstart in Germany was going to run Hindenburg out as chancellor. World upheaval was frightening to a young America, and it was to Britain and France too. Free democracies did not hanker to go to war again, what with the devastation of the Great War still fresh in the minds of many.

The barn was suddenly covered in shade by a large cloud passing overhead. The way the sign darkened just as he read it; Sean did not usually put much stake in premonition, but he did find that somewhat foreboding. Sean worried there would be no escaping troubled times ahead for his country.

Of greater calamity would be the trouble heading straight for Sean's own family, trouble that started about the same time Preacher Bowman noticed the Marshall's Model-T was loaded up and heading out of town with only Sean and the boy inside it.

Chapter 28

It was time to get the strawberry plants they'd dug up before the first frost and get them planted in the ground for spring harvests. Blair had spent most of the morning making certain her rows were straight and far enough apart from each other. Her back was giving her pains, but she kept at it, hoping to have all two hundred plants in place when Sean and Victor arrived home the next afternoon. She reached into the wheel barrel for another plant. Her mind wandered, and she thought of her little boy's glee when he finally laid hands on his treasured trike. She loved that boy intensely and delighted in spoiling him. Whoever would have believed she could be that happy? Despite the cause for its induction, her marriage was a solid one. She adored her husband, and he seemed truly content with her. And the child; Victor showered her with total, unconditional love. She patted the earth solidly but not too packed around the base of the plant and reached for another. A cloud must have just passed overhead because the wheel barrel was suddenly bathed in cool shadow. *No-no...* A chill skipped down Blair's spine, and she realized even before he spoke that he was near.

"Your husband has left you alone, wayward child."

Blair turned her head slowly to see the preacher looming over her. He wore the wide-brimmed hat that blocked out the sun and obscured his face. She put a hand over her eyes to see him better and rose quickly to her feet, backing away from him as she did so.

"You have no business here, Preacher. You're not welcome." She would never again refer to him as her father. She would not dirty the name she had used for calling Wyatt Marshall.

The preacher studied her. He hadn't opportunity to look at his daughter close up, because she had not visited him or the church in nearly four years. She was the image of her mother, the beautiful Jennie, even more so than before. Her youth had traded itself for more prominent, mature bone structure. Her lips were fuller, her cheekbones more pronounced. If anything, Blair had only grown more beautiful. She was twenty years old now, a woman, *his* woman. He took a step toward her and reached out to touch her cheek. Blair slapped his hand away.

"You leave me be, you hear? I want nothing from you and nothing to do with you."

"You are still my wife!" the preacher thundered.

Blair looked around quickly to see if anyone was near enough to hear the obscenity. There was no other person in sight. Will was working at the grist mill since dawn. "You are *drunk* you, you philistine!" she hissed. "I was never your wife. I was your child. I was only a child, and you—the terrible things you did to your own flesh and blood! I was never a demon, old man. The demon is inside of you!" She turned to run for the house, where Mavis was resting.

The preacher grabbed hold of her arm and spun her back around. With the other hand, he slapped her hard enough to send her sprawling.

"How dare you say such filth to your father? I have watched you go about your days with that Sean Marshall." He nearly spat the words out. "I stood by while he raised my son! I have imagined the things he does to you in your marriage bed, deeds which are, by right, *my* privilege! Oh, you are surely a demon, Blair. Be on your knees demon child!"

Her eyes grew wide with fear and shock. She had thought that she was safe from him, so safe that she never even gave thought to him anymore. She hadn't needed her inner-voice in a very long time, had succeeded in making it go away, but she needed it now.

Please! Her mind screamed. *Help me!* She was running. Somehow, she had found her feet and began running for the house, for safety. But he caught up with her, and they struggled.

The day was already growing nigh. Blair had been laying on the back breezeway for what must have been a very long while. The voice penetrated Blair's cloudy thoughts It told her she was an unclean, pathetic creature again.

Gone was Sean's devoted wife. Gone was Victor's loving mother. Cindy picked her battered body off the ground and made her way through the back door to the main house. She bathed herself with mechanical quality. She dressed and then began packing Blair's belongings. The trunk closed and ready, she sat at the small vanity and began writing Sean a letter. She couldn't just leave. She had to tell Sean what had happened to Blair. She wouldn't want him to think that her leaving was due in any part to something he had done. He was too fine a man for that. Cindy loved Sean too. She signed the letter and tucked it into a pretty pink envelope. She didn't want anyone else to find it and read the letter, so she looked around for a private place to leave it. Her eyes found the box Sean kept under the bed, where he stowed the money he was saving for college. She took the key from the vanity drawer and unlocked the box. She withdrew the money and put the envelope in its place. She wished she did not have to take Sean's savings, but Sean would understand. She locked the box but left it sitting on the vanity so that he might think to look inside when he found her gone. She looked around the room and said good-bye to the only joyous times Blair had ever known. Then, her stare hardened and her fingers snapped her small handbag full of money crisply shut, signaling the closure of Blair Bowman Marshall's existence.

Chapter 29

"I spy!" yelled little Victor with glee.

The top story of the house could be glimpsed from the downside of Hebo Mountain. Sean reached over and tousled the boy's hair. In spite of the adventure of going to the valley, the boy was obviously as excited to return home to Blair as he was. The trip was the only time Sean had been apart from Blair since the day they were married, and the intensity of his homesickness for his wife surprised him. A wave of inexplicable anxiety washed over him at the mental uttering of her name, and something spurred Sean to get home fast. He applied more pressure to the gas pedal.

On final approach, Sean could make out the figures of three people on the front porch, but none of them Blair. He saw his mother, well enough on that day to leave her bedroom in favor of the front porch swing. One of the figures was obviously Will, who was identified by the three quarter curl of his handlebar mustache. Sean had to strain his eyes to make out the third person. His anxiety quickly turned to dread. The noisy auto ground up the gravel drive. Sean pulled the red tricycle out of the back and lifted Victor down so he could play with it, and then he walked quickly to the porch, stumbling and nearly falling over a large rock, giving away his nervousness. At the top step, his brother grabbed his hand in an effort to steady him as much as to welcome him home, but the crack in Will's voice gave away a level of emotion Sean had never witnessed in his brother before that moment. It made Sean's legs feel like they were formed of water.

"Little brother, I can't spare you any pain, so I might as well come out with it. Blair has left you."

"What?" Sean was incredulous. "What happened, Will? And what's he doing here?" He jerked his head in the preacher's direction.

"Listen, Sean." He pulled his brother over to a bench seat. "I left yesterday morning early to see to the milking, and Blair was in the garden, makin' it ready to replant the strawberries. When I came back for dinner yesterday, there was no meal and there was no sign of Blair. Looks like she left her gardening right in the middle of her work. She left for somewhere without even seein' to Ma's care. She didn't put the garden tools away…" His eyes relayed his concern for the absence of his sister-in-law, a woman he had come to love and admire. "Sean, she ain't come home all night. Nobody's seen her."

Sean looked accusingly at the preacher, and he half rose with a threatening posture. "What did you do, Preacher? If she's gone, it's gotta be your doin'. You tell me what you've done or, so help me God, I will kill you!"

"Bah!" retorted Bowman. "Whatever you say. I'll be makin' it known to the whole town how you mistreated my daughter. That's the reason she's left you, Sean Marshall, and for no other cause." And then the preacher uttered words that sucked the wind from Sean's sails. "It won't do for my grandson to remain in this violent atmosphere. I believe he'd be better off with his grandfather, his only blood relative. My attorney agrees that it is right for the boy to come with me immediately." He descended the porch stoop and continued down the walkway to the drive, Bible in one hand, prepared to retrieve his grandson.

Sean was dumbfounded by what the preacher had said. He looked around wildly, seeing confusion in his mother's silence and grief in his brother's. By the time he realized that the preacher had left, the old man was within reach of Victor. Sean bolted down the walkway and twisted the old man around.

"I don't care what you say! I know you, Preacher. I know what you are! You'll not put your hands on my son. You hear? I know that if somethin' foul has happened to Blair, then you surely had a hand in it. You'll not get my son, you louse!"

"Your son? Was it you then, Sean Marshall, who was the rapist? Did we hang the wrong man?"

Sean seethed. "I ought to kill you where you stand. No. I should have killed you four years ago, when I saw what you did to your own flesh and blood."

The admission surprised Bowman. The preacher's eyebrows lifted in a way that told Sean the old man had believed his black secret to be sealed.

"That's right, old man. I saw you down by the river. I know what you are! And I'll see you in hell before I let you have my Victor."

"Well, you might find it to be a lot like hell, Marshall. But it will be a court room where I'll be seein' you. Mark my words, Victor is mine."

Sean reached for the man, but a stronger arm stalled him.

"Let him go, Sean. We will fight him legally. I want to give that miscreant a knuckle sandwich too. You can't imagine the garbage he's been spoutin' to our ma 'bout the way you treated your wife. Ma knows better, of course, but I tell you, Sean, that man is no preacher. He's evil. We'll get him, Sean, legally. So don't give him anything to use against you in court by using violence now."

Will shook him by the shoulders, unsure whether the glassy stare in his brother's eyes had kept his ears from hearing. They both watched as the preacher picked the small boy off the tricycle and carried him off to his car. Victor didn't cry, but he did look frightened, and his cry for help was a quiet one emitted from behind wide, questioning eyes.

Chapter 30

"I want my twi-shwicle!" Victor looked up at the fat man dressed all in black.

Bowman looked over at the boy, scowled. "Bah! We will not be needing anything from the Marshall family. Not after what they done to your ma, Victor."

"Mommy?" Victor's bottom lip had begun to quiver and his eyes brimmed. The dark man said nothing. Victor missed his mommy. He had not seen her in two days' time and that was the longest the child had ever been separated from her. High pitched *hnn, hnn, hnn*'s escaped the little boy's closed mouth as he rocked and soothed himself, and tried to keep himself from crying aloud.

"I won't hear it, boy. Are you a big boy or are you a baby?" He glanced sideways and saw the small child had already lost his battle with self-control. Tears were freely sliding down his hot little cheeks.

"I want my mommy," he cried.

"Your mother is gone, Victor. Sean Marshall drove her away. You may as well accept that you will never see her again."

"You're mean! And scary! And *old!*" Victor screamed at Bowman, who did not bother to answer or even turn his head toward the youngster.

"I want my daddy!" The four-year-old wailed and crossed his arms petulantly. He didn't like the dark man.

Bowman casually reached over and back-handed Victor across the face. It doused the boy's tears and crying like flour on a grease fire. He was stunned. Victor had never been hit before.

"I want to go home," he sniffed.

At that moment, Bowman's buckboard turned left to penetrate the dank, shadow-struck ingress to the squalid cabin. "Behold, Victor Bowman, you are home," the preacher said.

Chapter 31

Next to Cindy on the train was a finely dressed young woman returning to her home in Chicago, and she had a gift for gab, as she phrased it. Cindy did not want to be unfriendly, but she did wish that the woman would grow bored with her and take up gabbing with someone else for a spell. She tried laying her head on a pillow against the window glass and feign sleep, but the woman was not to be put off.

"Well, I guess I've told you all about me. What about you. Cindy, right? Where are you headed?"

"Indiana. To visit my aunt there."

"Oh," the young woman said in evident disapproval. "Not much society there, you know. I can't imagine leaving easy country just so to visit Hoosiers."

"Easy country? Why would you call it that?"

"Oh, I meant no offense. It's a good thing, I think. Oregon is…countrified. It has the feel of lemonade stands and church socials. Easy country is just a *nom de guerre*, what city folk in Chicago call hinterlands like Maine and Oregon." She pronounced it "Or-ee-gone."

"Oh."

Cindy realized that she was not going to have an opportunity to sleep. So, she reasoned, she might as well put out a glad hand to Percival and learn something about being in a society. She tucked the pillow under her seat and crossed her hands in her lap cordially.

"So, what's Chicago like?"

And for the next few hours, her newfound friend, Percy, devoted all her leisure in exposing Cindy to glimpses of the Chicago lifestyle.

Cindy was conditioned for trouble, which would certainly be a surprise to Percy, who considered life in the rural Oregon country as the daughter of a Baptist preacher to be "easy." Percy's misconceptions made Cindy want to snort with contempt. But when she stepped from the train and rested her eyes on the landscape of Chicago, everything was notably different from what she expected. Smoke-laden air carried along enticing smells from food specialties of at least three different countries. Brick structures jutted out among wide, people-filled streets, some towering sixteen stories high. Some structures were just steel skeletons of what promised to be. The men wore suits and bowties beneath their coats, and the women all wore fancy, touch-me-not finery. Will would have called them all "lollapaloozas," but Cindy thought they looked swell. She looked down at her own modest dress she had donned for comfortable travel and immediately determined to change her appearance. Why not? Blair was gone. Cindy needed a look all her own.

As she stood, admiring the city, hearing the noises and laughter of people on their way to and from jobs, shopping, dining and Lord knew what all, she became aware of a clanging that was growing louder, drowning out the other sounds until someone yelled, "Look out, miss!"

Cindy stepped back to see a bright red-and-brass street car bearing down on her. She had been standing right on the track, though she had not noticed it through the light covering of snow.

Chicago was everything Cindy could have hoped it would be and so much more. She breathed the city in and exhaled with satisfaction.

Indiana. Fiddlesticks. I belong in this city.

She hefted her satchel and started down a very busy street, looking for the first order of business: a place to live. Within minutes, she found a three-story brick building with elegant glass-etched double doors from which hung a placard reading, "Room for rent. Ring bell."

The buzzer bellowed with a hollow, gonglike sound. It was necessary for the buzzer to make a good deal of sound in order to be heard over the sewing machine's clatter from the first floor renter. Mrs. Warrington, an aging widow who never lost hope of finding another husband, primped before her mirror before hurrying down the stairs to welcome the visitor. Oh how she hoped it would be a renter for the top floor room in the back. That room had remained vacant for all of the last two months. Without the revenue from the back room, her overall profits were slight at best. She opened the door with a flourish and a grand smile.

"Won't you come in, my dear? Are you here about the room?"

She gave Cindy no opportunity to respond, as she continued prattling on. Cindy began to suspect that perhaps all of Chicago's womenfolk chattered nonstop.

"It is small but comfortable." She led her up three flights of stairs. "We get steam heat from the building next to us. The bed has a lovely set of springs, and the bathroom is only one floor below, but of course, you have your pitcher and basin here. I was formerly collecting three dollars a week, but I could let it go for…" She sized up the potential renter quickly, taking note of the humble attire and lack of coiffure. "You may have it for two fifty."

The strangely quiet girl was attentive and polite as the landlady continued with the advantages of renting a top floor room in the back. She was more than surprised when the silent girl opened a purse crammed with bills and handed her five dollars for two weeks' rent. Mrs. Warrington tended to regard any cash-carrying person as generally trustworthy until proven otherwise, so she did not require the usual exchange of references. The room was rented for cash, and that was information enough.

Chapter 32

March, 1932

Cloverdale, Oregon

In the early part of the twentieth century, protections for children came from nongovernmental societies, if they came at all. In rural areas, which Cloverdale, Oregon was, activists for the SPCC's (Societies for the Prevention of Cruelty to Children) were nowhere to be found. Small town rural governments witnessed shocking increases in the number of child cruelty, abuse and neglect reports, as well as in the number of calls for reform. The government's answer, "Juvenile Courts", took up the wider-umbrella of "Child Protection". The success spread quickly, and by 1919, Juvenile Courts were in every state but three. Politicians saw to it the remaining hold-out's joined up in short order.

The judge, in the case of Bowman v. Marshall, was an elderly gentleman who sported both a full mustache of solid white and a pair of bifocals through which he would survey a witness with an expression of mild curiosity. The white hair lent the judge an air of wise perception while the bifocals caused witnesses, mostly those conceiving of ill testimony, more than a little trepidation.

Will Marshall was an honest man, and as he testified his sincerity could not be questioned. Still, the judge made him nervous to the point that he began twirling that handlebar mustache of his, unintentionally conjuring a slightly fiendish image.

"You say, Mr. Marshall, that you never saw your brother strike his wife or in any way harm her during the four years of their marriage?"

"Uh…yes, sir. That's a fact."

"Did Mrs. Marshall seem happily married to you, sir?"

"Blair? Yeah. I mean, no one ever saw her happy until she married my brother. Then, after that, she didn't want anything to do with the preacher, like she was scared of 'im."

"Please do not make any suggestions to the court, young man."

"I…yes, sir. Sorry, Your Honor."

"Are you acquainted with the plaintiff?"

"How's that?"

"Do you know the Reverend Bowman?"

"He's no reverend. He's only a preacher because my ma and pa built him a church and the congregation said it was all the same to them if he wanted to preach for 'em."

"So then, Preacher Bowman does preach for your church?"

Will looked helplessly at Sean, who merely nodded for him to answer. "Yes, sir. I guess I know him as a preacher at my church."

"What is the relationship between your brother, Sean Marshall, and the preacher, as far as you see it, Mr. Marshall?"

"Do you mean, do they like each other?"

"Yes, sir."

"Well, I would have to say no, sir, not at all. It's just this way: Blair didn't want him around her or the baby, and so Sean saw to it. Seems there was nothing Sean wouldn't do for Blair."

"Did you ever see the preacher mistreat his daughter?"

"No, sir. Truth is, I never even noticed Blair until she became family. Then I never saw the preacher around his daughter at all. That's the way she wanted it."

"How do you know that was the way she wanted it, Mr. Marshall?"

"Well…uh…Sean told me it was so."

"Did Mrs. Marshall ever tell you this?"

"That she didn't want to be near her father?"

"Exactly. Did you ever hear this from her directly?"

"I guess not, like, in words, no. But whenever neighbors would gather"—he stopped to instruct the good judge that theirs was a close-knit community and there were many get-togethers, such as salmon bakes and picnics, barn-raisings, and church socials—

"and I would see him trying to…uh…layin' to make a touch on her, I could see that Blair always looked real uncomfortable. You could jus' tell she didn't want him around her."

"You sort of perceived her contempt toward her father, but you never actually overheard her say she was afraid of him?"

"What's that, sir?"

"Never mind, Mr. Marshall. You can step down."

"Yes, sir." He looked over at Sean miserably. He'd felt impotent up on the stand, talking face to face with the judge, and he feared that he might not have helped his brother.

Sean shook his shoulder and smiled wistfully when his brother took his seat next to him. The judge asked the preacher to take the stand next.

When the oath was administered, Bowman raised his hand higher than his shoulder and answered in his most arrogant, rumble-bass voice, "Of course."

"Mr. Bowman, some of your neighbors have testified today that your daughter seemed to be frightened of you. Not a single person has been brought forward who could testify to your claims that Mr. Marshall abused his wife. Do you stand by this accusation?"

"I do."

"Well, Mr. Bowman, how do you account for your own daughter's fear of you?"

"I was the only soul she could share her shame with, sir. The same reason no one else can testify to Marshall's assault and battery is the same reason she was afraid of me. You see, I had ordered her to leave him more than once."

"Well, Mr. Bowman, if that's so, then why didn't your daughter leave him or at least file charges of spousal abuse?"

"She was afraid of what he might do. The Marshall family is a wealthy one. And with that wealth comes power. Why, you and I both know how rich folks can pull strings and get away with most anything. I would not be a bit surprised to know that the Marshall money has tampered with this court!"

The judge rapped loudly and glared over the tops of his bifocals. "No impertinence, Mr. Bowman. No impertinence!" while Sean's attorney muttered loud enough to be heard all over the court room, "This is an outrage!" which it was, since Bowman had just won his case with that one inflammatory remark.

"You are excused, Mr. Bowman. Mr. Sean Marshall, please take the stand."

"Your Honor," Sean's lawyer objected. "I would like a chance to question Mr. Bowman about his motive for slandering this court the way he did."

"Well, sir, we all want things we can't have. Now please have your client take the stand."

Sean's lawyer blustered and ran an impatient hand through his hair and generally stomped his feet like a misbehaved child, but the judge paid no attention. Sean looked cautiously to his attorney as he remonstrated, but when he received no guidance, he decided to take the opportunity to say his piece.

"I do," he pledged solemnly in response to the judge's question of oath.

"Mr. Marshall…Mr. Marshall, are you the natural father of the child, one Victory Marshall?"

"No, sir, but I am his father just the same. I raised him, and I love him. I watched his mother give birth to him. I was there, holding her hand. His mother and I were the ones to rock him gently into the night whenever he took ill. I feed and I clothe him. I…I teach him…things…" Sean's voice broke. "He's my son…" Sean nearly sobbed and could not go on.

"Would you like some water, sir?"

Sean just shook his head no.

"Did you ever lay violent hands upon your wife, sir?"

"No! God, no! I would never do that! I felt sorry for her is why I married her, but then…then I fell in love with her, and we were, we were happy together. She's gone. I don't know why, and all I have left in the world is my son, *my* son, Your Honor."

The judge was a gentle man who was firmly opposed to domestic violence. He held that the man on the stand below him was telling the truth. Few justices can rebuff a strong man who is reduced to tears. He took a sip of some water to soothe himself before continuing. "Mr. Marshall, why did your wife leave you then, if not because you raised your hand to her?"

"I don't know, sir." Sean's anguish was palpable. "I swear I never hurt her. I love her. I tried to save her." He looked up at the judge with eyes which glistened. Then his face changed right before the judge's eyes. The lines in his face grew deeper, the hollows beneath his eyes and below his cheeks grew darker and his skin turned gray. "I could never harm her. I'll tell you who abused Blair…" He caught himself. He couldn't say it, not even then. Could he? What if she chose to return? She could be home right now for all he knew. And if she did return, her reputation would be ruined if he were to tell the court what he knew. He had promised he'd never do that. He'd promised Blair he would keep her secret forever. Forever was a hell all its own. He looked despairingly up at the bench.

"Mr. Marshall, you were going to tell the court you knew of some abuse your wife has sustained."

"No, sir. I can't say any more."

Will bolted upright and shouted at him. "Sean, for Christ's sake, man, if you know somethin', now's the time for sayin' it!"

Sean just looked at his brother and shook his head. Then he glanced the preacher's way and was met with a cunning smirk. Sean Marshall knew as sure as there'd be rain in April that he had just lost his son.

He was not cross-examined. In fact, the court room was deathly quiet. The judge rapped twice on the scratched and marred bench and cleared his throat. "I have heard the arguments and must admit that I remain in doubt. The court has heard no convincing evidence that Mr. Marshall has abused his missing wife. However, that is not the focus of this case. I am to decide the custody of a small child, whether that child is to live with the natural grandfather or remain with his now-wifeless stepfather."

The judge's good sense was in conflict with Bowman's alle-gation that the wealthy automatically emerges the winner. Fortunately, he formed a rule of conduct for just such an emer-gency: when in doubt, decide in favor of the plaintiff and order the defendant to pay all costs. He would bend his rule of conduct just a bit this one time. "In the case of *Bowman vs. Marshall*, I rule in favor of the plaintiff, Preacher Bowman. I dismiss all charges of spousal abuse against Mr. Sean Marshall. Each party shall pay his own costs. This court is adjourned." He rapped twice more and quickly exited the court room with a taste in his mouth that was thoroughly sour.

Chapter 33

"Can we get goin' a little faster, Will?" Sean's impatience was tangible.

Will snook a peek over at his brother. Sean was urgently tapping the outside of his door, through his unrolled window, with the fingers on his right hand; the other hand was busy keeping his hair from blowing in his face. The day was a sunny one, but that March air was brisk with the sting of winter still in it. Will had seen his brother that way before—every single day since he'd learned Blair had left, actually.

"There you go again, Sean. Plainly, you're still clinging to the hope Blair will be waiting for you when we get home." His declaration was met with breezy silence.

"Well it's either that or you're trying to drum the paint off the auto," Will tried. His attempt at light humor was lost on Sean, but Will was not the sort to be put off so easily.

"Sean, brother, she won't be there. I hate to see you keep working yourself up for it when it ain't gonna happen."

He did not turn his head. Instead, his eyes were focused on some place far ahead in the distance. "She might."

"No, Sean. She's gone. We tried everywhere. She was on that train to Indiana, but she never got there. She disappeared, little brother. People don't disappear by accident neither." He paused to sigh and to brace himself, too. He didn't like saying those hurtful things to his brother, but someone had to. He inhaled deeply. "She ain't comin' back. I don't mean to hurt you, Sean. I just can't stand to see you keep hoping the way you do. I mean, every single day, you're out in the fields or you're in the carriage house tearing apart old radios, an' I see ya go runnin' for the house 'cause you thought you heard someone. Sean, it's killin' me to see you this way. You gotta accept it or you're gonna go nutty. She's gone. Prob'ly forever."

Finally, his brother turned to him. So he had been listening. Will was never sure those days.

Sean fixed him with a hard stare. "No, Will. I won't accept it. I can't. Don't you see? I just lost my son. And the only way I can get Victor back is if Blair comes home. So she has to. She has to come home, Will. Don't you understand that?"

"I'm sorry, Sean." And he truly was.

Chapter 34

Sean lay in his bed, alone again. The pale pink envelope was clenched in his hand. The house was too quiet. It was absent the sound of a child. It lacked the industrious noise of a young mother getting that child ready for bed. The house was a void, like Sean's heart. In a room downstairs, Sean could hear his ma coughing.

Where could Blair have gone? he asked himself for the hundredth time. He knew she was alive, and that was all. *But not really even alive, was she?* He looked at the letter again. It was Blair's handwriting, but it was signed, "All my love, Cindy."

Sean grieved over the unknown. He knew the preacher had done something to make Blair leave. Sean had said he would rescue her; he had failed. He should never have left her alone. He punched his pillows. He threw the envelope across the room. But the small defiance did not make him feel any better. It seemed that nothing could take away the pain. He quickly threw his boots on and grabbed a flannel shirt. He slung his camera around his neck and reached for the flash. It was his only means of escape, that and his ham radio, but there would be no receivers on at that time of night. Sean had never felt so alone.

March 1932

Cloverdale, Oregon

Rebecca arrived by horse, and when she came through the front door, stomping her feet and shaking off her hat, she looked as pretty as ever. She was one of the few women Sean thought could look just as natural in pants as in a dress. She was right on time, but Sean had been waiting nonetheless. Rebecca had figured on that being the case.

"Will, Beck-wheat's here," Sean shouted up the stairs.

Will was taking the rainy morning to do some accounting work on the farm's books. He closed the books, grabbed his raincoat and headed down the stairs.

"You be careful, you two. Will, I'm countin' on you to keep him out'ta trouble, ya hear?" Said Rebecca.

"I'll do my best, Mrs. Tjaden," Will joked. Then with a degree of seriousness Will turned to Sean and asked him, "Are you absolutely certain you want to do this, uninvited?"

Sean grabbed his coat and hat off the rack in response.

"Alright, Sean. I'd be glad-hearted to see Victor, too. But you confound me by saying it's 'cause you need a witness. I still don't understand why you should need one. The man has said some hateful things, but he ain't gonna get physical with you."

"I told ya, Will. You're Victor's uncle and he'll be glad to see you. And, I need you there as a witness in case preacher decides to try and kill me."

At that, Rebecca's eyes widened. "The preacher? Try to kill you? Really, Sean. I know you two have your differences, but aren't you being a might blasphemous?"

Sean just smiled at her. "We'll see. Thank you again, Beck-wheat, for sittin' with Ma while we're gone." To his brother, Sean said, "Boy, I'm glad you said you'd come along, Will."

They tied their horses up to some trees standing to the left of the drive. Will stopped to remove a wooden spinning top that Elrod Tjaden had carved for little Victor out of a chunk of fallen spruce. Rebecca had asked that it be given to Victor as a belated birthday gift. He tied the pack closed again and turned around to stare blankly into the business end of Preacher Bowman's shotgun. It was pointed directly at them.

"Hey there! What?!" He looked incredulously at Sean.

Sean raised his hands innocently and walked slowly toward Bowman, smiling all the while. "Did I tell ya, Will, that he'd greet us out of sight, tip his hat, roll out the red carpet, welcome us in his most mannerly way?"

Will followed Sean's lead, raising his hands too, and walked a half step behind him. His smile never faltered, yet he admonished Sean through the side of his clenched teeth. "You just didn't want to rob me of the excitement, huh, Sean? What have you gotten us into?"

Sean acknowledged him with a wink. "C'mon, Preacher. What kind of a greetin' is this? You must think I'm here to cause trouble. Now, that wounds me, Preacher. What about turnin' the other cheek an' all that?"

"You've come far enough, Marshall. We shoot trespassers 'round here."

"Well, how 'bout forgivin' us our trespasses and let us look upon Victor for a spell? This here's his Uncle Will. We miss seein' the little fella."

Preacher Bowman tipped his head in Will's direction. "Will," he said in a form of greeting. He descended the front porch steps and walked toward them and then circled around and went for Sean's horse. He was checking for weapons.

Will could hardly believe it. "Preacher Bowman, I—I'm nearly beyond words. I don't believe this behavior in you. I know you an' my brother are fire-and-petrol to one another, but you gotta give him his due. The man's got a right to see his son. So? Can we look upon Victor, or not?"

"Not. Now you two go on. Get off my property before we have us a good ol' Tennessee barn fight. You'll not be poisonin' my son with your stories today."

"Your *son*, preacher?" Will had caught him off guard.

"My grandson…er, the son I never had." He waved the shotgun at them as he inched back toward them. He noticed that Will was looking with disgust at his boots. He looked down. "Aw, Judas priest!"

While the preacher was distracted by the horse pucky on his boots, Will lowered his hands, tapped his brother's shoulder and motioned with a nod toward the small window near the front door. Victor was watching them. Preacher resumed his advance, waving his shotgun as he did, pressuring them back toward their horses.

"You know, Preacher, if you keep making the mistake of menacing us with that thing, I'll have to take it away from you."

"That so, Marshall? You and what army?"

"Hey, hey, c'mon now. Let's siphon it down some," Will tried. "Preacher? You once told my Ma you spoke three languages. How is it you don't know how to say, 'welcome' in any of 'em?" He turned to Sean. "And, brother, you didn't come here to fight, you came to see Victor. That's right, ain't it?"

Sean swallowed his pride and nodded. Will turned to the Preacher. "Ita?" He surprised the Preacher with his knowledge of Latin.

Preacher Bowman wasn't feeling particularly charitable or welcoming. "No," he snapped.

"I'm gonna pop him so hard his great-grandchildren will feel it," Sean promised his brother.

Before their eyes, the corpulent face of the preacher grew an angry red, and he blustered. "I don't recognize what it is my Blair ever saw in you, Marshall. But you better believe I'd just as soon shoot you where you stand as look at you. Now get on!"

"Well, 'course you wouldn't recognize it, Bowman. It's a peculiarity called humanity. I don't doubt you never heard of it. But look. Why don't you start practicin' some now and just let me see my son?"

Will nodded, his smile full of encouragement. "We wouldn't stay long, Preacher. We wanted to give Victor a birthday gift that Elrod Tjaden carved for him." He held out the toy to Bowman, who refused to lower the firearm and take it from him. "C'mon, now. It was carved from that giant spruce on their property that lightning struck and split in two, last storm. Struck it twice in one night. It's a toy but it's also for luck, too." He held it out for a good long while but the preacher wouldn't make a grab for it. Will stashed it in his coat pocket.

Meanwhile, the heavy rain of earlier had since become a steady cascade. They would have been drenched had it not been for the canopy provided by the solid walls of trees. It was looming darkness all the way to the preacher's doorstep, save for only tiny patches of light amid forlorn shadows and chill depths. Will shivered, not from his wet clothes but from the depressing landscape that surrounded them. It was dank and austere and cheerless. He understood why Sean was so obsessed in getting Victor away from that place. It was no atmosphere in which to nurture a child.

Sean could see that the preacher's face hadn't cracked into any expression of mercy, nor had he lowered the barrel to his shotgun any. He turned to the boy in the window and shouted to be heard above the noise from the rain against a million leaves.

"Victor! Son! I love you, Victor! You hear me, boy? I love you!" He took a step closer, his arms outstretched to the boy, who continued to stare at him, his chubby hands splayed pathetically against the grimy glass, his little boy eyes filled with tears.

The shotgun touched Sean's chest.

"I'll do it, Marshall. Won't be any skin off o' my behind to do it. Now get on out of here."

"Forget it, Sean. Might as well be polishin' cow patties," Will said. He grabbed Sean's sleeve and pulled him around. Sean looked back at the window one more time with silent envy, feeling like his blood was being siphoned out of him, leaving his body cold inside. Within that coldness lay a primal desire to chop the preacher's head off with a dull shovel. The fleeting thought emerged with such passion that it frightened Sean. He swallowed the painful lump that had taken form in his throat and they trudged back through the mud to their horses. Sean untied the animals, mounted his, and turned back down the drive to the main road.

Will looked over to his brother. "I would still like to give him a knuckle-sandwich, Sean," he hollered over the rain.

"And I would sure like to watch him eat it, Will," Sean answered.

Chapter 35

"I think he wanted an excuse to kill Sean. I really do!" Rebecca told her husband. "Anyway, that was what happened when Sean and Will tried to visit. Also, he wouldn't accept your gift for Victor." She handed the carved toy back to her husband.

"Well, I don't have a mind to involve ourselves in the Marshalls' feud with the preacher, but he ain't gonna threaten my friends with a shotgun an' get away with it. Someone's gotta talk to the man, and it might as well be me."

Rebecca stopped him merely by touching his arm. "Don't, El. Don't go over there. I fear for what he's capable of doing. The Marshall's believe the man is fit to do murder. I saw it in Will's eyes when he was telling me all about it. It frightened me. The preacher's not right in his head, El. Leave it alone. For me." Her eyes pleaded with him, and he could not refuse her, though the Finnish part of him angled for satisfaction.

"Say he's got a few lanterns out, eh?" He chuckled.

Rebecca was relieved to see her husband place his hat back on the peg.

"It worries me, El. You know the hateful things the preacher has been sayin' about Sean. Sean Marshall's a good man. You know that as well as I do. But he's quit the church, and all folks know is that his wife's run off. He won't tell anyone, not even Will, what really happened. Now his word's no good over the preacher's. Things are just gonna get worse for him, El. And things are already so bad for Sean it makes me want to cry."

Elrod patted her hand gently. He knew the feelings his wife had for Sean Marshall, but he didn't begrudge either of them for those feelings. Sean had been her first love and she his. One never forgets their first. Elrod Tjaden also knew that Rebecca loved him, and that Sean Marshall had truly loved Blair. Her leaving had caused him a great deal of pain. "I don't know what I can say, Rebecca. If there was something I could do to help Sean, you know I would do it. He's been my best friend since we were both tadpoles."

"Just promise me, El, that no matter how bad the gossip gets about Sean, you'll stand by him. We Tjaden's are his only true friends, and he needs us."

"Of course, Beck. Sean's a fine man. He's earned my respect many times over, and that ain't gonna change because of some fool gossip. Besides, the man can't be a monster if my wife was in love with him once."

She looked, but she could see no bitterness in the remark. His eyes twinkled at her, and she knew that he'd meant what he'd said as a compliment. She was proud that she had married such a good man. Rebecca had been in love just twice in her life, and both men were among the finest to be found in Tillamook County. Rebecca grabbed her man and planted on him a deep, long kiss before hugging him for all she was worth.

Chapter 36

March, 1932

Chicago, Illinois

Cindy fast developed a taste for Parisian dining, strong coffee in tiny cups, and the theater, all of which bled her purse to near empty. She had paid her rent a month in advance, and had enough money left for a few days' meals, but after that? She had to do something to get more money. She did not know how to use a typing machine, and her sewing wasn't anything she was proud of. She was a good cook, but the dining styles in Chicago did not cater to huge slabs of meats, bowls of potatoes, and dangerous sections of homemade apple pie.

There was really only one profession the preacher had prepared her for, and she was good at it. The music man had said as much. He'd said she was better than any of the whores he'd had. All she had to do was allow Blair to stay hidden in her oblivious state and submit to the whims of men willing to pay for it. Maybe it would be sort of cruel to Blair, after Cindy had promised her she'd never be hurt again. But hadn't she always come to Blair's rescue when she was needed? Cindy needed Blair's help. It wouldn't be right for Blair to refuse her.

Besides, will she even be mindful of what is happening to her? I think not. Hmmm, Chicago must be full of men looking for that type of entertainment. But where does one go to look for them?

She made her way to a stool at the bar of the speakeasy and ordered wine.

When the bartender placed it before her, a gentleman sitting two stools down half rose to take a bill from his vest pocket. "I'll buy the lady's drink, Tad."

Cindy murmured a polite thank you and emphasized it with a demure batting of her lashes. She had developed a passion for wine with dinner, but that would be her first time drinking in a speakeasy. She'd been surprised how easy it was to obtain bootleg wine in Chicago.

As she sipped, the payer moved over to the stool beside her. "You're not from around here, are you?"

"I am. I've rented the top back room on Bishop Avenue. One can always reach me there by sending along a discreet note. Why do you ask?"

"Oh, well…I've just never seen you here before. Name's Wendell, ma'am. Ever enjoyed a meal in the Table D'hôtel? It's French. Pretty darn good food really." He noticed that she wore no wedding ring.

He'd noticed quite a lot about the young woman, actually. He had been watching her from the moment he saw her lovely image peering through the front windows, seeming to contemplate that barstool she eventually chose. She might have a room down the block, but this girl was not Chicago-born, nor had she been in the city for long, Wendell guessed. This was a country girl, possessed of country strength hidden behind mild manners and closely-checked fear. Wendell fancied she might have been raised on a farm in the Midwest, as he was. For one thing, although she wore rather fetching garb, no city girl would attempt a night out with nothing more than a bit of emphasis about the eyes and a dab of rouge on the cheeks, although Wendell wished they would try. Then there was the girl's air of awkwardness. She did not appear to be very much at home inside the Speakeasy, and Wendell guessed this was her first visit to such a place. But, as if to confound him with contradiction, a look into the woman's eyes bespoke volumes of experience quite beyond her years. Perhaps hers was not a country life of the gentle sort.

"Kind of you to pay for my drink, Mr. Wendell. And, yes, I have dined next door. I agree. It's quite good."

"Oh, it's my first name that is Wendell. I was rather hoping we'd get to be first name friends." Wendell lifted her left hand from the bar and held it in his.

"Mine's Cindy. Nice to meet you."

She gracefully slipped her hand from his, but not before Wendell saw the tan line where a wedding ring must have resided until recently, or before he felt the calluses of hands which had known a fair bit of toil. *This beautiful creature was such a contradiction!* Wendell thought to himself.

"So, Wendell, after you enjoy such a fine Bohemian meal, what do you do to work it off?" She looked at him pointedly.

Her provocative reply made Wendell break out in smile. He sidled up a bit closer to her and whispered in her ear, "Decorum demands that I say I would take a brisk walk after. But the best way to do work off a rich French meal is to do what the French profess to do best." He sat back and awaited her reaction.

She said nothing right away, and Wendell worried. "How much, Wendell?" Cindy finally replied.

"How much?"

"For the entertainment you proposed. You did just proposition, did you not?"

He cleared his throat, and his cheeks turned a might pinkish. She was pretty fresh when you got right down to business. "Five dollars is what I've paid…well, what I mean is, I didn't realize you were—"

"I'm worth six dollars if I'm worth anything, Wendell. I'm not your average whore."

"I can see that."

"First, I would like that dinner you mentioned. And you must supply the room."

"Sure thing, Cindy. Uh…so, have you done this many times before?"

"More times than you have fingers and toes, Wendell. And never a dissatisfied customer. I can guarantee a good time."

"Well then." Wendell's initial uncertainty changed immediately to a feeling that was good and feisty. "Let's drink up and go have us some fun, Cindy."

March, 1933

Chicago, Illinois

Mrs. Warrington had not so much as asked her last name. The girl, 'Cindy', was quiet but disturbed the other renters nonetheless by the strangeness of the hours she kept. She remained in her room all day, sleeping, Mrs. Warrington presumed, but then would leave her room in the evening. She usually returned at seven o'clock in the morning and then mysteriously remained in her room the full day again.

Mrs. Warrington felt she should never have allowed this to go on for so long a time. It had been almost a year. But the manner in which her newest tenant arrived and departed was one that begged no acquaintances, and so Mrs. Warrington was at a loss for learning anything about that beautiful and strange girl with the most variable habits. One time, she did grasp the opportunity to ask what deliveries there were in the form of plain white envelopes, to which Cindy responded they were tickets. She'd claimed to be an avid fan of the theater, which she was. But it seemed to Mrs. Warrington, and also to the other renters who watched the girl's room with unconcealed curiosity, that the envelopes arrived in a most curious manner; sometimes twice in one day, other times once in three or four days. Finally, her curiosity got the better of her and she poised herself at the top of the stairway one morning and waited for Cindy's return.

"My, but you do get in quite late for such a young woman."

Cindy turned and smiled. "Yes. I'm afraid a woman in my profession must keep strange hours." Then she quickly darted into her apartment and locked the door.

Mrs. Warrington was dismally disappointed. She felt like she should know more about her renter. But the girl had quite a put-offish manner that precluded any exchange of pleasantries. Still, it was her duty to keep the building clear of undesirables. She must question the girl. The building owner set her shoulders square, and with her most firm demeanor, she rapped on the girl's door. At least three other tenants waited anxiously behind cracked doors or peepholes to hear anything they could about the renter of the top-floor room in the back. The door was opened immediately, but the girl seemed surprised to see that it was Mrs. Warrington standing in the hall.

"The silliest of things, my dear. I tried this morning to write you a receipt for your rent you've been paying for the year. Do you know I never even asked you your surname?"

"It's Marshall."

The eavesdropping tenants nearly groaned aloud in their disappointment at such a common, unimportant name.

"Oh. Very well then, Cindy, um…Marshall. If you don't mind my asking, what type of work is it that you do, exactly?"

"Oh. Yes. I see. I have gone and made you nervous with my comings and goings. Hold one moment please." She left the door open just a peep. Mrs. Warrington stretched her neck a ways to look inside, but the girl came back before she glimpsed anything at all.

"In answer to your inquiry, I am a stenographer for the night courts," she lied. "I have tried to be very quiet when I leave the building in the evenings. Have I created a disturbance?"

"Well, no, my dear. Not a disturbance—"

"Wonderful." Cindy breathed with relief. "Oh, and here is another month of rent in advance." Before the nosy landlady could press for further details of Cindy's life, the girl pushed ten dollars into Mrs. Warrington's hand, which the landlady understood was a not-so-gentle hint that Cindy Marshall did not wish to talk about herself further.

Cindy put her back to the door and began counting her money. She hoped it would be the last interruption from her nosey landlady for a spell. She brightened when she saw that Artie had left her a ten-dollar tip for the "special" favors she had performed the night before. Cindy had fun with Artie, who happened to be Wendell's closet male friend. Cindy considered Wendell her best friend in Chicago, but as a client, he made love like he brokered stocks; he was careful. Sweet Wendell might not be much of a lover, but he certainly had an abundance of friends who were. Cindy had asked Wendell if he could pass her name to a number of the other gents at the Board of Trade where he worked, which was how she met up with Artie. How those stockbroker types loved to spend their money on the ladies. Either Artie was a might more successful a trader than Wendell or else he was quite generous with his earnings. Cindy's wealth was growing in leaps and bounds.

Cindy thought of Mavis Marshall, and silently thanked her mother-in-law for her success. During the four short years Blair had lived in the Marshall household, she had studied Mavis's style, manners and carriage, and tried her best to emulate them. Under Mavis's tutelage, Blair became a lady. Had she not been exposed to Mavis's upper-class ways, Cindy never could have infiltrated the Chicago elite. But infiltrate she did. Cindy could hold her own in Chicago society *and* command a premium. A touch of sadness and longing crossed her mind at the calling forth of Mavis. Thinking of Mother Mavis naturally conjured up thoughts of Sean and Victory as well. All the attention and good loving in the world could not rid Cindy's mind of Sean and her child. That sinking feeling, like her stomach was dropping to her feet, started to overwhelm her and Cindy quickly tucked away her sadness before it woke Blair.

I have not seen or held my child or husband in over a year. They must think me dead, she thought to herself.

She hoped Sean would think of her as dead and go on to marry another. She loved him so, and she wished him every happiness. But she had never told him so. She frowned. Maybe she should write him a letter just to let him know she was well and that he should go on with his life. Perhaps all that time, he'd been worrying for her. She went to her desk, pulled out a single sheet of scented stationery, and began writing a letter to her husband.

11 March, 1933

Dearest Sean,

I have made a new home for myself and Blair. I cannot tell you where we live, but I will tell you that it is in a city and that we love the excitement of theater and streetcars and snow in the winter months. I am taking good care of Blair, and we are both well. I hope you understand that Blair's life depended upon her being free from that evil man. Sean, he came while you were away and Will was milking. If Mavis had decided to leave her sick bed awhile and had per chance witnessed his brutality, I've no doubt he would have killed her as he killed your father. I, we, brought his wrath upon the Marshall home. Words can not convey our sorrow.

We love you and our son, Victor, so very much it causes us genuine pain. But we can never return to Cloverdale. We are so grateful that Victor has a loving father in you, Sean. We know our son will be raised by a good man in a loving home, and this has made Blair's escape possible. I beg you, Sean, to marry another. Find happiness. And know that your unselfishness and good heart saved this wretched girl from certain death. You did all you could, Sean. We have no regrets.

All our love, Cindy

She would give the letter to one of the businessmen to mail from another town, and Sean would never find her, should he take it in his head to come looking. Traitorous tears leaked out and tracked down her powdered cheeks. She wiped at them and willed the ice ball in her stomach away. Anyway, he would never think to search for Blair among Chicago's wealthiest inhabitants.

Cindy had a regular clientele that could legitimately be referred to as an elite crowd. She had been on dates with train officials, men from City Hall, journalists, and bankers. She was fast becoming the toast of Chicago among the more discreet, wealthier circles of men. Her bankroll was growing thick, and she thought she might take Wendell and Artie up on their offer to invest some of her earnings in the stock market. She had her eye on property, too. Wyatt Marshall had taught her the importance of owning land. And, practically speaking, life as Chicago's most successful prostitute couldn't last forever. But feeling fairly flush on that night, Cindy decided she would indeed take in the theater, followed, of course, by coffee at the Table D'hôtel.

Chapter 37

April, 1933

Cloverdale, Oregon

When the pale pink envelope arrived at the Marshall home, Will was tempted to burn it and never let his brother know. But he couldn't do it. Sean seemed to live only for word from Blair those days. Without her return, Sean would never recover his son. It was with a heavy heart that Will Marshall handed over the letter.

"That pink envelope!" Sean tore into it. "It has to be word from Blair, Will!"

He laughed gaily and unfolded the letter quickly, his eyes darting across the page hopefully. And then he looked up with an expression that clearly said bad news, and Will wanted to take the pain for his brother, if only he could have.

"She's told me to marry another. She says she can never come home…never." He wadded up the sheet of paper and threw it far away.

"Sean, brother, I'm so sorry. I…Sean, I wish there was some-thing…what can I do for you, brother?"

Sean had sat down on the front door stoop and bowed his head. Now he looked up at Will with glistening eyes. "She don't even know about Victor. If she did, I know…can you find her and bring her home, Will?"

"I don't think so, Sean."

He watched as Sean buried his head in his strong, callused hands, and Will thought to himself that that was no way for a benevolent God to treat a good a man as his brother.

"Well, Sean, maybe we can give that a try. Where's that enve-lope at?"

Sean looked up skeptically. "Here." He unwadded it. "What are ya thinkin', Will?"

"I'm thinking we look at the postmark and then go fetch your wife and bring her home. Hmm. Looks like it says Springfield, Illinois."

Sean jumped up to have a look. "It does! Her letter…" He ran to where he pitched it and hunted it down. Smoothing out the sheet, he read it again. "She says she's in a city where there are street cars and theatres and it snows. Is that Springfield, Will?"

"I don't think so. Not street cars. As I recall, they have them contraptions in New York, Chicago, St. Louis and San Francisco. That's all, I believe. But I could be wrong, brother."

"Did you say Chicago?"

"Say, that's not too far from Springfield. If she didn't want you to find her, she might mail the letter from somewhere else. It's what I would have done." He smiled at Sean.

Sean was dancing around the porch, boxing the air and taking fantasy swipes at him.

Will laughed. "I guess we'd better get to Chicago, then, and no time to waste. Your mind's nearly gone already!"

"You're wrong, Will! I've half a mind to go get my wife and bring her home!"

When the two men hopped off the last step and they beheld a bustling Chicago before them and a hissing, grunting monolith of steel behind them, their expressions must have been something like that of Christopher Columbus when, instead of falling off the edge of the earth, they beheld a new land. It was so foreign that it both excited and frightened them at once. The Marshall boys had never traveled outside of Oregon their entire lives.

"Look at those tall buildings, Will. Have you ever seen anything like it?"

"I never seen nothing like that." He nudged his brother in the rib and nodded his head toward two beautiful women walking toward them. "How 'bout those two lollapaloozas?" They had the shortest skirts Will had ever seen, and hosiery and floppy hats and gloves. "Say, Sean, this pamphlet from the train says Chicago is the windy city." Will rolled his eyes heavenward and said, "God, give me wind, and right now!'"

Sean laughed. "C'mon, Will. We're supposed to be looking for just one woman in particular. I know she's here. We just gotta find her."

They walked straight down Maxwell Street, through throngs of shoppers meandering up and down the open-air market. They dodged vendors with their pushcarts full of wares, sticking out like two sore thumbs, to a large but inexpensive-looking boarding house on the corner of Halston Street. They paid for two nights. Will flopped himself down on one of the saggy beds with delight. "What do we want to do first, little brother? Let's go to a show."

"Will…" Then Sean just shook his head.

"Oh, c'mon, Sean. We can still have fun whilst we look, can't we? She said in her letter that she loved the theater, didn't she? Let's get out and see Chicago. Neither of us will probably ever get here again."

It was a place to start, Sean conceded.

They went downstairs and asked the man at the desk where the nearest theater was. The man pointed them to a new Chaplin movie playing at the Bijou and an O'Neil play at the Pavillion. Will and Sean shrugged their shoulders. Chaplin movie, hands down.

Will's stomach was growling fairly fierce, having awakened to a skimpy breakfast on the train instead of a good ol' farm breakfast. "Say, little brother, I always did want to have me one of them long hot dogs you can get from one of those fellas with the little wagons. What do you say to that?"

"That sure does sound good, Will. I…thank you for coming along with me, Will. You're the best brother a man ever had. And it was awful good of Rebecca to offer to stay with Ma while we're gone. We should pick her up something special, something that she couldn't get back home maybe."

Will gave his brother's shoulder a chuck, "how 'bout some of them stockings we saw getting off the train?"

"How long you gonna go on about those stockings?"

Will just smiled playfully. "Well you don't find 'em back home. That's for sure."

"That might be a bit personal. Might offend Elrod some if I got them for her. You go ahead and get her some stockings and I'll buy her some fancy perfume or something from one of those street vendors."

"Hey! There's one of them hot dog carts over there!" They raced each other down the street.

Sean enjoyed the movie as much as he could. Every time a figure cloaked in shadow passed by or walked down the aisle, Sean's head and eyes were turning every which way, looking for Blair. But Will had the time of his life. Naturally, Will was introducing himself to every girl he saw, and even though they almost always looked over at Sean and asked, "Who's he?" Will didn't mind at all. He knew that Sean got the best of the looks in the family. But, as he often told his little brother, he got the wit and personality. Sean agreed. No matter where Will went, there were always people who knew him and greeted him like a long-lost friend. Will had friends everywhere. In fact, when they were leaving the theater, two swell-looking girls called to him, "Bye, Will," waggling their little fingers at him.

Sean looked at his brother with amusement. "You are unbelievable."

"What?" He held his hands out innocently.

Chapter 38

Back at their modest accommodations, it was hard for Sean to sleep in the windy city. It seemed like it was also the city that never slept. All night long, cars rattled; the bells of streetcars and open-air buses rang; the horse of a mounted policeman clop-clopped; and, most surprising to Sean, he heard musicians on the street below playing saxophones and other instruments for tokens from passersby. Sean thought that the music was wonderful, and he would have liked to listen for a spell, but he needed a good night's sleep more. Will had no trouble. He was snoring the second his head hit the lumpy feather pillow. But Sean could not stop thinking that he had only one day and one night to find Blair, so little time to save his life. And that's how he looked at it; without his son or his wife, there seemed little point in waking up mornings. He threw himself sideways for the tenth time, sending the squeaky bed frame into concert again, and hugged his pillow fiercely. Eventually, fatigue got the best of him, and amid the hustle and bustle of Chicago streets at two in the morn, he dreamed of Blair's homecoming.

They ate something called a bagel with white soft cheese stuff heaped on, which they devoured as they walked. The bagels weren't bad at all, but nothing could talk Sean into putting raw fish on top of his. They both carried a picture of Blair and put it in front of the faces of people they passed by.

"Seen her?" they would ask, and folks would look real quick like and shake their heads no, hurrying on.

"You notice how everyone in this town is in a hurry to get someplace?" asked Sean. "I never seen anything like it."

"Yeah," was all Will could manage with a mouth full of bagel and cream cheese. He leaned over and pushed the photo in front of a man waiting at a trolley stop. "Seen her?" Will asked, and quickly moved on.

"Looks familiar. "

Sean didn't quite register what he'd heard until he'd gone several feet farther. He turned around and ran back to catch up with the man his brother had last shown the picture to, before he boarded a trolley for destinations unknown. Sean could hear the clanging of a trolley's bells approaching. "Excuse me, sir. Did you say you've seen this girl?"

"No. I said she looked familiar. What do you want with her?"

Sean's heart pounded almost painfully. "She's my sister. She ran away from home because of a bad fight with a beau, and, well, we want to try and convince her to come home," he lied.

He didn't think God would mind a little white lie. It was just that he didn't think people would tell them anything if they thought she'd run from her husband.

"I see. Let me take another look. Yes, that does look like Miss Cindy Marshall." Will and Sean exchanged quick, excited looks. The man looked the brothers over carefully. He quickly sized them up as nice young men who meant well. "I'll tell you what I know of her. I believe the woman in the picture sparks an uncommon resemblance to Cindy Marshall. She has a room at the boarding house on Bishop Avenue, next to the Table D'hôtel. Miss Marshall is...well, you should do well to prepare yourselves for a change. I don't mean to insult you. You look like nice men. Not from these parts, I'd doubt. But the lady earns her living by accepting dates with strange men, if you follow me." He raised his eyebrows in question.

Sean and Will traded confused looks.

"Makes a living accepting dates?" Sean asked dubiously.

The man cleared his throat. "A concubine, if you will."

"A con-kew-what?" Will scratched his head in question.

The man shook his head in frustration. His street car was here. "A whore, gentlemen, a prostitute. And quite successful, or so I've heard. Good day, gentlemen." He tipped his hat and hurried on up the steps.

Will looked at Sean with fright. "That couldn't be Blair… she'd never…would she?"

"A prostitute?" Sean was dumbstruck.

Will clamped his hand on Sean's shoulder. "He said the name is Marshall, Sean. It might not be her. But it might be as well. Do you want to get back on the train now, or do you want to find her at any cost, brother?"

"I have to know, Will. If she is…if that man is correct, I just want you to know, I won't judge her. I hope you won't either. There's some things you don't know about Blair, and I can't tell you. But it could be her. And if she is, you know, selling her body…it ain't her fault. Can you believe that in your heart and hold her faultless if I was to tell you it was so?"

Will looked at his brother curiously. "I know she was a pitifully sad girl until she came to the house to live, Sean. I don't have to know why if you promised her you wouldn't say. And if she ran away and is prostituting herself to get along, I promise I won't judge her. 'Sides, Sean, don't you know that I love Blair like a sister? No matter what we find on Bishop Avenue, I won't hold any judgments against her."

"Then let's go see if we can find her and bring her home."

It took the two country boys a while to figure out how the streets of Chicago crossed and numbered themselves, but they finally found Bishop Avenue and came upon the boarding house. It was clear across town from where they had started out, on foot, in the morning. It was late afternoon when Sean rang the bell. Eventually, a woman peeked out behind a sheer curtain at the window beside the door and then came to the door and opened it a crack.

"I am full up, gentlemen. If you need a room, try Smythe's across Temple Avenue."

"Uh…no, ma'am. That is, we're not looking for a room."

"That's right," Will interjected. "We're looking for a woman."

"Well!" Mrs. Warrington nearly slammed the door in their faces.

"No. Please. Ma'am, what my brother meant was that we have a picture of our sister here, and we were wondering if you've seen her." He brought the photo up to the crack in the door.

The woman looked at it and then stepped out a bit to see the photo, and the men holding it, a bit closer up.

"Why do you need to find this woman, if I may ask?"

"Well, as I said, ma'am, she is our sister, and we would like to convince her to come home."

"She doesn't look like your sister."

"Well, she's a half-sister. That is, our father was remarried."

"I see."

Mrs. Warrington could tell right off the photo was of the girl who rented her top back room. That room had sat empty for quite some time, and her pocketbook had only recently begun to reflect the benefits of its steady rental. If they were to talk her into leaving with them, how long would it be before she found another suitable renter? And though the girl had strange habits, she was quiet and she paid in advance in cash.

"I'm sorry. I haven't seen her." She handed the photograph back.

"But wait!" Sean nearly jumped inside the door. "We were told she lived here. Isn't that so?"

He looked so hopeful that it could have brought a good-hearted woman to tears. But Evelyn Warrington was not a good-hearted woman. She was a businesswoman, a successful one, and she didn't get that way trading income for long-lost sisters.

"She does hold a strong resemblance to Miss Cindy Marshall, but Miss Marshall moved out in the middle of the night several weeks ago. She gave me no notice, told me nothing of where she was going, and left owing me twenty dollars in rent." She eyed the two men pointedly.

Sean looked down at his boots and could have kicked himself for getting his hopes so high. The wind was taken right out of his sails. He couldn't say anything or look at either of the people around him.

Will reached into his pocket and counted out twenty dollars to hand the woman. "Sorry about the trouble, ma'am." He pushed the money and a calling card into her hand. Then, as she closed her greedy fist around the windfall, Will grabbed her fist and held it quite firmly. "But you will let us know if you see her, won't you, ma'am?" His grip was tight, a bit too tight, and a certain message was delivered with that pressure. "This is where we're staying tonight. After tonight, we'll be heading home. The address and telephone number is on the back of that card too. You'll be sure to call?"

She pulled her hand away with a slightly intimidated look. "Certainly. Of course I will. Good day, gentlemen."

And the door closed before them. As they turned to leave, they could hear a deadbolt sliding into place.

"We'll go back to the downtown area, Sean." Will tried to get his brother to look up at him. "You know, if Blair's a...if she's looking...we could hang out near the theatre and show the photo to everyone we meet..."

Sean simply nodded. Chicago was enormous and filled with thousands of residents. They would walk all night, and they would show their photos of Blair to every passerby. But they would be getting on that train tomorrow without her.

Chapter 39

Will went ahead and bought them tickets home in a compartment. His brother looked so wrung out to him, he was hoping a good night of sleep would set him right. He didn't think Sean got a whole lot of shut-eye on their trip, and leaving empty-handed didn't help—especially after they'd phoned Rebecca and worked it out so's they could spend one more day looking. The men felt they'd gotten real close to finding Blair—like she'd been snatched from them just as she was in reach—and neither one of them wanted to leave without trying a little harder. But they'd goose-egg'd. Sean hadn't said a peep since he'd bought that paper and laid down to read it. He just looked so sad to Will.

"Dang-it!" Will griped under his breath.

"What's that?" Sean laid the newspaper on his chest and looked over to Will's bunk. "Did you say somethin' to me?"

Will was staring at the ceiling. He had his arms crossed over his chest, his ankles crossed over one another, and was twirling his mustache with one hand while flicking each of his fingers with his thumb on the other hand, over and over again.

"Will? You angry with me? You look angry."

"No, brother, I ain't angry with you. I'm angry with me." He sat up and swung his feet to the floor, immediately feeling the rhythmic rumble of the train on its tracks—not an altogether unpleasant sensation at all. "Did you believe that landlady we talked to? I mean about Blair leaving owing her money?"

Sean sat up, studied his brother. Then he contemplated the floor. "I don't know. We ain't in any position to call her a liar."

"Yeah. Except the more I think about it—about her, that is—I think, she don't strike me as the kind of landlady that a homespun girl like our Blair could pull one over on, move out all her stuff and herself without that woman knowing about it. D'you think that really happened?"

"Are you sayin' you think Blair was there all along?"

"No, not necess—well, maybe." He gave his brother a thoughtful squint. "I think that woman knew where Blair was, though. I think she just told us that story to pick some money from our pocketbooks."

Sean didn't answer right away and when he did it was only to let out a heavy sigh.

Will said, "I know you don't know your head from your heart where your wife was concerned, and you probably don't know whether to jump up and yell, 'let's go back!' or—"

"Is that my heart or my head talkin'?" Sean interrupted.

"Why don't you answer that one?"

"Well, I guess that sounds like the rash sort a' thing a heart would say," Sean said.

"Right. So then, little brother, what does your head say? Because whatever you think we ought to do, that's what we'll do."

"You wanna go back and call on one of them girls, you old birddog," Sean smiled weakly.

"Naw," Will reached into his front pocket and withdrew several calling cards with dainty handwriting scrawled across their faces. He fanned them at his brother. "I only kept 'em as a kind of reminder of our trip—even though I know we, we didn't find… we didn't do what we came here for—but, well Sean, it's the only time we ever went *anywhere*. They're just souvenirs. To tell you honest, fancy-type ladies of the big city don't interest me much. They're pretty and fresh, and a little more worldly-wise, but they wouldn't hold a shine standing next to an Oregon girl. Guess I'm old-fashioned," he shrugged. He tucked them back into his pocket. "But, my offer's still good."

Sean studied his brother for a moment, then moved his gaze to the darkening landscape whizzing past their compartment's window. "Will…I love you, Will. And I know our failing to find Blair would eat at you, because you would always wonder if we did enough—heck, you're doing it already. I don't want that. My head says we did what we could, and then some. Another day didn't make any difference, and another week probably wouldn't either. Chicago's just too big a city for hide-and-seek. Remember, Will, she don't want to be found. For whatever reason, Blair had reached her limit. An' our pocketbooks also have a limit. I wish it wasn't so, but…" He shrugged and turned back to Will. "Like it or not, we have other responsibilities. It's spring, and we gotta get back."

Chapter 40

May, 1933

Cloverdale, Oregon

Bowman was getting a little twitchy. Otis was late. He *hated* the man—he'd thought about killing him. But, Otis was six-and-a-half feet tall, and even though he was thinner than broth, the man was strong as an ox from hefting all that swill and ale. Besides, Julius was no longer confident in his own strength and agility. He was old, portly, and his hands shook when he waited too long for a nip. He extended his hands out in front of him and watched them jitter. He looked over at the boy, saw he was watching him intently. The preacher dropped his hands and busied himself by getting a fire ready to go in the woodstove for later, in case temperatures dropped.

It was a surprisingly mild May for the Oregon Coast. The day before, temperatures reached sixty-eight degrees. It was cooler today. Bowman glanced over at the boy. Victor was looking at a picture book given to him by a lady from church. The cabin held no other books or toys for the boy. In truth, the preacher didn't really know what to do with him. Julius Bowman had fixed his entire adult life's sights on getting a son. But Bowman had always assumed there would be a mother to care for his heir. *How Blair could run off and leave her son behind, I can't fathom. A female dog wouldn't willingly run off on her pups.* Here he was doing twice as much laundry and having to worry about proper nutrition for the boy, and whether or not the cabin was warm enough. All the chores Bowman was loathe to do were doubled with the boy around. And the preacher had to hide his nips—in his own home!

He could not have the boy slip up and say something in public about the preacher's minor indulgences—or the way his blasted hands shook when he went too long without a nip. Children will say anything at anytime, Bowman had learned in the year spent with Victor under his roof.

Where in hell was Welby?

Victor lifted his head from his picture book when he heard the sound of Mr. Welby's truck coming up the long drive. The little boy squeezed his eyes shut.

"Victor, I need you to think about your truths," Bowman told the boy.

"Nooooo", Victor started to sob.

"I won't hear it, boy!" His deep voice boomed, scaring Victor straight out of his chair. "You will go into your box on your own, or my hand will help you."

The five-year old climbed inside the box, closed his eyes and began sucking his thumb furiously. The preacher rolled his eyes heavenward as he dropped the lid. Just then there was a familiar knock on the door.

Bowman crossed the room in three steps and yanked the door open as he barked, "You're late. It's about time you—"

"Preacher," Otis greeted him. "This is my son, Lytle. That's a family name on my wife's side. His nickname is Tiny. Thought he and Victor could play together. They're the same age. Boy don't have any friends." Otis looked around the cramped, rustic cabin. "Where is he?"

"I, I...well, uh, he is being punished. It's not an opportune time."

Otis dropped his head to his left shoulder and kind of squinted at Bowman, like he often did. "I don't care. Get the boy."

Bowman grumbled but he did as he was ordered. He trudged over to the box and lifted the lid. "Did you think about your truths, boy?" he asked with relative indifference. He was humiliated by Welby and was sorely licking his wounds.

"Yes, grandfather," Victor answered hurriedly as he scrambled to his feet.

Bowman grunted. "You have a friend to play with." He jerked his head toward Welby's boy.

Victor looked at Mr. Welby, then to his son, and a great smile spread across the boy's face—likely the first in a year's passage of time. He jumped out of the box and ran over to the boy. "Hi! I'm Victor. Do you wanna play?"

"Is *that* your room?" the little boy wanted to know.

"No. I don't have one," Victor said.

"Oh. Do you have any toys?"

"No." Victor looked ashamed. He looked at his feet.

Tiny looked up at his dad. "How'r we supposed to play, Daddy?"

Otis Welby wasn't the world's best father. But stick his own flesh and blood in a buggy old banana box, he never did—and never would. "Your marble bag is in the truck. You boys go on out and shoot some for a little bit an' let us adults jaw awhile."

When the door closed Otis faced the preacher. "That's pretty low, Julius. Ya stick the boy in a box. Ya don' have a single toy for 'im. I hate to think I kep' my mouth shut during his Juvenile Hearin' for this. I don't give a hot ticket how much you hate his pa, I won't be party to it."

Bowman walked to the kitchen area and sat down heavily in a chair at the table. He glowered at Otis Welby. "You're late," he growled again.

"I got your swill right here," he opened the door a foot and retrieved the brown jug he had set on the stoop, carried it over to the table and set it down. He kept his hands firmly on the jug. "I got deliveries tomorrow. I'll be hitting the roadhouse last. If you are interested in riding out there with me, I could stay and enjoy a cold one for a spell, if you're of a mind to—"

"Yes. I'll ride to Grand Ronde with you," he cut Otis off. "Ah, but, what about Victor? He can't come with us anymore…gettin' too keen. Er, your wife, would she look after Victor?"

"She would. Be by about noon to fetch him. I'll come back for you around 1 or 2." He squinted again at Bowman. "Get some toys for the boy, Julius. That's an order. Ya hear me?"

Chapter 41

"Baby goats!" Victor yelled with glee as he hopped off the truck bed. He couldn't remember ever having so much fun as he just had riding on the flat bed of Otis Welby's delivery truck. The boys held on to wooden sides that Otis had added to the flatbed to keep his cases from tumbling off, and they yelled and shrieked with joy as the truck bounced and dipped its way up the dirt road, way up the highest hill, to Welby's camp. When the Welby property came into view, Victor thought they lived in the biggest fort he'd ever seen. It looked like they made their fort the same way Victor made his make-believe forts, out of available furniture, pillows and blankets. "Wow!" Victor yelled. "You're so lucky," he told his new pal, Tiny, which made Tiny Welby smile.

"That's my mommy and my baby sister, Nedra." Tiny pointed out the toddler and his mommy in the middle of six baby pygmy goats. The goats were trying to nibble on Nedra's shoe laces and hair, and one had a hold on her diaper on the backside and was pulling up on it, causing the little girl to belly laugh and nearly topple. Nedra's mommy was laughing too, sometimes swinging a bottle around and sometimes twirling with her baby girl.

"Can we play with 'em too?" Victor wanted to know.

Tiny had a hammock for a bed, which Victor thought was the best kind of bed to have, now that he knew what a hammock was. The wall that divided Tiny's room from his baby sister's was heavy blankets. The boys were playing marbles on Tiny's side of the blanket. This time, Victor had his own marbles to play against Tiny, and he was winning all of Tiny's marbles.

"I don't want to play anymore," Tiny said. "You won my favorite marble. You wouldn't even have marbles of your own if my pa hadn't told your pa—or grampa."

Victor blinked rapidly. He didn't want his new friend mad at him. He'd thought he was supposed to try to win all the marbles. "I don't want to take your favorite marble, Tiny. I wasn't going to keep any of 'em. Honest," he said. He held out all of his winnings for Tiny to take. The boys picked up the rest of their marbles and put them in their leather pouches, pulling the strings tight. "Your daddy tol' my grandpa to get me the marbles? Why?"

"My pa said it was wrong you din't have any toys or nothin'. So he tol' your—isn't he your grampa? Why did he call you his son?"

"He called me that ever since he took me away. He said he was my mommy's daddy and…I don't wanna talk about it." He had one of Tiny's metal trucks and was running its wheels across the floor. It took only a few seconds before Victor realized he did want to tell his only friend something he'd been growing afraid of. "Sometimes I can't remember what my mommy looked like. I used to see her in my dreams. She was the prettiest mommy in the world. But I don't have those dreams anymore. I haven't in a long time, and now I can't remember." He looked up at his new friend. "I miss my mommy." Victor's eyes had started to mist.

"Where's your daddy?" Tiny asked.

"I don't know," Victor sobbed a little. "My daddy was Sean Marshall, but grandpa said I'm not aloud to say that anymore." Victor wiped at a sniffle.

"Why not?" asked Tiny.

"Grandpa doesn't like him." Victor tried to say that like it didn't matter to him, and he spun the truck wheels again and shrugged like he didn't care, but the loss of his hero at the tender young age of four was too much for the little boy, and tears spilled over. "He never came to get me."

Chapter 42

August 14, 1933

Nestucca Bay, Pacific City, Oregon

When Sean and Will finally arrived, the party was in full swing. El Tjaden had taken over as 'the smoker'. He'd learned the art well from watching Angus all those years. The alder-smoked salmon, skewed on the long stakes set in the sand by the bay's shoreline, were giving off enticing aromas that made everyone's stomach rumble with anticipation. The clams and oysters were baking in a pit covered with seaweed. Corn ears in their husks and potatoes in their skins were lying right on top of the hot coals in the fire pit. Sean pulled off his shoes the instant he jumped from his shotgun seat in the shiny new family car. Not waiting for his brother, his bare feet dug into the cool sand. He walked straight up to Elrod and punched him on the shoulder, his smile wide.

"Say, how goes it JXN3?" Sean pronounced it, "Jackson three."

"What? You mean it?"

"Got it on the back seat. Have yourself a look, El."

The two men raced like kids back to the convertible, and Elrod reached in and touched the ham radio with awe.

"Say, Sean, she's a beauty. Is that why you're late getting here? I have never seen you late to a get-together where food's involved."

"Well, and you know I'm double hungry now, so I'm gonna have to eat twice as much. That salmon better be good, El."

"Hey, Marshall, you might be the master of the shortwaves, but I'm the master of bounty from the waves. Don't you forget it, WP."

"How can I when you keep reminding me? Say, we could try it out this evening. I mean, I know it will work, but I'm always anxious to christen 'em." He looked around the small beach. "Rebecca's not here?"

"Oh, she's here. She ran up to the house to get a salad. It's almost dinnertime."

Sean surveyed the friends and neighbors milling around the day camp. Their little community had been holding those annual picnics for more than a decade; in early May, if the weather was dry, or at the end of summer, like today, if they had a soggy spring. Most of the guests had been like a second family to Sean. It stung him that the preacher's gossip had made more than a couple of them question Sean's character.

"Seems we lose a couple every year, doesn't it, El? I mean, first my pa and then yours. Then Blair…" He trailed off. The pain was still fresh more than a year after she had abandoned him.

"I take it your ma wasn't feeling up to it, Sean?"

"Naw. She wanted to come, but she don't hardly get out of bed anymore. Ever since that sickness got her chest, she just can't seem to rid herself of it. It's worse mornings and nights, but the coughing leaves her tired the rest of the time. I was hoping I might get a plate to take home to Ma, if that's okay."

"Sure. Rebecca will wrap something up for Mavis. You be sure to tell her she was missed."

"I will. She's been knitting up a storm to keep her from boredom, so act surprised when you get a sweater for Christmas this year."

"I can always use a good sweater." Elrod smiled wide.

Sean laughed. "I didn't say nothin' about it being a good sweater, but, heck, she's enjoying herself. Anywise, you Tjadens seem to be making up for our declines. How many kids does your sister Ellie have now?"

"Five."

"And how many do *you* have?" Of course Sean knew the answer to his own question, but he could not pass up another opportunity to needle his best friend about the business of growing a family.

"None, and don't you get started on that and ruin a perfectly good clam bake."

"I won't say nothin' about how glad it is to become a father, Elrod. Didn't plan to say a thing about how your children can give you an enthusiasm for living you didn't even know you were missing."

That made Elrod fidget uncomfortably. "Say, Sean, kind o' along this line o' conversation now…my Rebecca invited the preacher here today. She was hoping to get you in close proximity to Victor. I just don't want you to be taken by surprise if he decides to show."

Sean squinted up at the blue sky and sighed. It had been more than two years since he'd been close enough to talk to his son. Seeing the boy without the luxury of touching him had not grown any less painful for Sean. But building radios, keeping his hands and mind busy, gave him less time to think about his loneliness.

"Do you think he'll come, El?"

The naked hope poked at Elrod's heart. "Well, this smokin' is tantalizing enough to reach all the way to his cabin. And we both know the man is a glutton to the point of sin. I think maybe he will. You know, I think I best check my piles of chips. I'd guess we got a half hour more to go 'til eats. Come watch a master at work, Marshall."

They ambled over to the smoking area, where Will was nosing around, mentally noting how Elrod had set the fish up. El had learned from his father, and Angus Tjaden had learned from a Siletz Indian many years back in return for bags of his kelp-ore. That was during the seven-year itch that raked the coastal region, and it turned out that soaks in tubs with the ore stuff took away the itching discomfort for days at a time.

The men paid attention as Elrod basted the long, skewered salmon and then checked the depth of the smoking alder chips at the bases of the stakes. He'd started the smoking early in the morning of the day before, he explained to the watching men. It took about thirty-six hours or so to get the flavoring and texture just right. He'd camped on the shore of the bay the night before to keep night vigil over the fire. He withdrew his pocket knife and sliced a portion off the side of one fifty-pounder. He tried it himself, smiling hugely, and then passed the sample and the knife to the next man, all of them took their turn groaning with pleasure at the first taste.

Rebecca walked up to the circle of men around the smoking pits. "I'm glad you could make it." She smiled at Sean and Will.

"Me too!" Sean exclaimed. I just tried a taste of that fish, and it is at least as good as I remember Angus making it. Ya married well, Rebecca."

"Happy you approve." She laughed. "That is why I married him, after all. You know I can't cook."

At that, all the men laughed since rumor had it what Rebecca claimed about her cooking was true.

Suddenly Sean's jaw muscles tensed and his body went rigid. His gaze was somewhere out on the bay. "He's here, isn't he?" He said to no one in particular.

Rebecca turned around and surveyed the partygoers on the beach. Sure enough, the preacher had arrived, leading Victor by the hand.

It's funny, she thought, *that he should come to a clam bake in the middle of August wearing his black suit.* It occurred to her she had never seen the preacher in anything but that austere black suit with the wide-brimmed hat that cast his features in shadow. "He is, Sean. I'm sorry if his being here upsets you. I did the inviting. I did it so—"

"El told me. It was good of you, Rebecca, for you to think of that for me."

"Sean, how did you know he had arrived? I mean, how—"

He interrupted her. "I could feel him. It comes on like a weight. Actually, I feel the air get hefty when he's around. Then I get this icy cold sensation that starts around my hairline and shoulders. The iciness crawls real quick-like, straight to my heart and squeezes it like a death grip. Then I know he's around." He looked at her and saw how his words disturbed her.

Her expression looked both shocked and remorseful. The others, too, were staring at him.

He tried to laugh it off. "I guess evil weighs heavier on a man than virtue is all. Anyway, you asked how I knew, and that's how. I'd really be beholding if you'd approach Victor with me, Rebecca."

"I'm right beside you, Sean."

They walked slowly through the sand toward the little boy. He'd grown so much. Sean stood two feet away from the boy. The preacher did not pause even a moment in his conversation with Charlie Berklund, the husband of eldest daughter Ellie Tjaden. The small boy sucked his thumb. He was a beautiful, plump-faced boy, nearly six years old and losing his baby fat as his limbs took length. The little boy just looked at Sean but made no move to go near him.

"Victor, my boy. I've missed you, son."

The boy said nothing but kept his thumb in his mouth and tightened his grip on his grandfather's hand.

Sean dropped to his knees before the child, trying to let the boy see him at his own level. His voice was shaking now with the fear that the boy had forgotten him. But it was so much worse than that. "Victor? Can you…do you think you could give your ol' pa a hug?"

"No!" The little boy snapped and plopped the thumb back in. His eyes held Sean's steadily.

The preacher's conversation came to an awkward halt. Charlie found an immediate excuse to visit with someone farther down the beach.

Sean looked helplessly up at Rebecca, who wanted to cry but dared not.

"Son, maybe you don't remember me too good, huh? That's okay. It has been a long time since I've seen ya. But, do you remember me?"

The boy just continued to stare at him, all the while clutching his grandpa's hand. The preacher pretended to ignore the scene below him.

Rebecca tried. "Victor, do you remember living in the big house with your pa here and your ma?"

The boy looked up at her with a gaze that held little but annoyance, and still, the child said nothing.

"Do you remember that your ma and pa loved you…love you very much, Victor?"

The boy glared at her. He took his thumb from his mouth and pointed right at Sean's face. He screamed, "You made my mommy go away!" Then he turned his face into his grandfather's pants leg.

Sean was shocked by the emotion in the boy's words.

"No! Victor, I didn't! I swear to you, boy, I didn't make your ma go away. Victor, will you look at me?"

The boy would not take his face from the folds of black fabric. "No! Go away! I don't like you!"

Nothing could be said that would console Sean. "Rebecca, my boy hates me. How did that happen? My own son hates me."

Rebecca patted his shoulder.

"I've lost him forever, haven't I? My son is dead to me." Sean sobbed quietly, breaking Rebecca's heart not for the first time or the last.

She looked over at her husband, and her eyes begged for his help. Elrod came over to the broken man, about to invite him for a stroll down the shore, when his eyes located an orange glow in the distance, crowning northeast above the trees of Gales Creek.

Elrod tried to think. Didn't Elmer Lyda say he couldn't come today because their logging company had won the Gales Creek bid? He searched the ridge for sign of flames and, within seconds, received his awful reward. Licks of flame could just barely be discerned. They were leaping through the treetops and building on their own updrafts. Elrod realized that in that hot, dry weather, a fire in the canyon could become a holocaust. And it would. August 14, 1933, would be known as the fateful day of the Great Tillamook Burn.

"Horse pucky!" Elrod shook Sean's shoulder urgently. "Sean! Look! I think that's Lyda's camp. Holy cow! I think fire's broke out up there!"

Sean lifted his eyes from his hands and blinked the moisture from them to see the unsettling sight.

Though it was still in its infancy, radio would grow quickly, being fed largely by the natural isolation of rural Tillamook County. For Sean, shortwave radio, what was technically known as low-frequency transmitting, was his salvation. It didn't take long for him or others to realize that he had a natural gift for building the transmitting and receiving handsets. He was already receiving checks in the mail from folks who wanted their shortwave radio built by Sean Marshall, a.k.a. WP, or as some of the radio enthusiasts called him, 'The Whip.'

The Radio Act of 1912 required all amateur radio operators to be licensed; this was done as much to protect commercial radio stations from interruptions to their broadcasts, as it was to protect military wavelengths from being infiltrated for nefarious purposes (during the Great War, amateurs on shortwave radio sets had been found forging naval messages and faking distress calls). The United States Department of Commerce and Labor was the empowered branch that oversaw the Act's administration, including the imposing of fines on those who broke the new federal law. Sean had made a friend in the state office in Salem. Before he knew it, he had the first call number in the region. Within months of that, he became known to a fast-spreading number of comrade voices in the night as WP7E.

When Sean's eyes found the fire on the ridge, he realized that his assistance would be needed for the conflagration. And he just happened to have Elrod's new ham set in the backseat of the car. Somehow, Sean needed to get that radio to the watch tower on the north side of the canyon.

"C'mon, Elrod. It's time for you to learn just how to use that radio I built for you. But first, we'd better stop off and switch vehicles for the farm truck. And we can pick up my radio and the one I built for the Bell farm in Blaine. That way at least three towers will have communications. Ha! I guess this is going to be your baptism of fire, El. Literally!"

Elrod kissed his wife quickly. "I'm coming!"

He hollered back at Rebecca that the food was ready, if she could get Charlie and some of the others to dig up the pit and take the fish off of their stakes. Then the two men ran slapdash for the car, leaving a frightened Rebecca to stare after them.

Chapter 43

There was a tug at her pedal-pushers that took her completely by surprise. She was watching her husband and her best friend drive away, into just what she did not know, but it frightened her; and then the boy was at her side, tugging, and she was startled.

"Oh my, Victor. You surprised me."

At first, the boy just studied her, and then he pulled his thumb from his mouth and said, "Where was that man going?"

"That man, Victor, is your father. I believe he is going to try to help fight the forest fire. See?" She pointed to the ominous orange light becoming steadily more visible as the afternoon grew late and the sunlight shrank from the horizon.

"Are you scared?"

It was her turn to study the little boy. When she answered, she could not still her bottom lip from quivering a bit. "Yes. Are you?"

"He made my mommy go away," the boy said without hesitation, seemingly by rote.

That was too much. She didn't care if she was butting into Sean's personal business or not; it was just too much to take, letting the boy go on thinking that the loss of his mother was somehow Sean's fault. She knelt, took both his hands in hers and looked into his eyes. Somewhere in those depths was the happy youngster she had known years before.

"I don't know why someone told you that, Victor. It is simply not true. Your father loved your ma. They were very happy together, more so when you came along. You can remember how they loved you, can't you, Victor?"

The boy just stared at her.

"Victor, do you remember going on a trip with your dad to get a red tricycle?" She saw a flicker cross the boy's face, and she knew she was getting to him. "When you and your dad got back home, your ma had disappeared. He doesn't know why she left. He misses her badly. Victor, your pa misses you something terrible too. He loves you, boy. Believe me."

"I'll thank you not to fill the boy's head with your fatuous supposition, Mrs. Tjaden." A gravel voice accompanied by a somber shadow hung over her.

Sorrow gripped Rebecca's heart. She was so close. She'd seen recognition in the boy's face … She rose dispiritedly.

"You know as well as I do that I spoke truth to the boy, something I reckon he hears little of from you."

"Such lack of respect for a man of God. Tisk-tisk. Seems just keeping company with Sean Marshall can cause an otherwise good and obedient lamb to wander from her shepherd."

"Mr. Bowman, I am not your lamb, and you sure as sight are no shepherd. But I will apologize for my rudeness."

"Well, no need. I wouldn't say you were rude necessarily."

"Ah, yes, but I'm preparing to be. I had you invited here today Mr. Bowman, but that was my mistake. Here's the rudeness: I'm uninviting you. I'd like for you to take leave."

The preacher looked around, flabbergasted. "I don't think my invitation here was yours alone to decide, child. I believe there are others here who appreciate my fellowship."

He looked directly at Signey Tjaden, the family's matriarch, capturing her attention away from the other picnickers who were wildly seeking signs of forest fire on the ridge and speculating lively on how far it might spread. Might it grow big enough to oblige the hire of firefighters? The benefits of Roosevelt's New Deal had not yet been spotted on the untamed coastal region of Oregon. Many of the local citizens were jobless in the current economic crisis and cared more about the prospect of work and a chance for some pay, than about the tremendous loss of wildlife or the impending quarter-million-acre loss of prime timberland.

Sig strolled over to take by her daughter-in-law's side. She smiled at the preacher. "Beg pardon, Preacher. Did you motion for me?"

"Well, now, my dearest Lady Signey, how do you do today?" He toadied.

Rebecca rolled her eyes immoderately, which Sig Tjaden noticed.

"I'm well, Preacher," she answered solicitously.

"Your daughter-in-law has just informed me that my company at this here get-together is unwanted," he said this as though the idea were ludicrous. "She has gone so far as to invite me to take leave."

The little boy was taking in the whole scene intently.

Sig raised her eyebrows at her son's wife, as though to inquire if the allegation was true. When she received one of Rebecca's more determined facial casts for an answer, that was enough for her. Only the briefest of moments passed before she made reply.

"Forgive me, Preacher Bowman, but if Rebecca does not feel comfortable with your presence here, perhaps that would be best…?" she ended her reply as a question.

"Well, I have never!" he blustered.

He looked around, noticing how people were noticing him. He was losing face in front of the better part of his dwindling congregation. He quickly assessed the damages and weighed them against the tantalizing aroma of the Tjaden clam bake. The men were just removing the salmon from their stakes, and his mouth watered. But there seemed little chance for him to maintain any dignity if he chose to stay, unwelcome. Finally, he grabbed the boy's hand and stormed off without another word. But silently, he promised the Tjaden's would pay for the embarrassment caused him that day.

Sig looked after him for a while before she turned to Rebecca. "What on earth, Rebecca?"

"Oh, Sig, he's an awful man."

"Rebecca!" Then she whispered conspiratorially, "Details, daughter."

Rebecca laughed. "Do you know he once pulled a shotgun on Will and Sean? He pointed it right at their chests and threatened to pull the trigger."

Sig looked both shocked and amused by this.

"Lately he's been telling that boy of Sean's that Sean is a wicked man and that it was his fault that Blair ran away. I can't tell you how I know, Mother, but I know there is not a shred of truth to it. And telling a man's son he's no good! Mr. Bowman is evil, Sig. More so that he is a man of the church."

Signey nodded. Like other women in her family, she had a touch of sixth sense; just a touch, but it made her able to judge a character with indisputable accuracy.

"Yes, Rebecca, I do believe you're right about that." She placed her hand on her daughter-in-law's forearm. "Do you think Elrod is safe, dear? I'm so worried."

"I hope so." Then she laughed. "Did you see the way those two took off from here, like that fire was a circus come to town?"

"Well, so long as they don't start acting like a couple o' clowns and get themselves hurt." She pulled Rebecca over to the food to distract her from the real danger the girl's husband and dear friend were in, but also to keep her own mind busy from conjuring up unwanted images about the impending disaster.

Chapter 44

Once started, nothing could stop the outbreak, which shortly became a giant holocaust. Ten days after the first flame licks were sighted by the picnickers on the Nestucca Bay, the fire literally blew up, ravaging 240,000 acres of forest and all of her critters in less than twenty-four frightening hours. The fire's explosion, likened to an atomic bomb's effects of a decade later, went on a high-speed rampage and destroyed everything in its path. The mushroom cloud boiled fifty thousand feet into the atmosphere, visible for hundreds of miles at land or sea. Ash and debris were two feet deep on the beaches and at the bay. Ships five hundred miles out could not see daylight through the black smoke. Great clouds of it could be seen from Idaho and Montana.

Wishes came true for the local boys and men of Cloverdale. They were quickly dispatched as firefighters, along with three thousand arrivals from places unknown. The crews were greenhorns, special volunteers from back East who'd never seen a forest fire, and they were generally helpless when the breathing, fast-moving flames leaped trails and jumped fire lines. It was inevitable that some of them would become trapped.

"Look out, Sean! She's changing directions again!" yelled Elrod.

Sean jumped back, and both men fled their immediate area. They'd been trying to control a crown fire, but the impossibility of it became immediately apparent. With the updraft wind blowing small fires into full flames within seconds, the men in the nearby fire camp began grabbing for all they could safely carry, and the outpost was quickly evacuated, once more, to a more accessible outpost.

Their small band of ten men, including the fire chief from Forest Grove, Walter Vanderveden, was one of two crew shifts responsible for holding at bay a fifteen-mile front of fire along the forest's northwesterly edge. To Sean, it was an awesome orange wall of flame that refused to die.

"Time for a spell, Elrod. It's five hours now. If I don't hit a chow line and water myself down, I'm gonna die in this here mad canyon."

Elrod swiped at sweat-dripping locks before he swung his dig axe a final time. "I can't hardly heft that axe again 'til I get me some grub," he panted. "Tell me again why we're doing this?"

"We're doin' this 'cause…"—he labored between huge swallows of fresher air as they backed away from the fire line—"these monster fireworks is feeding on our land's beauty." He stepped over the charcoal remains of a five-point buck and shook his head dismally. "An' if this thing don't stop soon, we're gonna have a new American desert."

"Just makes me sick to see it, Sean." Elrod referred to the dead stag. "I've crossed bear, cougar, and a million birds in that same state just today. You know,"—he hesitated and then said more quietly, "I hear tell it this whole thing happened because the Lyda crew wanted to pull out one more log after Johannesen told 'em to shut it down."

" I think that's a lot of loose talk. This fire was underway when he got here to shut down logging activity. Heck, conditions are such that I think a deer could have rubbed two branches together just passing by and we'd have fire." Sean muttered.

"Maybe so. They're gonna investigate just the same." Elrod said.

"Well, they got to find something or someone to place blame on, I suppose." Sean grabbed for a platter and a cup. They were the last of their ten-man crew to break loose from their combat for some food and rest. They would be needed again in five hours' time, so Elrod and Sean wasted no more time talking.

Distance communications were wiped out. But thanks to Sean, a few of the camps had shortwave radio contact with each other and could coordinate their efforts. They had only been able to sleep about two hours when Sean was shaken roughly awake. He was so groggy he could only move his sore, stiff body in slow motion, and something in his head kept buzzing between his ears. It was a fighter from the other crew who was poking him awake. Sean groaned. It couldn't have been five hours yet. He felt as though he'd only been asleep for ten minutes.

"I'm real sorry, pal, but we need your help." When Sean was slow to raise himself, the man shook him roughly. "Hey, wake up! This is serious, Marshall. We got a major problem."

"What? Yeah. Huh?" He shook his head recklessly, trying to clear it.

"Another fire has been started."

"Started. What do you mean started?"

"Someone could have started it intentionally. It's just northwest of our camp, and it is starting to shift toward us. We need you to work your magic with that radio of yours and get us some help or we ain't getting out of here alive."

That woke him up. He turned to shake Elrod awake. "C'mon, man. Get up. We've got big trouble."

"What's going on?" Elrod was feeling equally silly from sleep deprivation.

"We got another fire jumping right up our backsides. We gotta go!"

The other crew man yelled at Elrod as he helped pack up gear, "If the two meet and become one, she'll gallop in every direction. She'll eat us up along with everything else!"

Elrod blinked himself awake and turned wide-eyed to Sean.

He was already jamming personals into a canvas bag. "El, finish this up for me, okay? I gotta get on the radio and get us some help."

Help could not be found on the shortwaves. Every single outpost must have been on the move. Sean packed up the radio last of all, and the spur-of-the-moment camp was evacuated in great haste. They'd been on the northeast fringe of the fire. A new fire was brewing just north and west of their current position. The men discussed it quickly and decided that heading toward the coast for Blaine, via Hell's Canyon and the Devil's Playground, was their only good option.

They trailed through some old burn territory, deciding that bleached-out snags and burned soil was the safest place from new fire. Camp was again set up. It was almost night by then, and the men worked steadily in the humid heat. Several times before getting to the new spot, they had actually seen the fast-traveling fire and felt its heat. They had crossed the Nestucca River five or six times for that temporary refuge. Sean thought that they should keep going until they reached the safety of the coast, but so many of the twenty or so men were too tired and battered to make the trek. Sean and Elrod decided to perform some reconnaissance of the immediate area, checking the blackened timbers for signs of heat. The loss of wildlife they happened across was unimaginable. All that the forest provided shelter to, from deer to the smaller squirrels and rabbits, lay charred and strewn about. Some of the trees not too far from the camp were still smoldering.

"Sean, them smolderin' stumps are awful close to the camp, eh?"

"Yeah." He kept walking, stopping to inspect some boot prints in the freshly denigrated soil. On one knee, he touched the forest floor. "Still hot." They walked on in silence. Elrod walked north-northeast a few yards to inspect some odd markings he'd spotted in the soil, perhaps made by a fireman's ax. Sean took a southeasterly track toward more boot prints. Both men could see that they were heading into the fire.

"What does that mean, Sean? Footprints out here. No other camp nearby. That's a mystery to me."

"To me too. El, I think someone has been following us."

"Who? Why?"

"It'd be real helpful if we knew, wouldn't it? You know, that lineman, when he woke me, said Vandervelden was suspicious of the second fire. He thinks someone might have started it purposefully."

"Hell, why would someone do that? I mean, starting a fire deliberately on the other side of a camp of men? A man wouldn't do that just to perpetuate his job. That'd be like attempting murder."

"What if it wasn't about a job, El?" he hollered over his shoulder. "What if it is attempted murder? Do you know any of those men? I don't, and I don't know who their enemies are either. I know I have myself an enemy who would like to see me dead, and a fire would be a convenient means."

Elrod whistled low. "That's a troubling notion." He could not make heads or tails out of those marks he'd spotted. He stood again and looked Sean's way. "Say, Sean, I can see blaze over beyond that creek bed. Too close for my comfort."

Sean ventured ahead a little bit further, and again he stooped to examine the forest loam, both for heat and for evidence that they were not alone. *Hmm, I need to talk to Vandervelden.* To Elrod, he yelled over his shoulder, "I agree. This area ain't too stable. We should go back and let the crew know." He knew that Elrod was still a good ten feet to his rear so he'd hollered loudly. Their reconnaissance had proved to Sean that the camp they'd chosen was still very much in danger. Sean was thinking that if the crew refused to move on, perhaps he could convince El that the two of them should head home. He did not relish the idea of seeing another Tjaden, this one his best friend, die among surrounding flame and falling timber. *Falling timber?* He registered the dangerous crack too late, his senses dulled by ten days of intense labor and little sleep. He turned while still in his crouch and could see the huge, blackened pine coming straight for them.

"Elrod!" he screamed.

The heat woke him, very hot weather and extremely hot fire. He realized that he was nauseous and his head was aching something frightful. When he tried to move, pain radiated through his torso. He was on fire. He looked down. No, he was not on fire, but he was in dire trouble just the same.

"El? El, can you hear me? El?"

There was no answer. Sean tried to push the heavy tree off his chest. He came to the cloudy realization that he was only alive because he'd been ten feet farther out from the falling timber than Elrod had been. Sean had been caught and slapped down by the very tip of the burned snag.

Oh my God! Elrod!

Now adrenaline was pumping through Sean, and he pushed mightily at the dead tree, pushing the excruciating pain it was causing him to the back of his mind at the same time. He wiggled and rolled beneath the weight until he was finally free. He tried to stand, but his legs wouldn't hold him. Something was wrong with his back. He had a hard time taking breaths as well, and he knew that a couple of ribs must be busted. He tried to pay them no attention. He crawled down the length of the tree a few more feet and found his friend. Sean had no idea how long he had blacked out for, but his friend had been dead a while. There was nothing Sean could do for Elrod Tjaden.

Sean howled up to the treetops, "No!"

He'd tried to roll the tree off Elrod, but with all his serious injuries, he lacked the strength. The camp was too far for him to crawl, and the fire was raging too close. It was doubling back, the heat preceding it, which was why Sean came to when he did. He worked his way to the creek bed and rolled his beaten body down into it, spent. It might just be deep enough for the fire to pass over without incinerating him. It was the only hope Sean had of surviving. He used his arms to sweep the immediate vicinity of anything flammable and then pushed his face toward the creek's floor, coming face to face with a scorched chipmunk. He shoved it away and instantly succumbed to the inky blackness that had been creeping in from the edges of his consciousness.

Chapter 45

He'd done this once already this week. He knew it was dangerous. He wasn't rattlebrained; he might be reckless... But he'd weighed the chance he'd be recognized against the incredible number of firefighting men who came from all over the south, west and further, and swarmed the town of Tillamook. He then considered the propitious number of whores who had descended upon the town in response to all those men. Finally, the squalid room he'd rented was on the opposite side of town, about as far as one could be from the downtown strip, and Bowman was satisfied he would remain unnoticed. Not even Welby knew where he was at the moment. *Get a radio so I can contact you whenever I need to. Let the boy keep his pa's gifts, or plan to replace 'em yourself. Don't go celebratin' without my permission... (chug) you ain't respectable, you ain't worth a box a' hair to me...*" he wagged his head from side to side as he silently mimicked Otis Welby in a most unflattering way. A slow smile stretched feline-like across his narrow-lipped maw. He took a good long pull on his brown jug, looked sideways and saw the whore was watching him. Then he took another long chug, that time splashing a little on his mushrooming midsection. He hated Otis Welby. The man had been ordering him around—intimidating him—ever since the Tjaden wedding. *Four years of extortion, that's what it was.*

He looked her way again and the whore quickly averted her eyes. But he'd seen enough to know the woman was a little fearful of him. Bowman liked that. It made everything so much more exciting. Tied with her hands to the iron headboard, face down, Bowman had promised her she would not be hurt, but he could see she did not entirely believe him. Yes, there was that fear, that trepidation...my God, how he'd missed that... "Have you ever heard of the Marquis de Sade, my dear?" he asked.

Chapter 46

August 1933

Cloverdale, Oregon

The small cabin was modest at best. At worst, it was a haven for every kind of bug. Places where wallboard gaped from the floor boards, and the spots were numerous, provided access to the roly-poly's, spiders, carpenter ants and beetles. Fleas were so prevalent they could be seen jumping around the dirty floor. They were more in number on that night because the heat was driving them inside. Young Victor slapped at his ankles and scratched bites until they bled. He couldn't sleep.

The preacher had left a single light burning before he departed in the morning, and there were a hundred moths flitting around it. The living room area was shrouded in an eerie, nicotine-yellow cast. Save for the insects, the room was too quiet. His grandpa had not come back all day. Maybe he would never come back. It had been dark for a long time, and Victor had missed dinner. He didn't want to admit it, but he was scared. Then his ears picked up the sound of his grandpa's jalopy pulling in the long drive. When Mavis Marshall donated the family's old car to the church in Tillamook, she should have stipulated that neither the auto nor any funds derived from the sale of it were to wind up as property of Preacher Bowman, but she didn't, much to Sean's chagrin. Victor jumped up and raced to the window. A sticky strand of web stuck to his face, and he wiped at it, but his hands were no good at finding it. He peered through the black glass and saw his grandpa wrestling himself from his car. Something close to a smile formed on the little boy's face.

The old man stomped the dirt off his feet just before the threshold, like it mattered, hung his hat and a pair of binoculars on the peg behind the door. Victor was a bundle of questions. "Where did you go, Grandpa? Did you go fight the fire? Did you see that man who's my father?"

"What was that foul thing you said there, boy?" The preacher paused before putting his coat on the only other peg.

"W-w-w-what, Grandpa?"

"That obscenity about some other man being your father?"

The boy realized his error too late. Grandpa got furious when such things about Victor's ma or pa were mentioned. Gone was the little boy's tentative smile. His chubby face was suddenly frozen in fear.

"Your imagination has got the best of you, boy. You need to reflect on the truths as I have given them to you. You know what needs doin' now, don't you, boy?"

Tears escaped the little boy. He wished he wouldn't cry, but he could not help it. A hard rock was in his tiny throat, and his childish voice quivered. "I didn't mean it, Grandpa."

The old man said nothing as he crossed the room in two large strides and opened the lid to the antique banana box. With one hand holding the lid, he gestured to the boy with the other.

"No, Grandpa. Please. Please don't make me go in the box. There's spiders in there!"

"Spiders! Bah! They're no match for your size and strength. More importantly, there are truths to be found in there. When you discover those truths, then you may come out."

The box was the size of a child's coffin, and it felt like one. It was dark and close and especially hot in this warmest of Augusts.

The child whimpered as he approached it, his thumb jammed back into his mouth. "Please, Grandpa. I'm hungry." He looked inside the box. Its bottom could be seen, with tiny little black specks here and there. "Please, Grandpa. Don't make me go in the box!" The boy cried openly.

"No more of this nonsense, boy! Get yourself in there. When the evil that has crossed your mind is gone, you may come out."

Victor climbed in. The lid closed with a *whump!* The little boy began sweating immediately. He closed his eyes in the blackness and tried to pretend there was nothing else in there with him. His tortured mind raced. Trickles of sweat ran from his hairline here and there, making like vermin as they tracked across his skin. Fleeting images of a red tricycle came to him. Then a foggy memory of riding on a horse with a pretty, dark-haired lady, who must have been his mother, drifted into his thoughts. Victor pinched himself on the upper arm, hard. But it didn't help. His mind's eye saw the man from the picnic. He was throwing Victor up in the air, laughing. Victor remembered that from when he'd been a baby. *No! That man was not his father.* Victor pinched himself repeatedly until he could think of little else besides the pain. *The pretty lady was not laughing and smiling. She was sad. The laughing man was mean and made his mother leave.* The little boy in the big black box made himself believe those "truths" that his grandpa recited for him regularly. Victor found those truths in the miserable confines of the box in great haste. He pushed open the lid and jumped out hurriedly, relishing the cool air on his clammy skin. The preacher had taken the opportunity to swig from his brown jug while the boy committed his 'truths' to memory. At the sound of the boy jumping from the banana box, he set the jug inside the deep sink where the boy's eyes could not reach. He turned around and faced the boy.

"I saw it all, Grandpa! That man was mean and made my mommy leave home…she was always really sad. I was sad too, until you came for me." The boy looked at his grandpa hopefully.

"Is that the truth, boy?"

"Yes, sir. Boy, Grandpa, the truth can sure make ya hungry."

The old man turned to the sink board and began slicing ham to go with eggs and bread for their dinner. "Sit yourself at the table, boy. It is time for the truth to be rewarded."

Chapter 47

August, 1933

Chicago, Illinois

News of the great Tillamook Burn traveled coast-to-coast. Cindy dated several successful reporters, and even one newspaper mogul, so it was not difficult for her to get details about the Tillamook County destruction.

On her date the night before with Chester Lasley, who, as one with controlling interest in one of Chicago's largest newspapers, had up-to-the-hour information, she'd learned Oregon had lost more than 300,000 acres, and over 24 billion board feet of prime timber. The loss of forest creatures numbered in the millions. He also confirmed for her that lives had been lost among the unskilled, volunteer firefighters. Cindy had wanted to question further on the matter, but not from Chester. As far as that man was concerned, she had no more and no less interest in the Tillamook Burn beyond a natural curiosity. Chester Lasley made Cindy a bit nervous. Truth be told, he reminded her of the preacher, and she didn't want him knowing details of her past life. He was willing to pay a small fortune for a single night with her, though, and he'd always remained a gentlemen. Nonetheless, Cindy counted her chickens for the day she could afford to bring to an end her dates with Chester Lasley, without becoming one of his enemies. Especially since, in recent months, Lasley had been making it known to Chicago's upper-crust he had political aspirations.

Her friend Wendell did not like Lasley at all. He had begged her to step lightly about the man, if she absolutely *must* date him. "He's a bully. A silver-spoon'd scoundrel in hundred-dollar suits.

Believe me, I know the type," Wendell had said. He believed the man held his wickedness in check only because he had a reputation to protect. "Beware," Wendell had warned her just that morning, "of Lasley's formidable anger."

Cindy thought her friend was spot on about Lasley. And there was something more about Chester that reminded Cindy of the preacher, his word had reputation and influence over that of most others. He, too, may be untouchable.

She'd happened by a favorite watering hole of another reporter she dated, found him there, and learned worse news out of Tillamook: Sean had been a volunteer firefighter and he'd been hurt. Thank goodness he'd survived. Elrod Tjaden had died in the fire. Elrod was Rebecca's husband, Cindy knew, and she was heart-broken for Rebecca. She'd always counted the couple as Blair's closest, truest friends. *Think of something else.*

Cindy sighed and looked about her room. She was going to move. Her top-back room was cramped. And she could never have men visit her there. Her meddlesome, ever-inquiring land-lady would never hear of it. She could manage those nuisances; Cindy was easy-going about most anything. But, there was the arrangement of her bath; she was growing less facile about her bath being shared, and located a floor below her room. The only thing Cindy did like about her current apartment was the three flights of stairs to get to her room. She'd rather liked getting the exercise.

She'd saved up money enough to move across town to a spacious apartment with a water view—and it's own water closet, of course. It was not one of the swanky new ones they were building on the water. Those didn't appeal to Cindy. Instead, a few streets back away from the water, she and Wendell had happened upon a swanky *old* one. It was a small two-story publishing house, pur-pose-built in 1888, of brick and floated glass and tall ceilings, and capable of accommodating heavy industry equipment. It had been erected during a construction heyday, created by abundant available space near the rails, that came about after the fire of 1871. By the turn of the last century, the whole row had become a magnet for the printing industry. All of the other old buildings on the street were multiple stories high, and were being converted into luxury apartments. But no investor had taken up the restoration of her little two-story, deeming it hardly worth the trouble.

Cindy fell in love with the vastness of private space and the dazzling natural light pouring through tall windows. But what had sold her was the character of the building. It had functioned in a specific way for a long time, then found itself transformed to function in another way—something quite different, but beautiful and grand—precisely because of that first function's influences. The space lived two lives.

She'd instructed Wendell, who acted as her agent, to release the necessary funds, and Cindy purchased the space on the spot. She'd had the building split top-from-bottom, and renovated into two luxury residences. Cindy would be taking the top floor, with its tall windows and water view; she had a renter in the form of a quiet, elderly gentleman for the bottom apartment. The new place was the first thing Cindy can remember being truly happy about since—*No. That was not your life and it does you no good to think about it.*

But she was homesick for Oregon. *Careful…Don't let the panic in your heart get started…Slow your breathing, slow your heart beat.* She missed her husband and her child so awful much. It had been not quite 2 years since she'd run for Blair's life and took the helm; almost two years since she had felt the soft skin of her child's cheek, or smelled his baby-scented hair. *Oh…God…* She grabbed her stomach and curled fetal-like on her bed, willing her sudden nausea to go away. She tried to quickly tamp down thoughts of Sean and Victor whenever they bubbled up to her consciousness. But sometimes the blues swamped over her, leaving her depressed and fairly bereft of hope she would ever see her family again. She knew Blair was not strong enough to return to Oregon.

Anyway, Cindy had sent a letter to Sean months earlier asking him to forget Blair. Rebecca was widowed, and Cindy had told Sean to marry another.

Cindy fought her depression by getting up and going shopping on Navy Pier. She'd stopped at the bakery window and paid for a cinnamon roll and coffee. She strolled a few shop windows farther, then stopped to gaze through a jeweler's window at a darling watch piece. The gold neck chain was spaced every few inches with pale pink crystal beads. The front of the piece was beautifully scrolled, but what caught Cindy's eye was inside. The shopkeeper had opened the piece to show a porcelain face, hand-painted with pale pink calla-lilies. *What a guilty pleasure it would be, to wear something close to my heart which so reminds me of the Marshall home*, Cindy mused. *It's too expensive. You mustn't.*

"Oh, young lady, you simply must!" The shopkeeper had walked out the open door to engage the beautiful young woman who was contemplating the ladies' timepiece. He'd only placed it in his front window that morning. "The watchmaker no doubt had you in his mind when he crafted its beauty. Come, let me show it to you," the shopkeeper said, bowing deeply.

Cindy could not resist. She followed the shopkeeper inside to see the timepiece up close. It was exquisite. And, Cindy had reasoned, her twenty-second birthday was coming up. When she'd handed it back to the man to wrap up, he asked her, "how would you like it engraved, Miss?" Cindy was momentarily stumped. She did not know if she should put her name on the piece or Blair's name on the piece. But the man, wrongly sensing her hesitation at paying extra for engraving, interrupted her thoughts saying, "Tell you what, Miss. I will put on there for you a name, a special date, a favorite proverb, you just name it. And I won't charge you but for half the standard engraving fee."

Cindy thought a moment. "You can put a proverb on it?"

"On the backside, yes Miss."

Cindy smiled and turned coyly away from the man as she reached into her bodice and withdrew the treasured Emily Dickinson poem. She had long since transferred the strangely soothing words onto a piece of pink stationery, which she handed the shopkeeper. "Can you engrave all of those words on the backside?"

The jeweler read the words to himself and smiled as he finished, nodding. "I, too, am a fan of Miss Dickinson. Haunting yet alluring, do you agree?"

"Yes, I do." Cindy replied. "How long will that take you, sir?"

"Oh, by the time you walk to the end of Navy Pier and back to this spot again, it will be ready for you. I'll get to it straight away."

Chapter 48

September, 1939

Cloverdale, Oregon

Lorette moved into the Marshall's house six years earlier, soon after Sean was found near dead in a dry creek bed smack in the middle of the Great Burn. Will could not be expected to run the farm and gristmill by himself and look after Mavis and Sean too. The solution became obvious; they needed to hire a housekeeper and nurse companion. Lorette nursed Sean back to some semblance of health, fetched Mavis whenever she began wandering through the house in her confused state, and cooked and cleaned for the men. Lorette was an extremely busy young woman. She was buxom and a little on the ample side. She was not a great beauty, but neither was she unattractive with her bouncy blonde hair that fell below her shoulders whenever it wasn't pinned up, and generous lips. Sean was certain that his brother sometimes watched Lorette for too long whenever she exited a room, but Lorette never seemed to notice any of Will's attention. She was simply a young woman who was grateful for a full-time job that included such grand room and board.

Two months before the second Tillamook Burn, Lorette's job became a little easier. She suddenly had one less patient to worry about. She'd been out in the garden when Mavis rose early from her nap and began wandering the downstairs rooms again. Her cataracts were as thick as jelly wax, and for some time, she'd been unable to make out anything more than shadows. When Lorette found Mavis, she was cowering in the corner of the music room in extreme distress over being lost and not knowing where she was. Lorette did her best to calm the elderly woman down, but the experience had rattled Mavis's final reserve of strength. She died in her sleep later that same night.

No one blamed Lorette except Lorette. She atoned by lavishing attention on Sean, who grew rankled by the constant care. Her hovering finally forced him out of bed each day and pushed him to his limits, something that saved him from wasting away. The tip of the tree had hit Sean square across his midsection. It had cracked four of his ribs, damaged his spleen, and had broken his back in several places. The injuries resulted in making his heart work all the harder just to take breaths. Now his heart was abnormally sized and working twice as hard as that of a healthy man. Sean knew that he needed to take life easier, but he refused to lie in bed like an invalid. If that would be his existence, he would just as soon die.

That day, Sean rose early and got right to the business of picking through old photographs. He had started his own business turning his historic, scenic photos into picture postcards. They were much in demand, since the Tillamook forests ceased to exist, having been devoured by fire, twice. The forests of the scenic Pacific Northwest lived only in the minds of those who could remember and on Sean Marshall's postcards. The postcard business and Sean's sideline of making ham radio sets didn't just add to the family income; they gave Sean Marshall a reason to live. Once again, Sean had saved nearly enough money to attend the college and become an engineer. He was registered for the spring semester. Sean sat cross-legged on the large braided rug in the parlor. The room had three floor-to-ceiling windows to provide the light he needed, but he swore that he could still smell his mother's strong cologne emanating from the bedroom just off the parlor, and it persisted in making him feel melancholy about all the people missing from his life. He picked up his pencil and began rating each of the photographs on a point system. Then he went back through the pile and began numbering them in order of quality. He decided he would send off only the top twenty-four and see how they fared. He was cataloging the remaining photographs as he returned them to their boxes when Will burst through the parlor doors.

"Sean! You're not going to believe this! Guess who I just heard is getting himself a ham radio set?" He did not bother to wait for his surprised, mildly annoyed brother to answer before he blurted the answer. "Preacher Bowman! That's who!"

"Baloney!" Sean laughed. "He'd never dream of asking me to build him a set. I'm not sure I would even if he paid me double."

"Well, he ain't gonna ask you. I guess there's a guy up in Garibaldi who builds 'em now. Your friend Osborne from over there in Salem was just by and stopped to say hello. I didn't know you was up or I'd have asked him in, Sean—"

"That's okay. Get on with it," he urged.

"Right. Anyways, he got a set built by this Garibaldi guy and applied for his license. Osborne says everything checks out, so…I guess we're gonna have us a new voice in the night to chit-chat with." The mirth in Will's eyes was unmistakable.

"Glad you're having so much fun with this, Will," his now-dour brother answered. "We'll have no peace—the deviate's voice can intrude into our very own parlor, day or night."

"Yeah." His chuckle had been full of good humor, but Sean raised a negative Will had not considered. Still, Sean clearly missed what it was about the news that had lifted Will's spirits. "But listen. I thought that maybe, just maybe, the preacher might allow Victor to, you know, talk on the radio now and then. I mean, Victor's at an age now where the preacher might just have trouble keeping him off'a it."

Sean looked over to the radio sitting idle on the desk by the window. "Victor," he said, looking up sadly at his brother. "You know, Will, I was thinking last night when I couldn't fall asleep, that I can't really picture Blair so clear in my head anymore. I'm forgettin' what she looked like unless I study the portrait. And I don't remember what she sounded like. Her memory's fading as fast as my blue jeans."

The mirth drained from Will's eyes. He crossed the threshold and sat in a chair across from his brother's position on the floor. He studied his hands for a few seconds, but when he finally looked at his brother, he was as serious as a heart attack.

"Sean, brother, it has been more than seven years since she left. Seven years. We don't even know if she's alive. Rebecca's alone now too. She still loves you, you know. It'd be far better to drift off to sleep with images of a woman who is real, who's here and who loves you, than to pine for someone who's never coming back." He paused. "Little brother, I promised myself I wouldn't intrude on your privacies, but I think it needs saying for your own good. Sean, your wife is never coming home to you."

"I know."

Sean went back to flipping through photos, but aimlessly. Will studied his hands some more, twirled his mustache, coughed. The silence grew louder by the second.

"So, whaddya think of the preacher doin' a radio broadcast? Maybe he's planning to do sermons on the air or something like that."

"Nah. He's just a lonely old man, like the rest of us."

But Sean was thinking how unlike other men the preacher was. Sean knew that Bowman was not merely old and lonely but old and dirty. Sean's fingers stopped flipping photos. He looked up at his brother as the thought occurred to him, and slowly, his mouth turned into a devious grin.

"I think I know something that will spark up anything the preacher has to say over the airwaves."

Will was relieved to see his brother smile and to have the tension empty out of the room. "I recognize that grin. What have you got up your sleeve?"

"I think it'd be much more fun for you if it were a surprise, Will. I'm gonna go give Ozzie a call."

Chapter 49

Cindy celebrated her twenty-eighth birthday on September 1, 1939, with an abundance of champagne, provided by her date, and dinner with friends at the Table D'hôtel. The milestone was punctuated by Germany's invasion of Poland and an ultimatum that would set off the beginning of the Second World War. But Cindy's spirit for celebrating had been dampened first by the news that Tillamook forests in Oregon were again gripped by a fire holocaust. Much the same as the fire of six years earlier, this one raged between the Wilson and Trask Rivers, blackening more than 200,000 acres.

From pictures in the papers reaching as far as Chicago, one would think there was little left for a fire to eat. But flames found food among the deadfalls, debris, young seedlings that never had a chance to grow, and thousands of bleached snags jutting for steep miles across the area of the huge Burn of '33. Cindy looked in horror and disbelief at the destruction evident in the photos. Much of the region of her childhood was unrecognizable, and she could find none of the familiar landmarks. They were all gone.

She had been surprised by the intensity of her own grief over the news. Her life in the county of Tillamook had certainly not resembled any fairy tale, save perhaps the wicked fiend who was the preacher. But the forests had been her asylum whenever her existence reached the pitiful lows that it had time and again, and in many ways, Sean Marshall had been her prince. Now those forests were dead, maybe forever.

Cindy knew that she'd been blessed with those short years living in the Marshall home and being the recipient of their love and kinship. She also knew that she would not be grieving over people she did not feel a genuine love for in return. So, perhaps grief is the price that must be paid for the privilege of that love and kinship, and the deeper the love, the deeper the grief.

She had been immensely saddened six years earlier by the report of Elrod Tjaden's death. The papers had lauded him and his seriously wounded friend, Sean Marshall, heroes for risking their lives in order to set up radio communications for the fire-fighters. Cindy worried who she might lose this time. The loggers were calling the area jinxed, apparently in the Biblical sense. They were predicting the fire plague would continue every six years, three times in a row.

To the surprise and amusement of her date, she silently prayed before her plate of cherry-roasted game hen. She prayed to God that she lose no more of her friends to Satan's little games. Her date, Chester Lasley, completely mistook Cindy's prayerful concern as being about the day's events in Europe. He thought it funny that a high-class whore should fret about world crisis, and he patted her hand patronizingly as he refilled her champagne glass.

"Don't put another wrinkle in that pretty forehead of yours, Cindy. Britain and France will march over the very faces of those Nazi brown-shirts if they have to. You'll see. Anyway, it's not our fight, and it's never going to be, so let's drink to that." He picked up her hand and kissed the back of it lightly, promising, "But if Nazis ever do invade us, I will protect you, my dear."

Eyes around the table rolled in unison.

Cindy pulled her hand away angrily. "I have family in Tillamook. I am worried about them, fool." A few at the table snickered—Lasley wasn't one of them.

The longer she'd known Lasley, the more she grew to despise the man. She could hardly disguise it any longer. Cindy had told herself years ago that when she was secure, financially, she would retract from dating men like Lasley. She was secure, and yet here she was on another date with the man. It was the birthday. She had gone from needing to acquire security for herself in later years, to worrying about her earning potential in those later years. How long does a prostitute have before age threatens her career? Cindy was almost thirty. *You're drinking too much.*

He raised his brows at the others in the group. "You mean to say you're Oregon grown? Well, Miss Cindy Marshall, we're finally learning something about you. And I must say that they certainly grow them pretty in Oregon country. Say, doll, your family isn't a bunch of firefighters, is it?"

"Not hardly. No. My father was not cut from heroes' cloth." *Stop talking,* an urgent voice intruded upon her thoughts. But the warning went unheeded as Cindy took another drink, then reflexively, habitually, massaged the Lady Racine timepiece she wore around her neck. "But I did lose someone, a friend, in the last fire," she admitted. "And someone else, someone who was dear to me, was harmed. I'm not anxious to see anyone else hurt is all." She had never talked to anyone about her personal sorrow over the Great Burn, not even Wendell, her best friend. But that didn't mean she was not emotionally invested. On the contrary, her hurt and heartbreak over the obliteration of Tillamook County ran too deep to discuss the subject.

Cindy's date made a mental note to check into the facts that his date gave up so carelessly. One never knew when leverage over someone might be useful, and somehow, he felt like knowing Cindy Marshall's past could be very serviceable indeed. She might be just another whore, but she had money and important friends. He folded his napkin into his lap and reached to pour his lovely date some more champagne.

Cindy got up slowly, keeping the ice pack pressed to her forehead, and looked over the contents of her cupboard. She finally settled on some corned beef hash, a brown egg, and a thick slab of French bread slathered in butter. Even though she was queasy at the thought of food, she knew she would feel better after eating something. She needed to soak up the champagne that she could almost hear swishing around in her stomach. She asked herself for the hundredth time how she could have been so insipid as to drink nearly an entire bottle of French champagne.

She knew why she did it. She had several reasons, the first being that she'd celebrated another birthday, her twenty-eighth. That was hard for a woman who made her fortune with her looks. Then there was Chester Lasley, her date from last night, who kept refilling her champagne glass for her. He frightened her. There seemed some barely checked savagery brewing in the man, which reminded her of the preacher. But he consistently shelled out two hundred dollars for Cindy to spend the entire night with him, and he had always remained a gentleman in spite of Cindy's fear. And then there was the Burn, and this one dredged up all the unsettling emotions she'd experienced six years before upon hearing of Sean's injury.

He had almost died, the papers had said. She wondered how he was faring. It was none of her business really. She had abandoned him, after all, and had no right to concern herself with the Marshalls. But she had done him a favor by leaving, hadn't she? She'd wanted to spare him any more suffering. She should never have saddled such a good man with a mentally ill wife; a bastard, incestually conceived son; and the wrath of her evil, abusive father, who'd murdered Wyatt Marshall, Cindy knew. No, Sean was better off without her. Of that she was certain. But she still wondered.

She ate greedily, was immediately sorry, and lay back down on her chaise with a fresh ice pack, that time placing it under her neck. She fleetingly considered whether she had said or done anything while under the influence of all that champagne, anything that would have called attention to her "problem." She was relatively sure that Blair would not have come out while Cindy was on a date. Still, something nagged at the back of her mind, something *she'd* said, something *she'd* done wrong, something that flashed a danger warning, but what? A few minutes later, Cindy was beyond wondering what all she had done during her birthday celebration the night before. She was fast asleep.

Chapter 50

September, 1939

Cloverdale, Oregon

"You have to hold this button firmly in when you talk, and then you must always say, 'Over,' when you're done sayin' anything. And don't forget to give your call sign every single time you go on."

"I know, I know. Can I go first?"

"Now, Victor, I have waited a long time for someone to build me a radio. I do believe it is only right if I go first."

The boy kicked at a huge carpenter ant scurrying across the floorboards. Like any almost-twelve-year old with a new game, he was disappointed not to be able to play with it immediately. That was the only thing even close to a toy that his grandfather had ever brought home, except for a stupid bag of marbles, and he'd bought it for himself. *Figures*, Victor thought. He felt cheated, though he dared not say so and chance incurring the preacher's wrath. *Not that it was easy these days for grandpa to catch me, let alone deliver any sound blows,* Victor thought. Victor had grown up. His grandfather had grown old. And the swill the preacher had been drinking for as long as Victor had known him, made him unsteady.

Victor had spent every birthday (which happened to fall on Christmas Eve) and Christmas he could remember in the crappy little cabin, and there had never been anything resembling a gift or a holiday feast. When others were dining on roasted duck and turkeys and hams, Victor and his grandfather ate boiled wheat and boiled peas. At least they had electricity and an indoor toilet in the cabin, and a phone for the cabin was in the works—Tiny's camp didn't have phone service or indoor toilet. The church in Tillamook had Federal money that was provided those within the burn disaster area, so they paid for the cabin's renovations and a repainting of the church.

On the one occasion when Victor had made the mistake of crying about a toy he didn't receive, he got himself mottled black and blue for his tears. His grandfather used to joke that the cabin doubled as a boys' town for wayward young men. He'd kept a peeled alder wood stick in every corner and stripped new ones when the old ones became too brittle for whipping properly.

Sean Marshall, who claimed to be Victor's father, came to the door each year with an expensive gift, given for both Victor's birthday and Christmas. Thanks to Sean, Victor owned a fishing pole, a Swiss Army knife, a hunting knife, and a camera. Victor remembered back to his birthday last December, when he'd turned eleven years old. As Mr. Marshall had done every year for as long as Victor could remember, he'd arrived on Christmas Eve with a beautifully wrapped box. That year, there was a shiny new Winchester 30-30 inside. The preacher had not bothered to get Victor any gift at all, as usual. It prompted Victor to ask his grandfather why he wanted him to live in the cabin so badly when all he ever did was yell at him and bestow on him unmerciful beatings. To that, the preacher just laughed at the boy and told him, "The verse of the Bible I pin my faith on is the one that says if you spare the rod, you spoil the child. You are my one and only son, so no one will argue I do my full duty in that respect, boy."

It was not an answer to Victor's question, but since he didn't have the gumption to approach the question again, he would never understand why his grandfather insisted on being his parent. *Was it simply that he wanted to cheat Sean Marshall of his desire to be my father?* Victor had a hunch that was probably it, but it didn't matter anyhow. *Marshall never came for me…he never fought for me. He left me in this God-awful place. All the gifts in the world could not make up for that.*

Victor sighed loudly as he watched his grandfather fiddle with the radio. The old man was sucking all the fun out of it by repeating over and over how every single thing is done.

Heck, it ain't no buzz saw. It's a radio. How hard can it be?

The preacher made a flourish of pressing the button on the arm and clearing his throat. He smiled benignly at his grandson as he repeated the call sign he was assigned, according to the letter received in the afternoon mail from Osborne at the Department of Labor and Commerce, in Salem.

"Breaker, breaker. This is ADV8 coming on. Anyone out there? Over." He released the button.

The static buzzed and hiccupped, and some broken words were coming back. Bowman fiddled with the frequency knobs a bit. Then they heard the words plainly, and the smile vanished from the preacher's face.

"I say. This is D4WL in Tillamook. I'm a bit of a deviate too, but I don't advertise it! Over."

"Damnation!" Bowman yelled.

Uh-oh. His grandfather was seriously mad. His face was contorting and turning all purple and red.

"That Sean Marshall is behind this! I know it sure as I know he ran your mother off, Victor! Damnation!"

"Grandpa." The boy was trying really hard not to laugh. If Mr. Marshall did arrange that call sign, he had to hand it to him, that was a really good joke, a down-n-dirty all the way. "Maybe it's just an accident."

"Helsinki no, it's not an accident! Ain't you got nothin' but straw between your ears, boy? This is a deliberate attempt to slander me!"

Victor shrank back some. Grandpa took things too serious, Victor thought. "Well, I don't mind using that call sign. Can I, Grandpa?"

As if throwing a tantrum, the old man tried to heave the handle across the room, but the cord brought it bouncing back. Victor bent to retrieve it, and when he stood back up, he was just in time to see the front door slam closed. Then he heard the old car start up, and he knew that the old man would not be back until late, if at all. Once again, the youngster would be left to mind himself for the long evening ahead, alone in the shabby cabin. He picked up the handle and looked it over. It did not appear to have suffered the preacher's fit of rage. He pushed the button and put his lips to the mic.

"This is ADV8 coming back. Pretty funny, whoever gave us that call sign. Mr. Marshall. Are you out there listening?" He released the button and waited, and then he remembered and pushed the button again, saying quickly, "Over."

Will and Sean were rolling on the floor in tears from laughing so hard. "I'm gonna split my gut!" Will howled.

"I can see him now…"—Sean gasped for air, holding his side that ached from laughing—"his face turning red as a beet!"

"You were right, Sean. Good surprise! Golly, I hope Rebecca was listening tonight!"

He slapped his thigh and tried to make it sting so he could stop laughing for a minute. But every time they stopped, one of them pictured the preacher when he realized what his call sign had sounded like on the air, and they started laughing all over again. The sound of Victor's voice over the radio cut right through their levity like a blade. The laughing stopped, and the two men looked at each other.

Finally, Sean jumped up and grabbed for the handle. He hesitated, not knowing what to say. He pushed the button. "I'm here, son. Over."

"Boy, is grandpa peed off at you. Over."

"Why is he mad at me? Over."

"You did it, didn't you? You got his call sign for him, right? Over."

Sean looked over at Will and shrugged. "Okay. You got me there. I did it. Over."

"That was funny. Over."

Sean's other hand covered his right. He gripped the handle like it was a part of Victor and brought his mouth close to it. He drew in a deep breath and pushed the button. "Victor, I…I want you to know that I didn't do anything to make your ma leave town. She was happy here. I swear it to you. No one knows exactly what come about on that day when you and I went to the valley for your birthday present—a red tricycle—you remember that, don't you? I…I still can't figure what happened to Blair. To this very day, I still wonder. Only thing worse than losing her was losing you. I love you, Victor. No matter what your grandfather told you, we were a close family. This house was a happy one when we were all together. I loved you, Victor. I still do. Over."

The radio was dead. Nothing but air buzzed on the frequency. They waited for the silence to be interrupted. Will laid his hand on Sean's shoulder. A wound that had been healing for years, in a matter of seconds was fresh again. Will could do nothing but squeeze his brother's shoulder as he bowed his head.

Mr. Abelbaum was not well-liked by children. It was by design. The Abelbaums were not fond of children, so they were cranky around them, and that kept the neighborhood kids away. What the Abelbaums were fond of was their garden. They raised twenty-two different colors of iris, and the hydrangea went as high as the house eaves. There were several varieties of lily; numerous shades of tulip; and, of course, the clowns of the garden, daffodils. They sprayed children who got too close with their garden hose and sprinkled the vegetable side of the garden liberally with slug killer, which Tiny Welby swore killed his dog. The rumors about the Abelbaums' many evil deeds grew with atomic proportion.

So it was inevitable that two lonely, rowdy boys who happened to have little supervision, would choose the Abelbaums as targets for their hostilities that night. It was really Tiny's idea, but Victor went along with it.

"They killed my dog, man. C'mon, Victor. They deserve it."

"Yeah. Okay."

And they climbed to the top of the garage, over the peak, and onto the eastern side of the roof overlooking the garden. Systematically, the boys ripped the shingles off one by one and threw them into the garden. They kept mental score of how many plants they each wiped out with direct hits, giving bonus points if a ruined plant was one of Mr. Abelbaum's prized irises. Before they knew it, they were out of shingles.

"We better get out'a here before someone sees us. Geez, Tiny. Look at the mess we made of old prune face's garden."

"Who's there?"

A voice cut through the night about the same time the beam from a flashlight found the boys on the bare roof. Tiny was so startled that he slipped. He scrambled and clawed for something to hang on to but was falling too fast down the slick pitch. He landed at the feet of Mr. Abelbaum, on top of a pile of damaged shingles, holding his leg under him and rocking back and forth, crying that it was broken. The flashlight beam caught a surprised Victor, and he knew he was in trouble, big trouble.

"Come on down from there, you ruffian. I see ya. You're that preacher's grandson, ain't ya? Yeah, that's you. Get yourself down here before I call the police."

"I already called them."

Another voice joined the first. It was Mrs. Abelbaum.

Victor carefully climbed down from the roof. The minute his feet touched the ground, Abelbaum grabbed him by the back of his collar and dragged him into the bright light of their meager kitchen.

"What about Tiny?" Victor pleaded, trying to turn around and look after his friend who had still not gotten up off the ground.

"He can sit there 'til the police come. Ain't gonna strain myself toting another hoodlum inside."

Victor was shoved into a straight-backed chair. His eyes squinted in the bright light of the kitchen as he looked around. From the way they kept their yard, Victor had expected the inside of the house to look sort of fancy. His eyes found Mr. Abelbaum's face. It was not a pleasant face to look upon under normal circumstances. But now that Mr. Abelbaum was agitated…

"I figure I got about thirty dollars or so tied up in that roofing that you and your friend ruined. I figure my garden's probably worth another thirty or so. Now you're gonna tell me how you're gonna pay for it, boy."

"It was Tiny's idea," Victor ventured.

"It was Tiny's idea," Abelbaum mimicked cruelly. "Your friend's family lives like dogs. They don't have a pot to pee in or a window to throw it out of. His daddy makes illegal swill and spends most of his time in jail. Everyone knows that. No siree, I ain't wastin' my time tryin' to squeeze blood from a turnip. This is your problem, boy. Ought'a pick your friends better."

Victor looked out the open back door to the garden area, and saw that his friend had bugged out on him. *Busted leg, huh Tiny?*

"I don't have any money, either," Victor pleaded. Victor was too old for the box, but not for the switch. Even though his grandfather could not muster hard blows anymore, he could still switch him pretty good.

"You better think of something, boy, or I'm gonna have you arrested." Mr. Abelbaum informed him.

The two old folks stood with their arms folded firmly, scowling at him like he was covered in cow dung.

"Maybe…could I use your phone?"

The old man pointed to a generic black Bakelite phone mounted on a nearby wall.

"Do I just dial zero?"

The old woman nodded, exasperated. He reddened at the thought that the Abelbaums, who were obviously poor folks, had a telephone in their home but the cabin he lived in still did not. He felt inferior in their presence, and it angered him some. He heard a switchboard operator ask him for the party he was calling. He glanced back at the Abelbaums. They were still scowling at him. He turned his back a bit so they could not see his discomfort.

"Could I have…uh…the home of Mr. Sean Marshall?"

The phone started ringing on the other end, and then someone answered. It was a woman's voice.

"Uh, hello. I…uh…is this the residence of Sean Marshall?" He tried to speak so that the Abelbaums could not hear him.

The woman said she would call Mr. Marshall to the phone. Victor's heart was pounding painfully in his chest.

"This is Sean Marshall speaking."

"Uh…hi…uh…Mr. Marshall?" Victor's voice was shaking now.

"Victor, is this you?"

"Yeah…uh…I'm sorry I'm calling so late, sir."

"Can you speak up, Victor? I can't hear you too well."

"Uh, Mr. Marshall? I…uh…I'm in a lot of trouble. Can you help me?"

Sean almost laughed. "What's the trouble, boy?"

And Victor told Sean all about the vandalism that he and Tiny Welby had inflicted upon the Abelbaums.

"I don't know why we did it. It was stupid. I just can't let my grandpa find out, Mr. Marshall. You don't know what he'd do to me."

"I'm afraid I can imagine."

When Victor was done, he waited for Mr. Marshall to speak, trying not to let Sean or the Abelbaums hear how heavy he was breathing. His hand was slick on the molded handset, and he wiped the sweatiness across his blue jeans.

"Stay where you are, Victor. I'll be there in a few minutes."
He hung up.

Victor turned around to the Abelbaums, who were eyeing him suspiciously.

"He said he was coming right over. I think he's bringing money," Victor mumbled softly.

Chapter 51

"Whoa now, brother. Let's stop and think a minute here. I don't want to see you racing out of here all excited like Victor's suddenly gonna become the boy he was when he was four years old. He's almost a teen, a wild child, and he hasn't so much as cussed in your direction in years."

"He's my son, Will. And he's in trouble. What's to think about?"

"You're taking money you saved for your tuition. You're already enrolled for spring. God a'mighty. Think about it. This is not your problem."

But Will knew that he was beating a dead horse. Victor had called Sean to ask for help. It was a dream come true for his brother, and Sean didn't have many dreams left. Will only hoped the boy would read the love behind the gesture and would not hurt Sean that time. Sean was counting out the money he kept in that old wooden box of his. He was removing nearly all of what he had saved.

Will shook his head miserably and grabbed his jacket. "I'll drive you."

Chapter 52

"So our little Cindy is from Tillamook County, Oregon. I'll be. And you say there was only one death of a local resident as a result of all that devastation six years ago?" Chester Lasley whistled low. "A man can't ask to have things narrowed down much more than that now can he, Stu?"

"No sir, Mr. Lasley."

Lasley set down the few typed pages of the research his assistant had gathered from the newspaper Lasley partnered. "This Tjaden fellow then was the friend she lost. And the man who was with him, the injured fellow, is named Marshall. That's no freak coincidence. But is he her husband, father, brother?"

"No telling, sir."

"No. No telling. Hmm." He paced around his plush front room apartment on Chicago's east side. "Cindy Marshall has some of Chicago's most important men wrapped around her little pinkie. If I were to even be hopeful of becoming governor of this fine state, I'm going to need those men on my side."

"Sir, yes. But if I may remind you, your reviews and editorials have alienated more than a few." Stuart Piston stood ramrod straight beside the leather wing chair Lasley had vacated.

"Yes. But that is exactly the reason why I need Miss Marshall to champion me to her consorts. I need some means of control over that woman."

"Well, sir, she does seem fond of you."

Lasley snorted. "Fond of me! Ha! Fond of my money, you mean. She only takes clients who can afford her exorbitant rate these days. She makes more money each day on the stock market than I do. She doesn't need to prostitute herself anymore. She does so only when her outrageous fee is met. Even then she is sometimes…particular." Chester Lasley spun himself around with a mean glint in his eye. "Stuart, we're going to Portland, Oregon. This Tillamook Burn is still big news. I believe I'd like to peruse the devastation and perhaps sample logging camp cuisine for my readers."

Stu blustered and nervously patted his oiled hair. "But, Mr. Lasley, Tillamook is a long ways from Chicago society. We know nothing about logging and lumber. I'm certain conditions will be…somewhat crude, sir."

"Think harder, Stuart. We would not need to leave the luxury of my private Pullman railroad car if we choose not to. Arrange it. I wish to leave immediately."

He hid his grimace. "Yes, sir. Right away."

Chapter 53

September, 1939

Portland, Oregon

When Chicago's own Chester Lasley rolled into town in all his pomp, it was a day to remember for many Oregonians. A welcome crowd, formed at Portland's Union Station, was awed by the ornate splendor of his Pullman Car. Replete with striped awnings, silk and brocade in the drapes and upholstery, crystal chandeliers and wall sconces, and gold leafing on the Victorian age furnishings, the car was a world of contrast from a western logging camp. But the gathering was soon disappointed in Mr. Lasley. He emerged from the Observation Deck as though of royal blood, stood at the decorative railing with his silly looking Afghan hound, waved crisply, and then ducked back inside his luxurious womb, never glimpsed again by the locals and commoners who had traveled great distances to see the man.

"Ah, these admiring fans can be so tiresome. Have you located this Marshall fellow?" He did not bother to take his eyes from the magazine.

"The fellow lives in a small coastal town approximately ninety miles southwest of here, Mr. Lasley. If you like, we can hook up with a train going right into Tillamook. That would put us within twenty miles of his home. Apparently, Mr. Sean Marshall is considered fairly wealthy for these parts; he's an artist."

"An artist? Wealthy? Why on earth would a relative of his prostitute herself?"

"Perhaps he is not a gentle man with the ladies, sir. Miss Cindy could be a runaway."

"Yes, perhaps. And yet she said he was someone dear to her. See that we get to Tillamook, Stuart. Tonight."

"Yes, sir. Right away."

Chapter 54

"Fifty, fifty-five, and sixty. That square things for ya, Martin?" Abelbaum made a point of recounting the money in front of Sean.

"It'll do. Mind you, we're makin' an attempt to be charitable here. Perhaps your young hoodlum son will take this opportunity to straighten himself out."

"And we do appreciate your charity, Martin, Emma." He nodded in the wife's direction.

She crossed her bony arms and sneered for her reply.

"Don't we, Victor?" Sean continued.

"Yes, sir. Thank you, sir. It won't happen again."

An idea occurred to Sean. "Martin, perhaps it would do Victor good to see how much work goes in to a garden like yours. Maybe he could arrange to spend his free time over here, helping you put it right."

Victor wanted to scream. They were paid what they asked for to keep quiet. Why did Mr. Marshall have to go and offer his labor too?

"I ain't fond of kids," said Martin Abelbaum.

Thank you, God, Victor prayed inwardly.

"But seeing as how I got little time left to replant everything, and I have a garage needs roofin' now…"

Victor's head was shouting, *No! No! No!*

"Fine then. Victor. I want you to promise Mr. Abelbaum that you'll come over whenever you have free time and help clean up the mess you made. You hear?"

He glared at his boots and mumbled his, "Yes, sir." *Dang Sean Marshall anyway.*

In the car, driving Victor to the preacher's house, Sean could not help but notice Victor's angry silence. Will said nothing as well. When they pulled up, Sean asked where the preacher was.

"Ain't none of your business, Mr. Marshall," he yelled viciously. Will winced.

"Well, son, it's past eleven. You're only twelve years old—not even, yet. It alarms me to think he'd leave you alone so late. Do you think he'll be back soon?"

"Probably not. When he gets real mad, like he was tonight about the call sign, he goes off somewhere for the night. He'll be back in the morning, and you don't have to worry 'bout me. I'm used to takin' care of myself."

Sean was not to be put off by the boy's hostility. "I noticed that you didn't do so good a job of taking care of yourself earlier tonight, Victor. Isn't that why I'm here?"

"Well, I'm sorry I called you already!" The boy's face turned red with anger.

"Victor!" Will Marshall yelled at the boy. "Your pa bailed you out of a bad situation just now, and at no small cost to himself. You think we got sixty dollars just sitting around our house for mad money? That sixty dollars was supposed to get my brother through his first semester at the university. Thanks to you, now he won't be going. I think you owe him a little respect if you won't give him your thanks."

"Yeah? Well thanks to him, I'll be working old prune face's garden 'til men fly to the moon." He spit on the ground. "Thanks for nothing!" He marched up the steps to the front door.

Sean followed after him. He opened the door and ushered the boy inside.

"Sit down," he ordered.

Victor plopped himself down.

"Listen, Victor. I volunteered your effort to Mr. Abelbaum in order to teach you a lesson. You can call me anytime you need help, and I promise I'll come to help you. But you still have to make good yourself when you do wrong. You can't expect me to come bail you out and not have to do anything yourself. How else are you going to show that you're sorry?"

"I'm not sorry. I don't care about prune face's stupid old garden. He poisoned my friend's dog. I'm sorry we got caught is all. Now I'm sorry I thought to ask you for help."

"Would that be the friend that ran off and left you behind to hold the bag?" Sean asked. Victor said nothing but that clearly angered him. "Once you've had time to think about it, you'll understand why I volunteered you to work."

"You say. How would you know anyway? You don't know me." The hatred was evident in the way the boy spit out his words. *Talk about Tiny leaving me in a mess! Look around, Marshall. You left me here!*

"I know you, Victor. You're my son." Sean looked around the meager cabin. His son was growing up in that shabby place, without the love of a mother or father. No wonder he was bristly.

"I'm not your son!" he tantrumed. "You keep saying that! I asked my grandpa about that, and he stuck me in the box for saying it. All you do is get me in trouble!"

"Stuck you in a box?" Sean followed Victor's extended finger to the banana box against the far wall.

"Yeah. When I was little, he'd make me stay in there until I saw the truth. Like when he came home from the fire last time, on that day when you got hurt. Like, I asked him if he saw you up there, and he made me stay in there for hours without dinner. Every time I mention you, it gets me in trouble. Just stay away from me!"

"Wait a minute, Victor. Are you saying your grandfather went up to the burn last time?" Something crawled up his neck. He slapped his hand over the spot. Nothing. It was his imagination.

His ma used to say that feelings like that meant someone was walking on your grave, hinting that space and time could cross invisible boundaries.

"Sure he did. I mean, he didn't talk about it, but he smelled like a wildfire and he was gone from morning to night. And when he came home, I remember my binoculars were broken. He'd borrowed them and said the glass was accidentally broken out of them. Anyway, I asked him if he saw you up there. That's what got him riled, 'cause I referred to you as my father. And he made me go into the box." Sean was staring at him in an unsettling way. It was kind o' scary, like he was looking through him instead of at him.

"Are you sure about that, Victor?"

"Course I'm sure. I'm not a little kid, you know. Anyway, he was an old man an' he still came out of the first burn better off than you."

Victor didn't know why he needed to always try and hurt Sean. Maybe because every time he'd ever tried to embrace the idea that Sean Marshall was his father, he was severely punished for it. Somehow, he felt like Sean was partially responsible for all his suffering, though he didn't know if he truly believed that man had abused his mother. Aw, he didn't know what he believed anymore. It seemed to Victor like the older he got, the more things didn't make sense.

"I guess you're right. You're not a little kid anymore, Victor. I'm going to leave you now. I don't want to be here in case your grandpa comes home. I don't want to cause you any more pain." He squeezed his son's shoulder affectionately. "I love you, son. I'm here to help if you need me. Your grandpa doesn't have to know about us talking. Deal?"

"Yeah. Um…thanks. I…I'm sorry I said some o' those things."

"Forget it, Victor. I'm just glad we had a chance to spend some time together. I'd really like to do it again, under different circumstances I hope."

Victor laughed. "Well, maybe this deviate will call you up on the radio sometime, if I get a chance."

"I'll be listening, son. Now, why don't you put yourself to bed?"

Victor looked at him funny. He patted the broken down davenport. "This is my bed. There's only one bedroom, and it's Grandpa's."

Sean looked away quickly. Victor's disclosure dredged up some pretty awful conclusions for him.

Chapter 55

Will threw his hat down, emphasizing his anger. "What are you saying, Sean? Preacher Bowman started that second fire? That's a pretty serious allegation."

"Will, listen to me. He said Preacher had gone up to the fire the day Elrod was killed. The fire marshal always said that fallen tree was a might suspicious. It wasn't a snag; it was a fair sized tree. He told me it looked to him like someone had dug pretty deep around them burned-out roots on the one side, looked to him like a tool done it, but he didn't have any proof."

"I know. I remember."

"He couldn't figure how it could have toppled over on its own. It was dead, and it was cracked, but it still would have taken a sizable push to get it to topple. They said no other tree had fallen into it, but they did find some curious indentations in the ground several feet behind that tree. It could be he dug up them roots on the one side with a shovel and then used a fulcrum. And, Will, they never did determine whether the second fire was accidental or deliberate, but the investigators still believe it was set."

"Yes, by someone struggling financially and wanting to perpetuate his job as a firefighter for a while longer." Will insisted.

"Well, that's the theory they finally settled on. But ain't it awful coincidental that the second fire was started on the border opposite the fire line of the camp I was in? And Victor said that the preacher had the binocular glass punched out of his field glasses. That's what they determined started the second fire! The fire marshal was certain it was the two lenses they found."

"If there's any truth to what Victor told you, you realize I'm gonna have to go and kill that heathen preacher."

"No. You're going to leave it alone. We don't have any proof, Will, just hearsay. I just wanted you to know in case you, you know, ever doubted me."

That made Will hang his head ruefully. He loved Sean. His brother was the only family he had left, and he'd almost lost him too. "I never doubted you, brother. I know you were good to Blair. I lived in this house during those happier times. Her youth and beauty was what brought so much sunshine to our house. I was here that night you rescued her after…well, you know. I was here the night she gave birth to another man's child, and I watched you accept the child for your own. I never saw that girl smile until she became Mrs. Sean Marshall, so don't ever think I doubted you, brother. I never have."

"Thanks, Will. You're the best brother a man ever had. I'm going to turn in now. I'm awful tired."

Will watched as his brother trudged with drooping shoulders toward his bedroom. It had been moved to the downstairs since his accident.

That night, his brother did look tired. It made Will worry for him. That night had been a roller coaster of emotions for Sean, and it had obviously taken its toll. He made a mental note to try to keep his brother from thinking or talking about Preacher Bowman. It almost always seemed to punch the life right out of him.

Chapter 56

Bowman surveyed the old whore through her reflection in the dressing table's mirror. She lay on her front, with the sheets tangled around her pale, purple-veined legs. She had her bleached head buried half under her pillow, but he could see one make-up smeared eye struggling to wake. The sun was peeking in under the tacky beige shade over the window. Her name was Myrna, and she didn't like mornings. In spite of that, Bowman boorishly made plenty of noise getting himself dressed.

"It's five bucks when it's for the whole night, big fella. Jus' leave it on the dresser, and lock the door on your way out," she mumbled.

Bowman finished his primping and left the bill as instructed. "Be good," he said to Myrna before closing the door.

"Yeah right, honey." Her head dropped back down to the mattress. The old whore yawned once, covered her head with her pillow, and dropped back off to sleep.

Bowman had a hearty breakfast in the coffee shop downstairs. While lingering over his second cup of coffee, he heard several people at tables around him talking animatedly about Chester Lasley, the wealthy railroad and newspaper man. He turned to the table on his right side.

"Pardon me. Did I hear you correctly? Chester Lasley is here in Tillamook?"

"You have heard correctly. He arrived late last night in his private Pullman Car," replied a tall, lanky man in a white-collared shirt.

"Well now, that's quite a laurel for our little Tillamook, isn't it?"

"Certainly is. I hear he wants to tour the devastation, as he phrased it, and partake of an authentic logging camp meal."

"That so?" Bowman stood and put a bill on the table.

"It's so," said another smaller gentleman. "And he's looking for someone who'll take him to see that Marshall fellow, the photographer. Don't know why he wants to see him. Must be a collector of postcards."

That surprised Bowman. He hurried from the coffee shop as though his life was at stake. He sped across Third Street and headed the three blocks to the train station. It wasn't difficult to locate the Pullman Car of Chester Lasley. It looked like the boudoir of a French whore. Bowman had no plan for speaking to Lasley. He was simply spurred on by a frenzy of jealousy. Just as he reached the platform, he heard the door of the car open, and knew that he must come up with a reason for approaching the great man.

"Hello there. I'm Preacher Bowman, from Cloverdale. I've been asked to visit on behalf of Sean Marshall. He's a very ill man and not up to travel or company."

The assistant beckoned him in. Bowman had no time to rethink it. Up the metal grate steps he went. They led straight up to an ornate, wrought iron doorway through which he bounded, and there ahead of him was Lasley. A big, lanky hound sat next to Lasley in his stately wing chair. The dog growled at Bowman but held its place.

The manservant was whispering in the mogul's ear. He was a man of prodigious build. Bowman guessed that he was several inches taller than six feet, with broad shoulders; bulging chest and gut; and a stumpy, once-muscular neck. Lasley's heavy face was impassive. He nodded up and down, all the while studying the preacher.

Bowman returned the steadfast gaze.

Lasley smiled in a pseudo-friendly manner. Finally, he spoke directly to the preacher. "How is it you've heard of my request to visit Mr. Marshall, er, Preacher Bowman?"

"I take occasion to visit some of my former elderly parishioners in a home up here. I stopped to have breakfast at the coffee shop on Third Street and heard of your plans to visit Mr. Marshall. I took the liberty of coming here in case I could be of assistance to you."

"And how might you assist me, Preacher?"

"Well, I could answer any questions you might have. I've known the family a long time. The man was married to my daughter."

Lasley winked at his assistant. "Would that be Cindy Marshall from Chicago?"

"Cindy? No. My daughter's name was Blair."

"Was, Mr. Bowman?"

"Well, she disappeared almost eight years ago. We've assumed the worst after all this time."

"What a shame." Lasley said it in a way that made it sound like anything but. He paused dramatically, then exclaimed, "Eight years! Why, that's the same time Cindy Marshall arrived in Chicago! I believe it was in late February." He watched for the preacher's reaction and was rewarded. "A dark beauty she is. And a wealthy woman with prominent friends. She is heavily invested in stocks and bonds and Chicago real estate these days. I dare say she makes more in a market day than I ever did. Is it possible that she could be your long-lost daughter, Preacher?"

Lasley caught the preacher lost in thought. He cleared his throat loudly.

"I said, Preacher, why do you suppose she ran away? Or is that too personal a question?"

"It is, rather," Bowman responded.

"Well, I suppose I could always ask Cindy, or Blair did you say? She's always said her life is an open book," he lied. "We could test that claim."

"No! I mean, I doubt she would tell you the real reason. It is a difficult thing for a father to admit of a daughter, let alone a preacher about his child. Blair was a bit…unharnessed." He noted the skepticism on the faces across from him. "She was a bit of a runaround, filled with prowess of a sexual nature. I thought a husband might palliate the girl, but it soon became evident that he did not provide enough titillation. Sean Marshall is a gentleman, you understand, and Blair's tastes brinked the unsavory. I personally believe she ran from boredom." He put up his index finger and, with an exaggerated brain cramp, recited the Marquis, "'The horror of wedlock, the most appalling, the most loathsome of all the bonds, humankind has devised for its own discomfort and degradation.'"

"Ah, you are a devotee of the Marquis De Sade? 'It is always by way of pain one arrives at pleasure,'" Lasley recited from memory. "You are alarmingly well-read of the Marquis, Preacher Bowman."

Lasley was intrigued. Assuming everything the man said was true, how would a preacher know such a thing about his daughter? He whispered something to his assistant. Stuart left and then returned shortly with a silver tray laden with good claret; fresh Jewish bagel breads; creamed cheese; fresh, thinly sliced salmon; and rings of Washington Walla Walla sweet onions. The preacher's jowls juiced like a hungry wolf's, and his eyes seemed to gobble up the tray. The fine food looked a sight better than his usual fare of greasy fried potatoes and eggs. Though he'd consumed a large breakfast only an hour before, the preacher could not wait to be invited to partake. Lasley noted the hungry gaze and graciously encouraged Bowman to fill himself while he poured three glasses of the claret. Bowman never took notice that his was the only glass being refilled time and again.

It was not long before he was sloppily throwing his bulk around the dainty settee, howling at amusing stories that Lasley seemed to have hundreds of, and drinking still more. When the preacher's eyes were altogether glazed over and his speech perfectly slurred, Lasley leaned forward conspiratorially and said, "you know, I feel I must confess to you, Preacher. I've been with Miss Cindy Marshall myself. She's a tigress."

The preacher's response nearly caused Lasley to choke on his claret.

"I know. She pretends not to like it rough, but it's the only way she wants it. Take my word." He laughed obscenely. "Don't spare her the rod, if you know what I mean."

Chester Lasley was no gentleman. He had done dark deeds in his time and would do still more. But what the preacher had just admitted to was beyond even Lasley's warped capacity. If he understood this preacher correctly, the man had polluted his own daughter, apparently more than one time. Now that was a secret Lasley was sure that Cindy, a.k.a. Blair Marshall, would never want told. Lasley could not believe his good fortune. He now had the power to make Cindy Marshall do anything, anything at all that he wanted. And apparently, he was in for some exceptionally spirited foreplay in the process.

He could not wait to return to Chicago. He instructed Stuart to cancel plans they'd made for the remainder of their scheduled stay and set about arranging their return to Chicago. Lasley did get his log camp meal later that day, but he was quite obviously disappointed with the chicken and dumplings. He expressed scant interest in the details of the burn, which the state forester had rushed to the Pullman to give him, and he refused to leave his car long enough to view the devastation. Loggers, officials, and Tillamook citizenry alike were baffled by Lasley's visit. Clearly, Chester Lasley was a bon vivant and not the outdoor type. But many wondered how he intended to write about the Tillamook Burns in his East Coast papers, having viewed exactly nothing.

Chapter 57

September 12, 1939

Chicago, Illinois

Cindy loved the fall colors. September in Chicago was windy and red, skin-tingling and orange, fresh and yellow. She took her daily stroll along the storefronts, hotels, and cafes to Navy Pier and back, admiring tissue-thin maple leaves as they skittered along the sidewalks. She absorbed the delicious smells from the delis and fine restaurants. Their fragrances, carried to her by the chill winds, were impossibly rich. She smiled at the clanging of the trolleys. She was bundled in an expensive fur with a woolen scarf wrapped comfortably around her head to protect her ears and throat. Cindy felt fine. She had come a long way from Cloverdale, and not merely in terms of mileage. Her good friend Wendell had accompanied her for the first half of her walk and had glowing reports for her regarding her wealth.

She was a woman of her own means now, a survivor. She had the money to do as she pleased. She'd gobbled up real estate that was undervalued due to The Great Crash, or as some called it, The Depression. Folks in Chicago liked the term, "Dirty-Thirties", but whatever you called it, when Chicago began to emerge from it, her holdings were worth ten-fold. She lived in her converted printing house, where she occupied the top floor, loft-style apartment. She adored her new place; especially the three enormous windows in her living room that all took in stunning water-and-city-light views.

The apartment had three spacious front rooms, which she had tastefully decorated in soft buttery cream and the palest of purples. She dated successful men; dined and danced in the swankiest locales; and no longer had to do anything she did not wish to do, except perhaps for her date that night. She had already agreed, days earlier, to take in a Friday night dinner show with Chester Lasley, though she wasn't certain why she'd accepted. She did not like Lasley and no longer needed his money. It seemed that no matter how affluent she became, she could never have enough security. Wendell and his friends had invested her earnings well, and her stocks had easily tripled her wealth. Still, what if the stock market were to take a drastic fall? She could stand to lose quite a lot. But she would not lose everything. She had her properties and, because Cindy's faith in the stock market went only so far, she also kept ample cash savings hidden in a small community bank across town. She even kept a last will and testament in a safety deposit box there, with Victor as her beneficiary and Wendell as her executor. Each week, she collected her earnings from her after-dark pursuits and escort services, which she kept in a sock in her top drawer, and then she caught a cross-town trolley to Streeterville, and made her deposit. She finished with a leisurely stroll to Navy Pier and back, which was precisely what she did on that grand autumn day. She had come to love that particular routine of hers. Cindy had come to terms with the life she'd inherited from Blair, and she determined that, although Blair had been born unlucky, it didn't necessarily have to stay that way for *her*. They'd had their share of blessings bestowed upon them, few but wonderful blessings of a loving family and friends, for which both Cindy and Blair were grateful. All in all, Cindy was content with life.

She pulled out the long chain she wore around her neck and checked her diamond Lady Racine watch. It was almost three o'clock. She should probably go back to the flat and take a nap. It promised to be a late night with Chester.

Chapter 58

By three o'clock that afternoon, every man belonging to the board of trade was desperate. Their short office coats no longer flapped open but were discarded over chairs. Their soft hats, usually pulled forward over one eye in a "don't care" fashion, were removed to afford nervous fingers opportunity to streak through their greased hair in a rare and undignified manner. By the time the trade market closed that day, Jackson Street was frantic. The market had not had so severe a drop since '29.

Wendell decided to square his shoulders and tough it out. He had his own money tied up as well as the funds of more than a dozen clients, including Cindy Marshall. Wendell understood that the war in Europe was making the market fluctuate drastically. Giving in to the panic and dumping stock now would only cause a greater drop and would result in severe losses of wealth. So, when the market closed, Wendell was still holding all of his stock. He postulated that he would only lose money for his clients if he sold their stock at that day's loss. But a patient, careful broker waited, knowing the decline of that day would reverse and rise back up, sometimes in less than a week, sometimes it would take years. The Crash of '39 would not set itself right again until well into it's third year due to world turmoil, but Wendell's clients invested in the long term. Some thought his was a risky stake. If it was, so be it. The market was no place for the faint of heart. Anyway, Wendell believed that the real risk was in chasing stocks when they were acting like runaway trains.

Wendell did not feel it cardinal to report to Cindy. She understood that the market rose and fell daily. That day's decline was not so severe, after all, as to cause investors to jump from high-rise windows. Besides, she would be getting ready for her date with Chester Lasley that night. On their walk earlier, Wendell had asked Cindy to dinner too, but she explained that Lasley already had tickets for the new show and it would be terribly rude to cancel at such a late hour. Wendell, of course, had disagreed.

"Your portfolio is doing very nicely, Cindy. You don't need to be with men like Lasley," he had argued. He saw that Cindy shivered slightly and pulled her fur coat tighter.

She smiled at Wendell, her best friend. "This will be the very last time, I promise you. I cannot put a finger on it. There is just something about the man that makes me nervous. Perhaps he reminds me of someone from my past. But, no worries, Wendell. Chester has always conducted himself as a gentleman."

Chapter 59

Life with Father was drole, the cordon bleu was dry and salty, and Chester was positively insufferable. He would leer at her bosom, say inappropriate things, and every once in a while, he would admonish her as if he were her parent, for nothing more than chatting with acquaintances she ran into.

Cindy found his behavior boorish, and as the driver turned onto her street, she could not help but be relieved. Her solitude would be much preferred over the company of Chester Lasley. Silently, she vowed that that would be the very last time she accepted any dates with the man.

"Ouch! Chester, what has gotten into you?"

"Why, what do you mean, my dear?"

She sighed with exasperation. "I mean you've been acting strangely tonight. You've been ogling me and reprimanding me, and you just pinched me and it hurt. It is truly mystifying behavior."

"My dear, I promise you I am full of secrets tonight. And if you are a very good girl, I will share one or two." He shared a wink with Stuart in the rearview mirror.

She turned and looked at him. He wore that irksome smile again.

The driver pulled alongside the curb. "I'm awfully tired tonight, Chester. If you don't mind, I believe I'll go straight to bed."

"But I do mind, my dear. I had hoped I would be invited up. Am I to receive no thanks for entertaining you this evening?"

She stepped out of the car. "It didn't occur to me that this date was to be considered a down payment for my services, Chester. I made no promise to you beyond dinner and a show, and frankly, I have a headache. If you like, I'll happily reimburse you for my dinner ticket. How much was it?" Her jaw was firmly set as she snapped open her evening bag to count out cash.

Chester was nimble for a big man. He jumped out of the car and grabbed her elbow, spinning her around toward the front entrance to her building. With his fingers dug into the soft skin of her upper arm, he marched her past the doorman and growled under his breath, "I had other plans, Cindy. And I simply won't take no for an answer."

He led her to her flat in silence and waited impatiently while she fumbled with her keys. He frightened her more than a little. Her mind was racing.

What can this all be about? "Chester, please. I…I really do have a headache. If you're angry with me—"

"Just get that cursed door open, my dear," he hissed.

She obliged. Stepping across the threshold, she dropped the keys back into her purse. Perhaps if she poured on the flattery, he would settle down. *Yes, I'll play him like Blair's father. Be assenting,* her mind told her. She heard the deadbolt slide into place. She turned. "Chester, perhaps I could interest you in a drink?"

That's when he blindsided her. His open hand landed square across her left cheek and sent her to the carpet. She shook her head and tried to get her bearings on what was happening, but before she could react to the blow, he reached her in a single stride and pulled her to her knees by her hair, wrenching her neck painfully. Her face stung and then went numb. He repeated the strike across her face, then pulled her to her knees by the roots of her hair, and crudely motioned the act he wished her to perform.

Lasley pushed her roughly and she fell to the floor in a heap. "That was the worst I've ever had!" he screamed at her. He picked her up and threw her onto the bed. Then he straddled her and pinched her mouth painfully between his thumb and forefinger. "Tell me you like it, whore!"

She shook her head from side to side. "I don't! Stop, Chester! Please!"

He inspected her lewdly and then ripped open her gown. "No? Well then, let's see how Blair likes it! Does Blair like it?" He proceeded to ravage her with his slobbering mouth.

Cindy went slack as her mind raced to catch up with events as they unfolded. *How could he know?* Blair was suddenly awake and screaming inside of her. She was horrified. "Please, Chester," was all she could say. Her eyes glistened.

"Please? Please what? We both know this is how you want it. Your father told me so." He tore the rest of her dress from her. "Your own father! And then you abandon your invalid husband? And leave your child in the hands of that perverted preacher man to raise? You're disgusting!" He smacked her again and again, fiercely pitching her head from side to side. Her bottom lip split open.

She could feel one tingling eye beginning to swell closed.

"Your own father! C'mon! Tell me you like this!" He had her hands pinned above her head. "'The only way to a woman's heart is along the path of torment. I know none other as sure!'" He recited the Marquis.

"Oh Lord, please." She could not think. *This cannot be happening, not again!* She had escaped the preacher's evil. "I don't!" She sobbed. "He raped me. Chester…please. Please stop this."

Lasley ignored the heartbreaking pleas from the helpless woman on the bed, too caught up in his own excitement to hear anything she had to say. He wrestled her over on her stomach and pulled two nylon stockings from his pocket. He tied her wrists tightly to the bed posts, stretching her out painfully. Cindy made no more pleas, she just moaned in her humiliation as Lasley stripped off the last of her garments, leaving only her stockings and heels.

Lasley could barely check himself at the sight of the completely vulnerable beauty tethered naked and prostrate before him. His fleshy face dripped excited sweat and saliva onto her back. He would rob Miss Cindy Marshall of that which is most precious: her honor, self-respect, and her peace of mind. Oh, he would strip her of much more than mere clothing. When he was finished, Cindy Marshall would understand who she would be working for from then on. He reached inside his dinner coat and retrieved the small braided whip.

How long have I been lying here? Cindy grew aware of her condition little by little. She strained to listen to the sounds in her apartment, not daring to turn her head for a look around. The hum of the small ice box was all that she could hear. *Please, Lord. Is he gone?* she pleaded of a God she had never fully trusted. She wriggled a wrist and realized that she was no longer tethered, though she could still feel the nylon cutting into her flesh. She pushed herself up slowly, feeling stings and aches and flashes of hot pain from every point of her body.

She walked gingerly to her antique dressing table and beheld the reflection there. It was hideous. She could not even recognize herself. Her hair was a tangled mess. She had one severely blackened eye, and the other showed promise of brilliant bruising. Dried blood tracked from her nostrils. Her lips were swollen, and one was split and smeared with blood. She touched the bruises that covered her shoulders and breasts, feeling pain at her slight caress. The insides of her thighs ached terribly, and there was an unbearable, fiery pain radiating from her behind. She turned slightly to see her backside in the mirror and gasped. Her knees went weak, and she carefully lowered herself to the floor as nausea swelled in her stomach. Her days as a high-price call girl were ended. No man would pay hundreds of dollars to spend time with a woman so horribly scarred. As her hair fell over her face, Cindy put her head in her hands and cried.

She'd lost more time. Had she been in a heap on her living room floor for a few minutes or a few hours? She rose to retrieve a Chinese robe from her armoire and covered herself. The smooth, light silk felt icy cool against her skin, and the fabric blotted the bloody seepage that had been trickling and tickling down her backside. Next, she went to her small wet bar and poured bourbon into a tumbler, tossing it back in a gulp that made her cough and spit and rattle her battered body. She yelled at Blair to shut up. Suddenly Blair was not only awakened, she was shrieking, crying and accusing. Cindy could not rid her head of the girl's incessant sobbing.

Blair screamed back at her, "You said no one would hurt us again, that you ended it! I left my husband for you! I gave up my baby because you promised me this would never happen again—and now he is living in the preacher's home!"

"Shut up!" Cindy pressed her hands to her ears. "Shut up, shut up, shut up!"

Look at me! Look what he did to my body! Oh, Cindy, look what he did to us!

Cindy turned once more to the mirror. *Is it possible that I have become more unsightly in the last few minutes?* She heaved the empty tumbler at the mirror and shattered the awful image. "What do you want me to do? I can't always protect you! I thought I could, but I can't! Sean couldn't either. No mortal is a match for the evil of the preacher. Just what do you expect me to do?"

Cindy sniffed, wiped her hair back from her face, and closed her robe over her breasts bashfully and tied it snug. She walked to the front door, turned around, and put her back to it, facing the large view windows in her beautiful parlor room. She took a few moments to admire the city lights that comprised her view, the soothing colors in her decor, and the different rich textures that lent the room uncontrived serenity.

"What are you going to do?" a trembling, frightened Blair asked.

Cindy sniffed. "What I promised you. I'm ending it."

Acting before Blair could talk her out of it, Cindy sprinted as fast as she could across the living room floor and leapt, trusting herself to prayer one last time. Just before she'd reached the row of picture windows, Cindy had prayed to God that she would go completely through the window and not merely cut herself severely.

Finally, Cindy had a prayer answered.

Chapter 60

Wendell had gone no farther than the front steps of his own building when he heard the clanging of emergency bells. As he turned to see if they were near, an ambulance and police car swept past him, heading south. He turned up his coat collar and increased his pace. The sound of those bells always made him go cold inside. All of the sudden the racket ceased, and Wendell could just make out a flurry of lights up ahead.

Oh no! It looks like Cindy's building. *But that doesn't mean there is anything wrong with Cindy. Heck no.* There was an elderly gentleman living in the downstairs apartment of her building, Wendell knew. *That was it. Poor chap's time had come, no doubt.* Wendell didn't even realize he was running.

He approached the ringed crowd cautiously, both repelled and attracted at the same time to whatever sight drew the others. He squeezed past a bulging woman and peered between the shoulders of two men to glimpse a woman's shapely leg streaked with blood. A silver heel lay inches away. Wendell knew that shoe. Even as the ice ball formed in his gut, he was pushing people roughly out of his way, shouting her name, hoping she would emerge from the crowd, smiling, telling him it wasn't her shoe.

"Heavens no, silly," she would say.

But Cindy would not be emerging from the crowd. Wendell ducked under a blue uniformed man who held his arms out to hold the lookies back, and he saw her. Blood had pooled around her here and there, and one leg lay in twisted, gruesome fashion. Haunting eyes looked into his, and he dropped next to her and fetched her limp hand.

"Oh, Cindy, Cindy," he soothed, misunderstanding. "The stocks would have come back up. There's always hope…" But as

Wendell rubbed Cindy's hand in his, dissolving into weeps for the woman he had secretly loved since the first night he'd found her on that barstool years earlier, the Chicago wind provided him glimpses beneath the flapping royal blue silk. Wendell saw the marks Lasley's whip had made on Cindy's creamy, diaphanous skin, and he saw far more bruising than the fall that landed her there would warrant. He set his jaw and whispered in her ear as the medics worked to get her on a stretcher, "He will not get away with this. I promise." Her eyes closed.

Chester Lasley had run into an old newspaper crony upon departing Cindy's building. The two men stood in the brisk night air and shared a smoke and some old stories. Lasley was feeling robust and manful after his scintillating romp with Miss Marshall, feeling certain he had broken that little filly. He laughed heartily at one of Jake Smitty's lewd jokes when all of a sudden, there was a crash and shower of splintering light. A piece of glass tinkled inches from his right foot and sparkled in the reflective light of the gas street lamps. At the same moment, he felt, rather than heard, a *whump*. Lasley turned around to see a heap of royal blue silk, torn flesh, and the inescapably fetching eyes of Cindy Marshall. Lasley stood frozen in place, mouth agape. Suddenly, there were people everywhere, shouting and running. Police whistles competed against the noise from Smitty's puking, and a shell-shocked Lasley was shoved and jostled aside by strollers and nearby building tenants, who rushed to see who had jumped.

Within minutes, the block was a congestion of frenzied activity, but Chester Lasley was still too stunned to move.

He was utterly distracted when a nondescript man walked up to him and asked, "I think I recognize you—are you Chester Lasley?"

"Yes, yes," Lasley answered distractedly. He resumed his focus on the woman being wrestled into a medic wagon, when he was startled by a punch someone just landed him in his midriff. "What the—?" He looked back to the intrusive fan, but he was gone.

Lasley's abdomen began to ache something terrible. Still distracted and assuming he was reacting to Cindy's unexpected jump with a burgeoning case of indigestion, he pressed his hand there to stem the pain. But he quickly pulled his hand away and saw that it was awash with warm, viscous fluid. Lasley's shriek at the sight of crimson was lost in a sea of shrieks, and he looked down at his dinner coat in horror. It rather slowly occurred to him he'd been stabbed. That man, the image of the stranger, was already growing fuzzy. He'd seen that man before…Lasley shook his head to clear it, lost his balance, and fell. It took fully a minute before a bystander noticed the fallen man with the growing red spot on his front. But by that time, Lasley was dead.

Lasley's paper just one day earlier, reported that the railroad mogul and aspiring politician had an impressive number of ene-mies. Many of them, so the gossip went, had offered a price for his head. It was even rumored one such contract was issued by the governor of the fine state of Illinois himself, hearsay which most certainly would assure that the homicide would not be aggressively investigated.

Chapter 61

October 6, 1939

Cloverdale, Oregon

She moved her tile. Sean was pensive, thoughtful. Rebecca broached the subject again.

"Don't you think it's time, Sean? I have to agree with Will. I mean, it has been, what, almost eight years? I know you don't want to hear this, but…Sean, she abandoned you. You have every right to seek a divorce. Honestly, Sean, anyone else would have done it long before now."

Sean did not even look up at her. He made his move, a bad one. She was rattling his cage. "I do that and I'll never be able to lay claim to my son. Blair was…is my connection."

"Good Lord, Sean. You don't even know if she's alive. Are you going to continue loving a memory when there is a woman of flesh and blood right before you?"

That did it. He looked up at her, surprised. Then he smiled wryly. Rebecca was embarrassed. She hadn't meant to say everything she was thinking. "I'm sorry. I shouldn't have said that."

"Rebecca—"

"No. Sean, my husband has been in the ground for more than six years. I loved El, but he's gone and my bed is cold at night. You're lonely, and I'm lonely. We were in love once, remember? We're the best of friends, Sean. If that isn't enough for a strong marriage, I don't know what is!"

"Rebecca…" Sean started again but went blank as to what he would say next. Rebecca waited for Sean to go on, but apparently, he had nothing to say. He simply did not want her.

"Lord, Sean! I'm literally throwing myself at you! Say something."

"I can't marry you, Beck-wheat. I'm an old man."

"You're not even thirty-five!"

"I'm a very old thirty-four. I can't do farm labor, can't even chop wood for the stove, and I'm afraid you'd be very disappointed with me in that cold bed of yours. I'm not well, Rebecca. My heart is weak. I would leave you twice a widow."

"Your heart is broken, Sean. I can mend it. Give me a chance." She was blushing. She hid her face in her hands. "Some things are so hard to say, but…I know you could never disappoint me, Sean."

"I'm sorry, Rebecca. Lord knows I want you, but I can't. I love you, but…I…I'm sorry."

She abruptly stood, accidentally knocking her wooden chair to the floor, and looked down at the mah-jongg board with tears welling. "I'm starting to really hate this game!" she blurted as she quickly left the house.

As if his day was not going badly enough, there was the phone call. Victor had called from a pub in Hebo, obviously intoxicated, claiming that he and his pal, Tiny, had wrecked the Welbys' car. As usual, Sean drove out to get the boys and sober them up a bit. Then he went about the business of setting the boys' actions right with the Welby's, so that preacher Bowman would not need to be notified. It cost Sean a mere two hundred dollars to keep the Welby's quiet. The money would buy the family a much better truck with which to deliver their swill. Sean made it understood that he did not want his son driving the Welby's liquor truck, or making liquor deliveries, or gambling while Otis made deliveries. And, that if Victor should get into further troubles of the sort, these would be the last dollars the Marshall's would be paying the

Welby's on Victor's behalf. "Good Lord, Otis, the boy's not even thirteen years old."

As usual, Victor was less than grateful—even hostile. But Sean paid no attention. At least Victor knew who he could call when he was in a spot. That was something, wasn't it?

"Mr. Marshall, it's not a matter of the money. I assure you, there's quite enough in that envelope to cover my fee."

Sean had taken the remainder of his tuition money to a lawyer in Newport, Oregon, who was reputed to be very aggressive in custody fights and civil suits of that nature. "Then I don't understand." Sean had elected to remain standing when Charles Reynolds proffered a comfortable chair.

The lawyer walked over and sat down behind the large desk and made a steeple of his long fingers. "You say your son is growing wayward. You say he is allowed to carouse around all night with his incorrigible friend,"—he checked his notes—'Lytle Welby.' You say the boys drink heavily and vandalize, et cetera."

"Yes."

"But that's precisely the problem, Mr. Marshall. You say. Have you any proof?"

"I assure you these incidents did occur. I was there. I settled matters each time myself."

"Yes, Mr. Marshall. You covered for him. And in doing so, you covered up any evidence you would otherwise have."

"I had to. The boy is scared to death of the preacher. He's a terribly abusive man. He abused his own daughter, and I've no doubt he beats daylight out of my son."

"Again, where's the proof? You have nothing to support the abuse of his daughter and nothing to prove he would beat his, or your son. He never has, has he?"

"Victor told me he beats him where it does not show."

"I am sorry, Mr. Marshall. I believe you. But I'm afraid the wheels of justice don't turn on understanding and righteous belief. It takes evidence to grease those wheels. Until you can get me some evidence, I'm afraid I can't help you."

Sean snatched his cap from his back pocket and placed it on his head as he made his way to the door. With one hand on the door handle, Sean turned back to the attorney. "You're afraid. You're afraid to risk losing a case, afraid of tarnishing that sterling reputation you enjoy so much, afraid because the man I accuse is a preacher. I'll tell you something, sir. I didn't become the man I am by shying away from the difficult. I'm a man who takes on wrongdoing, be it easy or hard. And when I go to bed at night, I have no trouble sleeping with myself. Do you, Reynolds, after telling clients they should allow the abuse of their child just so they can get proper evidence to make your job easier? Do you feel good about yourself when you go home and take off your successful lawyer suit?"

"You're getting upset, Mr. Marshall." He stood to show his visitor out. "There's no call for getting personal about this. If you truly believe you can find an attorney who can make a case for you without any evidence, then I would hire that man. For the record, I like you, Marshall. I wish I could help you. And if you should obtain something on this preacher that I can use against him, I promise you I wouldn't let his backward collar get in my way. I studied law to rid the world of muck like him, or at least my little corner of the world. Get me something I can use and I'll give the man a dose of Hades on earth."

Sean nodded, a little ashamed of his behavior. His disappointment was just so great. He shook the lawyer's hand and made his way out.

Chapter 62

July, 1941

Grand Ronde Indian Reservation, Oregon

Tiny and Victor brewed their own trouble at the road-house on the Indian Reservation. The two teenagers had tapped a pony keg for themselves and a couple of drifters, who had told the boys that they enjoyed playing poker even if they weren't much good at it. By seven that night, Victor was thoroughly drunk, sick with a pounding headache, and he was two hundred and forty dollars in debt to the man they called Cleff. And Cleff wanted his money.

Tiny, Victor's fair-weather pal, was a chubby coward with a slight foot impediment, compliments of Mr. Abelbaum's roof. "Uh, I gotta go, Victor. See ya around." And he ducked out the door.

Victor had one cheek pressed to the cool wood of the table, his arms stretched out pathetically across the table, half of a beer sitting beside his elbow. "It's okay, you guys," he slurred comically. "I gotta rich uncle, sort of."

"Well now, is he a rich uncle or is he a rich uncle sort of?" Cleff breathed into Victor's face with breath foul enough to kill a blackberry bush.

Victor heaved all over Cleff's boots.

The man jumped to his feet and looked down with disgust at his boots. "That's two hundred and forty-six bucks you owe me now, you little puke!"

Victor just lolled his head on the table and laughed senselessly. The two men grabbed an arm each and relocated the drunken lad between them in the front seat of their truck. The bartender, Young Bear Johnson, went about his business of washing mugs and shot glasses. He wasn't gonna step into a mess like that for Victor Bowman. That kid was nothing but trouble.

At least Victor was sobering up enough to realize how extremely lucky he was. His grandfather was away again. Victor had long ago stopped wondering or caring where the old man went so often and stayed the entire night. He was just glad that that night was one of the old man's trips. He sat on the couch, feeling miserable, a hustler on each side of him. The man named Cleff picked the preacher's new black phone up off the floor again and held it in front of Victor's nose.

"Try it again, kid."

Victor dialed the number again. And again, it rang several times. He was just about to hang up when a woman answered, sounding out of breath.

"Oh, hiya," Victor said lazily. "Lemme talk to my dad," he mumbled. His head lolled sideways to give Cleff a goofy smile.

Cleff wanted to smash the kid's face in. But he wanted his money more. He shoved Victor's face away from him.

"Victor?" came a worried voice over the wire.

"Dad! Guess what? I'm in some trouble." He giggled.

"Victor, you've been drinking again?"

Victor didn't like the condemnation he heard in Sean's voice. "Hey, man! You said I should call when I need help. I need some help!"

Sean took a deep breath. "What kind of trouble are you in, son?"

"I owe some money."

"You mean you've been gambling again? I thought we agreed you wouldn't play cards anymore."

Victor was getting aggravated. "You said so, not me. Are you gonna help me or not? I got people waitin'."

"No, Victor, I'm not. Not this time."

"But you have to!" He was sobering now. "I owe these guys two hundred and forty dollars!"

"Two hundred and forty six," Cleff growled and pointed to his boots.

"No, not this time, Victor. You got yourself in to this mess, and you can get yourself out of it. Tell your friends you'll have to get a job and pay them back because I'm not handing you that kind of money. You don't respect it. And I think you're taking advantage of our relationship."

"Buggers, you say! I need the money, man! Hey! These guys aren't my friends! They'll—"

But his fury was wasted. Sean had already hung up.

From their end of the conversation, it didn't sound to Cleff like he was going to get his money. The little punk didn't have any rich uncle. He didn't have squat. The two drifters looked around the ramshackle cabin with disgust. Even they were accustomed to better living conditions than that rubbish heap of a shack. Still, he had invested an entire day and ample gasoline harvesting that kid, and he wasn't about to give up now.

"Ya know, I'm going to do you a favor, kid."

"Yeah?" Victor looked hopeful, and dopey.

"Yeah. I'm going to give you a couple days to get me my money before I kill you."

"Oh." Even through his beer-colored fog, Victor realized the threat.

"You got two days. Then my friend and I are coming back for my money. If you don't have it, we're gonna make fish food out of ya." He grabbed a fistful of Victor's hair and wrenched his head back to look him in the eye. "Understand?"

"Uh huh." He had no money and no means of getting any money. He was fish food.

"In the meantime, we'll need a little down payment. Sorry, kid, but you wanted to play with the big boys."

"Whaddya mean?" Victor looked left and right quickly.

The drifters stood. The big dumb one grabbed him by the collar. Then the blows came, one after another.

The hike up to Tiny's was a marathon. He felt awful, and the sun was beating down on his aching head. Every muscle in his body smarted, and he wouldn't have been surprised to learn that he had a few bones broken in the bargain.

Victor was on the last switchback. He stopped just before the inclining ingress to the Welbys' property so he could remove an annoying pebble from his boot. From where he was resting, he could hear the Welbys' dogs carrying on. Good thing they lived so far out that they had no neighbors. Every time Victor visited the place, the nonstop racket from untold numbers of animals drove him nuts.

Now he was approaching the, what, house? They called it a 'yurt'. The Welby's sheltered their children in something bigger than a tree house but a bit more rustic. It was comprised of old tires, scrap timber and board, and a canvas tarp for a roof, tied like a circus tent around a huge spruce for a center pole. The place had no running water, no indoor water closet, no telephone. The surrounding area was inches deep in mud since the dense forest blocked out any sun that would dry up the rain water. Wallowing in all that mud were an ornery goat named Gable, who liked to piss on himself and had the longest, sharpest horns Victor had ever seen, as well as several female pygmy goats who worshipped Gable, chickens, ducks, and angry geese—oh, and five big danged dogs that Mr. Welby kept locked up in a small fenced area until he needed them for security. Victor thought the animals acted like they had hydrophobia, but Tiny said they were mean because his dad wanted them that way. He kept the dogs a little skinny.

Overall, the smell was awful. It was some disgusting mixture of animal dung, unwashed bodies, and the fermenting corn in heavily bunged cast iron bathtubs lying around everywhere.

"Whoa! What happened to you?" Tiny asked when he saw his pal.

"Remember the two guys we played poker with?"

"Oh yeah." Tiny looked ashamed for about a fraction of a second. "So that's what I missed by leaving early, huh?"

"Yeah. By the way, thanks a heap." He paused. "They're coming back for me, Tiny."

"Whaddya mean?"

"I mean they told me if I don't pay them the whole wad I owe 'em in two days, they're gonna kill me. They're gonna nail my knees to the floor, pour gasoline over my head and light a match. Then they're gonna feed my ashes to the fish. It's what they said, I'm not kidding. You gotta help me, man."

"Whoa. Victor, be serious, pal. I ain't got no two hundred dollars."

"I know, I know. But you gotta help me think of some way to get it by tomorrow."

"I don't even know anyone with that kind of money."

"I do. But he turned me down flat. Couldn't believe it. I called old man Marshall and told him I was in trouble bad, and the old coot hung up on me."

"That's low. You try the dad routine?"

"Yeah."

"Hmm. Well, sometimes a man's gotta take what he wants. I mean, look, you're his only son, right? And he's old and sick. So, all that money's gonna be yours someday anyway. I say we go over there tonight and take what you need."

"You mean, like, hustle him?"

"No! Heck, no. I mean steal it or beat him 'til he coughs it up."

Victor didn't like the sounds of it. "I ain't beatin' up anyone. Maybe we could break in and just, you know, take it. But we'd have to be quiet, 'cause he's got a nurse and his brother's there, too. I don't wanna mess with Will Marshall." He could feel someone watching him and turned around quickly. Sure enough, there was Nedra, Tiny's younger sister, staring at him out a flap in the cordoned off area that sufficed as her bedroom. She smiled and then let the curtain fall back down.

Nedra was a weird girl. Victor called her the goat-girl, and pronounced her name as if he were a billy goat naying, "*Neeeeh-dra*", because she was always with those filthy goats. Nedra's mother was always stumbling around the place, bottle of swill in hand, but she didn't seem to have a bone to pick over her daughter's choice of bed partners. Sometimes Victor felt sorry for goat-girl.

Nedra never wore under-drawers. For one shiny quarter, she'd lift her dress and let Tiny's friends look at her private for as long as they wanted. Victor had paid her money plenty of times for a look-see. Just lately, she'd grown a little hair down there, and that made it more interesting. Twice, she let Victor get so close that he could have reached out and touched it if he'd wanted. But then she'd have to pay him a quarter, as dirty as she was.

"My brat sister," Tiny grumbled. Then he pulled Victor's ear real close to his mouth. "Know what? She let me rut on her the other day."

"Nuh-uh."

"Swear it to that God of yours, pal. She'd let you too if you asked. She likes it, man. Nedra likes you, too. I can tell."

"How much does she want for it?"

"A quarter, man. She let me do it for that. Swear to God." He crossed his chest. "Just lies right down and spreads 'em wide. That's why she keeps looking at you, Victor. She likes you, man. She wants it."

"Maybe," he said cautiously. "Anyhow, how am I gonna pay these guys off, Tiny? They're gonna kill me! Then I ain't gonna be ruttin' on goat-girl or anybody else. I'm fish food."

Tiny put his pudgy arm around his pal's shoulder. "Like I told ya, pal. We go over there tonight and we jus' take it. It'll be your money soon enough anyway."

"But is has to be tonight. And it's two hundred and forty-six dollars—and twenty-five cents." He stole a look back toward the flap.

"Sure thing, pal. Old dairy-farmin' guys like them probably turn in when it gets dark, and it's getting dark these days around ten. We'll go around ten-thirty."

"Okay."

"Okay? Hey, man, I'm giving you the only way to save your butt." He punched Victor's upper arm and Victor howled. "Sorry. Sore, huh? Hey, you got a baseball bat?"

"I think so. Why?"

"Bring it with you, dodo. Geez. Do I gotta think of everything?"

Chapter 63

July, 1941

Chicago, Illinois

"Blair?" Wendell's hushed voice called.

"Come in."

Wendell had a briefcase with him, which he carried protectively under his arm. He stepped from the foyer into the main room and saw her standing on the far side, in front of a bank of windows. She turned and flashed him a brilliant smile. Instantly Blair noticed the pained expression that fleeted across Wendell's plainly honest face, before he could hide it from her. Blair's heartstrings tweaked for her friend. But Wendell was adept at shrinking all of his sorrows into a single flash of dispiritedness, just before he squared his shoulders and returned her smile.

She'd broken his heart when she'd had to tell him the truth: Cindy was gone. She had never really existed at all, but inside Blair's own head. Blair had been mentally ill for many years, her doctors told them. She had suffered some fracture of her psyche early on, from repeated abuses upon her as a child. The trauma she'd suffered at the hands of Chester Lasley had shocked so deeply, it managed to reach those dark malicious pockets of insanity and root them out. Her psyche had fused together again during her ten comatose months. Her psychologist at the sanitarium, where she'd been residing ever since her release from the hospital almost a year earlier, told her she was healed. Her prognosis was sanity restored. Blair thought her doctors were absolutely spot on about her diagnosis. She prayed they were right about her prognosis. She had not heard Cindy's voice since she'd descended into a coma a year and ten months earlier.

Wendell had confessed his love for Blair when she was still in the hospital. He was crestfallen when he learned that Cindy, an alias for Blair, was married to another man and had a child with him. Until he'd learned that, Wendell admitted to her, he had harbored a secret hope that someday Cindy Marshall might consent to marry him.

In the intervening months since he'd discovered the inscription on the backside of Cindy's Lady Racine timepiece, the only item she had taken with her on her attempted suicide, the item that was clutched frightfully tight in her fist, he had recited aloud the poem for her. He did this over and over, many times each visit, which he made at the end of every workday, and every Saturday and Sunday. He knew it by heart, of course. Inevitably, he had come to adopt the verse as his own mantra, and it had helped him to keep his own secret hope alive. It had taken the passage of twelve months, the time since 'Cindy' awoke to the world as Blair Bowman Marshall, to dull the sharp pain of Wendell's new reality.

Blair watched as he swallowed a sigh and she knew what he was mourning; it was the death of hope. On his last visit, Wendell assured her he coping with his 'disappointment', that being the unfavorable recognizance that he would not be spending his remaining years with the only woman he had ever loved. He'd admitted to being heartbroken, but promised to have come to terms with the limits of his relationship with Cindy—now Blair. He professed to be and always remain her closest friend.

Blair used her crutches to meet him at an empty table in the middle of the room. "How's the leg, Cin—I'm so sorry…Blair?" he asked.

"It's getting stronger. I have walked all over this facility, for lack of something more entertaining to do. The doctor said this morning all the walking is indeed speeding my recovery. Tomorrow, I can begin walking Lake Shore Avenue to the Dock Street Navy Pier entrance, with my nurse and, of course, my very fashionable cane. If my leg can stand that distance, I may be able to leave here by summer's end. That would be the best birthday gift I could possibly give to myself, Wendell. I'd almost lost hope of ever seeing my son again before I die." She wrapped her fingers around her timepiece protectively.

"Does the leg still hurt bad?" Wendell worried.

"Oh my goodness, yes. But I have chosen to lie to myself and say it does not hurt too badly at all."

"The easiest person in the world to lie to is oneself," Wendell said absently as he rummaged through papers. He must have realized how morose he'd sounded and quickly looked up and winked at her. "Before I forget, I must give you these…" Wendell pulled two bars of soap from his briefcase pocket. "Of course, I have told my mother *all* about you—she did wonder where I went for an hour every day for the past two years and—" Crimson began to rise in Wendell's cheeks as he realized he was babbling. "Uh, but, she insisted I give you these." He nodded to the soap bars he held in his hands, his smile wide.

Blair looked baffled as she watched him place the soap on the table. "I, um, I'm not sure what—"

"Oh, goodness," Wendell turned a darker shade of red, and he hastened to explain. "My mother was born a Hoosier. She told me to give these to you, because it's, uh, an old Indiana healer's secret. See, you wrap each bar in some thin fabric, or maybe place them inside of summer stockings, and then put them under your knee areas, beneath your bottom sheet. Don't know why, but for ridding one of night cramps of the legs, nothing works better."

She smiled and placed one hand gently, intimately, on his forearm. "Thank you, Wendell. Please thank your mother for me."

The dear, sweet man had saved her life. When she'd been cast into darkness following her crash and fall, the only voice she could hear was her own. Even Cindy was silent. It was all so confusing. She had not known where she was or how she would find her way out of the darkness. Then Wendell's voice had broken through. Murky, vaporous tendrils of sound had slinked into the deeper crevices of her subconscious, and beckoned to her dormant ears.

She heard, *"Hope is the thing with feathers…"*, and suddenly there was a soft glowing light in the distance.

Wendell had sat with her in the hospital each day, sometimes holding her hand, while she lingered in a coma for many months. One day he'd noticed the timepiece Cindy had always worn around her neck, the one her fingers often rubbed and massaged, was laying on a bedside table. He picked it up, curious, and that was when he noticed the inscription she'd had engraved on the back. It was a poem he'd heard before but could not place, he'd since told her. Wendell had determined any poem meaningful enough to have inscribed on a piece of jewelry, must be fairly important to that person. So, he began reading the poem aloud for her each day. Blair had heard him each day, and it spurred her to find her way back from the darkness.

"How are you, Wendell?" she asked.

"I am very well, my dear. I have the paperwork from the court in Tillamook County, Oregon. I have furnished them proof you are alive, and used the Power of Attorney to have the papers drawn up to re-open the custody hearing for your son, Victor. These pages here challenge the preacher's custody rights." He placed them in front of her and pulled out her chair, so she could sit with the leg she had already had surgery on several times, stretched out in front. "These ones here, you need to sign where I marked. These ask for the new hearing. Once you sign and I file on your behalf, I am told we can ask for a date, possibly as early as the end of the year. I spoke with one of your doctors on my way in. He said he was immeasurably pleased with your leg's healing. More importantly, he told me your ment—er, your brain injury is fit as a fiddle, and has agreed to provide the court his findings."

He placed the papers in front of her, one at a time for signing, then stacked up all the pages and placed them in a portfolio for delivery to the courthouse. "I will have copies of everything delivered to your attorney."

"They won't contact the preacher, will they? I don't want him to have any notice. I am certain he thinks me dead and I wish to keep it that way. Until I am ready. Otherwise there would be nothing to stop him from trying again to have me killed."

"Yes, Cin—I am very sorry. Blair. Your secrets are safe with me." Wendell's cheeks were thoroughly scarlet. "New tricks are trying for this old dog, I fear. Forgive me, dear."

"Of course, Wendell. Think nothing of it, it's just a name. Oh, my! Can this be…?"

Wendell had placed before her several land contracts for the sale of some properties which Cindy had sagely purchased during the Depression, instead of more stocks and gold. The combined worth of the properties was over a million dollars! Blair had elected to divulge herself of Illinois property, with the exception of her printing house loft apartment. Although it had tripled in value since she purchased it, Blair had decided to hang on to the one place that made Cindy happy in the past nine years. If Victor wished to sell it when she was gone, it would be his choice to make.

Blair finished signing the real estate papers, and Wendell tucked them all back into his briefcase for the next day, when he would drop them off at the land attorney's office for listing them for sale. There was already great interest in the properties, so Wendell had no worries about getting their full value for Blair.

"There. We have the whole afternoon now, Wendell. Stay, please, and have tea with me. Tell me all about the theatre and what's new. Oh! What can you tell me about the moving picture, 'Gone with the Wind'?"

Chapter 64

July, 1941

Cloverdale, Oregon

It *was probably just a bear or a deer*, Sean figured. *We don't get much company here.* But as he looked out the darkened parlor's picture window for the source of the noise, he thought he could make out two men running around the front of the house. "Will!" Sean whispered hoarsely up the stairwell. He received no answer, and did not want to risk calling for him any louder. He let the lights remain off as he reached into his bedroom armoire for the shotgun. He slipped in two cartridges and clicked off the safety. Then he sat in the parlor in the dark and waited.

"I didn't say they'd be asleep by now, you did!" Victor retorted.

"Are you sure you saw someone at the window?"

"No. I'm not positive. I don't know if there's anybody home. Their car isn't here."

"Okay! That makes it easier. We'll just break in. We got bats, and the front door is made of glass. Just do it fast, smash and grab."

"Okay. On the count of three… Wait. What if just one of them is home?" Victor asked.

"We'll be in before he can get to a phone and call the cops. Got it?"

"Yeah. Count."

"One, two, three!" Tiny mouthed while counting down on his fingers.

They ran to the doorstep and leaped up the steps, and both boys struck the thick-paned glass simultaneously. The high-pitched shatter sounded almost soft. Tiny stepped through the opening and moved aside. Then Victor stepped through, lifting his head once safely inside, to see the same thing Tiny was staring at: the unfortunate end of a shotgun.

"Uh-oh."

"Victor, I'm surprised at you." Sean looked over at Tiny. "Not too surprised to see you, Lytle Welby. Let's see. You come here tonight to rob me or just vandalize my doorstep?"

"We come to kill you, man." Tiny tilted his fat chin up indignantly.

"Really? Then if I shoot you, Welby, in my vandalized parlor, it'd be self-defense, wouldn't it?"

Tiny backed up a baby step and zipped his mouth shut.

"Yes, Victor, what is this all about?" Will had left the mill late on that day because he had stayed to swap out grinding stones for a special order. So focused were the boys on Sean Marshall's shotgun, they never heard Will climb up the porch steps behind them. Will grabbed the ball bats out of the boys' hands as he passed between them to join his brother. "You plan on using the bat Sean bought you for your birthday last year to beat him up?"

Victor's eyes were downcast in his disgrace, but he said, "I told you I needed money. Those guys are coming for me tomorrow, and if I don't have it, they're gonna kill me."

"They're gonna nail his knees to the floor and set him on fire!" Tiny piped in.

Sean looked Victor in the eyes. He honestly couldn't recognize anything of the little boy he once loved more than life itself. *Is there not even a shred of decency left in him?* "You were going to kill me for the money, Victor?" His eyes went to the baseball bats resting against his brother's shoulder.

"I wouldn't have." Victor looked down in what appeared to be shame. "Tiny might have."

Maybe just a shred of genuine shame, Sean thought. *This boy is not my son. My son died the day the preacher took him.* Sean realized in that moment, he'd been grieving over the loss of his Victory for nearly a decade. That was long enough. Sean used the shot-gun's barrel to lift Victor's face up. "Those men you owe, they do all that to your face, son?"

Victor turned his head angrily away from the weapon and the man who wielded it.

Sean sighed. "How much do you owe?"

"Two hundred and forty-six dollars and twenty-five cents," Tiny said almost merrily.

Victor said nothing but nodded.

"What?" Will exclaimed. "How does a youngster your age get into so much trouble?"

"Wait here." Sean said, and left the boys with Will.

Victor wandered a few steps farther into the room. The place was vaguely familiar. He looked up to see a large portrait of a woman hanging on the wall over Mavis Marshall's piano, and he was mesmerized by it. She was beautiful. Sean returned with a wad of bills in his hand, the shotgun still cradled in his right arm. He followed Victor's eyes to the portrait.

"Your mother. Painted just after you were born. Recognize her?"

"Naw. Maybe a little. She's pretty."

"No. She's beautiful. And she was so proud of you." He shook his head miserably. His eyes glistened. "Here. Take it. It's what you came for. Now hear me, Victor Bowman. Don't ever come here again. Don't phone, and don't radio. I don't know who you are anymore. And I guess what I'm saying is, I don't want to be your friend."

Victor's reaction was puzzling, to Victor most of all. He cried. But he pocketed the money and left without another word.

Chapter 65

"You alright, brother?" Will asked. Sean nodded, downcast. Will set his jaw. "You go on to bed, Sean. Lorette and I will get this glass cleaned up." He waited for Sean to close his bedroom door, and then he darted out the open door after Victor.

He caught up with the youngster at the south end of their acreage by the old carriage house, and grabbed him by the collar at the scruff of his neck. With a single, powerful arm, Will turned the teen around to face him. "Did you think we were done here? I hope you got another think coming."

"Leave me alone," Victor tried to twist away. Will wouldn't have it.

"You really dropped a plunker back there, and you are going to tell me why, Victor Bowman."

"Why what?" Victor snapped.

"Why you go out of your way to hurt the feelings of the only man who has ever gone out of his way for you. Why you have to talk cold and cruel to the man who has bailed you out of every tight spot you've ever gotten yourself into—and there have been plenty of those. You're going to tell me how you can hate the man who has loved you so much all of these years, and has given so much of himself to you." Will shook the boy for emphasis. "Start talking." He released the boy's collar.

"Gone out of his way for me? Ha! Loved me? Given so much to me? Don't make me laugh." Victor spat on the ground. "He thought he could show up once a year with a birthday present and that was gonna make everything okay?"

"You think he didn't want to give you more? You think he didn't want to share his life with you, share his home and his love? How can you think that? He tried to get you out of that cottage—"

"He left me there!" Victor screamed. And then the tears pent up from nine miserable years fell like rain.

Will was stunned by the intensity of the boy's emotions. *Victor didn't know all that Sean had done to try and win the boy back. Good Lord.* Will ran a hand through his hair.

"Victor, you know your pa took the preacher to court to try and get you back. You knew that, right?"

Victor looked up at Will, seeming to distrust him.

"When he lost the case, he was devastated. We tried to come and see you after that, and the preacher pulled a shotgun on us. He threatened to kill us. You were watching the whole thing out the front window. Honest, boy? You don't have any recollections?"

Victor shrugged, but said nothing. Some of what Will Marshall was saying was triggering small memories, but memories were painful.

"When it was clear to us the preacher wasn't going to let Sean visit you, and he couldn't get custody unless your ma came back, we traveled all the way to Chicago, Illinois to try and find her and bring her home. Geez, Victor, all this time, how could you believe Sean didn't want you back? You were everything to him. Losing you and your ma…that's killing him faster than any injuries he received in The Burn. Don't you remember anything about your life here at all?" Will had never lost control of his emotions before, but his waterworks were turned on full-blast in confronting Victor.

Victor wiped tears from his face, too, then ran his sleeve under his nose to stop the running. He shrugged because he wasn't sure he would find his voice. Finally Victor said, "It doesn't matter anymore. He just got through telling me he didn't want to know me." His voice broke off and he shook his head sadly. "Doesn't matter anymore."

"You hurt him, Victor. You just hurt him one too many times and he's not strong enough to weather much more pain. The man's got a bad heart, among other problems. Doesn't help that you keep breaking it…Victor, do you really think after all the years he's been reaching out to you, that he could wash his hands of you? I can promise you, he wouldn't. If you just made the smallest effort…"

Victor's head hurt, and he was so sore and emotionally-drained he could have lay down where he was standing, and slept for a hundred years like Rip Van Winkle. He had chosen to believe the preacher over Sean Marshall, and now suspicion was marching up Victor's bruised spine. "I gotta go," he told Will. Without another word, Victor turned and walked away, leaving Will standing in the south forty with his heart in his mouth.

"He loves you Victor! He always has and he always will," he hollered softly to the darkness.

Chapter 66

The preacher was tooling around the kitchen preparing breakfast and making plenty of racket. He'd come home late the night before to find Victor asleep on the couch, trying to use a sheet to hide his blackened eye. Bowman wondered how much longer the boy was going to feign sleep before getting it over with and coming clean.

"Morning, grandfather." Victor shuffled over to the table.

"Yes, good morning, son." The preacher did not bother to turn himself around. "The church in Tillamook has sent us money. I visited a German bakery and brought us some bagel breads, and I have more of that creamed cheese and some Walla Wallas, and…" He turned with a rare smile. One look at Victor and his smile fell. That was a good deal more than a teenage workaday black eye. Victor had taken a severe beating. "What happened to your face, boy?"

Victor plopped himself down in a kitchen chair. "I got beat up."

"I can see that. What happened?"

"I owed some guys some money…"

"You were playing cards, weren't you, boy?" The preacher's face began turning that familiar corn-fed red.

"Yeah, I played cards. I played cards and I drank beer and the guys I set out to hustle hustled me instead. An' I couldn't come up with the money, so they beat me up. You might as well know, they're coming back today for their money."

"How much?" he asked cautiously.

"Over two hundred and forty."

An audible gasp escaped the preacher.

"You don't gotta worry. Tiny and me got the money already." Victor fiddled with his hands nervously.

"And how, may I inquire, did you and that street urchin, Welby, find that kind of money? And don't think of lying to me."

"We went to the Marshall house, broke in, and stole it." He changed the story just a little.

"Was Marshall home when you did this?"

Victor nodded. "We had our baseball bats, and we threatened to kill him if he didn't hand it over. It was Tiny's idea, but I went along with it. You wanna hit me now? Go ahead. Better take your turn while you can. I'm thinking I'm gonna take the money back to Mr. Marshall today. And after that, those two guys will probably kill me."

"You'll do no such thing, Victor." The preacher actually smiled. *Finally, the boy may have spurned and succeeded in shaking off the likes of Sean Marshall.* To Victor, the preacher said, "Marshall has been trying to force his fatherhood on you for all thirteen years of your life. Well, he ought to find out sometime that there's more to being a father than buying red tricycles."

Victor turned his head around and looked at his grandfather. "Red tricycle?" The preacher continued on. "I must admit that I am surprised to learn of such spunk in Tiny Welby."

He could not stand Otis's boy. The lazy loafer never worked a day in his life. Certainly, rowdy-riding in the Welby's delivery truck with his friend, taking nips and dropping off jugs, never qualified as honest work. The boys drank most of their earnings anyway, and the remainder was lost to gambling. It was the ne'er-do-well Tiny who got Victor drinking and playing cards in the first place, and playing cards badly.

"Of course, it was Tiny's fault you were playing cards while stinking drunk in the first place. You will never earn a dime playing cards so long as you drink. It is a handicap, a disability, in a game which involves seeking every advantage. I don't see how you ever expected to win." He placed the breakfast foods on the table.

The preacher sat down and really looked Victor over. He didn't notice any bones looking odd. Even the boy's nose survived the beating. They surely worked the boy over like a wool rug, but they'd been careful not to break anything.

"How badly was Tiny beaten? Does he look worse than you do?" He hoped so. Tit-for-tat and all. Anyway, Lytle could use a good cuffing. The boy was soft. He had taken after his mother: short, squat, dowdy, and a long-standing malingerer. Ironically, Otis Welby's pubescent daughter took after him, tall and slender, with long blond hair and long legs. The preacher allowed himself a moment to daydream about those long legs, and where they led.

"No, he's the hooch-supplier's kid. They didn't hit him once."

"Huh?"

"They didn't hit Tiny. Just me. Because I'm *your* son… or whatever."

"Whatever? Is that the truth as I taught it to you, boy?" Bowman was getting red again.

Victor followed the preacher's gaze to the banana box and his eyes narrowed. He gave a quick, forced laugh before he told the preacher unequivocally, "I'm done with the box." Victor held the preacher's stare. It was the preacher who broke away first.

"Well, anyhow, I'm proud of you boys—er, men. That took more moxie than I believed either of you possessed. That is, to go after what you wanted and take it."

"Tiny's just ornery and stupid. Guts or moxie or whatever never entered into it. We did a bad thing, Grandfather. I can't believe you don't see that. Don't it bother you at all? You're a preacher! I feel awful about what I've done, and I'm gonna go fix things after we eat."

"And let those men kill you, Victor? Did you think I have that kind of money to bail you out of this jam? Think again." The preacher tore angrily into a bagel with his bare, dirty hands, dove half of it deep into the pile of creamed cheese and shoved the entire wad into his mouth.

Victor put his head down in his crossed arms and cried. Now *that* bothered Preacher Bowman.

Chapter 67

Sean phoned his attorney in Newport first thing in the morning. He got Mr. Reynolds's secretary, who told him the attorney would be in around 9:30 that day. He had no appointments until 11:00 a.m. Sean asked her to put him down for the 9:30 slot. He needed to make a will.

"I can't say I blame you, Sean. But what was it, a year ago that you wanted to fight for custody of him? Now you want to cut him out of your will? Are you sure about this?"

"Quite sure. I am not going to be outliving my brother. It wouldn't be fair to Will, after I'm gone, if Victor, or the preacher, were to lay claim to everything Will's worked his whole life for. For the sake of argument, if I were a sole survivor and I were to die tomorrow, what would happen to my part of the estate? Who would get it?"

"Well, let's see. If you failed to name an heir, I believe your son would have no trouble staking his claim to it. You've claimed publicly that he is your son. It's even a matter of official court records. If he fails to contest, it would all go to your brother. If you survive your brother, it would all be sold, with proceeds going to the state. Now, I need to warn you that if you cut Victor out completely, it could be later argued that you were not sound of mind and forgot him, in which case the court would likely rule in his favor."

"So even if I cut him out, he could still wind up with everything. No. There must be something I can do to prevent that."

"There is." Charles Reynolds smiled. "You can leave him one percent. You leave instructions for your estate to be sold or auctioned. Name someone you trust to act as executor, and will to Victor one percent of your estate's net, or after sale, profit. Leave the rest to anyone you like: your best friend, your church, even your dog." Reynolds said.

"And that would be iron clad?"

"Mr. Marshall, the only thing that could imperil the legality of such a division of your assets would be if you were to commit suicide and leave a note behind that contained severe mental language. I trust you're not planning to do any such thing. With the one-percent inclusion, a court would plainly see that you did not forget Victor Bowman/Marshall and would discredit any diminished capacity contention."

"Very well. Let's do it. Of course I would want Will to handle everything, but if by some wild chance I survive Will, then I would like Rebecca Tjaden to handle my estate."

The men proceeded to divide up Sean's estate according to his requested bequeaths, ultimately leaving just one percent of the estate unaccounted for. That would go to Victor Bowman.

The attorney took furious shorthand notes. Then, looking up, he added, "I'm going to need a specific list of your real assets, Sean."

"I figured you might. Got it right here." He handed over the three sheets of paper. "I guess you can tell I'm a little anxious to have this business squared away. I'm not in good health," he added by way of explanation.

"I understand, Sean. I'm sorry too. You have my word that this will be completed by day's end."

Sean stood up and offered his hand to the attorney. "I'm sorry I came off at you the last time we met, Charles. That wasn't me. I want to thank you for seeing me on short notice."

"The pleasure is mine to be sure, Sean. Now go home and get some rest. You can take piece of mind that your affairs are now in order."

The next stop for Sean was a carpenter's shop in Newport. The man had said on the phone that he had one door with beveled glass inserted the length of it. It would have to do as a replacement for the door Mavis Marshall had been so particular about. His ma had always said the front door was the first impression of the family living behind it. She had commissioned the door in 1906, to have the glass insert beveled for dimension, in double-thick floated glass for strength and pureness, with acid-etched designs done by hand for deftness as well as grace. The replacement door would reflect no grace. But that had really died with Mavis Marshall anyway.

Chapter 68

July, 1941

Cloverdale, Oregon

Tiny's hard-shooting muzzle-loading gun reported with a powerful crack, and Victor howled.

"Gotta watch out for them coyanthers, Tiny!" He slapped his knee and laughed some more.

"Kye-whats? Damn it, Victor! Were you just funning me again?"

"Coyanthers, fool. You know, part coyote and part panther. They sit up there in the trees and keep on the lookout for their natural enemy."

"Oh yeah? You're so smart, what's the natural enemy of a coyanther then?" He looked doubtful.

"Tiny Welby and his fool gun!"

He howled some more. Tiny was looking peeved. "Come on, Tiny. It's a joke! Don't go getting all dandered up now. I told ya I didn't want to come hunting up here. I'm just making the best of it."

"Oh yeah? Well, pickin' deer outta the water ain't even sport, Victor. You got no sense of adventure."

"And I'll tell you again, I can't eat adventure. I can eat venison." Victor had managed to talk Evan Tjaden out of his skiff for a day and he had wanted to go deer hunting at the Cape of Kiwanda in Pacific City, just a couple miles west of Cloverdale. At night, the cougars would chase the deer down from the hills to the beach, where the deer would swim out beyond the breakers and stay until it was daylight, when the cougars were scared back up into their dens in the mountain. But clobbering the deer in the water with boat oars was too easy living for Tiny, he claimed. He wanted to hunt.

"Speaking of adventure, look out, Tiny! There's a hide-behind!"

Tiny spun on his heels and fired up into a tree. The report of the gun knocked him on his butt. Seconds later, the only thing that fell from that tree was a big branch, and it darned near hit Tiny in the head.

"Dag-nabbit, Victor!" Tiny yelled.

"Well, I never saw such bad shooting! Missed it by a mile! Heck, you'd prob'ly miss water if ya fell out of a boat!"

"Bull hockey! Ain't nothing in that tree. Ain't no such thing as a hide-behind or a coyanther. You do that again and I'm gonna whoop ya." He reloaded his gun with another shot.

"Yeah? You and what army, Tiny? And there are so hide-behinds and coyanthers. Hammer-tail cats too. I read stories about 'em. Sneak right up behind ya, making sounds you can hear but you can't never see them, and they whack ya on the top of the head with them deadly hammer tails of theirs. It's how they get their name. Must be such a thing, or else you've been shootin' at nothing all morning." He had himself another good laugh, falling to the ground and rolling.

"Hammer-tail cats! I'm gonna hammer your head!"

And with that, Tiny leapt at his friend and the two wrestled on the floor of the thick woods, among bramble and fallen leaves. They both stopped their laughing and punching for a second or two when they thought they heard twigs snapping off to their right.

"Uh-oh! Hammer-tails, Tiny! Better watch out!"

That earned Victor a solid punch in the gut, which was still sore from the beating he took a week earlier. And then, suddenly, out of the corner of Victor's eye, he caught a glimpse of something big and darkly furred bounding out of the service berries to the right of them. "Get up! Get off me, Tiny! I mean it! Get off!"

He pushed his pal roughly to the side. "There was something in the bushes there. Didn't you hear it run off?"

"More bull!" He drew back his fist.

"No, look!" Victor pointed in the direction he saw the blur run off to, and sure enough, there was a black bear cub bounding up the densely treed hillside. "Hey, it's a little cub, Tiny!"

"Whoo-hoo!" Tiny hollered, scrambling for his gun. He was a good shot when he had a legitimate target.

"Wait! What are you doin'? No! Hey!" Victor leapt at Tiny when he saw Tiny take aim at the climbing bear cub, but he was too late.

Tiny shot it. It fell dead in its tracks.

"I got it!" He jumped in the air.

"Man, Tiny. That's just a cub. Why did you go an' kill it for?"

"You were the one hollering!"

"Yeah, for you to look. I didn't expect you'd find sport in killing a baby!" And then something occurred to Victor. "Say, Tiny, that there's a cub. There's certain to be a mother bear close behind."

Tiny ignored Victor and was already making his way toward the fallen cub to examine it.

"Tiny, wait!" he yelled for his friend, but Tiny was still sore and was ignoring him.

Tiny reached the cub just as the mother bear emerged from the berry bramble. She made a beeline for Tiny; his scent was too close for any self-respecting black bear to ignore. When she saw her cub lying dead at Tiny's feet, she was one angry mother bear.

"Oh, sheez! Tiny, look out!" Victor shouted.

Tiny did turn around, just in time to see the bear charging for him. He lifted his gun and aimed, but he carelessly had failed to reload his weapon. Tiny tossed the rifle, turned, and started to run. The bear closed the gap and struck at him, tearing Tiny's hunting jacket from him in one swipe. Tiny ran for a tree. Victor was running full speed, trying to help his friend. He carried the Winchester that Sean Marshall had given him.

"Tiny, not the tree!" he yelled.

Grizzlies, it was widely known, could not climb. But black bears could. Tiny heard Victor's warning and changed course, but the bear overtook Tiny in no time. A single blow knocked him to the ground and tore loose his shoulder blade. Then the bear, with one or two strokes of her claws, tore most of Tiny's clothes off.

"Memaloose, Tiny! Memaloose!"

The Indians said that if a black bear attacked you and you played dead, the bear would leave you alone. *Memaloose* was the Indian word for "as dead." But this mother bear had apparently never heard that black bears don't molest dead men, because she angrily bit into Tiny's loins and back so that he screamed from the pain. The bear clawed at Tiny's head, turning him over to rip out his throat, but by then Victor was close enough to get the shot. The bear was all over Tiny, and Victor feared he might shoot his friend by accident.

He glanced at the sky and murmured a quick prayer. "If you won't help Tiny, Lord, please just don't help that bear no more." He looked down the sight of his barrel. "I got her, Tiny! Stay down!"

Tiny rammed his fist into the bear's mouth, making her rear up. At the same moment that the bear was crushing the bones in Tiny's hand, the report from Victor's Winchester 30-30 ripped into her. Victor killed the mother bear with one shot.

Tiny was still conscious when Victor crept up and nudged the bear with the muzzle of his rifle. She was dead.

Tiny's eyes met his friends. "I'll never see old Cloverdale again, Victor," and Tiny fainted.

Victor checked to see if his friend was alive. He seemed to be, just barely. When he tried to heft Tiny over his shoulder shot pouch-fashion, to carry him down the hill, it took Victor three tries. Strange thoughts went through his mind, like why Tiny Welby was called Tiny when he was so gol' darned fat. He'd have to come back for the weapons, which made him feel a bit vulnerable considering what had just happened. Trappers said that the black bears hang out together wherever their food source is. Probably all the shooting scared any others off, but you never knew anything for sure.

He managed to carry Tiny back to the clearing where they had wrestled. He laid his friend down and ran for the horses they had left hitched to a tree just off the trail. He had to lay Tiny across his horse in dead-man fashion. He tied Tiny down, grabbed for the horse's lead in his hand, and lead the horses out of the woods.

He took him to the nearest home, that of the Tjaden's. Thankfully, Evan and his older, married sister, Ellie, were at the homestead.

When Ellie opened the door to see Victor carrying a bloody Tiny Welby with hardly any clothing left on his body that wasn't shredded, she shrieked, "Ev, come quick!" She pulled Victor toward the sofa in the large living area and quickly threw a blanket down.

Victor let Tiny roll off his tired shoulder. "Bear," he said to her questioning eyes. "Tiny shot her cub. I never have seen a black bear charge a man like she went after Tiny. He didn't have a chance."

"Why didn't he shoot at her?" Ellie gingerly touched the flap of bloody flesh hanging loose from the bone of his shoulder. "Oh my," she looked as though she might be the one to faint next.

"What's all the commotion, Ellie? God's name! What's this?" Evan took in the torn and tattered man bleeding his life out on the Tjaden's sofa.

In response to his question and hers, Victor continued to explain. "He shot the cub and I guess he just forgot to reload his weapon. Then the mama came tearing out of the service berries on the hill and charged after him."

"Foolish, not reloading your weapons. To say nothing of hunting cubs for sport," Evan admonished. He watched as his sister brought over a pale of soapy water and a clean rag and began dabbing at Tiny's flesh.

"Yes, sir, I know." Now that he had Tiny in safe hands, Victor felt weak and a little out of sorts. His words started tumbling clumsily out of his mouth. "We were wrestling around a bit, and then we heard something. Tiny shot at it, I think before he even knew what it was he was shootin' at. And then, instead of reloading, he went to see what he shot down. Then, all of the sudden, Tiny was running for his life and that mama bear was chasing him and I was running as fast as I could carrying my rifle and I shot her." He had to take a breath. "But not before she did all this to him." Victor turned a shade of green as he looked over Ellie's ministering.

Evan handed Victor a double shot of bourbon and pushed him down into a chair. "Drink that. I'll get the doctor."

Ellie asked her brother to fetch Rebecca before leaving. "He needs a surgeon, Ev. You're gonna have to call over to Tillamook. And, Ev, hurry," she added unnecessarily.

She and Rebecca carefully washed out Tiny's wounds. Then, with sack needles and twine, they began sewing back into place the flesh that was hanging loose from Tiny's shattered shoulder blade. Meanwhile, the surgeon was at the hospital and was free to come, but the other doctor on duty was using the only vehicle to make his rounds. Evan Tjaden drove at full speed to fetch the surgeon. He agreed that Tiny needed one, and there was only the one doctor who qualified.

It took almost two hours for Evan to return with the surgeon. By then, the women had finished with the sewing, the bleeding had been controlled, and Tiny was beginning to come around.

The doctor frowned and ordered up a tumbler of whiskey for Tiny. "Be better off for him if he stayed passed out," he grumbled, opening his black doctor bag.

"The cleansing woke him. I'm sorry. I tried to be as gentle as I could," Ellie apologized.

"You gals did just fine, Ellie. Good as army field nurses. Good dressing too. But I'm afraid those are going to have to come out," he nodded at the stitches. The doctor busied himself by filling a syringe as he explained to Ellie that they had done a fine job, but the danger of infection from an animal's mouth and claws were much too great to be satisfied with soap and water. He set about ripping out the stitches to apply iodine to the deep gashes. The lacerations to the young man's scalp were terrible, and the surgeon thought Tiny would not live, but he did. The surgeon also thought the services of a particular bone doctor in Portland could fix Tiny's shoulder, which was so badly shattered when the bear ripped the bone loose. He told Tiny's parents the bone doctor could probably save the young man's arm. But Tiny's family had no money for that. The local surgeon did his best to fix it, but was unable to restore its strength and usefulness. Tiny's new nickname would be Lefty.

Chapter 69

August, 1941

Cloverdale, Oregon

Tiny "Lefty" Welby was quite proud of the bear skin. Rightfully so, considering what he gave up to get it. He got a bit wrapped up in his story during the retelling, and certain facts in the account had been changed to such an extent that Victor might as well not have been there at all. But Victor was willing to let that go. Tiny needed something to allow him to feel like a man. He only had the one arm, and had been kind of sickly-looking ever since the bear fight. He lost probably a quarter of his total weight, and he was reduced to helping his ma and pa with their homemade sour mash, work he would probably be doing for all the rest of his days. Ever since his bear attack, Tiny had been sipping high on his own supply and was almost never sober anymore. On this day, one of his worst days, he and Victor had a falling out.

"Hey, Tiny! Been lookin' out for them hammer-tail cats?" Victor still teased him, since it was one of the few things Tiny laughed at those days.

But on that day, Tiny was surly by nine in the morning, having woke with a stupendous hangover.

"Hammer-tail cats, hide-behinds, and coyanthers. Dang you, Victor Bowman. I wouldn't be a cripple if not for you and your half-wit humor." He scowled.

"Hey, Tiny, come on. You ain't gonna start blaming me for what happened."

Tiny glowered and took a big hit off his jug. Then he spat on Victor's boots. "Damn straight I am blaming you. If it hadn't been for you and your stupid wisecrackin', I wouldn't have spent both rounds on fool hammer-tails. I'd have a right arm today."

"You've gotten so carried away with your story that you plain forgot you spent those rounds shootin' to death a baby bear. An' if it hadn't been for me and my Winchester, you wouldn't have a head today or that foul mouth of yours."

"Oh yeah? If I had both arms, I'd whoop the tar out of ya! I suppose you're gonna tell me you saved my hide next."

"Well, I did, and you know it. You didn't even shoot the dang bear! I did! You shot her cub, and then you forgot to reload. Remember? Come on, Tiny. I just let you tell the story your way so's you can have some fun. Heck, I even let you keep the skin, so don't take your morning snake bites out on me."

"Let me keep the skin? *Let* me!" He jumped to his feet, was still sensible enough to recognize that Victor towered over him, and sat back down on the fence heavily. "Was too my skin. You didn't let me have nothin'. I shot that bear!"

"Okay, okay. *You* shot it, all right? I didn't come here to argue. I came to see if you want to take a ride in Evan's skiff. I'm gonna go pick me off some venison. Whaddya say?"

"I say it's a chicken shit way to hunt, same as before."

Victor was trying to be patient with his friend, but his patience was running out. "You're calling me a chicken, you one-armed son-of-a-beehive! You're the chicken, Tiny. Didn't have guts when it came to shooting bear, and you don't have any guts now. It's not my fault you fired your muzzle-loader at every fool thing in the forest and then forgot to reload it. It wasn't me who found sport in shooting that mother bear's baby. You know, folks are right about you Welbys. You're white trash, inbred and insane. A whole pack o' thieving, drunken liars is what you are."

"Did you say inbred? That's a snort! Your family tree don't even fork! And your grandpa's so crank that he's proud of it! Bow man for the king. Big deal! He probably calls you son because you probably are! I wouldn't doubt it none if he bedded your ma— he's sick in the head." He laughed cruelly and lifted the bottle to his mouth again. "I ain't too good on these family tree things. What would that make you, Victor?"

Victor's face darkened by a shade. "The guy who could wipe the ground with you. I could rip off your other arm and beat you with it for that insult, Tiny. I won't, but I could. Now you take it back."

"Nope! You know it's true. That's how come you're getting all fired. Hell, it's a one-room cabin with only one bed. Where do you think your ma slept, genius? Don't talk to me about inbreeding, mister bow man."

"She probably slept on the couch like I do, you danged demented gimp! What in the heck's got in to you? You sure do got a lot a gumption for someone who did it with his own sister!"

"I didn't!"

"You did too, for a quarter. You told me you did. You're the one who said she wanted me, and I know you remember that."

Tiny sneered over the top of his half-drank bottle of mash. "Don't matter. She's pregnant. You're gonna marry her."

"I wouldn't touch *Neeee*-dra with a ten-foot oar. So it ain't mine. Ain't mine, and there ain't no way I'd marry your filthy sister."

"I think you're mistaken. My pa aims to put it to your grandpa, or pa, or whatever he is to you, in a manner he can't refuse. He owes my pa for something and this makes 'em even."

"He can refuse. And he will as soon as I tell him it's a lie!"

"It's her word against yours, Victor. You lose!" He laughed uproariously.

"What? What are you talking about?"

"Nedra ratted you out, man. Yeah, it's my doing. But when I told her I'd kill her if she pointed her finger at me, I think she believed it. So you're it, no matter whether it's true or not. You gotta face the facts, Victor. Your grandpa thinks more a his'self than he does of you. Everyone knows that. He just needed you to carry on the family tree is all, you know, the one that don't split off that he's so proud of."

Victory stomped over to the fence, sinking his boots in all that stinking chicken crap and muck, and smacked the bottle Tiny was holding at his mouth to the ground. The contents began to pour out over the mud. "What kind of bull are you trying to lay on my head?"

Tiny reached down and picked up the spilt bottle with his one good arm and swiped at the dirtied opening. Shrugging his shoulders, he took himself another long pull before he answered Victor.

"Ain't no bull. Hey, maybe it was a hammer-tail cat just hit you over the head, Victor! A man's gotta watch out for those. I hear tell they sneak up on you."

Chapter 70

August 30, 1941

Chicago, Illinois

Blair twisted and mashed her lace handkerchief as she stood in the slightly-chilly 'Great Hall' that was the waiting room at Union Station. With a vaulted, skylight ceiling over one hundred feet high, and marble walls, it was impossible to keep the room warm between rush hours. She shivered. She hadn't been this nervous on the train *to* Chicago, some nine years ago. Wendell noticed her shudder and placed his coat over her shoulders.

"Pardon me, Blair. I just need to get something from the coat pocket." Wendell reached into the pocket on the right side and withdrew a small velvet box. As it passed beneath Blair's vision, Wendell looked up sheepishly, with trembling hands and voice, and said, "There is no point in delaying this. Blair? I know that you are…not free," he clumsily, and rather adorably, dropped to one knee on that cold marble floor and presented Blair with the ring box. "I could not have you leave Chicago…leave me…without declaring …I love you Blair. When you get to Cloverdale, if you find that your old life is…not waiting…or, you find you are not that country girl anymore, I will be here for you. I'll be here loving you from afar. I would not know what else to do," Wendell shook his head for emphasis. He then looked up, forced himself to look Blair directly in the eyes, and proffered the ring box, now open and boasting a simple, beautifully-sparkling marquis sapphire ring set in platinum. It was Blair's birthstone. "If you do decide to return to Chicago, would you consider marrying me, and making me the happiest man on earth?"

"Wendell…" Blair's voice broke. She looked down at him, blinked tears away and nodded.

"Yes? You…you're saying yes? Oh!" Wendell sprang to his feet and threw his arms around Blair, causing her to teeter a bit on her impaired leg.

He had clearly been expecting a different answer. Mild-mannered Wendell laughed and clapped, and walked around in a tight little circle in the middle of Union Station, exclaiming, "All right!" and slapping his thigh. Blair giggled. He stopped when an announcement was made by the public address system. Blair's train would be boarding in just ten minutes. Shortly, this echoing mausoleum of a room would be crowded with bodies and frenetic activity. It sobered the couple.

Blair laid her hand on Wendell's forearm, which caused him to freeze. "Wendell, as you said, I am not free. I do miss my husband and son sorely. I don't know if my old life will be waiting. It's been a decade, nearly. He may not have any love for me in his heart after all of this time…after all I have done. He may be remarried. But I have to know. Wendell, if Sean has waited, and if he loves me still, I will stay in Cloverdale. I care for you too much to lead you astray with false hope." She self-consciously massaged her timepiece, feeling the inscription as if in brail. She wiped her tears away and took a shaky breath before continuing. "I am a lucky woman to be loved by you, Wendell. You are a wonderful man and the most cherished of friends. I shudder to think how dreary my life would have been without you in it all of these years."

Wendell took both of her hands into his. "I won't be saying good bye to you. I will only wish you good travels, and promise to be here when you, or if you, return."

Blair kissed him. "I will miss you, Sweet Wendell. Please be good to yourself."

Suddenly doors clanged and slammed from different directions and bodies began pouring into the great room. Above the din, Blair thought she heard an announcement for her train. She squeezed Wendell's hand. She had no idea what she would find in Cloverdale and she was feeling anxious. Wendell sidled up close beside Blair so that their shoulders were touching and he whispered conspiratorially, "Blair, take this," he slid over something wrapped in a handkerchief. "Don't let it be seen," he whispered.

Blair tucked the package beneath Wendell's coat flap and peeled back the cloth to find a small handgun. She quickly covered it again and tucked it into her handbag. "Wendell, how did you, *where* did you get that pocket pistol?" Wendell fidgeted uncomfortably. Blair told him, "No, never mind. I don't need to know. Thank you, dearest."

"Call it an anticipatory engagement gift." Then he whispered in her ear, "It's loaded. Do you know how to use it?"

Blair smiled, "You're asking if an Oregon girl knows how to shoot?"

"Dear me, what was I thinking?" he asked facetiously.

"That is what they call a 'Derringer', isn't it? I almost bought one for myself years ago, when I dated that gangster who worked for Capone. What does it shoot?"

"This is new. It's called the Lady Derringer. The whole length isn't even five inches, so it is easy for a small woman to conceal. Later, when you have a chance to look it over, I hope you will like the scrimshaw work performed on the ivory grip—I had it done special for you. But to answer your question, it is single action and it holds just two rounds. They are 32 magnum—I chose that because it is easy to shoot but it still has reasonable stopping power. It can put a man down.

"Hope, alone, is not a plan, Blair. You can not hope your enemy will act in a particular way; you can't simply hope that help arrives in time; you just can't plan your survival based on hope. You need to keep Hope alive; you need to keep it in your heart. But, you also need to keep that gun close. Please, promise me you will use it if you need to."

Blair placed her hand, gloved in white cotton, along the side of her friend's face, kissed him again and told him, "Trouble has always managed to find me, though I swear I scarcely went looking for it. But I know, as sure as there are windy days in autumn, all I need is that pistol and five minutes of dazzling courage, and I can recover my son. I don't know how to thank you, Wendell." She smoothed the worry lines from his forehead and whispered, "Yes, I promise…I will put him down."

Chapter 71

August 30, 1941

Cloverdale, Oregon

It was Lorette calling from the small gristmill half a mile west along the farm's border with the Big Nestucca River. She was breathless and excited.

"Sean, come quickly! Will's been hurt!"

Sean's blood ran cold as he grabbed his hat and keys from the sideboard. His heart pounded all the way to the mill. He jumped out of the car and dashed to the open door, stopping short when he saw Will lying on the floor, his head cradled in Lorette's ample lap, her breasts bobbing just above his face. He was sucking up her attention with a huge smile across his face.

"What happened? Lorette said you were hurt. Well, are you hurt, Will?"

His brother turned his head toward the door and smiled. "Took a nasty hit on my head, brother. I'll be okay soon as the room stops spinning. I guess I didn't see that small millstone resting up there on the ladder when I went to move it." He fingered the back of his head gingerly and winced. "Don't look so worried, Sean. Lorette got you all riled for nothing. It's just a bump on the head."

"Looks to be more than a bump, Will. You've got blood on your fingers. We better get you over to that hospital in Tillamook. C'mon. Lorette and I can help you to the car, and you can lie down in the back seat."

Will started to protest, but when he went to stand up, to show them he really was just fine, his legs went wobbly on him and his gullet went queasy. Before he knew it, he was bumping along the dirt road to Tillamook with his head happily resting once again in Lorette's lap. She was smoothing the hair from his face and caressing his cheeks and scalp. She liked him. Will smiled as he closed his eyes.

At the hospital, the attending physician probed the wound painfully and stitched up the scalp. He insisted on an x-ray. Will insisted that they could x-ray all they wanted but they weren't going to find a thing inside his head. That caused some laughter in the hallway as the nurses left the room.

The doctor was somber as he relayed his findings. "I've closed the flesh wound, but there is a crack in the occipital portion of the skull, quite a nasty one. Of course, there's much bleeding, and there's the danger of a hematoma forming. Your brother has a severe concussion and should stay the night here so we can keep watch over him. He cannot be permitted to sleep while in this dangerous stage."

"Fine," Sean agreed. He was worried. "Might make things easier all around if Lorette could stay with him, keep him occupied. My brother's got a pretty thick skull, if you'll pardon the pun, and won't let anyone dote on him 'cept Lorette."

The doctor nodded smartly and excused himself, leaving Sean to stand alone in the chilly waiting room. He stepped quietly down the corridor to his brother's room and peeked around the doorframe. Lorette was holding his hand and tracing his face with the fingertips of her other hand. Will looked as happy as could be, and Sean would not have worried at all, were it not for his brother's color. He was gray, and his lips were white.

Sean stepped into the room. "Uh, Will, the doctor thinks it would be best if you stayed here, just for tonight," he added quickly.

Will started to object. Sean rushed on.

"I told him I wanted Lorette to stay with you. You're not supposed to sleep with a concussion. It could be dangerous. I thought maybe Lorette, if she doesn't mind, could stay and keep you occupied."

"I certainly will. That is, if you want me, Will." She batted her eyelashes for him.

"Oh, you bet I want you. I mean, that would be swell, Lorette."

Sean finally got to sleep around midnight and rose at dawn to drive into Tillamook to see his brother. He took along fresh clothing for Will, in hopes that the doctor would let him return home that day. Then he stopped and bought a bouquet as a way of saying thank you to Lorette for all her help, though Sean was fairly sure she enjoyed being Will's companion more than a little.

He stepped through the double doors into the foyer of the two-story hospital. There were large living/waiting room areas to either side of the foyer, both with their fireplaces burning to ward off the morning chill. He saw nurses in crisp white uniforms carrying trays of juice and medications. He saw elderly patients in bed robes hobbling along with the use of canes and crutches. He heard, rather than saw, a woman sobbing in the waiting room off to his right, and was saddened to think some poor woman had probably just learned she'd lost her loved one. He took a step into that dimly lit waiting room and looked around. On a cushion near a far window sat puffy and red-eyed Lorette. The doctor Sean had spoken with the day before towered over Lorette, offering her a tissue and something in a little white paper cup. Some inner voice told Sean to leave immediately. He didn't want to investigate. He didn't want to know why Lorette was crying. And yet, some invisible force pulled him toward the scene unfolding at the other end of the room.

The doctor heard Sean approach and looked up, suitably sorrowful. "Mr. Marshall, I'm so sorry. Your brother…passed in his sleep."

Lorette wailed anew.

"In his sleep?" Sean asked, dumbfounded. "But"—he looked at Lorette with confusion—"he wasn't supposed to be allowed to sleep."

This made Lorette cry harder. She tried to explain to Sean as she sniffed and sobbed. "Will never closed his eyes, Mr. Marshall," she wailed. "He never closed his eyes. I was reading him Sinclair Lewis. (sob, sob) *It Can't Happen Here*," she wailed.

The doctor patted her hand. "It happens everywhere, dear. Death is part of life. This was not your fault, dear girl."

Lorette dabbed her eyes and nose and forced herself to meet Sean's stare. "I was reading to him, Mr. Marshall. And I kept looking over at him every few paragraphs to make sure he didn't try to sleep. Every time I looked, his eyes were open. And then… then I asked him if he liked the book so far, and he just kept staring away. So I…I…he…" She began crying uncontrollably.

Sean stood motionless. *Will is dead? He was only thirty-seven years old and he is dead. Why?* He looked at the doctor. "How?"

"A hematoma, Mr. Marshall. It was a danger we had hoped we could arrest with cold compresses and anti-inflammation drugs, but there was simply too much swelling. I'm so sorry. There was nothing more we could do. Your brother was made comfortable, and he died in his sleep. I hope that offers you solace."

Sean nodded dumbly. His feet were set in concrete. A pixie had stolen his voice. His brother was dead. Sean would miss him so much. And he had never felt so alone.

Chapter 72

August 31, 1941

Cloverdale, Oregon

Lorette had panicked. She'd had to drive Sean's car home, and then help Sean from the car, into his room, and even helped him change and get into his bed. That didn't worry her, the man was plum tired after a long and emotional two days. What worried Lorette was Sean's color. It was off. And he just seemed so…despondent. She phoned Rebecca to tell her the news about Will, breaking down when she had to tell the story again. But she regained her composure and told Rebecca her worries about Sean. Rebecca said she would come right over.

"Knock-knock," Rebecca whispered as she opened his bedroom door just a crack. She could hear the rustle of bed sheets.

"Is that you, Beck-wheat? Come in," he said hoarsely. He sat up higher and dabbed his eyes dry. Rebecca quietly opened the door just enough to slip through, and then closed it behind her.

"Lorette phoned me, Sean." She removed her sweater. "Oh, Sean, I am so, so sorry," she said as she approached the bed, kicking off her boots. "I just loved Will—he, he has always been like a big brother to me." She unzipped her riding pants and began unbuttoning her blouse. "I am so sorry," Rebecca cried openly.

Her pants fell to the floor, and she'd flung her blouse in the direction of the dresser. Sean found his voice as his childhood sweetheart stripped off the last of her clothing and stood before him in the late afternoon light. "Beck—" he croaked.

She wiped tears away from her eyes, then bent and pressed an index finger to his lips, drew back his bed sheets and climbed in beside him. "I don't want to talk about how awful sad we are, and I'm not going away," she told him. "I only want to give you comfort. I want to feel close to you, just…be with you. That's all. It is only for tonight, Sean. I'm going to hold you and grieve with you, for Will. I will be marrying Evan in the spring, but I have not answered him yet. I want to love you this one time before I do." She wrapped her arms around him. "I need this, Sean. So do you."

He'd had no intention of sending her away—not this time. He wasn't a saint; he was only a man. "Beck, I am so alone. In a month of Sundays, I never would have believed Will would go before me. I'm not prepared. I, I just wasn't prepared for that. I don't know what to do."

She answered him by initiating the sweetest and most emotional lovemaking she had ever known. Their merciful suffering of time had a healing effect. She'd given him strength.

Afternoon had drained into night. Rebecca was dressing, and a dark rain was beginning to threaten inside Sean's heart. He could feel anxiety rising. He did not know how to ask Rebecca to stay with him. She'd already given him so much of herself, he could not ask for her reputation, too. He could not ask Rebecca, someone he loved and respected so deeply, to stay with him—but only for one night.

It was soon enough a moot worry. She rose from the side of the bed where she had been pulling on her boots and, as if sensing his anxiety, told him, "I am going to get a tray of food for us. Leftovers, nothing fancy. You know I can't cook, and poor Lorette was so broken up about Will, I told her to go on and take the night. I will be staying with you." She noted his struggling smile and was relieved. "I am going to pull those parlor doors closed, and then you and I are going to sit and play Mah Jongg or cards or something while we eat, and we are going to honor Will, and grieve our deep distress. Tomorrow, the sun shining on a brand new day will begin to blunt our keen despair."

Chapter 73

There was indeed a new day and the sun was shining on it, this first of September in the year 1941. It was Blair's thirtieth birthday.

It was an Indian Summer in Oregon, and the Pacific coast boasted beautiful, sunny weather with temperatures in the upper 70s. The moment Blair stepped off the train in Tillamook, she knew she was home. This was the place she was meant to wind up. Poor Wendell. She really did love him. The man was her dearest friend, and he had saved her life. He was the only one to reach her when she was lost in the darkest recesses of her own tortured mind.

Blair collected her bags and motioned to an attendant. She withdrew a ten dollar bill and folded it neatly, twice. When the attendant approached, she pressed the bill into his hand with a handshake, Chicago-style, and said, "You look like the capable sort of fellow who could find me a car and driver to rent for the day. I wish to go to the coast. To Cloverdale, specifically."

The young man opened his gloved hand and saw the number 10 plainly printed in the corner. He snapped to attention with a tremendous smile. "Yes, ma'am!" He took off like a forest fire in July.

Chapter 74

September 1, 1941

Cloverdale, Oregon

They held each other in the late morning silence. Slivers of intense orange sunlight stabbed around the edges of the bedroom window's shade, leaving sword-like lengths of shadow intersecting across the double-wedding-ring quilt. Sean's life was suddenly wildly different from his life of two days earlier, he was starkly aware. There were no farm machinery noises, no upstairs boots against soft fir floor boards. No sounds of Will.

But there was the smell of strong coffee and the sweet scent of something baked. He didn't want to think about eating. But as sad and as spent as the two lovers were, they were both powerfully hungry. It got them up and going.

Sean knew he needed to make some arrangements for Will, and it was going to be hard. He was doubly-glad Rebecca was there to help. He went ahead to the kitchen while Rebecca readied herself at the vanity. He peeked around the doorframe and saw Lorette's backside as she worked busily at the sink.

"Lorette?" He called to her softly. When she turned it was clear to Sean she had been crying, hard. Her eyes were swollen from it. "Aw, Lorette." Sean opened his arms and stepped toward her. She cried against his shoulder for a spell as he stroked her long blond hair, and he murmured, "There, there. It's going to be all right. We'll all be sad for awhile, but it's going to be all right."

She sniffed and withdrew from his embrace, then dabbed at her eyes with her apron. "I, I had a touch of sleeplessness and thought I would bake for us and prepare a stew for our supper later." She wrung her hands in her apron. "I, I don't even suppose you have an appetite, but we must all keep our strength up. I have fixed up some thick French toast and banger sausages. I made apple juice and coffee, too. I have eggs if you think we need them, and I, I…" She looked down and her shoulders began to sag and then shake. "I'm so sorry, Mr. Marshall. It's all my fault."

Sean gave her a squeeze. "It was an accident, Lorette, and not of your doing at all. The doctor told me there was nothing you could have done to change the ultimate outcome. But you were there with my brother at his end. I know that made him happy. He had taken a real shine to you, and it was my fault he never acted on it. *I'm* sorry, Lorette. Will had his hands full with an invalid brother and a 160-acre farm and mill to run, almost by himself."

She sniffed. "Well, sir—"

Sean interrupted, "Please, Lorette, call me Sean. It is just the two of us. There's no need to be so formal."

She nodded. "I was going to say that I, I had feelings for him, too." She began sobbing anew, "but I never told him."

"I'm sure he knew. Will's a pretty…he was a smart guy." Upon uttering Will's name and having to refer to Will in the past tense, Sean could feel anxiety rise anew, like cold steel bearings pinging around his stomach and chest. He would need to push his sadness aside for awhile or he would not be able to function, and there was much to do. "Say, I could probably eat about a dozen of those pieces of French toast you got baking there," he lied. "Do I smell vanilla?" He aimed to change the subject.

"Yes, sir—Sean. And tarragon, too. It's my own recipe. I hope you like it. I seemed to have whipped up a good deal of food for just us and Mrs.—Rebecca." At the stumble, Lorette's cheeks reddened. She hastened to add, "I was so heartened Rebecca was able to stay and keep you company, Sean. She's a treasured friend to have, Bless her." Lorette lifted her apron and wiped it across her face. Dabbing was daintier, but it wasn't getting the job done. She forced a smile and a more erect posture. "But, Lord, look at all of this food. I wanted to keep busy and I …"

He patted her shoulder. "It looks and smells delicious." He pulled the coffee pot toward him and poured three mugs of steaming, robust Columbian roast.

The three friends had thought they would need to force themselves to eat beyond a single bite of food, but they fairly gorged themselves on Lorette's oven-baked French toast. They finished planning the arrangements for Will. The family plot was in the old Cloverdale cemetery, purchased years earlier. Lorette and Rebecca would do the inviting, the cooking and the readying of the Marshall home for guests after the burial. They alternately laughed and cried all the while they planned, but they finished the sad business. Lorette immediately got busy with her duties, grateful for the distraction, and Rebecca departed for her home, to write announcements and such. Ellie Tjaden's husband and older children were seeing to the livestock for Sean. He was left alone in the big house, and the quiet absence of his brother really hit him. He pulled a chair in front of the parlor window and watched the lazy cows and the occasional Red Tail Hawk as he sipped another cup of coffee and remembered better times, with Will.

Chapter 75

He noticed a nice town car motoring around the great curve of Highway 101—probably someone coming to stay at the Tjaden bath houses. The family still ran the business, but it was a much smaller operation these days. They called it a 'spa'. Sean was startled when the town car pulled into the Marshall house's driveway. He stood and walked across the dining area to the glass front door and was about to open it when the driver opened a rear door for his passenger, and she stepped out.

"Blair," he exclaimed through a quick exhale of breath, and then he couldn't replenish it. The air was knocked out of him. His enamel-ware coffee mug dropped and clattered noisily. For a moment time stood still. When it started up again, the syncing was off and so were his movements. He grabbed his heart with one hand, then he ripped the door open and stumbled down the steps, starting across the lawn, half-running. She saw him, dropped her bag and closed the distance.

"How? How can it be you? I thought…after all of this time. We thought you were dead."

"I was, Sean. Or, more precisely, Cindy was. Oh, Sean, I only found out about you and Victor being separated a short time ago, and on that same night I suffered an accident. I have been recovering ever since." She looked from him to her cane. "I came as soon as I could." She searched her husband's face as she spoke her next words. "I understand if it has been too long, Sean. I will understand if you want me to go away."

"Go away? Oh my, Blair, I have missed you so much." He grabbed and hugged her, kissed her. His emotions were scattered. Will was gone, and Blair was home. He'd just kissed her! She was really there! It was all so surreal. "It's really you? Blair, where have you been?"

"I will tell you everything, Sean. But, I didn't know if I should let the driver go or…I didn't know if you were…remarried."

"You can let the driver go," he smiled happily.

She turned and waved him on. As she followed Sean into the kitchen and gratefully accepted a cup of coffee, she noticed for the first time how thin and haggard he appeared. "You never married again, Sean? You really waited all of this time?"

"I never remarried. I have been trying to get Victor back, but I had no legal standing where the boy is concerned." He looked down, "I did wait, Blair. I waited all this time, until last night." When he looked up and met her gaze his eyes were teary. It was so hard for him to say aloud. "Will died. Yesterday."

"Oh no, Sean. Oh, no." Her eyes immediately filled with water and her balance teetered. She sat at the table. "What happened? Can you even talk about it?"

Sean shrugged reflexively. "It was an accident. He hit his head with a grinding stone and passed away in his sleep." Sean's eyes spilled over. "I was so sorrowful, so lost. And then Rebecca came and gave me comfort and, and something…happened. I needed… one thing lead to another; I don't ever want to lie to you, Blair. It was just comfort Rebecca was giving me. She's going to marry Elrod's younger brother, Evan, in the spring."

"I have much to share with you Sean. The one thing I need to tell you right here and now is that I never stopped loving you. I have confessions of my own. So many that I pray once I tell you all of it, you can still find a scintilla of affection for me."

He lifted her out of her chair and squeezed her tight. Perhaps a tad bit too tightly, but she was content to endure it. "Lord, Blair, if only you knew how much I love you. I know what worries you. Will and I went to Chicago to look for you after you left. I, we, ran into someone who knew of you, and he told us how you made your…well, it didn't matter then and it doesn't now. We all do what we have to do to survive. I mean, I believe God expects us to fight for our lives, don't you?" He released his embrace and held his wife's shoulders at arm's length so he could see her face. She nodded to him shyly.

"And that's all you did, Blair, circumstances bein' what they were. You don't have a worry, Blair. I don't blame you for a thing. And I never stopped loving you, either."

Somewhere deep within Blair's soul, a feathered-thing tweeted. Sean dropped his arms. "But, I failed you, Blair. The preacher took Victor away from me. I lost him in court."

"I learned about it, darling; it's why I am here. Someone told me. I'm here to get my son back for us, Sean. I have already sworn out warrants against the preacher and submitted documents to the court in Tillamook to reverse Victor's custody to us, immediately. The preacher will be getting a visit from the authorities any day." Blair did not tell Sean the preacher would be getting a visit from her on that very afternoon. She kept that to herself. "I just need to see a local attorney who I can put on record as my pleader for the formal Hearing, once scheduled. I was hoping you could recommend one."

"I sure can. I'll take us down there right now." It was as hopeful as Sean could muster in his current state of grief.

"Oh-no-no-no. You've been through enough, what with Will and all. If you can call your Counselor for me and allow me the use of your car, I could deliver a retainer fee and legal documents for his signature, and return within just a couple of hours. We could have Victor under our roof by this evening. Sean, I want to hold my son so badly it hurts."

Sean understood. "I have missed *you* that much. I hate to have you leaving me right away. But, yes of course, if you must see an attorney today, you may borrow the car. I will call my man, Charles Reynolds, for you." A wry grin crept into the corners of Sean's mouth. "I wish I could see the preacher's face when he learns you're alive and his bucket's about to hit the wall. His precious *almost*-title will be dragged through the mud…I'm sure glad you're leaving this business to the authorities. If preacher ever got his hands on you, he might try and wring your neck."

"He's already tried to kill me, Sean. That's how I earned these scars." She pulled her blouse away from her right shoulder and gave him a glimpse of the many raised scars left by Chester Lasley's whip. "Let him try again. I am ready for him this time."

Chapter 76

September 1, 1941

Cloverdale, Oregon

"There's a black wreath on the Marshalls' door, Victor. I guess he's departed. He'll bother us no more." Preacher Bowman seemed truly joyous.

"He didn't bother me none," Victor murmured. Victor had already heard about the wreath, and he had not been able to shake a profound sadness that had enveloped him ever since. He hadn't been able to forget the words Will Marshall had hollered to him in the dark night, weeks earlier. "I bothered him mostly, as I recollect."

"Bah!" At times, Victor's lack of reason revolted the preacher.

"It's the truth, old man!" Victor jumped up from the chair he was lolling in. "Every word, and you know it! You know, he tried to do a hell of a lot more for me than you ever did!"

He was mad at his grandfather. He knew there was no love lost between him and Sean Marshall, so of course he'd be glib about Sean's passing, but it angered Victor just the same. Victor was feeling cheated of something. All he knew was that he despised his grandfather more than usual at that moment. He lashed out.

"He never stuck me in no gall-danged bug-ridden box! He never left me alone for days without food or warmth to go off on drinking binges, or whatever the hell it was you were doing. He didn't even refuse me the money I needed to save my butt, which, as I recall, you did!"

"That's right, 'cause I had no money to give ya. Now Sean Marshall, there's a man who has plenty to give to ya. He won't be needin' it where he's headed. Ya know what? I'm gonna phone up an old pal—he's got a law degree—an' see if he can assist you with your claim."

"What claim? Don't you understand nothing, you old buzzard! Sean Marshall doesn't owe me anything! He tried to give me it all, an' you wouldn't let me take it. Why was that, Grandfather? Why couldn't you ever show a feeling for me? Why is it you wanted me so badly in the first place, just so's you could treat me so poorly in the second place?" He flipped his head sidewise toward the swollen girl on the couch, indicating abhorrence. "And Sean Marshall sure as heck wouldn't have forced me to marry a filthy Goat-girl, who'd lift her dress for anyone holdin' a quarter. That kid ain't mine, either, 'cause I ain't touched her. Maybe you could force me to marry her before I was an adult, legal, but you can't make me stay. I'm leaving. You want your stupid surname to continue on so bad, you parent the little bastard. I'm outta here, and you can keep that squalid cow for yourself!" He stormed out the door, slamming it behind him so hard that it popped right back open again.

"What the hay got into him?" the preacher asked, truly perplexed. He looked at the girl. She sat wide-eyed, chewing fervidly at the skin of her filthy thumb.

Victor approached the house slowly, noting that the doorstep did indeed hold a large black wreath. He bowed his head in respect and knocked.

Lorette answered the door with eyes red and puffy, her disdain for Victor immediately evident. "You again! It's no use, Victor Bowman. You won't be getting any of his money today."

"I figured." He nodded to the wreath. "I mean, I jus' came to pay respects, ma'am."

She snorted. The little crapper had things mixed up. He thought Sean had passed. "A little late for that, isn't it? Ya didn't show 'im none when he was alive. Broke his heart, you did. An' all he did was try to be a father to ya, although I can't for the life of me figure why. You ought'a be ashamed of yourself."

"I am. I truly am." And he did look properly contrite.

Victor tried to think of something more to say, though he couldn't even figure why it was important for that woman to realize how regretful he was. He hadn't come for money. When Will chewed him out following the break-in, he'd told Victor things he hadn't known or had failed to remember. He'd been thinking a lot lately of how Sean Marshall had tried to reach out to him. He vaguely recalled looking out the window of his grandfather's house when he was a small boy and seeing his grandfather pull a rifle on the Marshall brothers. He remembered a picnic where Marshall had told him how he loved him. Victor couldn't ever recall his grandfather uttering those words to him, not ever. And lately, whenever he conjured those fuzzy recollections, some invisible fingers flicked his heart, and it hurt—physically hurt. Victor knew without a doubt that he'd been a fool.

But how can I make this woman understand? And why should I care to try?

He bowed his head at the woman, squeaked out something in the form of a sorry and good-bye, and turned to walk away.

Lorette was fine to allow Victor to leave the doorstep believing it was Sean who had passed. She didn't trust herself to utter the awful truth of Will's death, and besides, maybe it would keep the wretched little beggar away and leave Sean in peace for a spell.

Sean heard Lorette conversing with someone and thought Blair may have returned from her appointment with the attorney. She should have been back some time ago, and Sean had been worried. He'd phoned Charles's office and was told Blair had concluded her business in no time at all and had left for home more than two hours earlier.

Blair had promised Sean she would not go to the preacher's cottage alone. But, she had also been single-heart determined on seeing Victor without delay. "Never mind, Charles. I think she has returned." Sean hung up the phone and approached the door in time to see Victor turning to leave. He called out to him.

"Victor?"

Victor whipped his head around at the sound of Sean's voice. "What?" He looked from Sean to Lorette in confusion. She folded her arms and gave him an angry *Hmpff,* before walking away.

"What are you doing here? Why aren't you at home? Is the preacher at home?" Sean was rapid-firing the questions with some intensity. Victor was rattled, thrown off balance.

"I thought you…she said…I thought you were dead. And the wreath."

"Victor, listen to me," he said quickly. "Is the preacher at home?"

"Yeah, I think so," he was baffled.

"Did you see your mother?"

"What?"

Sean grabbed his shoulders and shook him. "Your mother has returned, Victor. We're gonna have a lot to talk about, but not now. I can tell you she'd been in an accident, and was a very long time healing, but she's home again with us. She wanted to borrow the car and see my attorney, but she should have returned some time ago. She was itching to see you, Victor. If she went to the cabin and the preacher was there alone, she could be in trouble."

"Jesus! You think he'd hurt her?" Victor's head was about to explode. He wondered briefly if he was dreaming all of it. He'd thought Sean was dead, but he wasn't. He'd been certain his mother was dead, but *she* wasn't.

"Victor, he already has, it's why she left. And he's done worse. You don't have to believe me, Victor, but the preacher's done murder—more than once. And he tried to have your mother killed, too. We gotta get over there. Come on! Run!"

Chapter 77

Victor did believe it. He believed all of it. That was the reason he was running. He was running so fast, the tears in his eyes were being blown across his cheeks and into his hair. His teeth were clenched so tightly he thought they might fracture. *His mother was home! God, he missed her. He'd better not hurt her. He'd better not!*

"Victor!" Sean was sucking air and stumbling. He was slowing Victor down. "Go, Victor!" He waved him on. "Hurry!"

Victor looked back over his shoulder to see Sean waving him on. Victor never slowed his stride. He was pouring it on now, up the long dank ingress, past Sean's convertible and the preacher's Lizzie, to the door. He flew at the flimsy door, breaking off a hinge as it gave. Before him stood an astonished preacher with his hands around the throat of a beautiful woman. It was the woman in the portrait at the Marshall house. It was his mother. Victor's world switched gears from super-speed to slow-motion. The preacher took a brief wide-eyed look at Victor and then resumed his strangle on the woman's throat. Victor saw the tiny pistol laying on the floorboards. He reached for it, then aimed at the preacher. "Let her go," he ordered through his teeth. The preacher glanced back at him and increased his pressure on Blair's throat. She was not moving. Victor fired and hit the preacher in the kidney area. The report from the tiny pistol was deafening. Bowman released his hold on the woman to grab at his back, and she freely slid to the floor. He turned and stared at Victor.

"Is she dead? Did you kill my mother, you son of a bitch?" Victor yelled at him, the gun still aimed at his middle.

"Victor, son, I tell you honest, that woman is a demon."

"You will never call me your son again." He fired the second shot and dropped the weapon. It slid in the direction of his mother's body and when it came to a spinning stop, Victor noticed the ivory handle was carved with his mother's likeness on it. The pistol fired powerful rounds; it was small, beautiful, and deceptively mighty. *Why hadn't she used it?* He wondered, too stricken to move.

The woman on the floor stirred slightly and Victor ran to her. "Mother?" He knelt next to her, cradled her head. "Please don't die, Ma. Stay with me. I need you. Mommy, please, don't go."

Her hand reached to touch his and he held it. Her eyes opened. She smiled the sweetest smile at her son. His tears dripped onto her cheek. "Victory," she whispered hoarsely. "Is he dead?"

Victor glanced over at the preacher. He had crawled to the far side of the room and was sitting on the floor, propped against the wall, his gut bleeding heavily. "He will be."

"You are so beautiful. My beautiful boy. I love you so much, Victory. And, you must know this, son. I love your father, Sean Marshall. I love him dearly. He is a good man. He tried to save us. You need to know that. And he loves you, son. He loves you so much."

"I know, Mother. I know that now. I've been a fool."

"Vic—" the base of her throat had a funny swelling in it that was growing larger and she was starting to have difficulty with words. She motioned to her handbag on the table. "Money," she whispered. "Card."

Victor unsnapped the clutch and withdrew a clip with hundreds of dollars in it, along with a stockbroker's business card. He looked at her quizzically.

"Take it. Go to Wendell," her eyes went to the card and back. "Sweet man. Cared for me. He will hide you. My executor…my best friend in this world." She squeezed her son's hand. *She was touching her son!* Her other hand reached for her Lady Racine timepiece and she enveloped it in her palm. She felt her son's hot tears on her cheek and she silently thanked God that she could see and touch her son, and hold her husband once more before she left this world. "Your inheritance—you are wealthy, Victory. Now go. Go to Wendell. Don't let them catch you. Son, I love you more than life itself."

"I'm not leaving you!" he cried. Blair closed her eyes in reply. "No! Mother, please. Stay with me," he bawled uncontrollably. "Stay with me," Victor drew his mother to him and hugged her fiercely. Her hand went limp and fell away from his. He laid her head back down, patted her cheeks and finally bent his ear to her heart and listened. It was still.

Chapter 78

"Mr. Marshall! Oh, dear, Mister—Sean. Let me help you, sir," Lorette threw one of Sean's arms about her shoulders and she propped him up. "The boy can run fast, sir. You shouldn't ought'a be running at all."

"Lorette, we have to get to the preacher's cabin right away. He'll kill her," Sean wheezed.

"I heard what you told the boy, sir. I called Rebecca. She'll be here momentarily. Please sit down. You need to catch your breath. Whew. As do I," she huffed and puffed.

Sean looked about frantically then back at Lorette. "You told Beck it was life or death?"

Lorette blotted Sean's forehead and neck with a handkerchief. "I told her you was worried that vile preacher man was gonna harm your wife. Rebecca said, 'I'm coming' and hung up the phone. I believe she is dispatched with urgency, Mr.—Sean." She patted his hand. "Sir, I could hear your good lung squeezing at the close of each breath you took. I think you should let the boy deal with this. No one is going to hurt anyone in front of the boy. I should call the doctor, M—Sean. That lung might collapse."

"No. I'm alright. You say Becky definitely knew this was an urgent—"

"There she is, Sean. If you insist on going, let me help you up."

Rebecca's car slid to a stone-rattling stop and she popped open the passenger door for them. As soon as Lorette had Sean shoved into the backseat, and had jumped into the shotgun spot herself, Sean waved at Rebecca saying, "Go!"

Rebecca asked no questions. She had hundreds and there was simply no time for that. She raced around the bend, up the long, malignant approach to the cabin, and braked to a hard stop behind Sean's car. Lorette was out and jockeying Sean out of the backseat as fast as possible. The three made for the door. It was open and hanging strangely. Sean's stomach swirled and it fluttered into his chest.

Victor wasn't there. The first thing he saw was the preacher, sitting against a far wall and slumped sideways. There was a lot of blood pooled around him. He turned toward the kitchen and saw Blair on the floor, a small handgun was at her side. He ran to her. Her hand was limp. He lifted her head and called her name. She did not respond. Lorette put her ear to Blair's heart and listened. She listened for a long time. She did not want to lift her head and meet Sean's searching look, but she finally did.

"Oh my God," Rebecca cried, putting her hand to her mouth.

Sean was on his knees, at Blair's side. His head was bowed and his shoulders shook, but he was hushed. Rebecca went to his side and she held him and rubbed his back and told him how sorry she was. And then, suddenly, the lid to the banana box lifted and a wisp of a young girl stood up, chewing on her thumb.

"Lord? And who are you and what'r you doin' here, child?" Lorette asked the skinny, unwashed teenager who was clearly in a family-way.

Sean didn't give her a chance to answer, he was on his feet and dragging the girl to the sofa. "Were you here the whole time, I mean did you see—or hear what happened?"

The girl nodded, her eyes wide. "Is he dead?" She asked in a tiny voice.

Sean figured he'd best find out the answer. He rose and went to the preacher, who was still pitched over on the floor. Sean felt for a pulse but found none. "He's gone," Sean told the room. He looked back at the girl. "Please, can you tell us what happened here?" he asked sadly.

Nedra nodded. "She came to the door and he made me get in the box. But I heard her say someone was coming to take him to jail. She said she was taking her son because she had a 'cussty', and then she told him to stay back because she had a gun. I heard them fighting, sort of. Scuffling," she said brightly, having thought of just the right word. "Then there was a loud bang and I didn't want to come out of the box to see what it was. But I heard Victor and he told the preacher to leave his mother alone and then I heard a gunshot." She stopped to chew on her thumb.

Rebecca sat down next to the girl and squeezed the girl's upper arm, giving her a sad smile. "You're Otis Welby's daughter, Nedra, aren't you? I know it's ugly, sweetness, but we need to know everything you heard and saw. What happened to Victor?" Rebecca asked.

Nedra liked her. She was nice, and very pretty. "Victor told him again to get off'a her and I guess he didn't because Victor shot him again. And then Victor was talking to his mother, and he was crying."

"Did ya hear Victor's mother talking back to him, dear?" Lorette asked her. The girl nodded.

Rebecca asked her, "Can you tell us what she said?"

"She told him to take money and a card. I heard him with her purse latch. Then I just heard him crying and asking her not to leave him. It was so sad," Nedra starting sobbing.

"Nedra, sweetness, is there anything else you can tell us. Do you know where Victor went?"

"She told him to go to the man on the card. She said he would take care of him. But I don't know where he went." She sniffed and looked over to the woman on the floor. "I think she said the name 'Wendell.' And she told Victor he was rich. She was sort of whispering so I don't know…that's all I heard."

Nedra wasn't going to tell those people the whole truth—that Victor's mother was dead because of her. When she'd heard the woman tell Bowman she had a gun, Nedra dared to lift the lid of the box to see if the coast was clear for her to come out. When she did, it surprised the woman and the preacher knocked the gun from her hand. Then he was choking her, and Nedra had jumped back into the box and closed the lid.

"I know where Victor went," Sean said. He was back at Blair's side, smoothing her hair and straightening her clothing. "This isn't fair, Blair. You deserved so much better than this. We had you for too short a time." He went to hold her hand and found it wrapped around her timepiece. Sean looked at the watch, felt the inscription on the back and read it.

"You never lost hope, darling. You did it. You saved your son, Blair." He kissed her forehead. "I will always love you."

Chapter 79

December, 1941

Chicago, Illinois

"I will get you a horse, but not an auto," Wendell said from behind his newspaper.

"C'mon, Wendell."

He folded his newspaper and set it next to his plate of bacon and cinnamon bun, Victor's favorite breakfast foods, so far untouched. "I am serious, Victor. You are much too young for an auto. But there is a wonderful horse farm not thirty minutes ride from the city. They have cottages for weekend stays and they will board and exercise your horse for you the rest of the time. They are a top-drawer operation. Their horses are very healthy. So, you c'mon, Victor. Let me get you a horse for your birthday, and we'll spend Christmas on the horse farm."

Victor wanted to sulk. But one look at Wendell, with the hope worn so clearly obvious on his kindly face, and he couldn't. Here was a man who took in a fugitive kid—a killer of men who likely suffered mental impairments—with no more of a beefsteak than his mother's name and the man's calling card in his pocket. Wendell opened his home to Victor. And over the past few months, he had opened his heart to Victor, too. Wendell, who wanted to teach him a trade, who had made his mother immensely wealthy, wanted Victor's permission to buy him a horse and take him on weekend holidays to celebrate his birthday.

He could not help but think of his mother at times like these. He pictured her watching him at that moment and wondered, would she be proud of him? He had made a promise to himself: he would do his best to live in a way that would make his parents proud, whether or not they would ever be made aware. Victor was pretty sure his mother would want him to defer to Wendell, maybe even treat him as his adoptive father. Wendell said they'd loved each other, and she had accepted his engagement ring. He looked up at Wendell through those incredibly long and dark eyelashes and nodded. Then he sat up straight in his chair and took a big bite of bacon. "Thank you, Wendell. No one has ever offered to buy me a horse before. It sounds like a swell present—and a swell Christmas." He smiled and took a bite of cinnamon roll.

Something happened there. It had taken months of gentle prodding and nudging, but Wendell had the feeling Victor was finally taking to him. He'd prayed for it. He loved that boy. Every time he looked at him he saw Cindy. And even though the two were separated when the boy was just four years old, he had her mannerisms, her way of speaking, and her eyes.

Wendell broke into a huge grin, lifted his paper and slapped his thigh with it. "Yes, sir! It will be swell, Victor! I will make it the best Christmas you ever remember."

Chapter 80

December, 1941

Cloverdale, Oregon

It had taken Sean's attorney, Charles Reynolds, a few months to settle Blair's financial and child welfare matters with the courts in Oregon and Illinois, and to clear Victor of any wrongdoing in the killing of Julius Bowman.

Sean knew Victor was living with Wendell in Chicago. Wendell sent along regular updates about the boy. Victor didn't know he was not wanted by the law for murder.

Shortly after Victor arrived in Chicago, Wendell had sent word so that Sean would not worry for the boy. More recently, the two men had a long distance conversation, and it was decided not to tell Victor about the Alter Ego Rule of defense, or at least not yet. The men reasoned that Victor was thriving in Chicago. He had a future there. There was no future for Victor in Cloverdale. The boy was not raised on the farm, and he had no knowledge of, or desire to, run Sean's farm for the rest of his life. Sean knew his weakened heart could give at any moment, and there were no other family around for Victor. The Marshall's were all gone. Victor, who had legally changed his last name to Marshall, would be the only one left. Until he turned eighteen, it would be best for Victor if he stayed in Chicago, they'd decided.

The day Sean signed over guardianship papers in Charles' office, he'd cried. Sean was officially a very lonely man.

"This was Will's enterprise and he died. I don't have any family left."

Bierlitz nodded somberly that he understood. It was all the same to him as long as he was getting the gristmill. The tiny mill had made a fortune for the Marshall's over the past decade. It seemed like everything they touched turned to gold, like Midas. But there was a cost, and a steep one at that. Given a choice between fortune and family, well, Kyle Bierlitz was no good without his family. 'Course Sean Marshall was never given any such choice, Bierlitz was certain. Kyle's tiny wife and children were his life. But he was hoping he would be blessed with both family and fortune, with the gristmill operation.

"All I ask, Kyle, is that you toss a loaf or two our way each week with your payment. That'll help Lorette out some with her workload. I have left instructions with my attorney that if I fail to outlive those payments, the mill is yours, free and clear."

Kyle Bierlitz almost choked. "Are you…really Sean?"

"I chose you because I know you're a Christian man and you have eight children to feed. This mill should do real good for your family."

Bierlitz hoped the mill would bring him some wealth. Eight children is a lot of mouths to feed, which was why Marshall was willing to let it go to him so cheap. Marshall could have easily asked three times the amount Kyle was paying. And now he was being told by the man that financial obligations would cease when he did. The good people of Tillamook County had long agreed that the Marshall's were kind-hearted folks. Sean Marshall sure made a believer of Kyle Bierlitz on that day. He shook Sean's hand with firm appreciation.

Sean checked the mailbox on the way up to the house. He could smell Lorette's roasting turkey, and his stomach growled. Sean had not bothered to stop to eat all day and it was late afternoon already. He flipped through the few envelopes, noting one from the Baptist church in Tillamook, probably another request for donations. He flipped to the next one, and his heart skipped a beat. A pale pink envelope with lettering by a feminine hand. Rational thought told him it could not be from Blair. He'd buried his beloved wife months earlier. Still, he tore it open urgently. Seconds later, his heart hurt so powerfully that he had to drop the remaining mail and clutch his chest.

Well, what did I expect? Rebecca is a lovely woman, still young and vital. And her bed is cold. Sean sat on the porch step and stared out over the green pastures, watching the Holsteins graze and lounge lazily. They had not a care in the world. "God, please make me one of those cows next time," he said to the clouds above him. He picked the invitation up and looked it over.

She was to wed Elrod's younger brother, Evan, on Valentine's Day. Sean supposed he should be happy for Rebecca. He would be if it was truly what she wanted. Her happiness was more important to Sean than his own.

Chapter 81

February 14, 1942 rolled in on 80-degree sunshine. In a haste of last-minute preparation, the Tjadens decided to move the small ceremony to where the bath houses once stood, on Tjaden Hill, overlooking the bay. It was a supreme day. The bride was beautiful, and Evan Tjaden appeared to be the happiest man on earth. Sean attended with Lorette on his arm. Lorette still felt responsible for Will's death, and she was feeling rather lonely herself, so she fawned over Sean twenty-six hours a day. And Sean stopped minding the constant attention so much, since he had become such a lonely man himself. Besides, the woman could cook, and cook she did. Lorette had gained twenty pounds since Will's death.

Rebecca had invited Charles Reynolds to the wedding, too. They'd had several meetings over Sean's estate and the next thing, he was representing the whole Tjaden clan. But Rebecca intimated to Sean, secretly, the real reason she asked Charles to come: he was a successful bachelor who she believed had eyes for Lorette. It seemed Lorette had eyes for Charles as well. By the time the reception had wound down, Lorette and Charles were slow dancing all alone to the musicians' guitars.

The bride and groom had left for their honeymoon, which they would spend in Seattle. Sean asked Charles if he would mind seeing Lorette home—it was the least he could do for Lorette. Besides, he felt like taking a walk.

Visiting a graveyard in order to gain piece of mind might seem odd to some folks. Sean had gained solace from the place ever since Blair took him for a tour there. That was a lifetime ago. He walked slowly by the headstones, taking time to read each one. Some made him feel sadness for the loved ones who so plainly suffered with their losses. Others made him smile, like the little stone next to a giant one for a woman who died at an enviable age. The little one was for her dog. According to the inscription, Cece died only days before her master. Maybe after ninety years, the old woman decided it pointless to go on without her best friend. Those were the kinds of things Sean thought about when he visited the Pioneer Cemetery.

He stopped in front of an average-sized headstone with beautiful carvings in marble about the edges, and he dropped to his knees. The more masculine headstone on the far side could not escape Sean's attention either. That was Will's final resting place. It was still hard for him to believe that his brother was gone. On the opposite side, behind Sean, was Blair's resting place. Her headstone was a travertine marble slab, with "HOPE" inscribed at its top. The remainder of the stone was inscribed with the first stanza of Blair's favorite poem, followed by her name and the dates of her life. Blair had been born on September 1, in the year 1911, and she'd died 30 years later on her birthday. A small cry escaped him. He gazed at his father's marker with eyes blurred by tears and spoke softly.

"Father, I'm losing everything, everyone. I think maybe it's me who's lost."

Seconds ticked by. Maybe he'd hoped his father's voice would reach out to him. The breeze blew the boughs of the great spruce trees, and the only sound that came back to Sean was the rustling of needles overhead. Sean looked up at the sky.

"Why are you doing this to me!" he shouted at the heavens. His shoulders sagged, and then they shook lightly.

"Father, you said there would be little victories. I have lost my parents, my wife, my child, my brother…I had to watch Rebecca marry Evan today. I couldn't saddle her with an invalid husband, Pa. She'd already lost one husband. I think that was the right thing, the best thing for Beck. But, Pa, I have nothing left.

"I know I've lived as a righteous man. I deserved a victory, just one little victory. You said it might not come soon enough to suit me. Well, I waited. And while I waited, I lost my wife and Rebecca's married another. My son had to grow up under the evil tutelage of the preacher. It is a sad thing to admit, Pa.

"I have grown sickly and weak. I'm angry, Father. My heart is sick and I'm very angry. I don't want to feel like this any longer. Please help me overcome."

He'd been kneeling for a long time, and his legs were tiring of the position. He put a hand down to push himself up, and it touched something cool and damp. Sean whipped his head around, and there sitting in front of Blair's headstone, was a dog trying to get his head under Sean's hand by pushing at it with his nose. Sean didn't know much about dogs. The family had never owned one. But he knew he need not be threatened by this pup. It was wagging its tail and begging for a petting.

"Hey, where did you come from, fella? Oh. Excuse me. Ma'am? Are you lost?"

His fingers tousled her ears. She was a pretty dog, medium-sized with long, wavy black hair and not a speck of color any-where. She was a bit skinny for her size, and her coat, stuck here and there with burrs and twigs, looked like she'd seen better times.

"I'll bet you're hungry, aren't you?"

The dog barked once and wagged her tail again. She'd been somebody's pet once, but not for any time recently by the looks of her. Perhaps her master had been made a guest of the cemetery and the poor girl did not know where else to go. Sean knew just how she felt.

Sean looked back at his father's headstone. "A dog, Father? This is how you help me?" He looked back down at the atten-tion-starved animal by his side. "Well, it's something, I guess. Thank you." To the dog, Sean looked thoughtful before saying, "I guess you're gonna need a name, huh? How about Cinders, because you're all black? Do you like that?" Sean thought Blair would have approved of the name.

The dog barked and wagged again.

"Well, come on, Cinders," Sean called to her as he walked back toward his home, his gait a little lighter.

Lorette was so grateful to the stray for putting a smile on Sean's face that she gorged Cinders on table scraps. Stuffed and content, the dog curled up on the braided rug next to Sean's ham radio set and rested, keeping one watchful eye on her new master. Every now and then, Sean would reach down and pet Cinders on the head or tousle her ears. When it came time for Sean to turn in, Cinders jumped up and beat him to the bed, making herself at home at the foot of his quilt. "Oh no, Cinders. Until you've had a bath, you sleep on the floor." He laughed good-naturedly when the dog sulkily jumped down to the floor with her tail between her legs.

The next morning Sean rose with a touch of nausea and decided he had eaten too much cake at the wedding. He had felt himself giving in to melancholy, as Rebecca and Evan's reception had worn on, but when he ate the chocolate wedding cake with its impossibly rich butter cream frosting, he'd felt his mood brighten. So he'd kept right on eating it. If he thought about it, he'd been neglecting his diet and exercise for some time. There were some things his doctor said he could do in the way of light exercise and light chores, but Sean hadn't bothered. He'd been lolling around for quite a spell. He looked at the pooch who had sneaked up onto his bed in the middle of the night and was currently sleeping soundly with her head on his pillow. Perhaps if he had come upon Cinders sooner, he could have benefited from walking her daily. Perhaps today was the day he would begin to take better care of himself. He had to smile as he watched the little dog sleep. "Brother!" Sean said aloud. Just standing there was making him light-headed and short of breath. He knew he should eat something solid, but first, Cinders would get her bath.

"Cinders, it's high time you had yourself a bath, girl." The little dog was comfortable in the bed, but she dutifully raised herself and followed her new master out the bedroom and across the parlor to the front door. Lorette met them at the door. "Morning, Lorette. Giving the pup a sorely needed bathing," he offered her.

"Sean, why don't you let me do that? Your color is a bit off. It worries me. Are you feeling alright this morning?"

"Oh, my belly's feelin' a little pinched, I guess. I ate too much cake yesterday. But I'm fine. *Really*," he added when he noted her disapproving look. He led the dog outside to where the hose was tied up. He removed the soap bar and a currying brush from his back pocket. "Okay, girl. It's gonna be a bit cold at first." He turned on the hose and doused her.

To her credit, the canine stood still for the bath, even though the combing had to have tugged uncomfortably at her fur. When she was done, tangle-free, sweet-smelling, and soaked, she ran back into the house, shaking the water from her fur excitably.

"Well now, my little princess. Don't you look pretty?" Lorette tied a pretty bandana around the little dog's neck.

The dog preened and seemed to delight in the compliments.

Lorette looked out the front door. "Where on earth is your master now? I swear that man just goes and goes." She went out the door looking for Sean, fully prepared to admonish him for so much activity before he'd even broken his fast. She spotted water trailing down the drive in great rivulets. Rounding the corner of the house, she saw first the bottoms of his boots and she raced the remaining distance. "Oh, dear Lord. Mr. Marshall! Sean!" She patted his cheeks and lifted his head.

He was unconscious but alive.

"Please wake up, Sean! Please! Oh, Lord, please don't let him die. Oh Lord!" She hefted him over her shoulder and carried him to the house. She laid him across his bed and fetched cool water. Then she called for the doctor.

Chapter 82

The physician snapped his doctor bag shut. "He needs complete rest. His heart has suffered a sizable attack. He can't take much more."

"Yes, sir." Lorette twisted her dishcloth nervously in her hands.

"Give him meaty broths, and lots of it."

"Yes, sir."

"And don't let him get out of this bed. I'll be back to check on him in a couple of days. He is out of danger for now."

"Thank you, sir. I'll watch him very carefully."

The doctor left. The instant Lorette locked the deadbolt behind him, she fell into a parlor chair and sobbed. She peered into the shaded bedroom where Sean Marshall labored to breathe. Oh how she'd grown to love the man. She'd loved Will too, but that was different. She could not bear to lose Sean as well, and so soon. Cinders rose on her back feet and laid her head in Lorette's lap for a petting. The home nurse smiled through her tears and obliged, thankful for the company.

Two days later, the physician visited, as promised, and was happy to see the color improve in his patient's face. This nurse apparently knew what she was doing. He pronounced Sean healthy enough to take short bouts around the house, but he was to be restricted to indoors. It would not do for Sean to develop a cold in his weakened condition. He would surely develop pneumonia and would have no strength to endure it. Cinders jumped from Sean's bed and ran into the kitchen where Lorette and the doctor talked over tea. The little dog went over to Lorette's chair and sat next to it. Lorette quietly slipped the little tail-wagger a bit of her crumb cake.

"Cute little beggar. Is she yours?" The doctor asked.

"No, no, she followed Sean home on one of his walks—at the cemetery, sake's alive. Won't leave his side, except for food and such. The lass was in a state when he found her—or, she found him, as I heard him tell it. But she cleaned up right smart, didn't she?" She reached down and tousled the little dog's ears. Cinders preened as if she knew what they were saying about her.

"Was she sitting on the grave of her master, I wonder? Perhaps she had nowhere else to be," the doctor said. He shook his head in sad sympathy for the pup.

"I wondered the very same thing, doctor. But now I think perhaps she is an angel. One thing I do know is, they needed each other. I believe she is good for him. Maybe my broths are not the only reason Sean is perking up, I dare say. He's quite taken with her," she told him.

The doctor cleared his throat. "What I am going to say has no bona fide medical findings to support it. But, I think I see a like-mindedness in you, Lorette. I believe the canine is capable of extending a man's life. I base the theory on several of my own findings: first, I have seen illness depart shortly after loneliness departed, in a patient who was given a puppy as a gift. She has been well ever since. Next, it is a fact that a canine must be taken out and walked, several times each day, which would require the responsible pet owner to get up and out of doors and move. Regular, reasonable exercise and fresh air is monumentally important to good health and long life. And finally, I personally know of several elderly persons who admit to living for their pets. They do not wish to leave them orphaned or they worry for their care, much as if they were their children. It is frankly astounding how some people will cling to life for the canines they love. As I said, medical science can not confirm such an assertion, but I know it has merit just the same."

Lorette slipped Cinders another bite. "Oh, I am absolutely certain of it, doctor."

"As you feel Sean getting stronger, when he is ready for light exercise, accompany him on short walks with the pup. Be sure he is bundled up, this weather is a fluke. It is still winter." He rose and reached for his hat. He thanked Lorette for the tea and patted the little dog's head. "She's a dark beauty, isn't she? Her eyes tell me you are correct, Lorette. She's been through it, poor little thing. But this one is much stronger than she appears, eh?" To the dog he said, "you take care of Mr. Marshall, girl."

Cinders wagged her tail. The people laughed.

"Call me if you need me, Lorette. But I think he is in good hands—and paws."

Chapter 83

The summer of 1945 was long, dry and hot. The Tillamook Burn exploded again, convincing loggers and citizens alike that the tragic region was under a six-year jinx. It didn't seem to matter that laws were constructed to require spark arrestors on machinery and to ban burning and logging during dry conditions. Nor did it matter that the country was at war, and salvage logging was a war industry. Such laws were widely ignored. The fact was, the logging industry was of no substantiality to the fire of '45, at all.

The people of Oregon were convinced that a major fire would happen every six years, certain that nothing would alter the fact. The outbreak of 1945 only succeeded in lending credit to this anxiety, since the freak blow-up was caused by, of all things, a Japanese incendiary balloon. It had, incredibly, floated thousands of miles across the Pacific Ocean, apparently coming in contact with nothing on its journey until it reached the sands of Manzanita Beach where the surf met the forest. The explosive device seemingly had but one destined purpose: the igniting of another fire in the Tillamook Burn.

They'd been talking about Tillamook's six-year jinx on that afternoon, and gradually the conversation came around to Victor.

"Victor changed his name to Marshall, legally," he smiled. "Wendell tells me he is a natural on the trading floor. He's going to turn out alright." Sean rasped to Rebecca. It was May again. The boy was nearly eighteen. *That would make it the year of 1945,* Sean figured. He could never break the habit of telling time by his son's age, no matter how far away his son was or how long he'd been gone.

"How long has it been, Sean?"

"Since I've seen him? You were there that day. Victor ran away four years ago. Never even got to say good bye to him." Sean hacked mercilessly. Rebecca jumped up for more water.

"I'm so sorry, Sean," she said.

Sean reached out for her hand. "Beck-wheat, I think it's time we phoned Wendell. I want to look upon my boy, tell him I love him. I want the chance to say good bye."

Sean started the telling three days ago. Rebecca only let him go on a few hours at a time so as not to tire him too much, though she was as anxious to hear the whole story as Sean was to tell it. She didn't doubt its veracity, but it was a dreadful true life account.

Rebecca could hear bustling about in the kitchen. Lorette was awful good to Sean. She'd be bringing his lunch soon. Rebecca thought the woman was a saint. She was putting off her marriage to that nice attorney, Charles Reynolds, for as long as Sean needed her.

It won't be much longer, Rebecca thought sadly.

Sean's voice broke her out of her grim reverie.

"Did I tell you the preacher started that second fire in thirty-three?" Sean asked as he looked out the window and could see only darkness at two in the afternoon.

The smoke had so darkened the skies of the Oregon coast, that folks were complaining their chickens were laying at all odd hours, something that only added to their labors. Rebecca sighed. If Sean were right, then she'd lost her first husband because of the man called Preacher Bowman. She followed Sean's gaze out the window. The sight was nothing short of ominous. Folks talked of the portentous sequence of the great fires, 6, 6, 6, saying it was the mark of the beast. After all she'd heard in the last few days, she was beginning to believe that perhaps one of Satan's soldiers had been present in Tillamook County, existing in the disguise of a preacher man. How depraved that concept was.

"Yes, Sean. You told me. Dearest, I think your lunch is about ready. Why don't I go fetch it for you? We'll talk some more."

"Thank you," he wheezed, setting off another coughing fit.

He'd suffered several more heart attacks since the first one three years before. The last time, pneumonia had set in his good lung whilst he was recuperating. And as predicted, Sean had not the strength to fight it. Antibiotics like penicillin were the medical miracles of the 1940s, but they could only do so much.

Sean could hear Rebecca's light step approaching across the planked floor. He felt truly blessed that she was by his side, and was thankful beyond words. As if Cinders could read his thoughts, she jumped onto the bed and pushed her head under the palm of Sean's hand.

"Yes, Cinders. I'm mighty thankful for you too, girl." He massaged her soft fur.

It seemed fitting to Sean that he should be dying when circumstances were incredibly wrong with the world, when night turned in to day and fire ravaged the countryside. It was as if hatred and evil had decided to rage at Sean's pending ascent to heaven, for Sean had little doubt he had earned a place in His kingdom. He knew it because he'd had so few rewards in this life, so very few victories. Yet he'd lived as a righteous man. Sean Marshall knew where he was going after this life, so he had no fear of dying; instead, he drew comfort from his due. He drew comfort, too, from being able to tell Rebecca everything.

Sean thought that she should probably be told by him, rather than Charles, of the specifics in his will. Rebecca carried a tray to his bedside, placed it on the stand that swiveled over his bed at just the right height, and helped him sit up higher on his pillows. Lunch was the same as breakfast, which was the same as the day before and the days before that. It was the only thing he could keep down: crisp-fried French potatoes with black olives and a chocolate milkshake.

"I phoned Wendell as you asked, Sean. He will talk to Victor post-haste. He said to tell you they would be on the very next train out of Chicago."

"Thanks, Beck-wheat. Please sit by me. I want to tell you about my bequests."

"Sean—"

"No. Now, come on, Rebecca. We both know I haven't got many days left. Let's not play like we don't." He cleared his throat. "This house, the farm, everything I own, it's to be sold. I listed you as administrator. It should fetch a handsome sum. I left some of the proceeds to Lorette. I know that if Will were still with us, he would have married her. I thought she should be looked after. She has Charles now, and I know he will take good care of her, but…well…I owe her for so much. I want her to have something."

"She's been awful good to you, Sean." Rebecca smiled.

"I left ten percent of the net to the church in Tillamook, with some restrictions. Charles knows all about it (cough). They're going to use the money to build a new pastor's quarters onto our little church and expand the existing chapel. But they must thoroughly vet the pastor, and I stipulated he must be church-ordained. I figured it best to know exactly what kind of pastor the church is getting next time around—now that I know how hard it is to get rid of a bad one." For the small chuckle which he allowed himself, he endured another painful, racking cough.

"I left fifty percent to Victor. He won't need it. The boy was a millionaire at age fourteen. But, I wanted him to know I loved him and considered him my family, my heir. And as such, I wanted to take care of him. I failed so miserably at it in life, Beck-wheat. I hope I can show him, you know, after I'm gone.

"The rest is yours, Rebecca, for you and Evan. I wanted to give you myself twenty years ago, but fate had other plans. When you gave yourself to me, in grief over Will, I know I had no right to let you, but I had no will to refuse you. I want you to know I will take that sweetest of memories to my grave with me, Beckwheat. I didn't know how to tell you how I've loved you all these years. I guess that's why I never did tell you. But I do, Beckwheat. With all my heart, I do. And I want you to be happy."

Her eyes overflowed, and a stream issued down her soft cheek. "Sean, I love you too. Always. Dear me, I don't know what to say." She dabbed at her tears. "Thank you, Sean."

He waved it off. "Would you consider taking care of my girl here, when I'm gone?" He scratched Cinders's head affectionately. The dog looked up at him with pure adoration.

"Of course. I would be very pleased to have Cinders by my side, Sean. She's lovely, and a part of you, your family. I would… (she choked back a sob) I would be very pleased."

She could see his tiny reserve of strength was ebbing. "Maybe we've overdone it, Sean. If you don't think you can finish your lunch, I can take the tray away for now so's you can rest some." She helped him with his pillows and bedclothes.

He smiled and lay his head down on the pillow. "Yes, thank you Beck-wheat. Now I can rest easy."

She stared at the sleeping man thoughtfully and then turned to take leave with his lunch tray. She never saw Sean's eyes suddenly open wide, or the smile that took shape. He weakly uttered a single word: "Pa?" Then, just as quickly, his eyes closed. The slight smile that crossed his lips remained.

Partly because Rebecca thought she heard Sean say something, but also because it occurred to her that his, "Now I can rest easy," sounded an awful lot like a good-bye, she turned around and watched his nightshirt anxiously. It no longer rose and fell in the irregular rhythm she'd grown accustomed to. She dropped the tray and rushed to his bedside. Rebecca reached tentatively and touched his heart. There was no beat. She felt his neck. No pulse. She choked back a sob. She knew that it was inevitable, but she was caught unprepared nonetheless. He would not get to see his son after all. Victor would never hear those words from

Sean—words he had wanted to share with his son so badly. A great man, her best friend, was gone. He left this life the same way he lived it: quietly, yet full of purpose and good, always good. She would miss him so much. Rebecca hung her head and cried.

Chapter 84

She needed help. She didn't have an inkling of what some of Sean's personal effects were worth. She called up Charles and Lorette. "I've only got today to decide. Oh, Charles, say you'll help me!"

"Just let me clear my appointments for the afternoon, dear. We can be there in…oh, say two hours?"

"Bless you, Charles. You're a gem."

"So are you, dear Mrs. Tjaden. So are you. You know, I believe, in spite of everything, in many ways, Sean was a very fortunate man."

"Yes," she answered simply.

Evan was trying to price the radios and parts. It wasn't as easy as it sounds. There were boxes of parts, antiques mostly. After being run in the paper only yesterday, Sean's radio parts collection had the phone ringing all morning with anxious buyers. They were coming from as far as Montana and California for some of Sean's pieces. Then there were the cameras and photography collection; and the farm machinery; and Mavis's exquisite furnishings, some of which had been shipped from Europe, around the Horn, and still had the tags tied to the table legs. And then there was his grand Victorian farmhouse and property. What should she let those go for? Sean must have suffered some mental incapacity when he thought to name her executor. What could he have been thinking?

"Say, Rebecca, I've got most of those parts cataloged and priced, but some of 'em…whew! I don't have a clue. What's say the stuff we don't know about we just stick a note on 'em for folks to make us an offer?"

"You think that'd be all right?" she fretted.

"Hey, Beck, I don't think Sean would have wanted you to strain so over his estate sale. He's givin' a healthy portion of everything to you. And he don't…I mean, he didn't have a mean bone in his body. If you don't mind handlin' those things the way I said, I'm certain Sean would be just fine with it."

"Okay. But Charles is really good with antiques. He collects them. And he said he could be here in a couple hours. I think I should do whatever Charles says to do when it comes to Mavis's furniture."

"That's fine with me, Beck." He used his pet name for her and hugged his wife good and long. "Say, maybe he'll bring Lorette and she'll make us a swell dinner."

Rebecca knuckled him playfully and smiled. She didn't really take offense. She knew full well that she could not cook a whit. "I'm fairly certain you can count on it."

"Well, I'm gonna start in on the camera stuff then. Sean used to take me around with him before he, well, had his accident. I think I know his inventory pretty well. By the way, Ellie talked to Johnny Arthur and Henry Kellerich at the service. You remember the Marshall's old farmhands, Johnny and Henry. They said they would come over early in the morning to milk and whatnot with Ellie and Charlie and the two oldest children, and then they'll all stick around and handle the machinery and livestock part of the auction for us. Boy, am I glad they offered to do it."

Evan knew that his wife thought Sean had gone off the deep end giving her that job to do. But there was a method to Sean's madness that Evan both understood and appreciated. Rebecca was too busy to really think about Sean's passing. When things settled and Becky had time to mourn properly, it would be that much easier for her, bittersweet but not bitter. Sean was a thoughtful gentleman to the very end. He looked up at the ceiling.

"Thanks, Sean. I miss you already, buddy."

Dinner was a festivity of sorts. Lorette brought with her a half a ham and a large roasted capon. She asked Rebecca to help her in the kitchen. Charles priced the furniture, and Lorette instructed Rebecca on the finer points in preparing walnut stuffing. With mashed potatoes and fresh corn, garden peas, cranberry sauce, and homemade biscuits, it was like a holiday meal. Best of all, Rebecca and Evan would eat delectable leftovers for days. Charles had also brought along two bottles of very nice white wine to round out the evening. Poor Rebecca, unaccustomed to drinking wine and exhausted from strain and grief, drank perhaps a bit too much. But it did her a world of good. The four friends sat amid the stripped carcasses and dinner scraps, feeding Cinders and swapping stories about Sean. It reminded Charles of a good, old-fashioned Irish wake, albeit with a smaller turnout. Some stories made them laugh uproariously. Quite a few made them cry. All in all, it was soul-cleansing and helped ease the pain. Perhaps the most poignant moment was when Lorette exclaimed about the number of people present at Sean's service.

Each, in turn, thought, *Yes, an abundant number, but not unexpected considering the man.*

Ten in the morning came mighty early for Rebecca and Evan, since both were nursing slight hangovers. To make matters worse, by the time they arrived to unlock the door, there was a wall of potential buyers around the place at least ten feet deep.

"Sweet Jesus," Evan exclaimed.

"Oh, Evan, what are we in for?"

"Did Charles say he would be here this morning?"

"He said he would be, Ev, but that was before all the wine and reminiscing. He might just decide to sleep in on his Saturday morning."

But she no sooner uttered the words when Charles Reynolds's convertible scooted into the driveway. Both she and her husband voiced audible sighs of relief. She managed to get the door open and turn on lights before the first wave of seekers hit the door.

"I'm sorry, folks, but I'm bound by state law to wait until the official start of this auction. You're going to have to wait until ten a.m.," Rebecca informed the crowd.

"C'mon, lady! It's raining out here!"

"I'm sorry. I really am." She closed the door quickly, shutting out the grumbling and complaints.

Charles and Lorette came in stomping their feet on the rug and shaking their coats.

"What an awful day!" Lorette shouted over the downpour.

"Seems it hasn't discouraged too many folks," Charles gestured toward the crowds. "Rebecca, I believe everything was in order last night, so let us not delay the good people. Why don't we step on out to the veranda and instruct folks on how this will work?"

"After you, Charles. Geez, I'm so glad you showed."

"Rebecca, I'm wounded! Did you think for one moment I would let you down?"

Lorette smacked him on the backside. "Move it, Charles."

"Yes, ma'am."

Rebecca and Evan exchanged amused looks.

"May I have your attention, please? Folks? I hope you all can hear me. In less than four minutes, we're going to have an auction here the likes of which you probably never saw before. We have extraordinarily maintained vintage antiques. We have ham radio transmitters and receivers and a slew of parts you can't even find anymore. We have the same type of inventory in classic photography equipment and, of course, the farm, machinery, livestock, inventory, and this grand ol' lady here." He patted one of the pillars supporting the veranda. "Everything goes today. I hope you brought along your bankers or your cash. Let's see that everything finds a good home! If you are here to look at the livestock and farming machinery, please head on over to the barn at this time, where we have some knowledgeable folks waiting to help you. Now, for the rest of you, we can only have a handful or so of you touring the inside at one time. But the rest of you are welcomed to find shelter on the verandas here, and my lovely wife will be bringing around coffee and pastries. Folks, if you find something you like, you may feel free to make inquiries of myself, this gentleman on my left, and this gracious lady on my right." He nodded at Evan and Rebecca in turn. He checked his pocket watch. "Let the auction begin!" Charles proclaimed.

She would be considered a wealthy woman. Rebecca supposed that Sean never even knew how much he was worth. He'd never seemed to care about the money for himself. But she knew he'd have been pleased with the results of the estate sale.

Victor Marshall and his guardian, Wendell, were given the sad news upon their arrival, that Sean had already passed on. Victor had taken it hard. Wendell had not taken the news well, either. He and Sean had become good friends over the years. Both of the men had hoped for a chance to say good bye.

Rebecca studied Victor. He was all grown up, and a strikingly handsome man. He was charmingly shy around women, much like his guardian. Wendell had done a wonderful job of bringing up Victor, and they all told him so. But Wendell credited Sean with all of the changes in the young man. Victor wanted to be the best person he could be, to make his parents proud. He said it all of the time, Wendell told them. Victor had wanted to say it to Sean himself, but they had been too late.

Victor had walked over to the parlor and was staring up at the portrait of Blair Marshall. Rebecca strolled over and joined Victor, then she, too, stared at the portrait. Seconds ticked and a

blanket of sadness was beginning to suffocate the room. Rebecca wanted to talk to Victor, but the longer the painful silence wore on, the harder it was to break it. Rebecca turned suddenly and punched Victor in the arm. It surprised him—and everyone else, too.

"Ow," Victor gave her a funny look and rubbed his upper arm. "You can hit pretty hard."

Rebecca started laughing nervously, very much aware of how inappropriate her punching Victor—and then laughing about it—was. "Vic—Victor, I'm sorry. I honestly don't know why I did that." She looked over to her husband, who mouthed, *what are you doing?* She shrugged, embarrassed, and turned back to Victor. "I guess I, oh, I don't know. We were all getting so morose and… mired in sadness; I wanted to change the atmosphere in here. But I also wanted to get your attention—"

"Well, Mrs. Tjaden, you certainly got that," he smiled at her.

"Oh, Victor, you do remember me?"

"Of course!"

"I'm so glad. I am so happy to see you, Victor. You look so handsome, and you have your father's ways. Can we talk?"

"Yes, ma'am." He followed her over to some chairs by the window.

"Victor, I wanted you to know that your father's last words and thoughts were about you. He had thought he had more time. He told me he wanted to look upon his son before he died. He wanted the chance to tell you he loved you, and to say how proud he was of you. You see, Wendell had been keeping Sean informed of your life. He really was so proud of you, Victor." She saw Victor's face contort as he fought back tears. "Darling boy, you don't have to hide your tears around here. Lord, Victor, this house has seen an ocean of them."

The young man broke down and cried. Rebecca reached over and smoothed his hair. She traced patterns on his cheek with her fingertips, just as she had done years earlier as 'Aunt Rebecca,'

whenever she had held him as a baby. "He wanted to tell you he loved you, Victor. But, he was pretty sure you already knew it."

At that, the young man lunged forward in his chair and threw his arms around Rebecca, and she realized that as much as Wendell had done with the young man, there were some things he could not accomplish; Victor was starved for a mother's touch. Rebecca did her best.

After awhile Victor unwrapped himself and stood. Rebecca rose with him, keeping hold of his hand. She pointed to the portrait. "Sean wanted you to have that portrait of your mother. And, there is a red tricycle in the carriage house for you. Maybe for a child of your own some day." She fished around in a deep sweater pocket for the letter. "He also wanted you to have this. Sean said Wendell has told you some things about your mother. I'm afraid this letter does hint at some mental…strain. I didn't want it to be a shock to you. Your Pa said you had so few things to remember your mother by. That's why he wanted you to have it. " She handed it over.

"That's okay. As you said, I know about my mother's illness. It doesn't worry me. I think my mother's mind was brilliant. How she survived…all that she survived…" He looked up at the others. "My mother, she's my hero…and my father is also my hero." He turned to Wendell. "And you, Wendell, you are my hero, too," Victor said, and he'd meant it. "I never could have hoped my life would turn out like this."

Rebecca squeezed his hand. "And there's this, too." She had worn the watch around her own neck, beneath her sweater, so worried was she of losing it. She slipped it over her head and presented it to him.

They heard a sharp intake of breath. It was Wendell. "I'm sorry, I just…I wondered if the watch had been found. It was very special to your mother, Victor. That inscription there on the back, it was of some significance to her."

"That's right, Victor. Your Pa said those words had a soothing effect on your Ma. He even had them engraved on her headstone, so she could rest in peace," Rebecca told him.

Victor opened the watch. It was pretty.

Wendell stepped forward. "She told me the reason she bought it was those painted calla-lilies. She said it reminded her of this place."

Victor smiled. Yeah, he could see that. He turned the piece over to read some engraving he'd been rubbing his fingers over. "Hope is the thing with feathers that perches in the soul, and sings the tune without the words, and never stops — at all..." there was more, which he read silently. Then he looked up with eyes full of tears. He felt so close to his mother at that moment.

"Like I said, I never could have hoped my life would turn out like this. But my mother did."